Glenna Carroll
2515 39th St SW
Lehigh Acres, FL 33976

WORDS OF THE PIASA

Teachings of the Last Dragon

Duncan Glenns

AuthorHouse™
1663 Liberty Drive
Bloomington, IN 47403
www.authorhouse.com
Phone: 1-800-839-8640

© 2010 Duncan Glenns. All rights reserved.

No part of this book may be reproduced, stored in a retrieval system, or transmitted by any means without the written permission of the author.

First published by AuthorHouse 11/17/2010

ISBN: 978-1-4520-9299-7 (sc)
ISBN: 978-1-4520-9300-0 (hc)
ISBN: 978-1-4520-9301-7 (e)

Library of Congress Control Number: 2010915612

Printed in the United States of America

This book is printed on acid-free paper.

Certain stock imagery © Thinkstock.

Because of the dynamic nature of the Internet, any Web addresses or links contained in this book may have changed since publication and may no longer be valid. The views expressed in this work are solely those of the author and do not necessarily reflect the views of the publisher, and the publisher hereby disclaims any responsibility for them.

Introduction

Please allow me to introduce myself, for I would like to tell you a tale of our kind's successes and sadly several of our unfortunate failures as well. My name is Nicolas Fletcher and I am just an common man who has earned the extraordinary fate to have been the very first person who had been himself chosen by an amazing being for the task of the conveyance of his newly acquired lessons which are intended for all of us that call this planet home; I only hope that I can communicate the great importance that the following words actually hold. In any case I am now going to do my very best to tell you a story today that was recently recounted to me by a young man named Nathan Bellows; whom had just recently experienced this glorious, life changing occurrence and said that I was in fact the first person that he had been able to tell the story; additionally he hoped in earnest that I would become a beneficiary of this incredibly valuable knowledge and that if it touched me as he felt it would after hearing the and learning the importance of the lessons that he had discovered exist within the dragon's words; I would pass the story on to other's that they also may realize that it is we who happen to now live on this precious "Mother Earth" and that we are the only ones that just may hold the key to heed the dragon's warnings; and from them develop the wisdom and apply the love that I believe he has attempted to pass on to us that are really the only practices that will be finally, not only necessary, but the only acts that will actually enable us to accomplish success in our salvation!

Nathan began, "Please excuse me if I slip into and out of the first person for sometimes I believe he was actually quoting the Piasa and at other times I know he was just telling the story as he knew it had happened; for he had not only heard the story from the dragon by word of mouth, but in some mysterious way they had bonded and become one. I do not now fully understand it all, but this was the story as it was recited to me."

Phoenicians and Amazons
Approximately 2500 B.C.

The tale began recently with just another typically beautiful Midwestern spring day that found young Nathan exploring the woods by his home in Great Springs, Illinois. He, like many other boys his age loved the freedom and occasional adventure that could be found in the woods that remained there. After all, they were not like the primeval forests of the old times that his father and grandfather had told him of so many stories telling of times that they had been filled with bears, cougars and many other fearsome creatures that were said to have lived within them in the past. Actually he even wondered if the elders did not really embellish those stories at times just to scare the young boys out of exploring the woods and being exposed to the dangers that could actually exist there. But then there were the history books in his school that had some very interesting accounts of the woods occupants in the past that did seem very believable!

He had finished his chores quickly and told his mother that he did not want to go to Marion with her and his sister for lunch; that he was tired.

He couldn't tell them the truth; that he would rather go and explore the nearby woods than to ever spend another lunch listening to their "girl talk;" as a matter of fact he would really rather do just about anything rather than that, besides he felt that something, somehow was calling him back into the woods, he thought that somehow there was something special that he was going to find there. He had heard, after all that the Indians that used to live in these woods had said for many generations that in these woods there lived a magical beast and these woods in the southern part of his home state of Illinois were still mostly unspoiled by modern man and were thick, green and often mist-filled; if there was any type place in which magic could still exist, this was it!

He was a modern child that had been raised with computers, television, video games and all of the modern technologies so he was not nearly as likely to believe in ghosts, demons or dragons, but on the other hand, he was curious to find out what could have caused them to tell stories like that.

Nathan looked much like many mid-western boys of his age, his straight, sandy blond hair grew over his ears and down the back of his neck due to the distain that he held for haircuts and his aqua-blue eyes and light amount of freckles did not really tend to separate him from many of the other boys of his age in the area. The overalls and T-shirt that he tended to wear on most days, even though his mother told him to wear something else for a change, also tended to make him blend into a crowd. What separated him from most boys of his age was his preoccupation with doing what was the fair or the right thing to do. This had caused some notice at school and it was not always positive, although those that knew him well knew for certain that if Nathan gave you his word about something that he would most definitely keep his promise. This was something of which he was quite proud of and he also knew that this trait in his personality was definitely something that had definitely been instilled by his father.

These woods did hold a quality that stirred an excitement within him that could not be matched on any computer game he had ever seen and so on he walked, deeper into the thick forest.

He hesitated, somewhat absorbed upon arrival at the furthest point of his explorations to date; the narrow end of the wooded valley that he had been walking down that later expanded into the neighborhood in which his and numerous other beautiful homes had been built. It was boxed in on three sides by steep, thickly wooded mountains; well his Dad said that there were no mountains in Illinois, so that made them really big hills he thought, but to a youngster of his age they certainly appeared to be mountains. As he was inspecting the small waterfall that had first drawn his attention to this place he found an opening in the side of the hill behind it, there was a cave. He thought for a minute, should he go in? It could most likely be rather dangerous, although he remembered his father saying the reason that he had moved them here was that Southern Illinois was a good place to raise a family that it wasn't nearly as dangerous as St. Louis, so utilizing the reasoning skills of a young ten year old boy he figured that it would be alright to take a look.

It opened into a chamber that was as at least as big as his schoolrooms, but it was very dark, he was in luck though; with him he had a small penlight on his keychain. The light barely showed across to the next wall, but he could make out the three openings that existed there. One of them seemed to have a faint light coming from deep within its depths and so bravely this one was the path he chose to follow. The middle passage, it seemed to go on quite a long way and what was troubling him was that now that he was trekking down the passage, he could no longer see the light though he tried not to let it bother him, after all his father had told him that this was a safe place to live.

Nathan didn't realize it, but that couldn't have been further from the truth for following stealthily behind him since he had entered the woods were a couple of teenage boys that didn't show much promise at this point in their young lives. Both were products of broken homes, they had not adjusted to it as well as some in similar situations do; they were chronic drug users, though they rarely had the funds for the weed that they enjoyed so much, mainly they just drank whatever alcohol they could obtain and sniffed glue, paint thinner or whatever else there was around. This morning had been an especially heavy morning glue rush to get them started, and this put them in an awfully malicious mood. Bill McGraine and Danny Newton were their names and with a different set of circumstances or more of a father influence in their lives things may have been very different, but this morning their hearts were black and they did not like the fact that Nathan was one of the top pitchers on the school baseball team and he was more popular than either one of them would ever hope to be, but they were going to show him; he would not forget this day!

When he entered the mouth of the cave, they were thrilled, for this would only make the mayhem that they planned that much easier. They followed him inside the cavern and it was very dark once they got inside the chamber. They could have wrapped one of their rags on a stick and light it for a torch, as it would burn very nicely soaked in what they had been using it for, but that would eliminate their element of surprise. They paused for a moment trying to decide what to do and that's when they saw it! A faint light coming from the passage on the right, this let them barely able to see two others to the left but they supposed that it was the little "preppie" boy making the light, and so they continued their stalking of Nathan down this corridor.

They had to move sort of slowly because of the uneven rocks that littered the floor. There were large clefts in the floors and walls quite often and the two hateful teens could not believe that Nathan was making such good time on this stuff; no matter they were still very close. After they had traversed a short way, Bill and Danny edged through an opening into an immense cavern, clearly as large as their schools gymnasium, maybe even larger! The good news; however was that their prey had obviously made his light brighter and they could now see much better. It looked as though the subject of their coming cruelty had stopped behind a large collection of stalagmites at the far end of the cavern and that was perfect, he was going to be even easier to sneak up on.

Then, as they were approaching the rock formation that they knew their victim was behind, something inconceivable happened. The light went out, and they now stood in absolute and total darkness. They froze, partly to maintain surprise, but mostly out of utter fear! After a couple of minutes the darkness got the best of them and Bill said, "Danny, give me your rags and I will make a torch," as he began to fumble with the rags, not finding anything to tie them to and beginning to experience an intensely growing panic; but then the greatest shock in either of their young lives made a torch unnecessary.

Towering before them was a beast that has been known by many names; Piasa, Quetzalcoatl, Yinglung, Gas'hais'dowane are but a few of the names by which it has been known; (1.) (2.) (3.) (4.) (5.) but there it stood before the two with flames of fire slowly billowing from both of his nostrils; a huge beast, easily over two stories tall and double that long. It was also as wide as any two large elephants that they had seen at the zoo and its entire body was covered with thick scales that looked like they could easily stop any bullet. The feet that it stood on

Words of the Piasa

had huge talons as an Eagle had, but many, many times larger. Folded at his sides were huge wings and his head held gaping jaws lined with fearsome looking teeth, some approaching a foot in length. The eyes though, they set this creature apart from anything that they had ever experienced; these eyes appeared to look right through you, even as if they could see your past and even into your future and at this time these two contemptuous teens could only imagine one future for themselves; that was a certain death of most likely their becoming the next meal of this horrendous beast.

Then something even more incredible happened. The Dragon as that is what they realized now they were confronted with began to speak to them. He somehow just seemed to put the thoughts into their minds, yet it was very powerful. "Change your ways," He said, but then continued, "Today I am going to let you live, as I can see that you may have some promise in the future. "DO NOT EVER BOTHER THE YOUNG MAN THAT YOU FOLLOWED IN HERE AGAIN, I WILL BE WATCHING, NEVER RETURN TO MY CAVE OR TELL ANYONE OF ME, NOW BE GONE!"

Though the cave was absolutely quiet, the boys heard these words roaring in their heads and scrambled back the way they had come, and even though the light had disappeared they were out of the cave in only a very few minutes. They ran as fast as they could until they got back to the woods near Danny's house and as for the changing of their ways demanded by the dragon; that you will see is another part of this incredible story.

Meanwhile, the dragon made his way to where the center tunnel led for he wanted to be there when his guest arrived. He also wished to provide some light for the young human, as while this particular grotto was comfortable for him, it could prove dangerous for a smaller creature such as his approaching guest, besides the first time that one is met is a very memorable occasion, and so the huge dragon got himself settled in just as he wished and waited on his forthcoming young guest.

As the large brown dragon gained his placement, further up the corridor Nathan struggled with the footing that was becoming more and more treacherous. He was beginning to consider turning back, when there it was again, the light he had previously seen had reappeared down towards the end of the tunnel. As he traveled downward, it was beginning to really slope down towards the opening where he could now see the light. Luckily the floor was getting smoother, although the loose rocks were still a bother. Then it happened, he slipped and began to roll down the tunnel. Over and over he turned as he traveled down the path; finally he was thrown awkwardly through a small passage out onto the floor of a much larger cavern. There he beheld the most horrifying and at the same time; beautiful creature that he had ever seen. As he sat dazed gazing in the dim light at his first view of a very large dragon, experiencing an uncomfortable silence for what seemed a very long time as he and the dragon appraised one another an incredible thing happened; the dragon spoke!

"Greetings, I've been calling you for a long time, I suppose that my magic is not what it once was. I am glad that you have come and I apologize for placing the wanderlust in your heart without permission, but it was merely my way of coaxing you to come to me. I would tell you a story now, about yours and mine and the ones that I have known along the way. Come closer so that you may see me for I know that it is very dark here in my lair. You need not worry; you are safe, as I invited you here after watching you for most all of your mortal life for you see that is not so very long for me, as I am very old. Come and be comfortable, for I am not hungry and will never harm you, as I stopped feeding on humans long ago. However, I would but have the chance to speak to you, as you show much promise, and I feel you will listen and perhaps be the one to help to spread my words!"

"Please make yourself at ease for what I will tell you for the next few days that we spend together is not so much a story, as it is a condensed recital of your kinds history, and the "humans" that came before you, as short a time as it has been. For you and your kind are different than any being that I have yet seen in this world; and as I have told you, I am very old."

"I see doubt in your face and I believe that you wonder why I would spend my energy doing this; well let me tell you, it is, in fact for two very simple reasons," The Piasa stated.

"The first you may find rather selfish, but try to understand, for thousands of years my kind was all that were here on "mother earth" we would today be considered by your scholars the apex beings and most of all the rest we merely considered food items, or prey and we knew only that. Then long ago, even before my time, there occurred "the great calamity." This produced explosions, fires, floods, no sunlight for years, a great upheaval, as if some giant thing had struck our "Mother Earth." No, I wasn't here for that, for I am not that old, I know only from shared memories! Yes, Dragons share a portion of all their memories and it can be both a blessing and a curse. Before we are finished here we will share some too! A change occurred at that time to those like me, though most of us did not survive; the remainders of my descendants were divided into two groups."

The natural; those that remained dinosaurs and seemed not to have been able to develop the intellect or mysterious magical powers of my kind and soon disappeared, and also;

The magical; those of us that became what humans today now call dragons. There were many, many thousands of years that passed, in which my kind had domain over absolutely everything and prospered greatly."

The dragon continued, "Then, one year, many thousands of your lifetimes ago, but not so long for me for when even I was a young dragon I can also remember seeing the early humans. My ancestors began to see subtle changes in the apes and chimps, as it seemed as though over night they began to have less hair, make different sorts of sounds, and make shelters for themselves from the plants or caves. Instead of running when we came to feed on them; they even began to try to fight us off with sticks and rocks; soon with the things they later called weapons, though in the beginning they were seldom very successful. Still we reconsidered attacking them and I am certain that this is the reason that most of us began to choose easier prey. They also awakened a feeling in some of us that I would like to further understand. It was obvious that they cared for one another; they showed something that I now know they describe as love, which is what I treasured about them most."

"The second reason is quite a lot more complex. Try to understand this if you would. Being here for so long as I have, I have come to know nearly all of the many secrets, needs and powers of our "mother earth", and though I do not know exactly why or how as of yet, I know that somehow you humans are the key to her future. The problem from my perspective is to tell you why the other humans failed, yet at the same time educate you and your kind in the use of your gifts, which are considerable, even if most of you have lost sight of the wonderful powers that most of you possess. Before, you too lose your balance to the onslaught of technology, or some other obstacle and go the way that all of the other very promising of your kind have gone. The Atlanteans, the Phoenicians, (6.) the Mayans and so many others, all showed so much promise, yet their downfalls, some of which were quite destructive; was as simple a thing as losing their balance? I will dedicate all of my remaining energy to showing you the way for your people to avoid the same fate as that which the others have already met," The dragon gazed at the young boy and continued.

"I know that the real problem is, getting your kind to believe," The dragon said warily. "However, I will give my maximum effort, as I hope that after hearing what I say that you will also understand the need, as I feel that both "dragon" and "human" futures are intertwined."

"As the dragon began his recitation, Nathan gazed at the tremendous animal in awe and while the sharp teeth, claws, scales and sheer size urged the little human boy towards absolute terror there was also something about the beast that suggested a warmth and kindness that would not be expected at first sight of this fearsome, reptilian looking creature. Nathan explained to him, "I can tell that you are good, tell me your story and I try to help in whatever way that I can." Though I watched him nearly from his birth, it was not until his tenth season that I really knew how special a "human" that this young man Nathan really was, but at this time I was now certain."

"Very well, my small friend, it seems that I have chosen you well, I am very well pleased and so let me continue." There are many things, places and powers that exist, that are very difficult to learn about in the short time that you humans have to spend here. Even with our shared memories there are still many things that we of my kind do not know about, as the world we call "Mother Earth" is a very complicated place. It still holds many mysteries, even for those that have been here as long as I.

Words of the Piasa

Let me begin by telling you of one of the greatest and most powerful of the earth's mysteries, one that I learned of mostly through the eyes of "Ebirius" a brave, skilled Phoenician sailor. Try to understand that sometimes it will sound as if he is the one speaking to you, as we shared everything, for you see, he was the first "human" that I ever "impressed" with; it was Ebirius that was the first to show me the state was even possible and I suppose what really made it possible for us were two factors; my inquisitive nature and the pure, giving, honest nature Ebirius possessed."

"Let me explain, the state of impression occurs when, dragon and human link mind and life, usually through the sharing of a life and death experience. They become inseparable and form a very strong bond, stronger than any friendship or family bond that you can imagine; this is both its strength and its weakness.

The Piasa then spoke, "It was a warm, late summer day, Ebirius had been sailing the western sea, as he would often do, for he liked nothing more than exploring new waters. You could see a fire burning in him to learn of the world, it was a wondrous thing."

"He called his boat "The Osprey;" Being a gift from his grandfather Elburt, it was built well and hand crafted by a master shipbuilder, which is exactly what his grandfather was as shipbuilding was the main portion of the "Saluur" family heritage. Though it had quite a small cabin, its lines were excellent and it had a massive sail, this made it a very fast ship."

"I normally I had kept a very close eye on him; however on this occasion, the three previous days I had spent feeding (with the accompanying nap) and in that time Ebirius had traveled further west than he had ever been; to a spot in the sea that has been drifting west from its original location for many thousands of years, so it hasn't been heard about very much, until recently. This place is unique in that it produces conditions that make it possible for a human to travel "between" without the help of a dragon, though they did need certain crystals. If he were to accidentally discover how to achieve this I wanted to be there in case he needed my help, as it is very fatiguing, extremely cold and sometimes inescapable. This and the fact that I thought I could feel the presence of a black dragon back in our territory made me anxious to find him again. Black dragons, though very rare, are the largest and most powerful of my kind, they also tend to be of awfully bad temper, even to the point that yours would call them evil. They are the usual dragon that mankind has experienced so many problems within your early and middle ages, causing the horrible rift in dragon's and man's relationship over the years, however most of us are nothing like the blacks. Your kind has a saying that I think accurately describes the black dragons it goes, "Absolute power corrupts absolutely!"

"I had been flying back and forth searching, further and further in what your kind calls the direction of west the entire morning and was ready to change the direction of my search, when I saw him appear on the far western horizon. There is no mistaking his boat, even at a distance you can see the huge water eagle pictured upon his sail. I began to slowly spiral down to get a better look, as I had been close to him and his crew on many occasions and was not worried about them fearing me though as I drew closer, I could see a strange setup of unusual looking apparatus on his foredeck that I could not fathom. A large polished brass disc lay flat on the deck, clearly six cubits in diameter and triangulated around it were three ornate staffs topped with a large crystal each. Though his crewmen Durages and Flaxon were both looking directly into the circle, I could not see Ebirius anywhere. Stranger still is that they were not headed home, but they were sailing into the West. This was very perplexing, so I slowly circled downward in order to look more closely. Suddenly, when I had gotten to within three lengths of the boat, a strange luminescence appeared over the bronze disc on the deck of the "Osprey" and after a moment the light strange shimmering light that had been within the disk disappeared and Ebirius stood there. He was wearing a suit of brightly polished armor that did not at all look familiar to me and he held in his hands, a long staff that was again topped with the same sort of magnificent looking crystal. This one however was fashioned into a very formidable looking sharp spear point. This took me by surprise, as I had never known these young men as warriors and wandered what could have triggered this newfound and I thought rather negative interest!"

Duncan Glenns

"He began to wave at me, slowly at first and then franticly to come closer. I drew closer to his craft, as I wanted to talk to him about going between and I wanted not to be too loud, as it often frightens humans when we are so."

"When I finally grew close enough to hear him I just heard him say watch out for the "black" behind you, stunned I reacted purely out of reflex, as I know that most of my kind prefers to attack from above and behind I dodged appropriately. My dive took me uncomfortably close to the water, which would have probably been the end of me, where he missed me by no more than a cubit, but had to lose all of his speed to avoid the water, giving me a fighting chance. As he struggled for more altitude, I circled the boat to gain as much speed as possible and with my extra speed I began to think for a moment that I might gain the upper hand, at least enough of one to survive. Unfortunately, he was a wily one and when he gained sufficient speed, he turned directly back for the boat. Somehow, he knew that I would feel the need to protect the humans there.

As he sped towards the boat, I folded my wings and dove for him. I fell as a rock falls from the sky and in an instant I was there. Just as we met, I reached with my outstretched talons for his wing, in order to at least injure him enough that he could not fly, not thinking that he could still easily out swim speed of the boat. Just as I slashed at him, he folded his wings and rolled, so that all I slashed was the impenetrable armor of his back; this merely angered him! I still had most of my speed though and decided to try and use it to my advantage, as he once again needed to gain headway, I circled and dived slightly thinking that I may be able to possibly get a quick slice at his gut. But I was in for a shock and it happened so fast; when I got there, he began to turn and I saw his exposed belly, I made my lunge as he still turned. (He was most accomplished at the art of flight!) As I stretched for where his belly had just been, I was suddenly captured in his viselike grip by his upturned claws."

The Black spoke coldly, "This is not your best day, little brown, but it will most definitely be your last," he continued, "My children probably will not eat you, as they have more the taste for such as these humans and other more tasty morsels, but they will very much like to slash, render and torment you as you die and I am certain that they will enjoy it immensely, as will I."

The black then turned and began his flight go back to whatever desolation he called home, as I helplessly struggled to no avail to free myself. I was beginning to feel that my options had run out, as I could not begin to loosen his tremendous grip; when I began to observe behind my head the same strange light that I had seen on the deck of the "Osprey" a moment ago. Brighter and brighter it grew, then suddenly a flash and Ebirius was straddling my neck, just above my wings. I was astonished and taken aback, that this human whom I had already thought was very special, was also extremely brave. As I looked on in awe, Ebirius acted, he quickly searched for and found a weak spot in the black's armor. There were but two, the thin spots under the pits of his wings and the brave young Phoenician chose the pit of his left wing were he aimed true and drove the crystal spear home halfway down the hilt. Then for the next several moments all we could hear was the monumentally anguished death cry of the mortally wounded black dragon and believe me when I say that there isn't a sound in nature more horrible or terrifying. Then with his last living action, he wanted revenge desperately and I could see his massive head snapping towards us, jaws agape malevolently; when suddenly there was only the bitter cold of "between."

The young human had been the one to bring me "between" though I knew not how, for I did not even know that humans were capable of this, but I wanted to get back out, as it is terribly cold there and I knew that too long of exposure is very bad for dragons, and had to be even worse for humans. So for a moment I thought, and then it came to me, of course the "Osprey."

We reappeared on the quarterdeck. Immediately I could see that my bulk on this part of the boat was putting the boat at severe risk of capsizing, but Ebirius just nudged me towards the middle of the boat and this stabilized the boat somewhat; however it was still riding uncomfortably low in the water. Ebirius approached me sympathetically and asked, "Are you all right?"

We now found that we easily spoke to one another, "Shaken, but no lasting wounds," I said. I then told him, "You saved my life, and something else, we are joined!"

As we gathered ourselves back entirely to the present, listening to the stout planks of his hearty ship grown under a strain unlike any that they had yet been subjected to Ebirius gazed deeply into my eyes for quite a while and I found this surprisingly enjoyable. Then he spoke with a deep conviction and said, "I know; I do not know how, but I know that it is true that we have become joined in some manner." After a moment of examining his ship and I pruning and grooming the new marks left on my scales by the black, he said to his mates, "The ship wallows, the dragon and I have much counsel to partake, sail her to the "Ascension rock islands." If the wind comes back up this afternoon, you will be there tomorrow morning. If not, then it will take a day or two more, in any case, we need this time to confer, and we can check on you if need be."

"Aye captain," said Durages Hammil, of the ancient Phoenician Hammil clan; a family known for their abilities in navigation and the prediction of events celestial, "We will make it happen!"

Just as Ebirius was about to speak again I asked, "What happened to the black?"

Flaxon Ceals; his family renowned for their training of beasts and knowledge of plants, herbs and medicines then took his turn to speak of the tale that they had just witnessed, "We'll be having no more problems with that beast." He then gave me a somewhat fearful look possibly thinking that he had spoken out of turn, but I merely stated, "Yes go on."

Relieved, he continued, "My captain smote him with such a blow, that by the time he hit the sea he was near a quarter consumed, as we watched him try to swim, he fully dissolved in a boiling sea before our eyes. No he'll trouble nobody ever again!"

Ebirius stated, "Stow the netherworld equipment carefully and both of you give me your solemn vow that you will not attempt to use it, as it is very dangerous and we need learn more of it before we try to use its powers."

Nearly as one they said, "Aye captain, as my ancestor's bare witness."

Ebirius then turned back to me and asked. "Would you honor me with permission to ride on your neck?" I told him, "The honor is mine, but 'tis a long way to travel holding the width of my neck." Flaxon immediately came to the rescue as he flashed into the cabin and came back with very stout but well-worn leather strap, with a buckle on one end. Ebirius commended him saying, "The old sail strap, its perfect my friend. We secured the strap around my neck and to my surprise, or possibly even some sign of the fate to come it fit perfectly! Ebirius told them, "Fair seas and winds," As I added, "Be watchful," and we were away."

"The flight to the island that he had named would not take us very long. I merely climbed to a sufficient altitude and then glided down to it. What really surprised me though, was that as soon as he named it I could see it in my mind and of course new exactly where it was. I had no way of knowing the "human" names for places, as I had never spoken to a human before; yet now I even knew his language, yes something very important had just happened. I spied the island and as we drifted downward and it was as though we were at the same time, exploring one another's minds and vowing commitment to one another without saying a word. That was a very beautiful experience; one that I shall always treasure and soon we arrived at the island and I chose to land near a small waterfall as I was thirsty and knew for certain that he was too!"

"You saved me from certain death, though you were not obligated, but you prevailed over a black dragon to save me, you are full of ever more surprises than any of the others that I have encountered of your kind my little human soul-mate. Tell me of why you care what happens to this brown dragon; how you learned of "the Nether World," and how came you across a weapon that could dispatch a black as fearsome as that so easily? Truly, we have much to talk about!"

"Yes, we have much to say to each other, though I am also certain that we are linked for life and we will have the time to do it. Firstly, tell me what I should call you, as the sound that you answer to when called by others of your kind is quite foreign to me, afterward I will tell you of my discoveries and how I know, that in the future you to will save my life also," Ebirius said.

"You know what I am called," I said.

"Yes, your kind calls you GGGRRAAANNNGGGRRRR,"

Ebirius attempted. "I try, but it sounds more like a growl to me, would you mind if I shorten it to something that I don't have as much trouble with; perhaps Granger!"

"No, I do not mind at all," I said. "That sounds as though I will rather like it!

"That's wonderful," Ebirius said. "Let me tell you how we got to this point. It began last summer, as my mates and I were exploring and mapping the peninsula to the south of our home that is shaped as a boot. We call it Talia, the home of the garlic eaters because of the people that we have met there. We anchored in a small cove on the western side of the island near Talia, as it looked as though it may have a supply of fresh water due to the mountains which were located there."

"Once ashore, we spent the rest of the afternoon searching the island for things that we could use for portage. We found numerous edible plants, game and several sources of fresh water, one of which had something of a trail beside it. This we followed down to a clearing where we found the "netherworld" equipment set up as you saw it on our deck. We wondered who would have left something as magnificently made as this, set there all alone on a deserted island, so we decided to wait, at a discrete distance of course and see if anyone came back for it. We made a fireless camp about one half league away, further up the mountain. We chose a thicket where we could see the equipment and anyone around it without being seen and to our amazement; we were rewarded just after we had our evening supper. We first saw the bright light, and then appeared a man. He was wearing armor that appeared stout and well made, however it looked as though it was dirty and not taken care of as it should be; four others, similarly dressed soon followed him. They finished setting up a rough campsite and settled in for the night. They appeared to be drinking a lot, wine by their behavior, as they were load and raucous. They continued to speak loudly with an occasional argument, as they played some game of chance it appeared. We also saw them due cruel things to the animals. They would lure them to the edge of the light with morsels of food, just to shoot them with their slings. They killed because they found it fun; we found it despicable. They were quite the ugly group; moreover they sounded as though they were planning something wicked."

"We decided that we needed to learn more of their plans as quickly as possible and so we carefully slipped in close enough that we could hear more of what they said. Once we were within about fifteen cubits of the rabble we settled in to listen; our first actual experience as spies. They would occasionally brag about what they were going to do with the loot that they would have after they had crushed the singers and their silver boats. This statement told us that they were making plans to wage war on our people, or our Babylonian neighbors to the south, solely for material gain, it sounded."

"This however, left us confronted with a difficult problem. We had to do something about the "Osprey" for more of their comrades coming the same way that they had come, or arriving by sea would mean that they would soon spot our boat. We could not afford to be discovered, as we were but three! As we deliberated what we were to do, the solution came of its own. We noticed that all but two had faded off to sleep; good strong wine no doubt. Taking advantage of this, Durages and I crept the rest of the way into their camp and finished the job by carefully slipping behind them and clasping a compress of Flaxon's fermented poppy jelly over their faces as the opportunity arose; you see he trains animals and often needs to put them to sleep, but this is another of the many stories about my good friend. It has the same effect on men and is rarely fatal; though it does produce a terrible headache I have been told! We gave a dose to each of the others that dozed and began our work. We tried to memorize the exact way the equipment was placed, and then carefully collected it.

After bundling it, we were joined by Flaxon and got to the "Osprey" as quickly as possible and got under way. We had sailed for but a short time when we began to see the sun peak from behind the horizon that was dotted with clouds. A short time later, when there was sufficient light. We saw a three masted ship bearing down on the island. It appeared as though they would catch their comrades sleeping, and that could not bode well for them! As for them having seen us, that did not matter, as they did not have any chance of catching the swiftest ship in the Phoenician fleet! An act that would have normally been called theft had made us feel somewhat heroic. Still, as we sailed for home I knew that I must learn more of their plans if I was to enable my fellow countrymen to remain safe!"

"So began our experimentation with the "Netherworld." In the beginning, we were very exacting with our resetting of the equipment, even to matching to the identical points that the shafts lined up with the navigational stars, as we had taken note of this, skilled at the art of navigation as we both are. When we had reproduced everything to perfection is when our real headaches began. We tried chanting, burning different herbs, reflecting the sun in from different angles onto the disc, through the crystals, all to no avail."

"Then one day, as I sat discouraged in the middle of the disc, after yet another number of fruitless attempts at trying to fathom what made this equipment do what we had seen it do. That is when I thoughtlessly began to daydream about what I loved; being under sail on the deck of my ship, when I was suddenly engulfed in a fuzzy multi-colored light; then came an instant of bitter cold, colder than anything that I have ever felt, as cold as I could have imagined that death might be. Then a blinding flash and I was on the deck of the "Osprey." I had done it; by accident to be sure, but I had used the "Netherworld equipment" for the first time and I seemed unharmed, just severely drained and bone tired. I went to find my companions and share the news with them!"

"The next several moons were filled with a small number of experimental uses of the equipment. Only I so far have embarked on these journeys, as Durages is "waiting to see" and Flaxon will have nothing to do with it. The trips started as short tests, and then I became bolder. One morning when I was feeling unusually bold, I envisioned the cave at the top of the cliffs of the great jungle land that I had found by sailing south for nearly one half moon cycle. For that adventure I was severely punished by my parents, as I was but a lad. However, with the use of the "Realm" I shortened the trip; after my arrival, I was astonished to hear gruff sounding voices coming from the inside of the cave I had pictured and so I stole to the entrance where I could peer inside and not be seen myself."

"The torches that they had with them dimly lighted the cave and I could see three of the same type of men that I had seen on the island; with them, tethered with yolk and staff about her neck to keep her under control, was a tall, powerfully built and very beautiful young woman. She was wearing the most striking and brilliantly polished armor I had ever seen, and though she fought furiously she was no match for all three. She seemed not to have yet reached her twentieth birthday. They laughed and taunted her saying "After we are done with you, we will see how badly your mother wants you back, but not until we have had our fill," She cursed them and vowed vengeance, but didn't scream. She appeared to be an Amazon, as I had heard tales of these incredible women."

"My time was short; I needed to do something very fast. My days spent with Flaxon were about to pay off, for I imitated, with good skill, the sound of a great beast that he called an Oliphant. Inside, the obvious leader of the men called to the largest of the three, "Murdoc, go to see what that is! There will be plenty of time for you two when I am done, He grunted his acceptance and ambled out towards me. I tossed one of my pieces of jerky into the bushes down the face of the cliff and as he looked down the slope, I hit him square in the temple with a well-placed river rock from my trusty sling, he slumped forward into the bushes, out cold."

"The maiden continued her struggle, but was now stripped of all her armor and on her back on the ground wearing nothing except a small skirt and halter as she was no match for the large men. I had to do something so I made the call again, this time making it sound louder and even closer. Both of the barbarians turned and faced the entrance of the cave to face what they thought was some sort of a wild animal, just in time for the one holding the staff to receive a fist sized rock from my sling squarely in the forehead, this dropped him like a sack of grain releasing his staff. Seeing this, the maiden reacted instantly she swiftly kicked the other from behind in the groin; this brought him to his knees at once, while I leapt forward to capture him; only she moved like lightning and with a chop to the back of his neck and he was no longer awake; or possibly even alive for all I knew!"

She turned to face me, as if I was also an enemy, "Wait!" I said, holding my hands up to show them as empty, I am only trying to protect you. She realized immediately that I was speaking the truth. "Sorry" she said, "They are animals, let's finish the job!" She meant to kill them all; and it was not hard to understand after what they had been about to do.

I told her, "Would it not be better to leave them tied as prisoners, the three of them bested by one Amazon?"

"How know ye that," she said.

"I have heard many tales, but I did not truly believe, until now!"

She continued, "Yes, 'tis true. I am Amazon but what of you?

Words of the Piasa

You seem of fair and noble race, but not from this land or any that I recognize. What is your name and where is your home?"

I told her, "My name is Ebirius, sailing is my calling, and Phoenicia is my home. I would like to know your name to, as you are very fair and I would like to talk more with you, but now we must leave this place."

"You are correct about that at I am certain; I am called Desiree, let us secure this rabble and be off!" She answered curtly.

"Desiree," he said slowly. "That is quite a beautiful name," I told her as she tied them with a very interesting knot that even I, a most experienced seaman had never before seen, saying that it would only tighten if they were to struggle; this expertise with knots told me that her kind were most likely also seafarers although I had not heard this fact about the Amazons in the past.

As we began to leave I told her about not having the "Osprey" with me at present and how I came to be there, this stopped her in her tracks.

"You have discovered how to gain the realm. As I nodded yes she said, "This may be very dangerous for you! However, you have saved me from kidnapping and a certain assault and so I am certain that my mother will be pleased, she may even fancy you. How came you by the crystals used to gain the realm," She asked?

Ebirius continued, "I would not have normally come by them in the manner that we did, as I and my kind are no thieves, however we saw them appear inside of them and saw what was possible with their use; after listening to them for a while we heard that they were planning to attack either our people or our Babylonian neighbors near us. We thought that it would be in our best interest to take their equipment to stop them and learn what we could of its use!"

"Let us hope that you were right, for that leaves us with a problem. They brought me here using the crystals that you now possess, having stolen them from my people. Believe me when I say that it is safe for neither of us to escape in that way. You can still go back from whence that you came, the problem is really mine. I can only go home by going back with you first, and I believe that it is now possible as you have just saved my life and I am indebted to you; my mother will understand. I would ask Ebirius, now that you have saved me, would you please take me home?"

"It would be my honor to take you home but how," He agreed skeptically?

"Just look into my eyes and take me back to where you came from. When we arrive merely continue the gaze and trust in me, I will get us to my home," I took her strong but soft hands in mine and stared into the most beautiful green eyes that I have ever seen for a long and remarkably tender moment, then came the cold of between and the now familiar twinkling of multi colored lights. I'd have loved to seen the look on my mates faces, but I was so enamored with this surprising and wonderful young woman that I never looked away from her face to see their reaction; again with the accompanying cold and flash we departed from the deck of the Osprey!"

Suddenly we were surrounded by at least two score of very fierce looking, heavily armed warriors, all female and all quite angry looking. Desiree acted immediately, "Halt," She shouted. "He is my friend, he rescued me from the Gruumens and is under my protection, harm him and suffer certain punishment from my mother."

"Your mother," Queried this rather astonished Phoenician sailor?

"Yes, my mother Queen Andrea Perseii, the queen of the Amazons," Desiree said with a smile.

I smiled at her and whispered, "Princess Desiree."

"She merely nodded and returned my smile."

"We were escorted to the Amazon palace. It was different than any that I had yet seen in my travels, as while being full of murals, treasures and all manner of things of beauty on the inside, it readily blended with the forest when outside the walls. This made it very difficult to see until you where at, even nearly inside the doors. What an intriguing defense I remember thinking to myself, I had heard in tales about these prolific, beautiful warriors that they were not only very fierce and unmatched archers, but they also happened to keep all men prisoners." This was unsettling!

"At length we came to a room that served as both throne room and meeting hall, all around the hall there were placed large round tables with chairs for ten at each, while on the far end was a beautifully carved and jeweled throne fit for a queen. In this sat a strikingly beautiful woman, quite tall and garbed in flawless silver armor that shined as a mirror.

Words of the Piasa

Next to her, at arm's length was a cache of the most ornately carved and bejeweled weapons that I had ever seen. Some of these included the bow for which they had won such renown, a short sword, long broadsword, several lengths of spears and a collection of some rather sharp looking discs that looked as if they were made exclusively for throwing. These were all displayed beneath a shield that boasted a luxurious looking huge catlike animal with jeweled, glowing eyes, it was all magnificent to view!"

"We approached and Desiree ran and embraced her mother the queen, I was still shocked! The queen spoke, "So this is the one who delivered my greatly loved daughter from the evil that my warriors could not even find."

"Twas a land far away, your highness," I began to say, when suddenly the queen said "Silence! I speak with my daughter, no man," This was accompanied with a scornful look from Desiree; I took my cue and fell silent."

"Yes mother, he was heroic, he is not like the rest. He placed not, even his hands on me, except in help or tenderness. Also he showed intelligence and resourcefulness in the execution of my rescue, why he even possesses great expertise with a sling."

She was beginning to sound as though she was selling me to her mother.

After a few moments of silence her mother said, "From what I hear, it sounds as though you are thinking of keeping him for your future breeding stock; you may yet keep him, but it is surely not yet time and is something that I must first consider!"

"No mother, you do not understand," Desiree said. "I value him as a friend, possibly more; I do not want to keep him as a prisoner, besides we could not even if we chose to."

Her mother's face grew ever more somber as she asked, "What are you saying?"

"He has found the crystals that were stolen by the Raginites, and most likely once again stolen by the Gruumens; in any case he has learned how to gain the realm," Desiree explained. Then she defended me with, "That was my good fortune!"

"The queen turned to me and said, "And what does my young hero want as his reward for the rescue of my much loved daughter?"

"I looked at her and back to her daughter and said, "What I did was not for profit, but because of it being the right thing to do, and I want no reward save the permission to continue seeing your daughter if she would want it so," I paused, "Perhaps also to return home briefly by your leave to let my friends know that I am unharmed and safe."

"You are right my little elf, he is not like the others, however his requests make it necessary that he learn all of our rules that would pertain to him; how dearly we hold obedience to them and what will happen if they are broken. He may well be different, but he is still a man," The queen said with absolute authority!

"You will now tell him all that is expected of him, or shall I assign Therasil the task of teaching him our ways?"

"Therasil was standing further behind the queen in an alcove of the hall that somewhat separated her from the other Amazons in the room and she seemed to be surrounded closely by those that seemed to hold somewhat of a strong allegiance to her over all others; even the queen. She was as tall as queen Perseii, yet of more slender build; she also showed an unusual wiry strength and a strange, dark, foreboding beauty that while not altogether unappealing was somehow vaguely frightening. I realized at that moment, that to look into her eyes was most unnerving for most."

"I would rather be the one, honored queen/mother, as our fates now seem somehow linked and I feel something of a debt is owed," Desiree continued, "Therasil, I will also make the arrangements for the return of our crystals, so you need not bother my honored sister. I was later told by Desiree just how brutal that Therasil enjoyed behaving with the men."

Queen Perseii instructed, "Give him the necessary instructions my love and when you return you can continue his education during a feast to celebrate your safe return, however be of good trust my kitten as the chaperones will be always close by!"

Therasil appraised Ebirius with a most chilling stare and coldly interjected, "Yes, and when the chaperones judge the need to act I suppose that it will be necessary for someone whom is not so young and impressionable to show the young male our ways properly!"

"Thank you sister Therasil, but I will take great care to educate him correctly for as I said; I feel something of a debt is owed." Desiree stated calmly and firmly as she looked first to her mother, back to Therasil and then quickly and discreetly back again to her mother before excusing herself.

"They exited the hall quickly and rapidly she led him away down halls that turned inexplicitly into apparent forest pathways then back into beautiful hallways and he needed to use every last bit of his physical ability to keep up with her."

She spoke quietly as they continued to slip quickly through the woods. "Thank the stars that my mother was of good mood and allowed me to teach you of our laws, for Therasil is not satisfied with the way that this rescue came about. She is very ambitious and can be very cruel!" We must stay away from her and her "chaperones," Desiree whispered. "I would now show you a place that you must remember perfectly, as it is where you my come back to me through the realm without being discovered, do you understand?"

"Yes," I said.

"That is where we will begin, be silent unless I or one of us asks something of you or asks you to speak," She began. "Please, just listen for a few moments and stay with me step for step as I must show the chaperones that they have no hope of staying with me in my home. Hold my hand," She commanded. As she led me out of the castle, through a courtyard, under the huge roots of an ancient tree, through a long tunnel covered by thick jungle canopy with numerous turns and slants and then through a sheer leaf curtain, out to a beautiful meadow on the side of the foothills that approached a massive mountain that appeared to begin to reach to the very heavens."

"As she escorted me along this trail at break-neck speed she told me. For over two centuries we have lived with our men as prisoners. It was not always so, but we are told that the ancients grew tired of consistent bondage, beatings and other unfairness that the men of the past had made part of their women's everyday lives. They had decided that this is the way that all men behave and as they needed them for reproduction they enslaved all of them; for all time, they were said to have stated. The Raginites are their descendants that had somehow escaped and still support the old beliefs, as they are cowardly, dishonest and refuse to change. They would rather steal something than trade fairly for it and they would rather kidnap and subjugate than to win a maidens heart as we hear that the men of old did, and even some today I am beginning to see. They have laid down the following rules that must be strictly obeyed, as there is but one punishment.... That is Death!

"Men may speak only when spoken to, or asked to do so. When not caged a man must be bound hands, neck and feet or, escorted by no less than four warriors and men must obey all commands at all times. Men must also service whatever warrior has won the right of fertilization and failure to do so, be it willing or not, is a punishable offence. Last and most importantly telling anyone of our location will not be tolerated, as our sanctity is most sacred to us. Please obey these rules and I will try to convince my mother to be easy with you, as you are so very different. Do you understand?'

"I took her hands as before and gazed into her eyes and said, Yes Desiree I do, but your people need to learn that all men are not like those in your people's past, and that mine is a proud and honest people that treat their women with respect; however we will not be enslaved by anyone. Our people need to have counsel with one another."

Desiree pleaded with her eyes and said, "Our time runs short. I would like to see more of you and perhaps will come a time when we can share a future together, so please just promise me that you will bide your time for a while and I will make the arrangements that you would like in time. Just be patient," She paused and whispered, "For me!"

"When you ask, I cannot help but comply, for you have touched me deeply into my very soul." I told her. "However, I must be away for a while as I have dear and trusted friends that I am sure are very concerned with my whereabouts, and they need be warned of the dangers of the crystals. I will but caution them, put their worries to rest and make certain that my ship is secure and then make haste to return to you. We can talk of our people to one another and you will teach me your ways."

"When you return, please be very careful, as our warriors can be quite ruthless when dealing with men at times," she warned again. "Go back to your home now, but be aware that the next time you go, I shall have to return with you and bring back our crystals; please make them ready for me."

"But, what of defending my people from the Raginites," I exclaimed?

"They had but one set of crystals and it must be returned to us, this cannot be changed. They cannot travel via the realm to any place that they do not know unless someone that knows the place willingly takes them through the realm to that place after linking minds and that only happens rarely as far as I know. Believe me, your people are safe, but we will make certain of that when you come back." Desiree assured him.

Desiree asked, "How long must you have in order for you to set your affairs to rights?"

I thought to myself and told her. "I would confer with my friends, gather some things and be back to you before the sun grows low enough in the sky to disappear behind this mighty mountain."

"This is well," She said, "For there are dangers in this jungle, besides our deadly Amazonian archers. We have monsters here that I do not believe you have seen anywhere else in your travels; and unknown they can be of very great peril."

"Ebirius boldly stated, "I have been exposed to my share of danger and have always been able to take care of myself and those in my care until now!"

Desiree smiled and stated, "You do not have to prove you courage, or resourcefulness to this maid that you so recently rescued. Just be careful my love!"

We both looked at each other in astonishment, realizing that we both shared same intense feelings, "I will make all haste my love, just meet me back here in three hours."

She looked at me crooked-headed without understanding and it dawned on me. I had seen no sundials, no mention of the time of day at all, for they did not measure time as we did! "When the sun is about to hide behind the mount meet me here, my love." I stated.

"Yes, my love for I desire time at your side, as my love for you is burning" She cooed.

"Yes, I can feel the love burning intensely within me also."

"I will soon quench that fire," She said.

"By now I was becoming somewhat proficient at gaining the realm, and after the familiar cold and flash. I was once again back aboard the "Osprey." Durages and Flaxon were sitting down to their evening meal it appeared and the sun was getting low in the sky. This alarmed me somewhat as I had left Desiree only seconds ago and it was just past midday. I decided that I should just stick to the plan of three hours and learn what I could from her, as her people were the ones that had mastered this art of travel in what they referred to as the realm."

"I told them all that I could of my adventure in the time allowed; I was also careful not to mistakenly give information as to tell where the Amazons land was. (That was very easy, as I had not a clue where I had been, only how to get back!) I found this very strange and I was aching to return to Desiree. I added, as an order; that was exceedingly rare for me, as I never really had to. "Stow the netherworld equipment out of sight and safely, as there is more danger hidden in it than we yet realize. Then make sail to the west to "Guardian Rock" and anchor near the reefs there; as the fishing is good and I will meet you there on the third morn. If someone tries to board to search for the crystals, flee; you can outrun any ship in these waters! Do not worry my friends, I will return in three days. They both, nodded their agreement, gave me a friendly embrace and began to go about their business. They were really wonderful friends and crew, I was truly blessed.

As I prepared to gain the realm once more I noticed that it was fully dark, I thought to myself the sun was performing strangely today, I then took the needed steps and went back to Desiree!

"I was just a couple of minutes early by my reckoning and in a good location, behind the roots of a giant tree with lots of ferns to conceal me and recognized that it was nearly dusk, just the time I said I would arrive and somehow, I knew Desiree was nearby as I felt that I could feel her presence. Just then I heard some rustling in the treetops to my right and shortly after some low, but very audible clicks in the trees on the other side of the clearing. I began to edge around the roots, stooping as I went to remain out of sight and being as quiet as I could be. I gained access to an area where I thought I would get a better view, when I was suddenly grabbed from behind with a neck breaking death grip that I recognized as it was taught me by my father with one arm bent and the other hand over my mouth; I had been captured in a warriors grip, very strong, but strangely soft!"

Desiree whispered as a light breeze into my ear, "You are too clumsy in the jungle my dear, I must teach you better skills. They are hunting monkeys yonder, but they could have just as easily found their mark in you. I do not want that sort of accident to happen."

"Nor I," I whispered.

"Be absolutely silent and follow me; your man's voice carries far in these woods. I will take us now to a chamber to where we can have some privacy. We can discuss what has happened, our plans and anything else that we desire. The looks of longing that we shared with one another told us what we wanted; the love was growing very strong between us. I had never felt a bond such as we now had between us, that is, until later on in our relationship as the intensity always continued to grow!"

"While I was an accomplished sailor and navigator, and experienced at many things, I had never been close like this with a woman. The experience of lovemaking with Desiree was not only beautiful and unforgettable, but the most tender expression of caring between two people that I have ever known or heard of. While the details are personal, suffice it to say that after that evening I felt as though I would do anything for her; even die if it was needed in order to protect her!"

As the night transpired we spoke more of the rules of her people, and I began to think that we may be able to reach some kind of understanding, though I began to see that I was probably not going to be able to help their men captives immediately, that would take some lengthy negotiations. With the new love I had found here though, that process just might become possible in time I thought to myself.

The next morning we had a breakfast of fresh fruit, delightful rolls and tasty syrup that I was not familiar with, as I told her how delicious I thought it was, I thought to myself. Someone knows that we are here to have sent us this breakfast, could we be in danger? "That was very thoughtful," I said, and then I asked my beautiful Desiree, "Who arranged this wonderful breakfast?"

"Oh, my mother sent it," She beamed happily at me, "She probably wants you strong for tonight!"

I was caught completely off guard, "Tonight," I queried, "What happens tonight?"

"Why she will have you come to service her of course. She will command you and you cannot refuse," Desiree stated as a matter of fact.

I tried to get her to understand, "Desiree, my love, let me try to explain. My people have different customs than do yours; different but just as important as the set of rules that your people have adopted. When a man and woman of my culture find someone that they love, they honor that love with a vow of faithfulness and loyalty to one another that is lifelong, called marriage. The only way it will end usually is the death of one or the other. We promise ourselves to one another and no one else, it is our way and the way of our ancestors, and I would have only you!"

She smiled warmly at me and I could see that she was deeply touched, "You are so very different, but it matters not as my mother cannot be denied, she is the queen."

"Expert I am not, but I do know that I can return to my ship whenever I want," I tried to show that I was not entirely at her mother's command. "I will not live as a slave, Please let me talk with your mother."

She pulled on a gilded cordage on the wall and turned to embrace me, "Truly I want you to be all mine, and I for only you, but beware the Amazon ways. We have magic, potions and many wiles and I can only protect you so much, you must be very careful," She kissed me deeply.

Suddenly four guards burst into the room. I was seized and roughly pushed out the door and down a lengthy hallway to a different courtyard than the one I had seen with Desiree the previous evening, I was indelicately thrown into the room and Desiree walked in a few moments later. The place was an interesting mixture of the outside jungle with all of the conveniences that were to be had anywhere in the castle. On one side stood a pedestal and a very large and comfortable looking bed with sheets that looked of some fine grade cloth. The other side had two large sofas and a number of smaller chairs, where it looked as though could be held some of the more casual meetings. Beyond those on two walls was an ornate, yet sturdy looking façade with fine screen in the spaces; walls that could keep out the wild things of the jungle yet still are seen through. Most gloriously of all, in the middle of the courtyard, featured among splendid statues, exotic plants, gemstones and orchids of all colors was a luxurious tub; large enough to be called a pool by some was Queen Andrea. Splendid, yet still instilled with an aura of absolute power, even in her nudity. She sprawled languidly in the steamy water and appraised me for a few moments. Fortunately for me (I believe) I remembered to adhere to her rules, at least for the time, and held my tongue until she addressed me, "You are called Ebirius, and you are truly very different; so says my sweet young Desiree, come join me and let me be the judge of that."

I did not move, and tried not to look too defiant and for a few moments nothing happened; then several of her guards began to approach me. I stared questioningly at Desiree, not knowing exactly what to do.

Desiree broke the tension by saying, "Mother, he is truly very different and his people have very strange ways of living that we are not accustomed to. They are not bad ways, but merely different! He has asked to speak to you and I told him that I would make the request. I think that you will be glad that you did my mother. Please listen to him; he speaks with honor and truth.

Queen Andrea Perseii looked from her daughter to me with a heavy gaze and commanded me, "Approach me young man and let me learn what has touched my daughter so," The queen summoned. "I already know that you do not covet men over woman, as it can be seen," She paused, examining my demeanor carefully, glancing at the part of me that in fact implied just what she said. "Look at me, do you not find me attractive," She asked.

"Oh no Queen Andrea, that is not it, nothing could be further from the truth, I find you exceptionally, beautiful and quite attractive. You are the picture of what all men would fight and die for in a woman, although I would try to make you understand that it is a purely cultural difference. You see, in my culture when a man and woman fall in love with each other they make a vow of commitment to each other, forsaking all others for all of their lives. We call this marriage and it is deeply revered in my land. I would humbly ask your permission to ask your daughter if she would have me in this most sacred of vows." I paused for a moment while I tried to gauge what she thought of my words. She seemed to be accepting what I said thus far, so I thought I would continue. "My people also do not believe in, or practice slavery, save prisoners of war until the two sides can exchange their charges back to one another. Though I wish with all of my heart to be with Desiree, with your permission, I will not live as a slave, and I beg your pardon as I do not want to seem arrogant, but I do have means to escape if I see fit. I and mine are against the practice of all slavery. As an attempt to show my willingness to cooperate I added, "I believe your highness that both of our people can benefit from meeting and learning about one another and I believe that I can make the arrangements for it to begin to happen if you would give me your permission, for I am an accomplished navigator and can sail back here with my ship after I take some star sightings."

"Enough," The Queen growled. "Different you may be, but you will not come here and presume to change the way that Amazons have lived for many lifetimes. There will be no meeting of our cultures now or ever, unless I deem it necessary and as for your request of Desiree in marriage, I will consider it this evening, as it is an honorable request; the kind of behavior that I am told by our scrolls, our men once possessed. Lastly, we will keep our slaves, we Amazons have been happy, even our slaves for the most part, have been happy with this way of life for hundreds of years. The neighboring peoples around us fear our military might and so leave us alone in our jungle homes. We have abundance of food, room and treasure. We will not change a way of living that has produced all of this, and as for your learning of the realm, just remember, there are none who can achieve the realm faster than an Amazon arrow. As you have held your tongue when needed and have spoken well, I will dwell on your request this evening, after I have discussed it with my daughter. Take him to my library," She ordered, "And keep him safe, do you understand Therasil?"

"As you wish, my Queen," Therasil muttered silkily.

As I was led away Desiree and I crossed paths, as we exchanged glances I could see a great deal of relief in her face, still I wondered if I could have been too bold with her mother and what the consequences were going to be.

They deposited me into yet another room in this huge castle in the woods, with just a bit more dignity than last time.

"You may read if you wish to learn about us." The guards said as they walked out of the room, knowing that I could not discern what their scrolls said, so I contented myself with the beautiful artwork that I found inside of some."

What I believed would take a matter of minutes turned into several hours of waiting and as I examined a larger number of the scrolls, a picture clarified picture of their past began to emerge. The Amazons seemed to have been similar in many ways to my people of several hundred years ago; they even were quite gifted sailors and navigators. This was evident from the many maps that I had found within these journals. While their home is in the heart of an immense jungle, they used a great river that they had named for themselves; to gain access to the open sea. They seemed to have sailed great distances in all directions, but what I found most interesting were the maps that showed the voyages that were taken to the East and Northeast, after crossing a great sea, they had found and mapped the coasts of lands with which I was familiar, including my home. They were easy to recognize, being a mapmaker myself. The more I learned about the Amazons, the more intrigued I became with wanting to learn more of them.

Unfortunately, it appeared that several hundred years ago something horrible happened. I wondered what had changed to create the unusual type of culture that existed here now! I needed to ask Desiree all, about her peoples past. And just as I thought of her, she walked back into the room.

"I did not know that you could read our language," She hurriedly stated while smiling at me.

"I cannot, however the pictures and maps tell their own story," I offered.

"Perhaps you will be able to return, but for now we must leave and quickly!" She urged me. "We must gain a place of safety unknown to Therasil while she is busy with my mother, as I know that she entertains designs on us now that could be quite unpleasant. She is angry with me and has designs on adding you to her host of slaves. Do not think that you can always escape; she also is an Amazon princess, and we have our ways, spells, potions and the like. Also never forget the crystals, they have great power and it can be used in ways that you know nothing about, my love!"

"You knew what your mother was planning," I stated quietly.

"Yes," She said innocently, "It is all that I have ever known."

"Well," I began to scold her.

"I am so happy that you stood up to her, for I want you all for myself and am happy to love no other man except you for you are so truly different and I do not want to share you," She beamed. "Now follow me quickly!"

For the next thirty minutes or so we ran, skipped, swung through trees and crawled, until we came to small clearing in front of a large lake. Moonlit though it was, its aura was that of deadly menace, something that I could not quite fathom warned me of danger in this body of jungle water.

She pointed at a huge, ancient looking, gnarly tree that was easily fifty cubits wide at the bottom and clearly thirty cubits wide even seventy cubits up, "That is where we are headed.

"Do you have a boat; it looks like a long swim," I was saying as I took a step towards the water.

"Oh no, you must stay away from that water," She said with a sly grin. "The crocs and the cannibal fish would finish you before you got a third of the way across. This is my special place of solitude where I have set traps and other contrivances to protect my privacy, as when you are the daughter of the Queen it is very difficult to gain."

"As you say, my most fascinating lady," I merely took her hand and said, "Show me the way, as I know that you have something in mind!"

"Come," She said with a mischievous smile.

We backtracked forty cubits the way we had come to another tree, not quite as large as the one on the other shore, but huge none the less.

She turned to me and whispered, "Up this tree just as I; try to be quick and please do it as quietly as you can."

She seemed to be getting anxious; I followed as best I could. When she was at the height of about forty cubits she stopped and whispered again, "Lean against here and don't move." As I did what I was told, she reached up behind a crooked limb and I heard a barely audible click. Seconds later a stout looking rope appeared in front of me and I could see that it stretched across the water to the great tree. What is more, I saw clearly four loop trusses on it within our reach. "Grab the first one, wrap it around your shoulders step into the second and hold on until we reach the other side, I will follow right behind you." As I secured my hold, I heard another low click. We were pulled across the lake as if shot from a sling. I was forced to hold on very tightly, but it was rather exhilarating and we were across in just a few moments, the landing was quite comfortable and then as I turned around my sweet Desiree was tossed into my waiting arms.

"We are safe for now," She said as she returned my warm embrace, "Though my feeling is that we must do something about Therasil!"

"I do not understand," I said as I held her tight.

"She is never happy with what is hers, she always wants more. She thinks that she should be Queen, as a great deal of royal blood flows in her veins as well as my mothers, or so she says! It has never been proven conclusively and she is want to challenge my mother to prove it in combat, as my mother is most likely the fiercest warrior in all of our land. Therasil is more cunning than that; when she makes her move it will be far more sinister and I know it will happen one day soon. It will be using some strange contrivance, trickery or deceit, which would be her way," She pondered with a troubled look on her face. "She also wants you for her own very badly; I can see it in her face and I warn you again, beware for she is devilishly cunning, and has many warriors that are loyal to only her. She will pursue what she wants with great ruthlessness, until it is hers and I fear now this would put the two that I love most in the world both in great danger from her."

I only held her tighter, "Perhaps we can help one another." I said as I held her head up to give her an assuring kiss.

Again my love and respect for my sweet Desiree keep me from telling of the wondrous time of our passion. Suffice it to say that it was so much more rewarding than I had dreamed about for a large part of my young life. I was also amazed at the tenderness and power of emotion that we both exhibited; afterwards we fell soundly asleep in each other's arms.

"Allow me to interrupt her for a moment. As you are probably aware, I was speaking to you as Ebirius. We share much of the mind and sometimes it is difficult to keep the memories separate." Granger snapped back to himself and interjected, "You see, Ebirius had visions of a long life of living and loving with the beautiful Desiree, with his finding of the ways of the realm he must have had a certain perceived feeling of invincibility for you see the realm is mysterious in that way, however what you achieve is not always as you had intended. You see, Ebirius was a most honorable young man and not only wanted to help the brave and lovely young woman and her mother, but he wanted to do something to earn the respect and along with it the good graces of Queen Andrea, thinking that it would make the life with Desiree that he wanted so much to achieve easier to accomplish; regrettably he could not have been more wrong!

The next morning he was awakened to not only Desiree's soft and loving embraces, but yet another delightful fresh fruit that he had never before seen, "Have your ladies been here also," Ebirius asked?

"No, not here, not ever," She exclaimed! "You were sleeping so soundly that I went and gathered it myself, it was very near."

"I cannot believe I slept so well, I have always been a very light sleeper, perhaps the added comfort that you have added to my life," Ebirius claimed somewhat surprised at himself.

"Comfort or exercise," She chuckled? She then paused, smiling and then delicately added, "The realm is new to you, it can be taxing, and you needed your rest."

"I feel well rested now. Why don't you come here and hold me," I invited.

She showed a perceptive smile and sprawled into my eager arms; a little while later she told me, "Come, we have much to accomplish. We must meet with mother later today for we think it wise that we have a plan to deal with Therasil, in order to achieve this I believe that you need some further training in use of the realm."

"A good point," I agreed.

"First you must realize that it is not only very demanding of you, but it is also very fickle." She began her instruction. "You must be able to concentrate with a good deal of precision or you will become lost in the realm or end up somewhere that you had not planned; either of these can be fatal."

I remembered my promise to Durages and Flaxon and said. "I have promised my crew to meet with them tomorrow; I hope that this training will not interfere with me keeping that promise."

"Oh no," She said, "As a matter of fact, it will be part of the training.

We also must return the crystals. We will coordinate that with my mother, as I am sure that she wants us to return them to a location that she chooses. That will be the only way to protect them from Therasil's intrigues and this is something we most definitely need to do, as she will stop at nothing to fulfill her ambition to become queen."

"Why does your mother just challenge her to combat and best her for all to see, if she is such an accomplished warrior, I queried?"

Desiree explained. "That is not as simple as it sounds. Royal combat ends only in death for one or the other, and Therasil claims that she comes from an ancient line and a good portion of the Amazons are very loyal to her because of this."

My mother is hard set in her ways and can be rather harsh in her judgments at times, but she loves her people very much and that love always guides her actions, although she has acquired great wealth and power, she has done so not in the pursuit of such, but has come by those fairly in her dealings with our people. The well being of her people has always been her first priority and for this she is well loved by the great majority of all of them, save the ones that Therasil has corrupted with tales of far off beautiful kingdoms and vast treasures beyond our lands, across the great seas."

I interrupted to inform her, "Desiree, there are such places. I am a sailor by trade and I can show you many of the places such as she speaks and more, but all things in their own time, for now we are confronted with the problem of your mother's nemesis. We must create a plan that is certain to help your mother maintain her throne and protect her people and especially her daughter.

"Yes," Desiree agreed. "However we must be very careful; Therasil has a renowned system of spies that enable her to have great knowledge of matters that are supposed secrets. She has surprised many Amazons by knowing their plans, and always seemingly to her profit. The first thing we must accomplish is that we must put the crystals back to where they rightfully belong; The Raginites would not have been able to steal them in the first place were it not for Therasil's wicked stratagems. After that, we must find the location where her followers are mining the rough crystals, with luck we can do so before she gains the knowledge to produce her own working crystals and have the widespread power of gaining the realm at her disposal."

"Do not all Amazons have this power," I asked?

"Oh no," She exclaimed! "The realm is too perilous to give everyone the knowledge of it, there are dangers that even the years of training that we priestesses receive may not prepare you for. Letting all know of the ways of the realm would be far too dangerous; it could destroy my people, or even worse, just make us disappear forever within its desolation."

"Priestess," I asked, "You are a priestess?"

She explained, "Yes, I am as is my mother and her mother and hers before; you must first be a priestess to one day become queen. Ours is the religion of the "Druii"- worshippers of mother earth and nature. Therasil was ordained a priestess long ago, however she now only remembers it when it is convenient and blasphemes our beliefs much these days and I dread what the future holds for her, for it is the belief of most of us that nature repays in kind. In other words, your deeds of today shape your fate of tomorrow. What do you think?"

"I would have to say that I hope that this is true, as I try always to let fairness guide my actions and to do what I feel is right," I confessed. "Meeting you is really enough proof of the truth in my beliefs for me!"

"You," She whispered tenderly. "I will indulge in your charming ways later, but for now I must depart for a short time. Is your hunger sated, can I get you anything before I go?"

"My hunger for you will never be satisfied my love, but as for food I am fine for now," I told her. "If possible though have you any books here in your hideaway, perhaps one with maps and charts like the one I found in the library?"

"You are in luck," She told me. "The one book that I keep here has both and I think that it will interest you immensely. She opened a cabinet next to the bed and pulled out a huge volume twice the width of my hand and told me, "Keep yourself interested in this for a while and do not leave here, please, for it would be very dangerous for you. I will return in no more than half of the morn' with a plan that I am certain my mother will have for us. She kissed me and then stood up and disappeared into a sparkling silver fog.

"I could only marvel, as that was the first time that I had seen her venture into the realm. It was quite beautiful and looked to me much of magic, yet she has taught me that it was but part of nature; still I believe that nature is full of magic and do not see how you can ever really separate the two."

"My attention then turned to the great book that she had left with me. In the front was what looked like the title, but deciphering the runes that made up their written language would not come to me until much later I was convinced. What I did recognize, I thought were the symbols that mean her people's name; Amazon. I later found what the rest of it meant, so that I know today that I was reading the book called Lands, Seas and Treasures of the Amazon Empire. It also looked very ancient, could it have been written when the men were not yet slaves?"

"I leafed through the pages until I fell across some maps and that is where my interest truly lay. Theirs was a great land; it appeared far larger than even my home sea, the Mesopotamian Sea, named for the peoples that we had found traces of living in our lands before us."

"Throughout the entire land was a great river system that as far as I could ascertain was the one that bore their name. It looked as though the mouth of this great river was wide enough to hold many great cities or numbers of fleets with room to spare; it emptied into what appeared to me to be the western sea that I had begun to explore after finding my way west through the horns of Bospero. I felt this because of finding on the map a coastline at the extreme east that looked exactly like the one that my crew and I were just exploring weeks before that we called the "Dark Land," Because of both the thick dark green jungles that we had seen exist there and the curious black skinned people that we had also seen living there. I also saw the islands that we call "Ascension Rock," mapped to perfection. The map ended there, but I knew that a day and a halves sail to the east were the horns of Bospero and my home sea, I had been correct; I could easily sail to this land!"

"I also found what appeared to me to be the Capitol City of their land; it was at a fork in the great river and looked as though it was hundreds of leagues upstream from the sea. I felt as though that was probably exactly where I was now located and would ask Desiree about it later, for now I just concentrated on memorizing the map, as I did not want to damage an obvious treasure belonging to the Amazon people that was in the safekeeping of my new found love."

"When I was confident that I could find my way to the mouth of the great "Amazon" river from the Ascension Islands that I was fairly familiar with, I continued to study the volume. I desired so greatly that their written language made some sort of since to me, as there was much information to be learned, but that was not now possible."

I then came across what looked like a plan for one of their ships; it was somewhat larger than the "Osprey" with several interesting additions. In addition to the large area of sails that my ship was so well endowed with, they had spaces for oars, a convenience that I had wished at times that I had the required crew for. There was also what looked like a weighted keel that could be raised or lowered as the need arose; most ingenious. Additionally there were also several rather ominous looking features for at the bow there was a ram protruding out front, just below the waterline, and the wheel had a protective housing that could be raised into place. They were obviously warriors!

This made me even more curious about what had happened with the Amazons. Why had the women taken control? What had happened that the men had let themselves become slaves? And why were they no longer a seafaring people? They had, at one time been at least as accomplished as my people currently in their ways of the sea; the mystery was becoming more complex by the moment and there was much that I needed to learn! I continued in my reference work on Amazon history that I could not yet read, though while I kept trying to decipher their language I was unfortunately not having much luck. Suddenly I came across something that I recognized all too well, it was the equipment for gaining the netherworld, along with what appeared to be calculations and measurements to produce the crystals. The next page had some very boldly written and ominous looking symbols and an arrow pointing to the next page, but unfortunately it had been torn out of the book at an earlier time. This is becoming more interesting by the moment, I thought to myself.

I was startled from my studies by a sound that I did not recognize, as I walked across to the entrance on the opposite side that we had come in and slowly opened the shutter I saw that the day had passed and it was already well into dusk, below me I saw a huge brute of a boar burrowing into the soft ground after who knows what. That explained the sound, but what had become of Desiree?

I began to weigh my options. She had asked me not to leave, but

I was beginning to worry for her safety. I could go back carefully the way she had brought me last night; no too dangerous, even if I could reliably find my way, or I could use the realm to go to the place she had shown me to go to. No that could be equally as dangerous, or I could continue to wait here for her to return. While the opportunity to study more of this very remarkable culture was most inviting; none of these options suited me at all!

I began to search about for a suitable weapon so as not to be entirely defenseless, but found naught but a small dagger apparently more of a decoration than any sort of defensive tool; I picked it up and began to walk towards the back door.

Thankfully Desiree popped into the same door that we had arrived in almost noiselessly right then. She was very anxious, "Gather yourself quickly for we must make haste," She said. "Foul workings are afoot, we must leave at once!"

"What is it Desiree," I queried?

"I do not know how they did it, as it has never before been accomplished, but I was followed. They are close now and there are many," She warned.

"They come to fight," I stated, feeling the beginnings of a great anger that someone would so threaten my sweet Desiree.

"No," She said somberly; while a look of absolute certainty showed as stone upon her face, "They come to kill! We must use the realm to escape, as Therasil has the jungle thick with warriors. My Mother and I have prearranged a meeting, but she will not be there until tomorrow evening, we must escape now; I thought that you might take me to your ship," The sound of a whipping rope interrupting her for a moment, "Right now," she finished!

"Yes, I said, but how?"

"Just hold me and go," She nearly commanded.

I clinched her closely and pictured the "Osprey" in my mind. Then, as we were about to emerge from the lighted silver fog of the nether world I saw it! The face of a Dragon, and it was looking at me with something like compassion in his eyes. Desiree saw it too, but as quickly as it had come, he was gone and we were on the deck of the "Osprey" with Durages and Flaxon looking on in awe!

"Did you see it too," I asked?

"Yes, I saw it too," She assured me. "What was it, for it appeared quite fearsome, but at the same time beautiful and even pleasant?"

"Yes, truly I would not want to anger it, yet I feel that this beast and I share a fate closer than either of us can now imagine," I stated.

"It appeared that there was something," Desiree agreed. "But, at least we are safe for now."

"We need have no fear of that one," I offered.

"I then noticed the admiring interest that my crew had in my guest; after all she was quite beautiful. "Durages and Flaxon, my crew; allow me introduce you to Princess Desiree Perseii of the Amazons. She is, as you will soon see for yourselves the most wonderful woman that I have ever met and we are soon to be betrothed."

Flaxon nearly fell to his face performing an outlandishly formal, yet impressive in a slightly humorous way introductory statement, saying "It is our honor to make your acquaintance." He did this as he nearly fell over the side with imposed formality, making us all have a good chuckle and lightening the mood appreciatively.

Durages was not as flamboyant. He just stated, "The pleasure is mine and the friendship and loyalty that we show Ebirius is at your disposal, welcome!"

"There you have now met my well loved crew Desiree," I proclaimed. "Better and more dependable friends cannot be found. The three of us have trusted one another with our lives on countless occasions and we can speak freely with them. Let us tell them of the Amazon rules; accepting their pledge that I know they will keep; then have supper as we tell them of our situation."

Flaxon volunteered without delay, "I will prepare some fresh Red Grunt-fish that we have caught this morning. They will go well with the flat cakes that I made just a while ago.

Desiree, with an interesting look on her face that was a mix of both demure and melancholy disclosed. "I too have a few very close friends as you three seem to be. You will meet them soon. I have also lost some like them as well, what you have is very precious and will be most valuable in the days to come. I feel that all of our loyalties will be put to the test in the next fortnight.'

Ebirius spoke, "Desiree, tell us what we can do to help your mother put an end to Therasil's conniving ways and restore peace to your kingdom."

Desiree began sadly, "Let me explain it to you. Therasil is very ambitious and will stop at nothing to usurp power from my mother the Queen. She has not been able to succeed with any legal ways, so she is trying to utilize scheming and deceit. We also fear that she is illegally showing her warriors the ways of the realm and this is very dangerous, as they have not been appointed as priestesses and so have not been adequately trained. My mother says that this can only lead to disaster. As I have told my love Ebirius, there are things about the realm that even we that have been trained for generations do not understand; such as picturing something that you have only seen in a painting or from verbal description in your mind and arriving somewhere that you do not know. There are even stories of sorceresses in the past projecting things to priestesses' minds with a spell and making them disappear forever. I feel that I will be forever learning of the realm and yet it will still remain a mystery, for that is its nature! Though for now we are faced with the problem of returning the "Realm Crystals" to the safeguarding of a secure priestess stronghold; but not the temple where they were kept before, as Therasil and her minions have compromised the safety of that place and it may never again be restored."

"They used the Realm to steal the crystals," Ebirius interjected.

"Yes," She replied. "As you know, once you have envisioned a location and traveled there using the realm, you can return there whenever you wish." She explained. "So that place is lost to us. We also believe that she is training her warriors not only to use the realm, which will be rather slow without the crystals. I guess that is something that we can thank the Raginites for; but also to mine and create more crystals. Of this we feel a great concern, as I know that she has acquired a plan to cut the crystals."

It was then that I realized who had vandalized the book and I let slip, "That's the missing page!"

"Yes, it was Therasil, Twas not even a fortnight ago and I was finishing my lessons in the temple quite late at night when I saw for just a moment the silhouette of Therasil; she was walking out of the sacred tablet room and she appeared to be rolling something into a small scroll. Then came her scent, I would recognize that sickly-sweet flour smell anywhere, as I remembered it from when I was younger and she tried to force herself upon me. No one else smelled like that, the recognition was now complete. Suddenly I saw the foggy shine of the realm in the background and when I got around the corner, she was gone. When I walked into the room that stores all of our history I saw one of our greatest volumes, The Land, Seas and Treasures of the Amazon Empire opened to the page telling about the cutting and polishing of the crystals with the page of the drawings and measurements torn out. She had stolen the plans for our most sacred treasure, the Crystals for gaining of the realm; that was when I vowed then to recover them, but instead found the Raginites!"

Suddenly Durages exclaimed, "What if we need the crystals to protect our people from this surly looking clan that intends to attack our people, our neighbors or both?

"Durages," Ebirius exclaimed, halting his friend!

"Wait Ebirius, let me explain," Desiree gently offered. "Durages and Flaxon, neither of you know me or my people though my love says that you have heard of us in your travels. I just want to tell you that our keeping the realm from you or anyone is more for your own protection than for anything else, as we will endeavor to show you in the next short span of time. As for the Raginites, you have nothing to fear from them, as any bragging or boasting by them is totally unfounded. Anything that they have has been acquired through thievery and deceit and they would be no match for a well commanded warship, let alone a fleet. Though, I hear that in the days of old our men; for that is whom the Raginites are descended from; those Amazon men that escaped our control, were very competent sailors of the seas."

Desiree speculated, "In any case, it is going to come to pass that you will see the demise of the Raginites accompany that of Therasil's group, for the two mingle at times. We can only hope!"

If only young Desiree knew just how true and widespread this prediction was to become; she knew not that she had just unknowingly spoken of the fate of most all of her kind!

"My mother has a plan that we believe will cause Therasil to be the catalyst of her own downfall; First, she has hidden some of her guards at the mine; of this we are certain. We know Therasil has placed her own loyal warriors so that she will be provided with knowledge of what takes place at the mines and she believes that they will not be detected. My mother has also taken steps equipping her "special warriors" with a certain unique weapon that we call the "fork of darkness." It is more a capture device than killing weapon, as it will force anyone whom is not protected with earplugs to fall into an instant deep sleep. It was discovered by accident, so the story goes when they were making an instrument to use in the tuning of one of the giant harps that the ancients had produced. The Priestesses have now safely stored it as we have done numerous relics from our past."

"However, this will probably not be the way that we thwart Therasil, as she will most likely always just send others to replace those that we capture over time and she knows that to be caught at the mines if you are not a priestess means suffering execution. We have something else in mind that we believe she will not be able to resist; with your help we can take her and her clan to an island in an area that we know of where exists naturally occurring conditions that make it impossible to use the realm. If we banish her to this place, as that my mother is a very noble woman and insists that the punishment be banishment is according to Amazon law Therasil and her minions will not be able to return and make trouble ever again. That is where I will become involved; I will convince Therasil that you know of another mine location that has the same natural crystals that she wants. Using the realm, I will take her to our mine and we capture and imprison her there."

"She gazed into my eyes trying to gauge what I was thinking and pleaded, "Well, what do you think?""

"It sounds overly complicated to be honest with you," I stated.

"I am sorry my love, I ask too much of you. You have known me for such a short time and I ask you to risk your life to help my people, I am being selfish," Desiree lamented."

"Nothing could be further from the truth, my love," I assured her. "I would die for you, although I would rather live a long life with you at my side. So, this will take some clever planning and maybe the help of two of the most cunning people that the world has ever known. What do you say," Ebirius asked of his friends, "Does this not sound like the adventure that we have been seeking?"

"There will likely be a considerable reward, if I know my mother," Desiree quickly added."

"Princess Desiree, we do not seek adventure for the gaining of personal riches. Our wealth is from a different source," Durages began attempting to explain to Desiree.

"Will it be dangerous and with all odds against us," Flaxon interrupted cynically?

"You know it," Shot back Ebirius!

"Sounds like the quest that we seek," his mates exclaimed with ever broadening smiles.

"What could be better?" Ebirius exclaimed. "My betrothed, my best friends and shipmates at my side, going to protect my loves family and make right the Amazon's problems and protect all the good in their culture; Therasil had better beware."

"Make sail out into the great western sea, south of Ascension Island and set a course Southwest at maximum speed. I know how to find the Amazon's homeland and trust that queen Andrea now will accept our arrival," Ebirius commanded. "We will help them to achieve a new age of greatness!"

"If only it could have been that simple," The Piasa lamented as he continued.

Later that evening Ebirius was startled abruptly from a dream that he was having as he took a short nap on Flaxon's watch, he nudged Desiree awake and told her, "I must gain a weapon that will kill a large Black Dragon; do your people have such a thing as this?"

"Yes, we have mighty weapons stored that can kill even the huge river snakes and saber toothed cats that inhabit our jungle, but what is a dragon," Desiree queried?

"It is what we saw in the realm earlier, and I know that it is my fate to save that one as I know that he will someday save my life as well," Ebirius explained.

"Would you like me too take you there now," She gently asked? You see she understood the realm and new that it was possible to see a glimpse of your future at times and fully believed that he needed her help, just as she needed his, "Hold me," she said and a moment later they were in a huge, dimly lit storeroom. It was full of very beautifully crafted weapons of all shapes and sizes, ornately decorated musical instruments, armor that looked as though it was created for kings or queens, different crystals of all shapes and sizes, and beautifully crafted items that he had no idea what purpose they would have served. What he did know was that this room was full of Amazon history that he wanted to study and discover more about."

"She led him into a more congested area several cubits behind a large harp, which clearly appeared too large to be played by anyone that he had ever seen; he would inquire about that later."

"Suddenly he saw it, the most glorious lance that he had ever beheld; it was fully two cubits taller than him, carven with all sorts of pictographs, runes, and beasts of all sorts, some that he knew and some that he had not yet seen. The shaft appeared to be made of wood; however it was wood that was as dense and as hard as the ivory that Flaxon had shown him that were the teeth from the "Oliphant" beast that he had told him about. But it was the magnificent head of the shaft that set this lance apart from anything he had ever seen. It was carved from the same incredibly hard crystal that he had seen on the realm crystals. The difference was that this one was far thinner and came to a perfect and obviously very sharp point at its tip, and it seemed to have a faint glow that somehow bestowed it with a deep inner light and power all of its own."

"Desiree immediately warned me. Be very careful not to prick yourself or anyone that you do not wish to kill with this lance. My people call it "Saapwin." I suppose that would translate to your tongue as "life-drainer." It is a very dangerous weapon; there is nothing alive that it will not kill, in fact I am ashamed that my ancestors had ever created such a thing; though if this creature is as formidable as you say, I can see that you have an absolute need for its use, as you also "know" that your fates are intertwined and the creature we saw will someday save your life. There are those of my people that would believe that this is breaking the rules of its use; but the situation fit's the Amazon by-laws for its employment and as a high-priestess I have the authority to give you leave to use it on your quest, and this permission I now grant. Just remember that it can only be used against evil and we want it returned as soon as possible after you have achieved your goal."

"I will consider this a sacred trust and would only use it or anything at my disposal for good only," I swore.

"Of that I am certain, my love," Desiree whispered, as she gazed knowingly into my eyes."

"That is how I gained the weapon that I used to save my soon to be found soul-mate; the brown dragon that I would soon call Granger."

~~~~~~~~~~

Then, as Nathan watched; the great beast shuddered before refocusing his attention back to a warm gaze on the ever-attentive young man. He apologized instantly saying. "I apologize, but it is sometimes quite hard to recognize where that part of myself, which is the memory of Ebirius, ends and begins, as we were so very close. You see, normally when one loses one that they have become "impressed" with, the other cannot generally survive, as the pain is far too great. However, I believe that it is my commitment to the saving of the race of man which has kept me alive for the many seasons since his disappearance; also contributing is the fact that I have met and bonded with in sincere friendship with so many more very special "people," as you call yourselves. However I am becoming distracted; let us get back to the story of Ebirius and his sweet Desiree."

~~~~~~~~~~

"Well," Granger continued. "As I have told you, Desiree had arranged a meeting with her mother for the next day. Ebirius bravely chose this time to set up the "realm" equipment and locate the Brown dragon that he had seen. (More than just that time in the Realm; he knew that this was the dragon he had seen around his ship on many other occasions.) He prepared the crystals, as he coaxed all of the speed out of the "Osprey" that she could muster for he knew in his heart and with the help of the ancient Amazonian maps that if he sailed South-southwest he would find Desiree's homeland. It was further than they had ever sailed, but his crew trusted him implicitly and the coming promise of adventure was extremely enticing to the young men. They sailed into mild swells with a wonderfully fresh wind and the feeling of the salt spray in their faces so they knew that they would make very good time with the speed that their ship was known for and with an outright, absolute trust in their captain's word; this would be an unforgettable adventure!"

"So began the brave Phoenicians voyage that would bring them together with the Amazons and one very different brown dragon, named by some the Piasa."

"The next morning saw Desiree off to the meeting with her mother, Queen Andrea Perseii. She used the realm, so we did not know where it was, but Ebirius did know that she would be back soon. He decided to use the realm equipment to search for the dragon that he had seen; me. He set off with the "Saapwin" in hand just searching the realm with his memory of me, which is dangerous enough without such a horrible weapon. I am convinced that I sensed his inevitable danger and that is what brought me to the fateful encounter on this day. I guess that he tried several times that morning with no luck, for how was he to know that there is no need to search for your destiny, as it will always unerringly find you."

"As I described to you earlier, I had been searching for Ebirius for most of the morning and was very surprised to find him so far away from home."

The bravery and resourcefulness that he exhibited that morning in saving me from certain and horrible death at the whim of a black dragon twice my size is something that I will never forget. I also do not feel that I can ever repay the debt that I owe, as I feel that some of the traits that you humans possess are found only in your kind, but that is a part of my own personal journey."

"As it happened, he didn't find me; I found him and immediately after the Black found us! After the heroic struggle which I have previously described, we conferred on Ascension Island and I had the pleasure of seeing the beautiful Desiree appear out of the same magical light that I had seen Ebirius materialize from when he had saved me from the clutches of the black not so long before. Humans appear so differently from dragons when they use the realm as they have a large aura of light surrounding them, while dragons simply blink in and out with a much less pronounced aura of their own type; mine I have seen is a warm sparkling brown. However, when she appeared in her splendid radiance I was not at all surprised, but rather I had indeed felt her before ever meeting her."

Words of the Piasa

Ebirius was shocked, "How did you find us?" He queried as they embraced with obvious deep affection."

"Oh, I just followed my heart my dear, you could have done the same, but you merely haven't discovered it yet," She told him. As they spoke her attention turned to me; she stared at me in awe, but without what appeared to be any real trepidation and so for the moment, I just behaved as soothingly as I could and let the meeting unfold."

"I was taken by her extraordinary beauty when we first met, but as I came to know her, I was even more impressed with the absolute goodness of her soul. These two humans I would consider two the best examples of human kindness that this dragon has ever experienced."

"She was very cautious around me at first and I know that I must have been frightened mainly because of my size although as I talked to her and treated her gently she began to warm up to me until finally after hours of talking she even made herself quite comfortable on my outstretched wing."

As for her plan, I did not at that time understand the importance of why her mother the queen wanted to give her enemies the protection of the human laws as my kind had always merely battled our enemies and kill or been killed. At that time I did not understand the noble concepts that these humans were introducing to me and continue to this day to be astonished at their efforts at providing justice. I reaffirmed to her though of a large group of islands to what they called the west from this place. It was quite a long sail even for the speedy "Osprey." But as I told them these islands were the only place that I knew of where the realm could not be attained. They were in the southern part of the triangle that I may have mentioned before-where nature just doesn't behave in a normal manner. (Known today as the Bermuda Triangle) (7.) That meant that the only way to get the banished wrongdoers to their "confinement" would be to sail them aboard ship or fly them dragon back.

"I could see a curious mixture of interest and apprehension in both of their faces as I told them of the problems and blessings that these islands held."

Ebirius was the first to speak, "That sounds like the perfect place to keep Therasil and her bunch. I would like to see these islands and try to put our friends on one as far away from their homeland with as little material to build ships with as possible."

"So it was decided that Desiree would go and begin organizing the entrapment and consequent imprisonment of Therasil and her followers. She would first meet with her mother and acquire troops and the special weapons that they planned to use in the capture. I found it so strange; weapons that made your enemies sleep; that just seemed like a waste of time to me when I first heard of their plan; but now I consider it one of the many traits that the humans own that make them so very special!"

"I placed Ebirius upon my neck and as Desiree was beginning the tasks at her end, Ebirius and I began to fly to and search out the appropriate island with needed characteristics for our utilization. I warned him of the great storms that regularly passed through these waters when it was warm and that meant that we could not use one that was too small for these storms were capable of entirely washing a smaller island away, yet at the same time we did not want one that was large enough to support a mature hardwood forest as he did not want a great deal of shipbuilding supplies readily available for we knew that Therasil's lot were not only ruthless, but also resourceful."

"We had been flying for most of the morning lost in thought and reverie when on the horizon began to appear what seemed to be hundreds, no more likely thousands of small, flat, sandy islands. Our excitement built as we approached and began to fly amidst what seemed a multitude of possible sites, though as we inspected them one by one it began to wane and I prepared myself to gain the realm again and travel back home to my ship, Ebirius thought." But the Piasa urged me to persist and so on we travelled.

"As we continued to search this vast collection of tiny islands, hoping to find some that were somewhat more substantial. I told Ebirius of some of the different and wonderful islands that were in this area. The chain of islands behind us and much closer to Desiree's homeland were lush and beautiful and the islands to what you call the south of us are quite large and inhabited by friendly humans and all sorts of prey animals. They neither suit our needs in any case though as nature there is normal. The islands that we want to find are called "The Bahia islands" by their neighbors to the south; I believe that means "bedeviled" and today they are known as the Bahamas, though I do not know very much of human superstitions, that is the reason we need them, they lie in the triangle where nature does not behave normally; the Realm cannot be used there; they were perfect!

As I told Ebirius of these places and he vowed to investigate and explore them, as young sailors often do, when our hopes were suddenly answered as if on cue. An island appeared on the horizon that was clearly more than one hundred times the size of most of the other's we had seen to this point. We flew directly for it, and as we grew closer we could see it might possess the qualities that we needed. There were small mountains with trees, which would surely mean water and shelter. We made a pass over the island to investigate from the air and found several small streams coming down from the hills. We chose the largest of these, which happened to be on the lee side of the island and landed next to it for some refreshment. It was fortunate that the stream was so large, as we both now decided to take a swim. Both preferring fresh water to the salted that we had flown over for most all of the morning. This large stream handled my dragon's bulk without a problem. There were also numerous fish to which I helped myself on several occasions. I offered to catch one for Ebirius but he declined and said thoughtfully, "Perhaps later."

As I relaxed in the wonderfully cool fresh water for a while, Ebirius hiked up into the hills to see what was available for our soon to be dispatched guests, surprisingly he was gone for a large part of the afternoon, but just as I began to become really concerned I heard an incredibly high pitched whistle, rather like a Falcon protecting her young, but at the same time I knew that it was Ebirius. It had come from further up the mountain that he had gone exploring; I feared that he might need some sort of help, so with but a dozen or so beats of my wings I arrived at the point where the whistle had originated from. He was standing in the middle of a clearing that contained some carven stones of some sort and he had an interestingly amused look upon his face.

"I thought that you might have needed my help," I stated.

"I am sorry to have startled you my friend," Ebirius blurted out. "But I thought that you may have wanted to see this too!"

"I had no idea that you could make such a noise," Granger said, most surprised.

"Lessons from my good friend Flaxon, he smiled; I did not realize that you could cover distances so quickly," Ebirius stated, equally surprised. "Look at these closely," he pointed.

I asked him what it was.

"There have been visitors on this island before, though it does not appear to be recently," He said. "If my memory serves me correctly from the book I inspected, it was Desiree's people."

"What did you find," I asked?

"I am not exactly certain," Ebirius replied. "It appears to be some kind of shrine or alter made of stone of a sort that I did not see any place on this island. As a matter of fact the only place that I have ever seen it is thousands of leagues from here in the quarries not far from my home. It is very mysterious; it does not belong on this island of sand and coral. It shows great workmanship and appears to be for astrological sightings and such, though I would need to investigate further to be certain. This island would suit our needs; however, I believe that we should search further, for an island that perhaps does not have as many large hardwood trees."

~~~~~~~~~~~~~~~~~~

Meanwhile, many leagues away in the Amazon Queens private quarters, Queen Andrea had gathered Desiree and two of the most trusted officers from her bodyguard Charondele Helms and Victoria Pearce to "conference." Her use of the phrase conference told Desiree that her mother did not want her to speak of anything that she, as queen had not already mentioned. She found this odd for she knew that her mother and these two had been close since they were young girls together; though as always she dutifully followed her mother's instructions and complied.

They spoke at length of a plan to post many well-hidden spies day and night at the mines. They discussed arming them not only with bows, but also bolos and blow darts for live capture of those that they could as an alternative, if these plans failed; the staging of a distraction close at hand that would deceive Therasil's minions into thinking that the guard's attention was drawn and it was safe to sneak into the mines.

The meeting ended with Queen Andrea giving the orders to make it happen now and them all vowing allegiance to one another and to not rest until their enemies had been conquered.

As her two captains left to make her wishes a reality, Queen Andrea caught her daughter by the arm, "We must speak alone," The queen whispered. "You see that I do not fully trust even my dearest friends," she said desperately.

Desiree could see the pain in her mother's eyes, "Yes mother, I noted that you did not tell them of the "Fork of Darkness" but of other ways to capture the thieves alive."

"Yes, my dear, let us hope that it is an advantage of mine that she has not yet discovered through her spying," The queen lamented.

"Mother, you are very distraught, what troubles you so," Desiree pleaded? "You have strong and loyal friends surrounding you, your forces outnumber hers by nearly two to one and you have a daughter that would do anything for you. How can I help?"

"That is just it, my love. You are my last remaining weakness. Therasil is very ruthless and would stop at nothing to get at me," She said as she lovingly caressed Desiree's cheeks in her hands. "I fear that she would cast aside the fact that she is your godmother and do you harm. You must go to somewhere that is absolutely safe!"

After a few moments of thought, Queen Andrea looked at her and said. "When your man returns-

"Ebirius," Desiree interrupted!

"Yes, of course, Ebirius. A noble and trustworthy young man that I feel so certain towards that I am about to trust him with that which I value most. When he and his beast that you have told me of return I would speak with him and give him an old map to a place that I believe will serve us well. He can take you there for a time, for safety until we have captured Therasil and her group; at that time we will place them on one of the islands we discussed and bring you home," The queen finished.

The plan sounded compelling at the time, but events do not always occur as they had been planned in one's life!

In a clandestine location, not many leagues from where Desiree and her mother had been meeting with their loyalists. There was progressing another, somewhat more ominous plan that was being designed for a much more sinister purpose.

Therasil glared at the five of her lieutenants that she held in highest regard, you would not say that she trusted this five, as she did not really fully feel that for anyone. Though they had; I suppose come as close as anyone had ever come to gaining her trust. However, the power that she held over her followers through her expertise in use of not only all weapons, but the nearly witchlike understanding of the realm created an abnormally fierce loyalty in her followers. There were even stories of her warriors laying down their lives merely to follow her orders and please her, jumping from cliffs, swimming with river monsters and the like. It was well understood that the way to advance in Therasil's army was to please her explicitly. They also all knew that results are all she really cared about. She also had her even more treacherous side that was well known but seldom talked about; when she began to speak to any it was known that she always had their full attention.

"You must all do exactly as you have been told and my victory will finally come to fruition," She hissed. "Andrea pictures herself as such a great warrior and yet she leaves unprotected her most obvious weakness; her beloved daughter Desiree will soon be the tool used to cause her ultimate demise."

"Let me explain again!" She stated in a cunning and manipulative tone. "The twelve warriors that we have taught the access to the realm will divide into two groups. The first will keep the training of new "realm warriors" proceeding at best possible speed and the second will be stationed at the locations that I have specified for all of their waking hours. We will capture her at her mother's quarters, her hideout or the crystal mine. Within the next few days one of you will contact me through the realm with her location and I will come and join in her capture. This will begin my conquest of her mother and her followers for she will do anything to protect her sweet treasured daughter. With Desiree in our control, we will bait her mother away from her protective forces and very quietly kill them both to rid ourselves of their intolerable Amazonian High Priestess Values."

"Alas, if only this weary dragon had known of this at the time of its contrivance perhaps there would have been something that I could have done, for Therasil was unknowingly planning the extinction of not only her enemy and rival, but all of her kind. ~ Unfortunately, some of what is called destiny is beyond control of any being; it has happened and is now done and I remain, but to tell the tale!

As the Amazons conferred in their different secret meetings their plans would unknowingly set something inescapable and of much greater consequence than they would realize into action, but I suppose that they were just the unknowing tools of fate!

Ebirius and Granger had finally found an island that they felt would work for them. It was much further west and quite a lot smaller than the first one where they had stopped for a swim. It was perhaps only half the size of the first island, with multiple streams and even several small lakes. There was also a substantial amount of tropical jungle growth, but nearly all palms; nothing like the Amazon homeland as surely the summer storms that these islands endured thinned them on a regular basis. This was a really attractive feature, as they would have plenty of wood for building materials such as shelters and even the food that many of them provided, however it was not good wood for the fabrication of ships; the flora was much the same on this larger island as he had seen on the first except for the absence of any hardwood trees. He was relieved that without these good shipbuilding trees to use, they would have a very difficult time constructing any decent seafaring craft for Ebirius knew from experience that palms soaked up water like a sponge.

They flew around the island for a time to investigate any signs of occupation and save a multitude of birds, large lizards and fish, saw nothing. It was becoming late in the afternoon and Ebirius was beginning to indeed get rather hungry. He suggested to his new dragon friend, "Why don't we land at that lake below and if you are still so inclined I could go for one of those fish that you offered earlier."

"Yes, I would like that," Granger said. "I am growing weary of flying as well, would that we rest and eat."

"We will camp here tonight, rest ourselves and explore the island, and if this is as good as it appears to be, we can be on our way back to the Amazon homeland tomorrow morning. Sound good to you, my friend, "He questioned his large companion soothingly?

"Of course," Was Granger's immediate response!

Ebirius thought that he could sense the dragon tiring of the complications that humans bring to life and perhaps at that time he was, but it later turned to intrigue.

They landed next to the lake where Ebirius dismounted with an affectionate hug and couple of pats on my side that I would later become quite accustomed to and grow to enjoy immensely, we were building a very strong bond this young human and I.

Ebirius said, "I am going to build a small fire, as I am not as fond of raw fish as you are. I will be back in a moment.'

As he walked into the woods, I approached the lake that we had chosen and it was teaming with fish of many kinds. It also had a population of large and very tasty eels and was very clear fresh water. Perhaps too hospitable and nice of an island for ones enemies to be banished to, these humans had some strange ways about them, I thought. However, I had begun to wonder if there might be a way that I could help and began to ponder that as I caught an eel and two of the tasty pink-fleshed fish for my human friend.

When he returned I tried to tease him a bit about cooking all of the goodness out of the fish that I had caught him. He chuckled slightly, but I could see that he was lost in contemplation.

That is when the insight struck me, "You are worried about her, are you not?"

"Desiree," he affirmed. "Yes, very much so, for it seems to me that if I were going to try to hurt Queen Andrea, she is too powerful for a direct assault. Therasil's warriors are no match for Andrea's army, as they would be annihilated. In my mind that leaves only trickery and deception. If they were to successfully kidnap Desiree and hold her for ransom to be paid only by the queen, they may be able to capture both the queen and the princess and accomplish what we are trying to do with them, or even worse just kill them to get them out of the way, either way Therasil would be the new ruler of the Amazons and she will be teaching all of them the ways of the realm without proper training. It could be a huge disaster in the making! We must finish our business here as quickly as we can and get back as early tomorrow as possible to protect Desiree and Queen Andrea," Ebirius vowed.

We spoke further of the type of life that the banished enemies of the Amazons would be able to lead here as being too good for such as Therasil's lot deserved, of while the trees on this island while unable to build any kind of decent boat could still in fact build a raft that would float and possibly take them somewhere. Although we both agreed that with the prevailing winds and currents, it would not be in the direction of the Amazon homeland. As we conversed we watched the beautiful tropical sun radiate its last brilliant and beautiful beams of the day then slip under the horizon for its nightly rest.

That is when I noticed that Ebirius had fallen asleep lounging in the crook of my wing. I found this strangely comforting and soon joined him, for it had been a long and tiring day.

We awoke the next dawn to seabirds noisily arguing over the few remnants of the meal that Ebirius had cooked for himself last night. We both had a chuckle as they started and began to fly away when I began to stir. The exploration of the island went quickly, as it was mostly by air. Although there were a few times when we did land and take a much closer look. Finally, just a little later in the morning we decided that this was the island that we needed and that it was uninhabited. Reaching that point of understanding we started for the Amazon homeland with all haste.

We flew very high to take advantage of the wind currents at this height, so it was rather cool, but it did seem to cut the travel time. When we saw the islands that we had seen on the way out that we knew to be to the north of Desiree's homeland we then realized where we were and that we had only a short time left in our journey.

At this point Ebirius asked, "Do you think that it is safe now to use the realm to travel the rest of the way? I could take us to Desiree's special meeting place where she told me to always meet her when using the realm."

I turned and looked deeply into his eyes and said, "Using the realm is not something that should be done unless it is absolutely necessary, as there are dangers that most never know about until it is too late. Do you think that it is warranted?"

"Yes my friend. It is only a feeling, but it is a strong feeling that has been growing all morning and I think that it possibly is a life-threatening emergency. I feel that it is best if we go as fast as possible," Ebirius groaned.

"I am with you my friend. Show me where to go and take me with you. But remember do not remain for anything, use the realm quickly and get out. There are things that will try to deceive you and lure you to your death or everlasting captivity. Knowing this, let us go to your woman," Granger exclaimed; then they were gone!

The eerie luminescence, along with the bitter cold and was it voices; No matter, in an instant they were in the grotto where Desiree had told him to meet her when coming out of the realm. Surprisingly it was more than able to nicely hide the substantial bulk of a large dragon it seemed, as this Amazon jungle was very thick and formidable. As Ebirius began to collect his bearings to decide the proper way to travel to find his delightful companion, we were both astonished to see her step out from behind a very large tree.

"Whoa you two," Desiree called! "It is very good to see you back so soon. I trust that you have found the place that my mother has in mind."

As she signed for us to be quiet she said, "You will not be very easily hidden now we must approach the queen's domain in another way from now on. Trust to my mind and come with me."

Again we felt the horrible cold that no living being can ever become accustomed to, the faint, tormented sounds always seemed to be there, the background noise made from within the strange place that was the realm? Souls trapped inside wanting to find the way out? Perhaps they belonged to as of yet undiscovered, aberrant, hideous creatures that inhabited this very strange part of the natural or perhaps supernatural world that we were using quite too freely now.

Granger and Desiree reappeared almost instantly not far from the location above the mountain near the crystal mine. The thick canopy of trees was gone and Granger instantly felt better as he had freedom to take immediate flight and this made him feel more secure. But where was Ebirius? He had not rematerialized; Desiree and the dragon exchanged a long agonizing look with one another.

Desiree had just begun to call his name and he rematerialized and was there beside them both!

"What took you so long," She asked painfully? "You frightened me. There are so many ways to lose oneself in that place, I cannot warn you enough!"

Ebirius gazed at Desiree and then up at the dragon and merely said, "I was just trying to figure out what that noise is when we use the realm."

"You must not look at or listen to anything while in the realm. That is how it can make you forever its prisoner," Desiree pleaded.

"It was but a few moments, my love and here I am, please do not worry my love," Young Ebirius tried to calm her.

"No, you must listen she is right." Granger rumbled, sounding rather like far off thunder that was beginning to get closer. "You have but begun to train, her with most of her young life in training, even I with thousands of your years know next to nothing about what you call the realm and I fear that we never will. We will never know about more than a small part of the dangers that lurk there. That is why I have learned after my many encounters with it, just to leave it be and not to tempt fate by visiting that horrid place!"

Ebirius looked at the dragon with a strange dreamy look in his eyes and said, "I could not quite hear for sure, but it sounded like voices."

"There may be voices there or perhaps something else; that is but one of the aspects of that place that can trap you inside forever more. A few moments in the realm can be many lifetimes in the real world. Time does not exist and has no meaning in the realm. You must only focus on your destination; anything else can mean death, this I do know from my training," She pleaded as she approached to hold her man.

"I would be foolish not to listen to advice from two that I know have nothing but love for me and I happen to know have a far greater knowledge than myself on this very important subject," Ebirius responded. "I will not dwell on anything that I hear or see in the realm and what is more, I will stay away from use of it except for the most dire of emergencies, this I promise."

He had no way of knowing for certain at this point, but the number of what he deemed emergencies that would soon occur in his young and about to become very tumultuous life, were about to increase considerably!

The next part of the story is better told from the point of view of my young seafaring friend as for understandable reasons- stealth being the main I imagine. He asked me to fly to meet with the "Osprey" and show his trusted companions Durages and Flaxon the way to the Amazons homeland and it happened something like this.

"Your mother seems to be somewhat at a loss for people that she can really trust, Desiree," Ebirius observed.

"Yes, I noticed," She replied, "I believe that she is just being very careful."

"You can never be too careful," He said. "Two and no more than that are the friends that I will vouch we can trust with our lives, as I have on more than one occasion, they will help our cause."

"Agreed," She admitted not mentioning the trusted friends she had before.

"Granger my friend," Ebirius proposed. "How long will it take you to find the "Osprey" and lead her back to us?"

The dragon pondered the question for only a moment and then said, "I can find them in one or two days, but although your ship is very fast, getting them back here will probably take two of your weeks or so, without the use of the realm.

"That is still the way that we should approach it," Ebirius stated. "If I need you, can I get in touch with you, is this not true?"

The large brown dragon looked intently into his friend's eyes, as his changed and twirled with that strange multi-faceted light that only dragons possess he said solemnly. "All you have to do is call and I will hear. Call me from anywhere at any time and I will hear you."

"Thank you my friend," Ebirius responded. "I know that I would hear you also and that is well. Then please make haste and quickly bring back my ship and my friends."

Desiree hesitantly interjected. "If somehow we lose contact with you, just come back to the mountain and perch yourself on the ridge towards the sunset, my mother will be told of your presence and will contact you very quickly as I have spoken to her about your special nature. You will be safe there for the short time it will take for her to contact you."

Words of the Piasa

"You two are the ones in great danger. Please do not hesitate to call upon me if the need arises," The big Brown insisted. "My heart is with you and I will return with your allies as quickly as it can be done."

With this he arose on several mighty strokes of his huge wings and quickly disappeared over the mountain and was gone.

As they waved farewell to their large fierce looking, yet beautiful friend, they both felt the love in their hearts that the big dragon was talking about. Neither of them was at all surprised by the intense bond that they had developed with this wonder of the natural world; they in fact felt rather blessed at having the opportunity to have him as a companion and a friend. They shared that they both did indeed feel as though they shared a common fate with the indomitable, yet caring creature. They would miss him even for the short time they where apart.

Soon after their friend disappeared Desiree began to tell Ebirius of her mother's plan, "This area has been mined for the crystals for many of my people's lifetimes and the most complete knowledge of the catacombs inside is held by the priestesses. There are many numbers of maps done on many different dates, but none can really be relied on as totally accurate, due to the long years that we have been mining the mountains here and the large amount of rain that we receive in the jungle. Many people have become lost in the mines and paid with their lives, so please stay near me always!"

"Right at your side, my love," Ebirius assured her.

As Desiree led her man towards one of the lesser, yet still quite large, entrances of the mines, neither of them realized that hidden within the great catacomb hallway they were headed towards were several of Therasil's most trusted warriors, closely watching the couples approach. The commander of the three quietly spoke to the one that was furthest inside the cave. "Zin-Darlya, use the realm and tell Therasil of our discovery. Escort her back here if she desires to come at this time, return with her orders; Make haste!"

"Yes commander," She stated and was gone a moment later in the pale light of the realm.

Desiree and Ebirius approached the mouth of the cave and began to realize how large the entrance they were walking into was. In an attempt to be as cautious as possible they decided to walk along the left hand side of the wall, thinking that this way would offer them the most cover. Unfortunately it achieved this far better for their foes than they ever suspected, as they did not see Therasil and her warriors until the darts had pierced their exposed necks. The poison worked immediately and they both crumpled to the ground at once!

Therasil's brutal crew quickly gathered around to admire their helpless catch. Zin-Darlya kicked Ebirius roughly over onto his back so that they could all get a good look at this foreign and handsome stranger. "He will make a wonderful addition to your harem Lord Therasil," She said.

"Possibly; if he lives that long," Therasil responded. "He may even become a reward for one of my trusted warriors for exemplary service in the imminent change of power in the Amazon Empire. He will not be of any use for pleasure for several days until the effects of the poison wear off. For now, we will need him as a hostage, in order to keep his beast at bay. It was obvious that they are very close and the thing will try to assist him, I am certain. After we kill the beast we can do as we please with him, for now apply the disruption yolks and take them to the interrogation cells."

The Amazons planned to use the same weapon on Granger that Ebirius had used to neutralize the Black dragon when he met Granger and this was unfortunately very much possible as Ebirius had returned it immediately, just as he had promised.

~~~~~~~~~~~~~~~~

Already many leagues away and flying swiftly to close distance on the "Osprey" as quickly as possible, Granger felt a terrible feeling of something being very wrong. For a few moments he considered turning around, as he thought he was needed. Though he had not heard any call and knew that Ebirius would call if he needed him. He also remembered that he was given a task to perform and so he decided that he just missed his friends, he found a new resolve and flew on.

~~~~~~~~~~~~~~~~

In the meantime Queen Andrea was meeting with High-priestess Jenal al Arrief; from what I have been able to learn of Queen Andrea, I have found that she was a very progressive leader and was ahead of her time in many ways. She was very outspoken about caution in the use of the realm, until it could be further studied and more fully understood. Yet she knew more about it, and it's capabilities than almost anyone alive save this old priestess; but still she knew that she could use it as a weapon to finally trap her enemies. This unfortunate knowledge was the key to the Amazons final demise.

Jenal spoke slowly and quietly of times long past.

She said. "A similar situation was recorded as happening several generations ago when there was a great power struggle among the Priestesses at that time. A sect of Amazons had grown in power to the point that they rivaled the sisterhood; they were known as the Nuuns; they had begun to practice the use of some telepathic powers. It was already known that the use of these powers in conjunction with use of the realm can be not only a horrific weapon, but also very dangerous to those that attempt its use. This is why we have established the rules that ban from the sisterhood and excommunicate anyone who is found guilty of attempting to use these gifts in this manner, and as you are aware we have arranged for a number of the elders to be silent lookouts for any occurrences of this and to meet at the waning of every moon to discuss the months details and what if anything should be done. It has been very many seasons since there has been anything to report on, but it seems as though Therasil's lot has intent to change that."

Queen Andrea spoke with a knowing authority that Jenal found quite unnerving. "Therasil's ambition will be her downfall there are aspects of the realm that I know about that she does not even imagine. I am more than her match in powers of the mind, as well as battle!"

This produced an extended, somber stare from the High priestess Jenal al Arrief.

"Do not look so mournful, Jenal," The queen assured her. "I have guided my people through many a crisis. I will not fail them now!"

"There has never before been such a crisis as this," Jenal lamented. "I fear this one will be far worse than any that you can imagine. It could be that which leads to our end!"

Queen Andrea responded with an affectionate hug for the old woman, as she had been the one whom had the main responsibilities of raising young Princess Andrea, being her mother's nanny as well as a priestess at the time. She looked into her eyes and said. "Rest easy my friend, I will rid us of this evil and put things back to rights once again.

You can trust in me, I assure you," She concluded with another, slightly more distracted hug.

This Queenly display of assurance and affection did little to ease Jenal's feelings of premonition. They had, in fact made her feel much more ill at ease.

She had one more bit of advice for the queen though as they parted, "You are a great queen my beloved, loved and revered by your people. You were the most gifted and accomplished of any of my students and know more about the use of the realm than any person alive, perhaps even myself. However, do not let this blind you to the devious and subversive nature that dwells there for even the simplest aspects of it can become your undoing if you are not always totally aware of just where you are! Be very careful, for no mortal will ever fully understand everything about that mysterious part of nature!"

"Do not fret my old friend for I, as always will heed your warnings," Queen Andrea spoke so very soothingly, yet as she left the room she was already planning in her mind the way that she would use her telepathic powers to vanquish Therasil and all of her followers. She felt very good about her plan for she knew that it was now beginning to unfold just as she had planned. Although she did not yet have verification, she felt certain that her beloved Desiree and her man had been taken prisoner by now and while she did not relish risking her daughter like this, she knew that this was the perfect way to arrange the ruse that she would use to defeat her foes.

Later that afternoon, many leagues distant, aboard the fleet and sweet-lined ship known as "Osprey" Durages and Flaxon true to their word coaxed every knot of speed that they could from the quick little ship. They had been on the heading that their friend had told them to follow now for three days and were in what to them were absolutely uncharted seas. Though they both knew that if Ebirius instructed them to sail in this direction, they could trust that he would get them to where they meant to go. Ebirius was the most uncannily accurate navigator that either had ever met or for that matter, heard of! As they were discussing that, planning dinner and engaging in some other small talk, Flaxon began to stare ahead of the boat. He was not exactly certain what he saw at first, but then yes he was certain, for he could definitely see now, it was the dragon that their captain had befriended; it was Granger. He was flying towards the ship; something must have gone wrong they feared. They quickly cleared the deck and hailed, "Granger, our friend, please alight on our boat and take rest! Give us news of the adventure."

With that Granger let out a friendly grumble and with a few gentle flaps of his wings he was down on the deck and although he landed quite softly, he had to be very careful lest his immense bulk swamps the boat and they begin taking on water. However, after a couple of minutes of adjustments they managed to get Granger 'hunkered down' fairly comfortably in the middle of the ship curled around the mast. This not only made the ship more stable, but also managed to make the dragon more relaxed with his seafaring; something that dragons are totally unfamiliar with, and so very uncomfortable taking part of, and as far as is known to me no others have ever experienced sailing, Granger the Piasa was the first and most likely only of his kind to do so!

Contented with the stowage of their large friend they all exchanged pleasantries and Durages began the conversation in earnest. "Tell us our friend, why do you fly all of this way over the mighty sea to find us when you can use that magic place, is something amiss? What about Ebirius, were is he? What can we do to help?"

"Just a moment and we will get to it all!" The dragon said to them, somewhat surprised by their intense enthusiasm even after being forewarned by Ebirius of their extreme loyalty and fervor. "I have been told of your exceptional characters and I am sure that you can be trusted. We dragons can *see* that in you humans and as it is also in my kind, it is a rare attribute."

"What is it that you need from us; need we go back with you in the realm," Flaxon interrupted. "We want to help!"

"Very well," I began, as I thought to myself, dragons and humans working together, even when not *impressed* to one another, this is a new beginning. "I was sent by Ebirius to lead you to the Amazons homeland at all haste. There are foul workings afoot and we are trying to exile some very bad Amazons from their homeland and we will need you and your ship the Osprey to help us to accomplish this."

Flaxon appeared rather disheartened and queried, "It is actually

Ebirius's ship and there are none better, his grandfather is a master shipwright; is all well? No fighting or such!

"Not as of yet, my young friend, however you need be careful of what you wish for as you may get it," Granger said. "Besides, not only are the Amazons formidable warriors, but I also sense a ruthless characteristic in them that I feel shall soon surprise us all, although that is still to be seen. Desiree and her mother the Queen Andrea seem to be of good character and deserving of trust, but I have a strange instinctual feeling that is trying to warn me about every one of them in some way. We shall soon see!

"However, the matters which are now at hand for you," So continued the large dragon, which by now was speaking to the two young sailors as if they were members of his own brood. "First, you need to get to the Amazon homeland, with this ship as quickly as you can. I will be your guide, but you are needed there in as short a time as possible. When you arrive, you will first need to set things to rights as I feel that something is not as it should be back there. Ebirius has not contacted me, but I have had some feelings that I cannot deny and I have learned to trust them through the years. I cannot distinguish exactly what is wrong and I know that if he were in mortal danger, I would *feel* it. Although I do know that something is wrong. The three of us will be able to deal with whatever it is, I do believe. To set things right we will need to capture the Queens enemy, Therasil and her main supporters and banish them to an island that we have found. It is a place far to the west of here where the realm cannot be achieved. That is why we need you and the Osprey, and the quicker the better. Therasil is showing her warriors how to use the realm, with next to no training. The Amazon priestesses say that this is very dangerous to do, and I can only agree most strongly. They are going to be very difficult to keep hold of once that we capture them, because of this, but the Amazons know certain methods. We have a tough time in store, but with one another we should prevail!"

Durages said, "I am certain that I speak for Flaxon, in telling you that we will always be there for Ebirius when he needs us for anything, and it sounds as though he is trying to defend the rights of some very honorable people. We are with you, hail to defending the righteous people of the entire world!"

"Here, Here!" shouted Flaxon. "Dragon-friends troop is formed, we will fight for the rights of good and honorable people everywhere!"

"Yes, yes," growled the dragon, "I am beginning to see that we have the right crew to be able to succeed in this exploit. We are against great odds, but they will not stand against us, now though, we must make all haste. Allow me just a short rest and I will alight to make the ship lighter, so that you can gain speed."

With this statement from the great beast, Durages and Flaxon began to stare at one another. They slowly began to smile and Durages finally said to Flaxon, "We must be thinking the same thing, I am sure it will work. Why don't you tell our esteemed friend?"

Flaxon explained, "Yes I agree, it should help immensely. You see Granger, my friend. The art of sailing has everything to do with weight dispersal and sail area to weight ratio. While you are here amidships in the hold, it gives the impression of being more stable; there is a way of stowage that is as stable and yet lets the ship ride higher in the water thus enabling it to achieve much better speeds by adding much more sail. We have a simple adage - *More weight in the back means more sail on the mast.* If we can just get you to situate yourself as much onto the quarterdeck as possible and we will be able to rest. This it will enable us to add the maximum of sails that will in turn increase our speed and shorten our trip to the Amazonian homeland.

After helping to get the large dragon stowed as closely to perfection as his size would allow, Durages and Flaxon added all the sail that they had available and battened down for a very quick trip southwest to the largest river mouth that they had ever encountered. What they were yet to discover was that it would also be the most fascinating of their adventures with Ebirius to date and an encounter with beings, places and things that would change them for the rest of their lives.

The dragon thought initially that the trip would take two weeks, however the ambitious crew did it in eight days. During this time I, being a brown dragon and as such, the most sensitive to the realm, not to mention the only of my kind to have the sensitivity to regularly mate with the golden queens found myself very anxious at not having felt anything from Ebirius for such a long time. Though I also knew that I would be able to *feel* if he were in any mortal danger, that should have comforted me, but yet it did not. I felt as it did when he slept, but that could not be, not Ebirius, something was not as it should be. I could not decide how to best regain contact with my friends and allies without putting Durages and Flaxon, not to mention the ship in real danger, but after considerable thought on the matter I decided to fly on ahead. I instructed them "My friends, you are already in the mouth of the Amazon's mighty river. For yet another day you will need to sail this same course. By midday tomorrow you will be able to follow the map in that book that Ebirius has drawn for you, when you spot the great barren mountain the Amazon's city is at its base. Under no circumstances go to shore, not even close enough to be seen with one of your spyglasses. You cannot let them get a good look at the Osprey, as they will then be able to use the realm to board you, and you have yet to see the incredible range of these Amazon's bows. I will be back before you get to the capitol, but if something happens and I am not, just stand off out of range but in sight of the mountain. We will definitely contact you. Do you understand?

"We understand and will follow your advice to the letter my friend," Durages said.

"Should we wear our mail and have our weapons at the ready, my fierce looking brown friend," Flaxon queried?

"Well, my brave little comrade," I felt my eyes dancing with amusement as I appraised him. You need to be ready to defend yourselves, but I feel that if it comes to all out battle on this trip it will not go well for us, this battle will be won or lost with our wits; that is what you need to prepare."

"Yes, I suppose that is true," Flaxon sighed.

Durages interjected, "You let us know what Ebirius and yourself would like us to do and it will be done. Our lives, our swords to you, as you Granger and Ebirius are one. You will have all of our loyalty, unto the end."

We dragons had not normally felt much warmth towards the humans in the past, and to my knowledge I was only the third or fourth dragon that had ever been *bonded* with a human. Because of this I was very surprised by the affection that I was feeling towards these remarkable young men and I told them, "Go with the valor and loyalty that I can see you Phoenicians possess and nothing will stand in our way. I, Granger the brown will always stand by you, for now though I must alight and fly on ahead to find Ebirius and Desiree.

A brown dragon standing, stretching and alighting into flight must be seen by the humans as quite amazing, because as I looked down at them as I rose, I knew they had a serious need to shorten sail, yet all that they seemed to be able to manage was to stare upwards at me, these humankind have never failed to amaze this dragon.

It was a short flight to the grotto where I first went with Ebirius and I felt a real temptation to alight there and begin a search of my own through the dense jungle, but I remembered what Desiree had told me and considered that it was probably very good advice, I still wasn't sure exactly what Therasil's warriors were capable of and Andrea's people had given Ebirius the weapon that had destroyed the black dragon and saved me. Who knows what the other Amazons might possess? In any case I flew to the mountain and alighted in the spot that Desiree had asked me to, and began a most tormenting of waiting periods.

~~~~~~~~

Back in Queen Andrea's quarters, where the queen and an acquaintance that none of us had yet met as of yet were in the midst of enjoying each other's amorous company, in the queens luxurious bath; this I have later discovered was a common practice of not only Queen Andrea, but a long line of the Amazon leaders before her.

The queen stroked her partner's soft skin as they both lie languidly in the steaming water and spoke to her softly, "Tamara, I am trusting you with this most important of tasks for the well being of our people, not only because of my great love for you and the fact that I can trust you with all of my love and future, but all of the signs that I or anyone that I have assigned the research point to you being the priestess that is the chosen one to help us thwart the evil that has arisen from within our own ranks. You are the "radiant beauty as yet untouched by man" and in addition, you have the gift of telepathy that has not been seen among our people for many generations. The most important of the signs though is that you offer your help freely, with no desire for reward as you see it as being preordained, you are truly a treasure and I believe possibly the angel that will save our people."

Tamara gazed into Queen Andrea's loving eyes and softly said,

"My love for my people and especially you my Queen knows utterly no bounds."

As they settled once more into a loving embrace the queen asked softly, "Show me our special place just once more, my love."

At that, Tamara smiled and closed her eyes, as did the queen and an explicitly detailed and beautiful scene of an idyllic garden appeared in both of their minds, almost inviting them both to stay. As they enjoyed the envisioned waterfall, fresh fruit and the many other tempting objects that could be seen, the queen whispered, "Yes, this will do nicely my pet." As the queen snuggled even more closely and affectionately her young, sweet Tamara and thought of just how she was going to entice her foe into taking the bait and sealing her doom; she did not realize that it was a doom that would be shared by those more numerous than she could ever begin to fathom.

Meanwhile, at one of her many hideaways deep inside of the mountain Therasil and her lieutenants continued at what the priestesses of the sisterhood considered unauthorized training in the use of the realm; thinking that they had found the way to a newfound freedom and their seating as the new leaders of their people, but if they had only known, nothing could have been further from the truth and in a cell several levels from the training Ebirius and Desiree began to stir and finally awake from a drug induced sleep that had may have lasted for hours or even days, they really did not know. They had been bound back to back with a silken rope and each wore an ornately carved yolk around their neck that was made of a strange-looking greenish, cloudy crystal that seemed to have a faint vibrating energy all its own.

Desiree was the first to speak, "Ebirius my love are you all right," She whispered.

"Other than a headache more hard felt than I have ever endured from wine and being trussed like a fowl ready to be baked, I suppose that I am fine," He replied, but as he talked to her he began to examine his bindings, asking her, "And you; are you well?"

She responded quietly, "Besides being in the same fix that you just stated, I am fine! Be careful not to struggle with these ropes, as we

Words of the Piasa

Amazon warriors know of ways to tie knots that will merely draw ever tighter with any amount of struggling."

Ebirius retorted as quietly, "Would that you keep an eye on your side of the room and I will show you how Phoenician sailors have learned to deal with such ropes." She did as he asked, as he in turn slipped a long; what appeared to be a wire or thread from the waistband of his shorts. He carefully looped it around the rope and began to pull back and forth on the ends of it. In only a few instants time it cut its way through the rope and he was free.

"Aha," He said, and tossed her the rope.

"You just never stop surprising me, my resourceful sailor from afar," She praised him.

He then repeated the process on her and they were at least free of their bindings, although they still had the larger problem of being imprisoned in a place that they did not know and being entirely surrounded by Therasil's warriors.

They happily embraced, so very happy to be in one another's arms again and Ebirius quietly told her if ever I have seen a time to use the realm to escape a situation, it is now!

"I am sorry to tell you my love, but that will not be possible. Do you know what these are around our necks," She asked sadly. "They are called Quellenar and no power can remove them from us except for the special reflective light key that put them on, and what they are for, is to disallow our use of the realm. We will not be escaping in that manner, there has got to be another way!"

Ebirius looked deeply into her eyes and said, "Yes, my love, there has got to be and I will find it for you. Follow me and tell me if you recognize any passages. We will need to leave quickly, but very quietly and with the greatest stealth possible."

"Let us be on our way now then, for I am certain that they will return soon," She said. "Lead on, my hero and save me once again!"

Without another word they scurried down the dark hallway away from the noise that they believed to be some sort of training. With that in mind they felt as though they had a relatively good chance of finding a way out of the labyrinth that they now found themselves lost within, though their progress soon grew very slow, as the direction they were headed was no longer illuminated by the torches that they had enjoyed in their cell. They could tell, however that they were traveling downward and they were headed toward a fresh draft of cool air. As they traveled they continuously searched for an unlit torch or anything they could burn to make light.

Their progress was not as fast as he would have liked, but they felt that they were headed towards freedom. They just needed to keep from being discovered and find their way out of this mountain, a prospect that could be more difficult than it first would seem. As Ebirius mulled over his possible plans and probabilities for success, he found himself yearning terribly to find his new close friend and ally Granger, not only for the assistance that a beast that was as large and ferocious as he could be, but also for the comfort that the dragon would provide him personally. The closeness that he felt to this rare animal never ceased to surprise him, but it was especially so today, in this time of serious crisis and as he was feeling this he held his Desiree even more tightly and continued down the corridor; Desiree enjoyed this assuring sign of affection and felt her love for him build inside her.

As they continued down the passageway, they grew more confident in their possibility of escape, but unfortunately for the young couple, there were contrivances afoot that would have a very telling effect on both of their futures, and they had absolutely no control over any of them at this point.

~~~~~~~~~~~~~~~~~~~~~~~~

Dragons can be very patient when the need arises; they have been known to lie in waiting on known game trails entirely motionless for days, even weeks to ambush herds of prey animals for an extra large feeding, why there are even tales of greens and other small types playing dead within a cave for months to fool a larger foe.

That was certainly not the case with this dragon at this particular time; Granger had a terrible discomfort chewing at his very being, it had been far too long since he had felt the presence of Ebirius and he was beginning to fear for the worst. While he wanted to abide by Desiree's instructions, he had now began to lumber down and investigate towards the tree line.

Dragons are not normally unnoticed for very long. Queen Andrea had already been informed of Granger's return and was in fact going to greet the dragon personally, although her young devotee had insisted on accompanying her, as she just had to see such a beast with her own eyes and could at times be of very persuasive of her older lover.

Meanwhile, deep in the mountain, Therasil was in deep conversation with an elder Amazon priestess called Neandra-Luz. This old priestess was, in the mind of Therasil, the foremost living expert on mental projection. She was involved in experiments over one hundred years ago, when she was still quite young that not only showed great promise, but also nearly enabled the faction that she was involved with at the time to seize power from the leaders of the Amazon's at that time. She had told Therasil about a year ago about the narrow-minded ruling priestesses and how they had captured and excommunicated everyone that was involved, but she was able to use her abilities to escape and remain in her homeland. Though she had also sown the seeds for a long life of lies, hiding and deceit with all of her relatives and friends taken to somewhere that she did not know, never to be seen again, the pain that she felt from the missing of her mother, sisters and friends had festered in her for her entire long life; a life that she had lived in nearly complete solitude talking to very few and practicing what she considered her craft and in so doing she had become quite masterful at it; some would say "dangerously competent" at the art of projection; in any case that is how Therasil liked to describe her.

She had evidently seen a quality in Therasil that reminded her of her mother, and had decided then to become her ally. Neandra-Luz had but one thing on her mind, revenge; revenge for the taking of a perceived blissful life that had been stolen from her, revenge for the life that she had been forced to live, revenge on the few remaining priestesses that perpetrated this on her and all of the remainder of their living children. I do not believe that Therasil ever suspected the depths of the hatred that Neandra-Luz possessed, for it was a black and uncompromising, all devouring evil.

They were interrupted by an approaching warrior that was obviously well known and trusted by Therasil as she addressed her much more calmly than most of her other warriors, "Yes Kristine, what is it?"

Kristine, who carried herself with what could only be called a mix of grace and hostility, responded with gentle, quiet confidence, "We have observed that the beast has returned."

"That is good news my love, are the weapons prepared," she queried gently?

"The poison arrows and spears are ready, but the Saapwin is not where you told us it would be and though we have searched all of the priestess stores that we are aware of, it cannot be found," Kristine commented routinely. (Desiree had fortunately had the foresight to put it into hiding after her man had returned it as he had promised) "We are already more than a match for that beast, but one of our poisoned arrows will kill a giant river snake or a jungle sloth and we have thousands of them, not to mention the world's finest archers. We will kill the ugly beast at this very moment if you order it, my Queen."

"There now my brave shooting star, you will be able to legally call me Queen in a few more days time and your confidence is very admirable, but for now we must still use caution." Therasil instructed. "We must approach the thing unseen and have our archers in place before giving the signal to fire, lest he merely fly away with a few beats of his wings, trust me our patience will be rewarded."

Just then, Zen-Darlya, one of the most trusted of Therasil's warrior-priestesses burst into the room saying, "By your leave my queen, the prisoners have escaped."

"What of the yolks," Therasil asked venomously?

"They must still be wearing them," Zen-Darlya responded.

"How then did they escape," Therasil queried. "Who tied the ropes?"

"My Queen, the ropes were tied perfectly, but they were cut," Zen-Darlya volunteered. "I have warriors in pursuit of them."

Therasil mused, "They either had help from some of our own, which I seriously doubt, or this young Phoenician man child is more formidable and surprising than I would have ever guessed. Call to our warriors to let them just follow, they can escape but one exit with us behind pursuing them; we will be waiting for them at the appropriate time and place and that is when we will conquer her mother and lay claim to what is rightfully mine."

By now, too much time had passed for this dragon to remain waiting and doing nothing at all. I had begun the investigation of the edge of the tree line, when I was surprised to hear behind me near the rocky outcroppings that were evident from the top of the huge slab on which

I had been waiting up further up the mountain, a shrill whistle, rather like that of a hunting hawk. Quickly turning I could see instantly that it was no bird of prey, but a small group of Amazons. Initially I was very surprised that they could have gotten by me with so little cover. I supposed that they had either come from around the other side of the mountain or some interior passage, but then I recognized Queen Andrea; I knew then that this was a meeting of great import. I part hopped / part flew towards them approaching very quickly. When I alighted in front of them I noticed what looked like surprise on most of their faces. They were most likely not aware that a dragon could move as I had done, I noticed also that there was something about the small one that stood touching the queen that I did not feel at all comfortable with. I could sense an extreme callousness in her that felt as strong as to the point of evil, not unlike that of a black dragon. I wondered if any of her companions could also feel it; I wondered if the queen knew. I knew though at that time, that this one could be most treacherous.

The queen interrupted my short reverie, "We are glad that you are returned so quickly my interesting new ally. It is well that you came away from the trees as fast as you did, as Therasil will most likely have her archers and their poisoned arrows arriving at any time now."

I must have started somewhat and looked around towards the woods.

She noticed and attempted to calm me, "Do not worry, you are well out of range now and are with friends," She added.

"What has happened to Ebirius and Desiree," I queried, rather too loudly I imagine from the way that all save the queen started.

Queen Andrea addressed me calmly saying, "They have been captured, but do not fear for they are in no danger, they are being used as pieces in a game and they have a great importance now.

"A game," Granger asked?

Queen Andrea explained as well as she could, "They are being held captive by Therasil and her crew. Therasil is trying to use my daughter as bait for some kind of trap that she is hoping that I will fall the victim of, you see she has enlisted the aid of a renegade priestess that is known to have certain abilities in the power of mental projection and I am certain that she hopes to trap me and most of my commanders in the realm by some means. I however, have no intent of allowing her to succeed."

This is when I Granger the Brown Dragon felt as though I had been dealt a vicious blow, I felt that I was seeing a glimpse into the future, and these wonderful, vivacious and intelligent humans were no longer there and this is when I pleaded with Queen Andrea, "This path that you are on is wrought with peril; I have known of the place that you call the realm for many of your lifetimes and have ventured into it on many occasions. I still know almost nothing about it for it is one of the great mysteries of our world, but I do know this. It is not something that may be trifled with and to be lost in it is to be absolutely lost, now and forever. I have known of many dragons and numerous other beings that entered there and are now eternally lost for there is no knowledge of aught natural within this place. Do not ask me how I know this for I am not certain, but in truth I just do."

"I have been unfortunate enough to have seen the vision of a future without you and your wonderful people in it and never want this to come to pass," The Piasa pleaded. "Find another way to settle your differences and leave the realm alone. Please listen to me, for your people's future is what is hanging in the balance."

Queen Andrea obviously impressed by this dragon's lucid use of her language tried to calm her large friend as best she could, "My grand friend, please try to understand, our order of priestesses have been training in the use of the realm for hundreds of years and one of the first of the laws that we teach is to use the realm only when absolute need exists and that it is a sacred act of great importance, do you not see? This is what we are trying to uphold; Therasil is advocating the wanton and easy use of the realm for the gaining of power and even personal gain and she must be stopped."

The dragon repeated, "The realm cannot be taken lightly or misjudged; it is the seat of far too great a power; for your people's future and your own good find another way."

"My friend, you have my word that we will treat the realm with the respect that it is due, but in order to accomplish this we will first need to use its power several more times in order to capture and hold those that oppose us." Queen Andrea tried to appease the dragon, but she was adamant. "Once we have dealt with the problem of Therasil and her followers, we will purge those that wrongly practice accessing the realm to the islands that Ebirius and you have found and the control will again be in the hands of the sisterhood, where it belongs and things will become as they are meant to be, you shall see!"

I could not help but think as she spoke, if she was only aware that she was talking about nearly all of the Amazon population or if she knew that I was thinking that she had just prophesized the end of her fascinating people; I felt a deep and utter hopelessness that could not be denied!

Meanwhile, somewhere in the labyrinth far below, Ebirius and Desiree were now making much better time, as they had finally found the items that they needed to assemble a small torch for the light that they needed. As they trotted quickly downwards, hand and hand in near total darkness Desiree offered, "The only way that I know of to exit out of here in this direction is going to be guarded by Therasil's lot; we could surely use another way out of here."

"We will slow down when we draw closer to the exit that you know of and search to see if there are any other passages in the roots of this mount, as I've seen that often there are in caverns as great as these," Ebirius instructed calmly and then added, "Or perhaps I can find us a needed ally to provide us some much needed assistance!"

"Granger," She said, rather desperately. "The yolk will not allow you to reach his mind."

"No, but he will recognize my whistle," He told her, but then added. "If we can but get out from under this mountain."

They renewed their flight down the gloomy corridor towards what would be either escape or possibly the end of them and the life together that they both so yearned for.

As The queen of the Amazons, Andrea Perseii conferred with the fierce and majestic looking brown dragon near the top of the mountain and most would probably consider it a noble sight worth a few moments of wonder. The Amazons gathering just below the tree line however felt differently; especially their leader Therasil Zerca who murmured, "The beast does not even know how wrong its choice of allegiances is, or how fatal. Zen-Darlya, take twenty warriors with you and recapture the princess and her resourceful friend at the gate and bring them to me with most haste. Do not yet disturb the beast or the queen's guard. We will stay here and keep an eye on things. Neandra-Luz, you be ready to project to them all when I give you the signal. Everyone prepare to seize our future."

Neandra-Luz looked into Therasil's eyes and said, "I have prepared for this for all of my life, it will be done."

Therasil may have sensed something that made her rather uncomfortable about the ancient priestess, but chose to ignore it in the passion of the moment.

Near the top of the mount Queen Andrea and the brown dragon that the humans called Granger did not realize how deeply inflexible had become the events of this day; events that had already been set into motion to the point that there would soon be no turning back!

In the meantime, as Desiree and Ebirius neared the end of the passageway they had begun to slow and search for any other way out of the depths of the mountain. While there was a labyrinth of passages to chose from, they all in time seemed to return to the main passageway. They had, however begun to see some amount of outside light. Ebirius whispered to Desiree, "These narrow fissures in the rock may not provide a way out, but they just might enable us to arrange an escape. We must hide and remain undetected by Therasil's waiting troop, yet we must get close enough to the mouth of the cave to be within earshot of my friend."

"We may never be able to achieve that my love, we would need to be able to pass Therasil's warriors in a location of their choosing and they are very competent," She sighed adding, "They also enjoy what they do immensely."

He stopped and held her face in his hands and assured her, "I just need to be able to see outside and I can call him. We are going to make it, for I will always take care of and protect you my love."

They held each other tightly for a moment and then proceeded to pick their way through the rocky corridors carefully working towards the opening of the cave while always staying well hidden.

Therasil's troop was quickly growing in numbers and they had formed a half moon shaped perimeter entirely within the tree line that was perfect for an archers attack on an army; or a dragon except that both were still just slightly out of range. However Therasil was ready now for the next step, "Talya," She called her top warrior, "What news have you from Zen-Darlya?"

"My Queen, they have not yet been captured though it must be soon, as they have had enough time to make it to the mouth of the cave," Talya stated, "I will go and flush them out if it is your will."

"No, let them come to us, but begin to push them from behind. Create a calamity of sound behind them to herd them into our trap," Spoke Therasil.

"I will order it to happen at once my queen," responded Talya, she saluted and disappeared in the hazy light of the realm.

Therasil shrugged and said comfortably to Zen-Darlya, "I have surrounded myself with loyal and courageous warriors of the highest caliber, you are all learning of the realm with such ease. We are going to take the Amazons to a new age of glory.

Unfortunately, Therasil was living in a dream world which she believed that she could bring about in one afternoon with very little planning and no growth towards this complicated future goal at all. She seemed to desire that utopia just be given to her and she was soon to learn a hard and bitter lesson. The really heartrending part was that she was forcing the rest of the Amazon nation to learn the same terrible lesson, completely unawares.

Desiree was carefully picking her way towards the huge mouth of the cavern, as they could now clearly see daylight and so they were trying to move ever more quickly; when she felt Ebirius grab and hold her from behind. She met his eyes and he signed her to be silent, he then pointed back up the way that they had come and signed to his ears for her to listen.

She listened carefully and at first did not hear a thing, but then she heard it, very faint, but it seemed to be growing louder. It was the sounds made with the quick marching of warriors with armor and weapons. She whispered to Ebirius, "We are trapped."

"Perhaps not," He quietly responded. "We just need to get as close as we can to the outside and very quickly!"

They chose an alcove that would lead them closer to the outside, but at the same time it also took them uncomfortably close to a few more of Therasil's guards. They considered it a necessary risk, so they scurried towards the mouth of the cavern with all possible haste.

The warriors that Zen-Darlya had set to oversee the apprehension of the princess and her able new consort were very best of Therasil's militia, this is the reason that they were always chosen for the most important or the most secretive of tasks. Therefore, it is no surprise that they picked up on the noises that the approaching couple made, even though every attempt was being made to be as silent as possible by the two.

"Aliceria, did thou hear that noise, it can only be our escapees," Said Lorna, a very large and formidable Amazon woman by anyone's standards. "They are in the next hallway, and close. The queen wants them alive, but says that just barely so will do!"

The two approached Desiree and Ebirius from the side, with malevolent intent on their mind.

Our fleeing couple had seen them as they had passed by in the darkness, knew exactly their presence, which was in their favor, however they could feel the noose tightening around them and wondered if they would be able to get close enough to the outside world for their plan to succeed.

They could still hear the other guards that were pursuing them on the occasion that one or the other would slip on a rock or such and make some noise with their weapons, which was not any longer as far up the corridor as it had once been, but it seemed now as though they were getting uncomfortably close. Ebirius fully expected to be dodging either missile from the famous Amazon slings or arrows any time now.

They finally came to an opening into the main corridor where they could now finally see the trees outside. The room that they were now confronted with was very large with walls of smooth rock, yet offered no cover to speak of save a short ridge that ran along to their left, high enough to offer slight protection from sling or bowshot yet they would be in full view for all to see. Unfortunately this seemed to be the only way out, yet once that they were committed; there would be no turning back.

Desiree stated, "They will surely have guards at the end of that path and we will be the easiest of targets for their archers. We are going to most likely be captured, or killed."

Ebirius took her in his arms and said, "I did not come this far to lose you. I will whistle and then you follow me down that pathway as quickly as you can. Trust in me, our love will find a way," He then kissed her passionately.

He loosed her from his arms, stuck his fingers in his mouth just so and let out the loudest most piercing whistle that she had ever heard. Rather like an eagle or Falcon coming down on its prey. He grasped her hand and said, "Now run, stay with me!"

They proceeded as quickly as they could possibly muster down the small corridor formed by the immense wall and the small parallel ridge that they headed for and had chosen to cover their flight, but they were spotted at once by nearly a dozen expert Amazonian killers. They kept as low as they could and ran as quickly and low as possible.

As soon as the trapped couple made their move to escape, they were seen, Aliceria and Lorna's eyes met and they smiled at one another, Lorna said gruffly, "Alive, but just barely," They loaded their slings and began their pursuit.

Ebirius and Desiree were very quickly dodging stones from slings. This was not easy, as they could not see them coming and they were coming with such a fierce velocity. Luckily this speed of flight produced a hissing sound for the short flight, so at least they knew when to duck. They still ran as fast as they could, but their route was not at all straight and seemed so very long.

As they ducked below the ridge for the third time to hide from the missiles that were whistling towards them he loosed another extremely loud whistle that reverberated in the mouth of the cavern and even seemed to produce a tremendous echo. Therasil's minions knew exactly what he was trying to do and redoubled their efforts with their weapons. They did not want him to contact his large friend, as well equipped with the poisoned arrows as they were and despite what Zen-Darlya said about being more than a match for the beast; they increased their pace without delay.

Desiree had forged a few steps ahead of Ebirius and she saw them first, at least ten warriors in full armor waited at the end of the pathway that they had chosen for their escape. She stopped Ebirius and the two of them lowered themselves to hide in what appeared to be the last possible cover that they would be able to take advantage of.

Ebirius immediately produced the longest and the loudest of his bird of prey-like whistles. He felt certain that Granger must have been able to hear him this time; unfortunately Therasil's brood was also alerted to exactly where they were hiding. However there was no other choice; he needed the help of his large friend now like never before. They both ducked down in the tiny niche that they were in and Ebirius said, "Stay down; I think that our help will be here in a moment. I just hope that he has returned from the errand that we had sent him on. He is very fast when he needs to be, he will be here!"

Near the top of the mount there was a new development, Queen Andrea and the brown dragon Granger's discussion had been interrupted by a messenger of Therasil's that was questioning if the queen would like to negotiate the return of her daughter.

As the messenger talked, from a distance to the queen's officers, Granger thought that he heard a shrill whistle that he recognized, he cocked his head to one side to listen more carefully.

Therasil's messenger, Anna-Suz was rather apprehensive about touting the capture of Queen Andrea's well-loved daughter, especially knowing what an accomplished warrior that she was. But she did not let it show, she said with much bravado, "Therasil, the true and gracious queen, offers you this proposal. The safe return of your daughter and her man for the banishment of you and your inner court to a location of her choosing; no harm will come to anyone and no battles need be fought."

Andrea began to speak when all present heard unmistaken a loud, shrill, wholly piercing whistle. It had come from the entrance to the mining catacombs at the base of the mountain and Granger recognized it at once; Ebirius needed him!

Those that have not seen a dragon stirred to fierceness have not seen one of the most awe-inspiring sights in nature. The kaleidoscopic dancing colors of his eyes changes to a deep and brilliant red, as he tenses and flexes his muscles, apparently expanding his whole body. When he unfurls his wings to take flight, they seem to fill the sky. Stating only, "I am needed," The dragon took off with a hurricane force of wind from his huge wings nearly pushing the queen and several of the closer Amazons off of their feet. With but a few mighty strokes of his wings, he was air born and fully three hundred cubits over their heads and as all of the Amazons present watched in awe, he folded his wings and with a horrific shriek dove descending down the mountainside in an instant. He was outside the opening of the cave when he heard the last and most desperate whistle come from just inside the mouth of the cavern; he was on it at once. He landed inside the cave close to where the sound had come from and was at once confronted by more than a dozen bow wielding Amazon warriors. He shrieked a dreadful dragon challenge and this is when the Amazons let their arrows fly.

The mighty Amazon warriors knew in their hearts that no animal in the jungle had ever been able to withstand a hit from the razor sharp Amazon arrows loaded with the most toxic poison known. They were all shocked to total disbelief when their arrows simply bounced off or shattered on the dragons rock-hard scales.

Granger advanced on the location where he had heard the call that he recognized as his friend. He looked towards the wall and there behind a low ridge he saw his two young friends, hiding low to avoid the Amazon fire. He proceeded towards them while taking care to protect his eyes from the sharp, flying arrows that the air seemed to be filled with now. He then realized that his friends lay behind the rocks, somewhat protected and so with several powerful strokes of his wings for a few seconds, he produced a force of wind that cleared the corridor of the Amazons for nearly a hundred cubits, injuring some and knocking others senseless. It gave him the time that was needed as he looked over the ridge of stones just as Ebirius and Desiree began to poke their heads over to see just what had happened.

"Someone in need of a friend," murmured the fierce-looking brown dragon in an astonishingly gentle voice, considering his ferocious appearance.

"I'll say," Ebirius sighed with what can only be described as grateful relief.

At the same time, Desiree just moaned in appreciation, "Oh, thank the gods you are here Granger."

As the fierce-looking brown dragon inspected his two young human friends, making sure that they had no serious injuries he told them.

"Climb up to my neck and hold on to the joints of my wings we must take leave of this place as quickly as we can."

Even as their large friend spoke, they vaulted onto his back and began to make the climb to his wings and although the dragon attempted to assist by lowering himself as much as possible it was still a difficult task that took more time than they would have liked. The Dragon urged them, and vigilantly guarded their escape with his great body.

With the departure of the dragon, there began a number of important changes near the top of the mountain. Therasil's army had grown by several thousand warriors and now half surrounded Queen Andrea's army that had also continued to grow in size. The space that they occupied however limited them to a small force of not quite several thousand, though they were steadily being joined by more of their allies that was now spreading over the height of the precipice, these included a force of Andrea's warriors that was building behind Therasil's army further down the mountain, the combination of the two groups had succeeded in gathering nearly the entire Amazon population to this one mountain at this point in time it was an unusual and very strange twist of fate indeed.

Meanwhile, in a very heavily guarded tent in the very middle of Therasil's brood Neandra-Luz was in a near trance-like state. She had described to Therasil and others before the great difficulty that existed in deceiving so many into thinking that her projection was indeed "friendly" and someone that they should believe and obey, especially with so many souls involved. Therasil's troops did strive to maintain as peaceful a situation as possible for the witch's purposes and for the most part they were succeeding until the ear shattering calls from the beast began.

Still Neandra-Luz concentrated on the malevolent task at hand and she seemed to be very near readiness in turning the horrible deed to reality.

At this moment Therasil approached and entered the tent, discreetly leaving her guards outside. "How long until you are ready my friend," She asked?

The effort was obvious from the tension and small beads of sweat that could be seen in Neandra-Luz's weathered face. She replied, "When you spring the trap I will be ready my young queen!"

Therasil seemed very pleased with the way things were and said, "When you hear two short notes from my hunting horn, prepare. With the third, make it happen; I will spring our trap in just a short time before her army at our rear becomes too numerous," She then turned and left the old witch alone in her tent with the fate of all the Amazons resting in her hands.

Meanwhile sitting at Queen Andrea's side with her eyes closed seemingly oblivious to her surroundings, Tamara quietly told the queen, "She is ready to project something into our minds, and she is very strong."

"Are we in danger," Queen Andrea queried?

"No," Tamara replied confidently, "She is not even aware that I am reading her thoughts. We will definitely gain the upper hand on this day!"

"I knew I could depend on you to help protect my people with your considerable skills," Andrea said. "This will yet be an historic day for the Amazons," she told Tamara stroking her cheeks.

As Queen Andrea surveyed the situation and looked across the clearing at her adversary's troops she noticed a general stirring from behind, approaching the middle of the mass of warriors approaching her bodyguard. It was Therasil; finally the two faced one another on a field of battle. She knew then that this day would find a solution to the problem that faced her people, in some way.

Across the field of the coming battle Therasil said to Zen-Darlya, "What of the escapees, do we have them as of yet?"

"I have heard nothing your highness," Zen-Darlya responded, "But surely they are in custody by now!"

"What word from the messengers that we have sent," Growled Therasil?

Zen-Darlya began to feel a growing fear as she had but a weak response saying, "None yet, as they stopped the conference when the beast shrieked and took flight."

Therasil noticed the demeanor of Zen-Darlya and told her in an almost soothing manner, "Fear not, little one for we still hold the upper hand, as my trap below will dispatch the beast shortly and Neandra-Luz is ready with her sorcery even now."

She quietly said in a voice that seemed laced with poison, "Send word to Andrea that if she wants to see her daughter alive again she is to use the realm and follow me to a place of my choosing to negotiate a settlement once and for all."

"Yes, my queen," Zen-Darlya responded, "At once."

After just a few moments that seemed as though they had taken forever, the huge brown dragon realized that his passengers were finally secure and he leapt into the air, taking flight with an ease that they both were very grateful for. You see, in the few moments that it took Desiree and Ebirius to mount their dragon savior the Amazon warriors had regrouped and were again ready to sow the seeds of death that they were so well trained in delivering and once again the sky began to fill with arrows; only now the young couple had only the cover of the brown dragon's bulk from below. It was most unfortunate that the arrows came from many different angles. Granger immediately realized this and put the greatest of his effort into swift flight, gaining altitude very quickly, but the mountain now seemed to be filled with Therasil's archers. Dragons do not often feel fear, but at this time Granger felt a terrible fear for the safety of these two humans that he had grown to feel so strongly for.

Things then began to happen very quickly! Therasil and her messengers delivered the ultimatum to Queen Andrea even as Andrea's army began to surround Therasil's army from behind; Therasil's army was now threatened by the surrounding royal guard; and Queen Andrea, who now in turn was demanding to see her daughter.

Therasil not only could not produce her daughter, but also had just discovered that the young Phoenician and Andrea's daughter had just escaped with the aid of the great brown winged beast. Things were beginning to happen faster than she felt that she could ever hope to control. Just then something happened that made her think that her luck may be holding, she saw down the mountain and climbing towards her the beast that had been causing her the most disconcerting problem. It was gaining altitude but was still clearly within bowshot and to her delight two passengers were visible astride its neck. She quickly gave the order, "Concentrate all of your fire on the beast. Bring it down with its passengers at once!"

At the crest of the mount Queen Andrea waited and observed the new group of messengers approaching her guard under a flag of truce, with the communication that she knew would set the days climax into action in one way or the other.

She spoke lowly to young Tamara, "These will be the ones that set the trap into action. Remember to appear totally unaware, for I know that Therasil has been very close to all of her officers; most were her guests in the bath in the great hall on at least one occasion, and they all have been taught the basics of acquiring the realm."

"I, as always will use discretion my queen, you know that I have learned this well," She purred.

"That you have, my pet. Are you fully prepared to convey what our enemies must see, for the time is drawing near," The queen asked soothingly.

"I am ready, you will be proud, the old witch doesn't know the extent of all of my powers, she will be greatly shocked," Tamara bragged, "and she will not discover my spell until it is far too late."

"Very well my love," Said Queen Andrea, but she seemed to have something gnawing uncomfortably inside of her. Was Tamara was too confident? She just hoped that everything was as superior as she was being told, "We are ready then."

She strode out to meet the messengers herself.

Therasil had with the use of the realm positioned herself directly in front of, but quite a bit below the big brown dragon. He was no longer flying directly up the mount but was still threatened somewhat by all of the archers below and he though he was concerned he was quickly gaining altitude. Though with Therasil's latest order all of her warriors that covered this part of the mount let loose a ferocious barrage of arrows, and it pleased her to see that many were finding their mark.

Though a dragon heaves mightily, he cannot always achieve what is needed as quickly as is needed. Trying to evade the archers at the base of the mount he had flown up towards where he knew that Queen Andrea was waiting, and for a few moments it appeared that they would be safe in this direction, however they shortly flew over an even thicker concentration of the reprehensible archers. Upwards and downwards appeared to be blocked, so we began to fly away from the mount beginning at right angles to the combatants and then curling away and gaining altitude as quickly as I could when suddenly they were surrounded by a cloud of arrows that fortunately bounced off of my thick scales, but to our horror one found its mark in sweet Desiree's back. She groaned a mournful wail and began to fall, but Ebirius immediately grabbed and held her with his free arm; just at this time something most strange happened, the Quellenar's that had been fixed on the necks of Desiree and Ebirius just fell away.

At the same time the massive flights of arrows just stopped. Ebirius couldn't understand what was going on, but his confusion lasted only a few moments as he was then aware of the hazy light that he had seen before with the use of the realm and Therasil appeared on the same dragons back as he; grabbing Desiree with one arm and stabbing at him with the other. She was an incredibly capable warrior with exceptional balance and she stabbed deeply into his shoulder.

Her wounding him enabled Therasil to wrest Desiree away from him and disappear in a shimmering haze of light.

I, as a dragon not familiar with the ways of humans and caring greatly for the young man that was scarcely able to hold himself secure to my wing decided, with the help of a new volley of arrows headed our way that discretion was smartest form of valor and flew away from the amazons and their vicious bows to find a safe place to land and tend to my friend.

~~~~~~~~~~~~~~~~

Their Queen Andrea had departed to address her adversaries, so she did not see as her brave warriors that remained to guard Tamara, the strange and otherworldly light that began to surround the queen's fierce little doll. This sight alone produced a grave terror in those surrounding her, something that is exceedingly rare in a race of warriors that is

Words of the Piasa

most renowned for their bravery. Had they fully understood what was happening, they would have been far more concerned, of this I am certain.

~~~~~~~~~~~~~~~~~~~~~~~~~~~~~~~~~

At the same time Neandra-Luz had entered the height of her own spell, she was sweating profusely and continuously mumbling to herself, "Try as you wish you young kitten, you cannot begin to match this old cat, I will show you what real power is, and you and all of yours shall then be placed to the torment where you belong!"

~~~~~~~~~~~~~~~~~~~~~~~~~~~~~~~~~

Therasil reappeared at the head of her guard, across the clearing a short way from Queen Andrea holding Desiree. To her trumpeter she said, "Sound the first two notes."

The trumpeter obeyed immediately. She then turned to Andrea and said. "Would that you will save your daughter than follow me at once," She turned back to the trumpeter and said, "Sound the last note."

She was once again obeyed immediately, and only a moment later the wicked woman that desired her new place as the queen of her people disappeared in a strange glow with the mortally wounded princess Desiree in her arms.

Just after Therasil disappeared with the princess, all of her army began to disappear in much the same way as she had just done as one by one they faded away until after but a few moments none remained, but Therasil was not there to have seen it.

The Queen of the Amazons, Andrea Perseii was already crossing the field in pursuit of the traitor Therasil and her precious daughter when she saw what had happened. She wasn't surprised at Therasil's use of the realm and was ready for it, or so she had thought; she could already sense Tamara's projection and felt that it was working as she had supposed. Also she knew that she was probably one of the most expert of all the priestesses in the use of the realm. She hesitated for only an instant, but then cried sadly, "save my Desiree," and was gone in the same eerie not quite normal shade of light usually shown with her practice of the opening and use of this ghostly domain.

~~~~~~~~~~~~~~~~~~~~~~~~~~~~~~~~~

Meanwhile, towards the rear of Therasil's force, Andrea's warriors had begun to fight their way up the mount towards where they thought their queen and princess now needed their help. The main force battled their way towards a large tent just in time to see the sight of a demented looking witch just finishing her incantations with a strangely horrifying scream.

There was what seemed to be a brilliant flash of blood red color; did it surround them or was it in their minds, no one could tell for certain, but at that point nearly all of Andrea's troops disappeared in the same unusual hue of color with which their queen had just moments ago, falsely believing that they were to follow their queen to assist in the rescue of the princess; they all disappeared as well into oblivion.

Further up the mount, near the summit and down below where they thought that they were closing in on Therasil's troops for the kill, Andrea's warriors all "saw" the same picture in their minds and "knew" that to follow their queen to this place was to help the queen in the coming rescue Princess Desiree and maintain the Amazonian glory; nearly all of them fully believed this perceived falsehood and unwittingly disappeared into nothingness for all time just as their comrades had done.

Unfortunately for Neandra-Luz, Katlena Beez had seen that the old witch was the one responsible for the spells, and as she had been aware of what was really happening, she did not disappear with the rest. She instead dispatched the old hag with her razor sharp sword with the extreme skill of a master warrior; when she finished her grisly task, she rose up in celebration of her dispatch of the old witch to her compatriots, the witches macabre head in her hand above her head; but to her complete shock and dismay, she was standing utterly alone.

～～～～～～～～～～～～

Tamara was finished, her plan to rise into the greatest of power with the use of her sexual wiles and her hidden alliance to the new queen Therasil was now complete, or so she thought. She began to slowly and battling a great weariness raise her head to surmise the situation, just in time to see the unnerved warriors surrounding her for her personal bodyguard disappear. This was accompanied by the unmistakable laughter of Neandra-Luz and a quiet whispered curse that echoed in

Tamara's mind. "Young kitten catches and passes the old cat in age, but dies in the pain and dust of envy."

This curse was all that she could hear in the last moments as she watched her own skin slowly wrinkle and wither, her ample breasts sag and disappear, her teeth and gums decay and fall away, until finally she fell over dead and obedient of the curse turned to dust; a fittingly repulsive death was the reward for an overly ambitious young woman with a spirit that was of pure evil.

Less than a league away sat a very large brown dragon with a surprisingly courageous Phoenician sailor nestled comfortably under his wing. Though his wound was not mortal and a quick bandaging would have helped, it was still bleeding and Ebirius was in a somewhat weakened state, but still he insisted, "I saw where she was being taken I must go to rescue her. She is my life, my friend. She is my love and future."

"I am a Dragon my small friend," I said. "We are not the same as you humans, but I am beginning to understand about the love your kind feels. What I must tell you now pains me greatly, because of my love for you." I paused for a moment to take a deep breath and gather my resolve, for what I was about to tell him, I knew would utterly crush him. "From where she has been taken, there is no return. There is no way even to find her; I felt the evil here today. The casting of dark sinister magic took place here today. I felt and can recognize it, as there were those of my kind that were capable of such evil; to attempt to follow her to this place would only ensnare you forever as well. She has gone to nothingness none of them will ever return!"

The young man gazed woefully into his huge friend's eyes and said, "I must try my friend; I love her with all of my heart. I swear to you, I will be back," he vowed as he began what he felt he must.

As this Dragon watched the glow of the realm and heard those words echo in my ears, I sadly knew that he would never be able to fulfill this last promise he had made to me.

Now, as wild and filled with humans as this place was just a few minutes ago, gathering to have what they had called "a great battle," as if there could ever be such a thing; but now it had now become totally desolate and empty; I was entirely alone, save for three or four of the Amazons that for some reason or another did not disappear and their hoard of men prisoners down the mount at the "Castle in the Woods," the whole of the Amazon culture that had occupied this land but moments ago was gone; now and forever!

I lay in wait near the top of this mount for many hours. I was greatly saddened, thinking about the adventures that Ebirius and I had talked about that now would never happen, about missing the children that such a warm and wonderful union would have produced. Desiree's beauty and charm, Ebirius's kindness, heroism and bravery, they would have made exceptional little human progeny; but alas, now it was not ever to be.

And what was it that had really decided the fate of the Amazons?

They were such interesting humans, though my friend held that they were somewhat "misguided," they seemed to be so advanced in so many things that they had done. Their artistry in building, clothing and unfortunately, even weapons was very obvious. What would they have accomplished had they not been their own undoing?

They had committed the unfortunate error of arrogance towards <u>the natural world</u>; they had a firm belief that they understood all of the mysteries of "Mother Nature" and believe this old dragon when I tell you that no matter how long you live there will still remain mysteries in nature that are better respected and left alone. They regrettably paid the price with the elimination of most all of their kind and it will always remain a day of great, unforgettable sorrow!

After spending the rest of the afternoon pondering these things and crying real Dragon tears at the loss of my friends, I decided that I must go down and release the Amazons men and get to the "Osprey" to tell Ebirius's good friends Durages and Flaxon just what had happened. It would be as bitter for them as it was for me; possibly even more so if that could be possible, though I do not think that is feasible for one to feel more pain than I towards this occurrence.

They told me that they thought they had seen him in the haze of the realm on the quarterdeck, though it appeared that he was floating and lost, but he had not known where he actually was and just faded away. We all shared a most profound grief and I told them that if they ever needed me they could contact me the same way that Ebirius had done and tried to carefully explain it to them, though I fear that perhaps I did not explain it as well as I should have; or perhaps they were just too pained to try, for they have never once made the attempt as far as I am aware. I looked for them on the seas a good many times, but alas this "Mother Earth" is very large and there is also the possibility that they no longer sail, for this "adventure" most likely changed them in some most unforeseen ways.

Now it was the dragon's turn to be surprised for although he had been totally silent for the entire story that the dragon had recited, the young boy Nathan finally spoke, "You don't want to hurt us like everyone has always told me, do you."

"Oh no," I said. "Quite the opposite actually, I have continued growing ever more fond of humans throughout all of my long lifetime."

This brought to me an old, familiar feeling that I realized I had missed very much, I was beginning to care for this young human even more. You see, I had been watching and appraising him for quite some time before I finally called to him and arranged our meeting and I had grown to admire his personal attributes even long before we had actually met. It had been many human lifetimes since I had communicated with mankind and I realized that I had fortunately chosen well.

"That was a wonderful story," Nathan said. "But why did you bother to get me to come to your cave to tell me a story?"

"Oh, my young friend," I continued. "That is but one story, I know many more, but will only burden you with a few today. What I really seek is your help."

"Help," Young Nathan blurted out, "How can I possibly be of any help to you? You are so huge, so strong; why you can even fly. What could I ever do to help a being as mighty as you?"

"My young friend, you are correct that I have many powerful abilities, some of which that you do not even know of," I agreed. "But there is something that I must accomplish that I am certain I would not be able to succeed at without the help of humans such as yourself."

Nathan anxiously stared up at me and asked, "What is it?"

"I must convince your people to listen to me and heed my words," I said.

The boy did not understand, he exclaimed, "You are huge and fierce, you can make anyone listen that you chose to."

"No, no," I explained. "I cannot force the understanding of this on them; they must not only listen to my warnings, but they must heed them as well, for the future of our "mother earth" is in your people's hands. You see, I have seen many races of your people come and go over thousands of your years and I finally have realized that not only do the humans control their own future, but they control the future of all our home, Mother Earth; however you are now becoming dangerously close to being able to make the final mistake that will end life for all of us that call this place home. So you see I must convince you and yours to heed my warnings in order to save us; one and all!"

"And you need the help of a ten year old boy for this," He asked dubiously.

"Do not sell yourself short my young friend," I stated. "I have become a very good judge of human's character over the ages and I can see that you have some very remarkable qualities. I feel that you will grow into a very brave and honest man; someone that a dragon, or anyone would be proud to call his friend."

I paused for a moment and then asked, "Would you like to help an old dragon to save our world?"

"I will surely like to try," he said.

"That is very good and I know that you were the right choice," I told him. "Well then make yourself as comfortable as you can for even though there are many tales that are important to tell with many of your kind that have disappeared over the ages with a lesson in every story, I believe that now I will tell you of what became of the people who were called the Atlanteans."

While the first story was being told to young Nathan, something that would have been of extreme interest to a narrating dragon occurred, a couple of would be hunters Burt Slade and Gill Jess that were new arrivals to the area saw Bill and Danny come running out of the thicket like they were being chased by the devil.

There had been stories told; stories in the bars and other haunts the two frequented of sightings of a huge mythological-looking beast of some sort in these woods, a dragon it had been said. They had come with their large caliber/ high velocity rifles to investigate this properly. Its death would make them famous and most probably also very rich men; once again they each shared another swig from the flask that Gill had produced.

As Bill and Danny bound through the woods they were now in flight, making their escape, from something that surprisingly did not pursue; but that did not matter to them now. They slowed and saw behind them two men, armed with huge rifles that were walking towards the cave entrance they had just so recently exited. They paused and wondered; should they warn the men of the peril that they now approached? No, they decided, for they were well armed. Should they warn young Nathan and the monster? They decided on doing neither at this time and just continued along their path of flight somewhat puzzled now by the feelings that they now experienced.

The People of Atlantis
Unknown – est. 2000 to 1500 B.C.

Meanwhile, back in the depths of the cave the large brown dragon some called Granger, but today is probably more widely known by the name Piasa continued with his story about the land and peoples of Atlantis, (8.) unaware at this time of the possible danger that was growing ever nearer.

As young Nathan settled in against the brown dragon's outstretched wing to listen Granger began another even more fantastic story. "It began very long ago," stated the dragon. "Many of your human lifetimes before you began recording your history and several hundred of your years after my friend Ebirius and Desiree had met their destiny I came upon another unique culture of your kind who lived on an island that they called Atlantis.

The Atlanteans were a very advanced race of people in mainly every way; I loved to get close enough to their dwellings that we could hear their music, as it was very melodious and soothing. They were also very accomplished in the creation of what they and those after them called art. They created beautiful and sometimes very large pictures that were very pleasurable to gaze at, sometimes even using an entire mount or something as immense as one of mother earth's flat plains that can stretch as far as the eye can see as the medium, and at this they were a very gifted and talented people, though there was a side to them that I and my kind were most uneasy with; even the blacks who as I told you in the first story were not ever the type to fear anything of this world showed the Atlanteans a healthy respect by giving them a very wide berth, for they feared many of the objects that the Atlanteans had created. Their creators had given them the names weapons; and they were weapons like none ever before seen, beams of light that could burn a hole in our scales, stones that would explode when they were hurled at you, they even had platforms that they could sit inside of that would let them pursue us in flight. They had the ability to create so many amazing things that they at the time called Atlantean marvels, though you would now probably refer to them as *technology*; but unfortunately they were proven to be quite reckless in their pursuits."

"One of the very special beings of this culture that it was my good fortune to meet and befriend was called Shawna. She and I had shared a cove in which we met on her island home that was created from a small river slowly winding its way out to the sea. I enjoyed it because it's many, thick; short, bushy trees enabled me to swim and bask in the sun and I could thoroughly enjoy myself in this place without being seen and as I soon discovered these were the very same reasons it seems that Shawna was so fond of this place as well."

"As I discovered the day that she and I first met, for she was in the habit of swimming in the wonderfully refreshing water just as was I, without the encumbrance of the clothes that so many of your kind seem so prone to wearing. It was especially amusing for me to see the way that she was startled when she climbed upon me to rest in the sun and I opened my eyes to see this lovely creature stretched out upon me; it was even more interesting to see how quickly she became composed again and stretched out to relax once again, not even considering departing, she even then began to talk to me and although I could not understand her tongue initially, we still began to bond immediately."

"We carried on in this manner for quite a while; at least two lunar cycles, and in this time we began to understand one another and began to develop the ability to actually speak to each other. This, of course began with food, she arrived at our cove one day rather early when I had not yet gone into the water, but was on the shore when she arrived nearly silently behind me on a cart that somehow seemed to be self-propelled, my first real encounter with any of the many Atlantean marvels that I was soon to discover and will in time attempt to tell you about.

Duncan Glenns

You see, to find this secluded cove I had flown for a very long way, for not only was I trying to stay away from the battles that were taking place in the old land between humans and the black Dragons and even humans fighting bloodily amongst themselves, but as you will probably soon realize, I possess as one facet of my character, that which I suppose that you would call *wanderlust*. I have always wanted to find new places and explore them, especially when I was a few millennia younger; in any case, she got out of her cart with several large round striped melons. She held them up just under my nose for me to smell them and said, "I brought you some new foods, would you like to taste some Atlantean Muskmelons?" Surprisingly, I understood her and even seemed to have knowledge of a simple response, as I answered her, "That I would like!"

She immediately took a large knife from her satchel in the cart and cut the largest in half scraped out all of the seeds and expertly peeled off all of the skin. I rather thought that this was a waste, as I was quite used to eating fruits such as this whole, until she tossed a large piece of only the succulent meaty part of the melon into my open and waiting maw, and it seemed to nearly melt in my mouth with an unimaginable sweetness and it was also very strangely invigorating. I thoroughly enjoyed all that she had brought, especially since this lovely Atlantean creature was so graciously feeding me. I even told her that it was not necessary to remove anything that I was more than happy to eat them whole. Her response was, "It is my pleasure to do so, my large brown friend."

Once we had finished the melons, I wanted to return the favor and give her something equally as delicious to eat and so I asked her, "Please stay here for a few moments and I will return with a gift for you, too!" As she protested behind me I disappeared into the deep part of the water where I searched for, and soon found the small, golden fish that I later heard humans refer to as Trout-fish. While they are rather small for me, I have found their rich sweet taste rather remarkable and was certain that she would too! I soon returned and delicately placed them on a large flat rock beside her. She was very profuse with her thanks, but added, "If you don't mind, my friend I will not dine on them quite the same as you do. Let me show you how my kind prefers to eat trout-fish and she immediately went to her cart and came back with a large pane of what you now call glass, yet it was somehow very different. She set up the Sol-cooker as she referred to it over the fish that she had expertly filleted with her very sharp little knife, sprinkled something on the fish and waited. In only a couple of minutes it was sizzling and exuding a most remarkable aroma and I must admit I found it very tempting; in just a short time, she stated that it was done. This was to be my first experience in tasting food that was prepared in this way.

Shawna would, in the time that it was my good fortune to know her, show me many of her people's marvels. Some like this device that *cooked* the fish that I had given her and she had in turn prepared for me were exceptionally interesting and useful, although there were others that I would soon discover, that were unimaginably horrible things, weapons of such power that their very possession corrupted the beings that wielded them. Weapons that could pose such total destruction of our "Mother Earth," that they could be the end of the home of us all; Oh, I am sorry, my passion to tell the story overtakes my telling of the facts of the tale; let me continue.

Shawna placed one of the tasty fillets on her plate and the other five; she would patiently toss into my open mouth as she was eating hers. She called this "dining together" and we soon fell into the habit of doing it with a great regularity, although we did graduate to much larger portions for me. She did grow to like some of the deer and hogs that I would later bring her and she would then *cook* over an open flame splashing it repeatedly with a wonderful sauce that she had so expertly prepared.

One pleasant summer day after we had spent several moons dining with each other and by this time speaking to and understanding one another really quite well, not to mention building a really deep trust between one another she began to ask me a great number of questions that she had not deemed to ask before.

"Do you have a name," She asked?

"The one of the humans that I had known in the past would call me Granger," I replied.

"You have known my kind before," She queried?

"Not exactly," I answered, "He was a male, very different from you, also a Phoenician, a source of even more unique aspects of the differences of which I speak."

Words of the Piasa

"We have had reports of people that live far towards the rising sun that were sailors in past times, but they no longer seen as once they had been; are those his people? Whatever became of him? It seems to me that you were very close and you appear to miss him terribly," She stated observantly.

"He was lost in a terrible calamity," The dragon stated somberly.

"I'm so sorry," She said quietly.

"I will always miss him, as we grew to be very close. However, I have learned to live with it, though the pain that I feel will never disappear," I told her.

"Alas, there lies the two-edged blade of love, along with the intimacy comes the inevitable and sometimes unbearable pain. I am sorry about your loss, perhaps we can enjoy some times together and I can help to lighten the load of remorse that you seem to be burdened with," She offered.

"What of his people," She asked? "Why do they not take to the sea as they once did, I hear that they were a truly great race of seafarers."

"That is true," I responded. "But alas, there is great strife and war in his land now. I am convinced that it would sadden him to see what has become of his home."

"Yes," She stated grimly. "We have experienced how strangely warlike some of the other people in our world can be, that is why we have put so much effort into perfecting the great weapons that we can now wield. We are not a people that desire to conquer and colonize others, but mark my words; no one will ever conquer Atlantis, my father is obsessed with her defense and he is brilliant!"

Now that I think back to what she said, I see how prophetic her words came to be, and wonder if it was in fact their own attitudes that shaped what their future was to become for although I do not feel that she recognized it; I may have detected some of that strangeness within her on that day.

She then asked, "What of your home?

I then responded rather slowly, "I have had a good many homes over the expanse of time that I have lived on our "Mother Earth" some more comfortable than others, but what I believe that you are asking me is the location of my birth home. Alas that is even further into the rising sun than where Ebirius's People live. Three more days would I need to fly into the sun to arrive there, It is a realm of many very tall mountains and none but the hardiest of humans ever venture there and very few of them ever call it home, as it is very cold and so the hunting is not always so good, that is the main reason that I departed, but I do still return on occasion as I sometimes somehow seem drawn there by something.

"You fly there," She exclaimed. "I thought that your flights were just short and limited."

"Oh no," I replied! "I have been known to fly over great distances. How do you think that I came to be here?"

"Why, I took it that you swam in the sea as others that I have seen of your kind," She stated. "You seem naturally made for swimming in the sea."

"Oh yes, I do love to swim. However, the seas are quite large and they can at times hold many unknown dangers," I told her.

"Dangers for even so great a being as you Granger," She questioned? Using my name for the first time in natural conversation; it sounded wonderful spoken by this lovely creature and I was soon to grow very fond of her speech and especially of her, of this I knew!

"Definitely," I told her. "No matter how large and fierce you are, it is likely that sooner or later you will be confronted with something, which is larger and even more powerful than you happen to be, for that is a common fact of life!"

"I suppose that is also very true with people, but for one as large and strong as you. I find it hard to believe," She offered.

"But in any case, it is especially true," I told her.

"So you are afraid to swim in the ocean," She half asked and half stated.

"Well my young friend, I do not know if fear is the exact way to describe it, but those who do not respect that which could do them great harm are inviting catastrophe though they may not be aware of it," I tried to explain to her.

I hoped that she would remember these words for I could already see in her the Atlanteans attitude towards their use of the weapons that they had created, though at the time I did not yet know how truly dangerous this attitude really was; however this was soon to change!

"You are right, of course," She said.

Words of the Piasa

She paused and gazed at me for a long while and then asked, "Can you take me flying sometime?"

"Well of course I can," I told her. "Would it please you to try it now?"

"Oh yes," She gushed excitedly, "I would love to."

"Well you may find it easier if you have a rope or something as such to tie around my neck to enable you to hold fast," I said.

She had a very long sash in her cart that fit around my neck nicely, secure, but not too tight. She finished tying it and climbed up my down turned neck. She wrapped her muscular legs around my neck, just above the wings and seemed to settle in nicely.

"I trust you not to drop me," She said, "though I've never liked heights very much."

This was very touching to me and I was moved to say. "You need never worry about your safety around me. I will not drop you and what is more, I will always fully protect you when you are with me and so fear not; you will always be safe with me!

And then we were off; I quickly rose into the air and as I did she let out the giddy scream as of a young girl one quarter her age, while she was at once excited, fascinated, awed, slightly frightened and above all having an enormous amount of fun.

We continued to climb until we were at just under cloud level and flew out towards where the sun first began its daily trip across the heavens, I then turned to head in the direction that you and yours call north so that she could look down over our left side and see her island home in its entirety. From this vantage point her home, which was quite a large island could really be appreciated. The canals that encircled the capitol city could only be navigated when the enormous gates that had been built were opened and the outer part of each ring of land in succession between the ringed canals of water was shear, smooth rock cliff face. In the very center was the tallest mount on the island that appeared to have a large number of cavern entrances intentionally hewn into them. These housed the top government officials, scientists and labs I was later told. However between the canals and the top of the mount could be seen a number of springs and small cascading creeks that looked as though they were totally supporting the numerous trellised gardens that seemed to surround the mount, this made it obvious that the city appeared to be self sufficient and unassailable.

I was quickly gaining respect and even developing a strong admiration for this new group of humans whom I had found that called themselves the Atlanteans.

We flew around her island for a short time until I saw something that not only surprised, but even startled me, for I was not the only large body now flying in the air. I saw what can only be described as a bird that did not flex or move its wings, (9.) but still it flew and very quickly; it was rapidly rising towards us and when Shawna saw it she at once became incredibly shaken.

"Flee," She cried. "You must get away, for they cannot have any good intentions towards us. You need, for both of our sakes escape this place or we will surely pay with our lives."

I experienced some momentary confusion for I had never seen anything like this before. I remarked to Shawna, "It is very fast and will soon reach us, what is it?"

She answered almost pleadingly, "They are new, experimental and they are called War birds. They are very fast and they have horrible weapons; trust me we must escape it at once!"

Even as she spoke, the strange thing erupted with an intense beam of light that looked as though it was directed right at us, luckily it missed initially, but it was arching around and getting closer very quickly. I did not feel that even my considerable skills of flight had any chance of escape from this malevolent looking ray of light, so though I had vowed to myself to never again use it; I immediately took us *between,* into the nether world.

We were both engulfed immediately with the bitter cold, and I thought that I heard, very faintly the voice of my old friend Desiree calling mournfully for her love and my bonded friend Ebirius. I then realized my mistake and the dangerous folly and quickly pictured the marvelous cove that Shawna and I had grown so fond of, and we were there at once!

We were back at our cove where we had met and grown familiar with one another, but I feared that I may have lingered for too long in that horrid place as Shawna could not even speak because of the chattering of her teeth. She was obviously very cold and so I gently placed her on one of the large smooth boulders where we had dined together so many times, I also fetched from her cart one of the large cloths that I had seen her lay on and sometimes wrap around herself and covered her with it. She began to recover, albeit painfully slowly, but the warmth that the sun had provided to the rock was very beneficial and I remained at her side as she recovered.

Several minutes later she whispered weakly, "You saved us."

I dipped my head in recognition and to get a closer look at this human that I was growing so fond of and she reached out to caress me and said, "Thank you," as she stroked my neck.

She then looked searchingly into my eyes and asked me with a very puzzled look on her face, "What did you do, where did you take me, what was that cold, horrible place?"

I certainly at that moment felt rather guilty, "I am sorry to have taken you there Shawna, but I saw no recourse. It is a dreaded place that I had vowed never to return to, it is known as the realm and I feel that there is a strangeness there that can prove to be very dangerous, perhaps even evil. One must not be enticed to remain for too long, for if you do so you will be trapped inside of that place forever. I fear that I had you there for too long just now, as I thought that I could hear someone whom I used to know; for the Realm can easily deceive you!

"Yes, I thought that I could hear my mother telling me to go home right now," she countered. "However, my mother was killed in a laboratory accident four years ago."

"That is the trickery of the realm," I said. "You must always stay focused and never remain for too long, it is best to not venture there at all, for I've known many that have never returned from that place, as you cannot begin to fathom the dangers and trickery that dwells there. Please, do not ask me more about it for it would be a great disservice were I to teach you anything of the realm."

I had said my word about the realm and thought that my warning would dissuade her from her strange interest in the place that had caused so much pain for so many; and for a time it seemed as though I had succeeded in quelling her interest!

I was troubled though about what I had just seen and needed to know more about it. "Was that beam one of the Atlantean Marvels that I have been told of," I asked?

"Yes," she replied.

"And what is it called," I asked again?

"It is called the Atlantean Death Beam," She murmured. "It is very accurate and has an unlimited range, as far as we know. It will burn through anything that it touches, it is very dangerous, and you do not ever want to suffer its touch. It is but one of the many horrible weapons that my people possess, but there are many more!"

"You seem to know much about these weapons and dare I surmise that you seem to feel shamed by them." I offered.

"You could say that, but I am also very proud in certain ways," she whimpered.

"And why is this so," I asked in as comforting a tone as one my size could muster?

"It's my father," she said quietly. "He is one of the main creators of these so called marvels. You see, I love him dearly, but he has changed so since the death of my mother. He is one of our most brilliant scientists, all who know him call him a genius, which he most certainly is, for he has created many devices that were a real help to our people such as a machine that can distill seawater to fresh water, nearly instantly and he was also responsible for the creation of our Optiscopes, which enable us to see objects many leagues away as though they were very near. Why, he even created plants that can yield up to ten times the amount of food as before, but that was before the accident; now all he ever wants to create are devices that can kill; always better and deadlier."

"It sounds as though he seems to have been altered in quite a bad way by your mother's untimely death," I said. "Have you tried to speak to him of it?"

"Oh yes," She replied. "He merely hides what he is doing from me and tells me that I will understand when I am older and ends the conversation. I have already seen fifteen summers and I am not as young as he would have me believe, as I know what he is doing and I am shamed by it. You were right, he was changed and not for the better though I love him and desperately want to help him succeed, but fear what he has become as well!"

"He is now close to completing what I am sure will be his most deadly and dangerous creation of all. He and the others with whom he toils are within several weeks of finishing their largest, most powerful

"Death Beam" yet. They are mounting it atop Mount Sienna, right at the heart of our island and in the middle of our capitol, whoever controls it will have power over everything from horizon to horizon. It will have horrible possibilities for misuse that I think our people should be very suspicious of and it will even need a source of power that will be so great that my father is experimenting with something he has discovered that he calls anti-matter, and listening to him speak of it when I at times eavesdrop on him makes me think that this is the most fearsome of all of his discoveries. I fear for my father, he is not the same caring man that raised me, I fear for my own safety and most of all, I fear for my people for they seem to be traveling down a road to their demise and there seems nothing that I or anyone can do to stop it. They seem to have become obsessed with more and more powerful weapons and I fear that there will be only one end to this strange fascination that has enchanted my kind," she finished, looking utterly defeated.

"There, there now my passionate little friend," I soothed, "perhaps you are too close to the weapons and their production, as your father is so heavily involved. Maybe what you need is to back away somewhat and maybe you will become able to see it from a different perspective, it may not be as bad as you think."

She looked at me with such a look of resignation in her eyes that I could feel every bit of the sadness that now was filling her soul. She just said, "You don't understand my people the way that I do my huge friend and sadly, by the time that you do it will probably be too late. Just promise me that if I ask you to leave our island home that you will get as far away as you can, as quickly as you can."

"I will and I will take you also when the need arises," I offered.

"Perhaps," She sighed, "though I have many responsibilities, I must first try to save my father from what it appears he may have already become; I must somehow find a way to save him from his own hatred which I feel will soon entirely consume him."

"We can try together," I offered, "If you will accept my help."

"Of course I will," she sighed. "I'm just really at a loss as to what next to do."

"Well I suppose that the first thing that I should do is learn more about your people. It seems as though it might be more dangerous for me on this island than I had first suspected," said Granger.

"Yes," she chirped. "We need to have a place where you can stay without being seen, for you will not be easy to hide in the open, while you are beautiful, but very, very big. It will be difficult although I think that I may know of the perfect place, if you feel like another flight to the far side of the island I believe that I can show you another new home that you may rather enjoy for a time!"

"Climb aboard, my sweet Atlantean princess," I offered as I leaned down presenting my back for her to climb aboard to her place on the back of my neck, "show me the way to this promising new abode."

"Yes, alight my friend and head the opposite way that we traveled the first trip. To the mountains on the southern tip of the island and then just to the water side of them, that is where we will find the cave of the blowing rocks," She directed.

"Blowing Rocks," I repeated, "sounds like a rather tumultuous cave to live in."

"Yes, it looks like a very violent place and nobody would ever attempt to enter there because of the danger that it appears to hold," she said. "But I know better, I was swept into the cave on a giant wave during a boating accident when I was a child and I was fortunate enough to discover its entry secret."

As she spoke we approached the mountains that she had been guiding me towards. They were beautiful and lush and seemed to be the perfect habitat for the type game that I so liked to feed on. I was beginning to like this place immensely, then suddenly I began to feel the updrafts coming off of the peaks and realized that I could glide on them effortlessly all day long, this island was getting better by the minute. I enjoyed this for a few moments, but was disturbed from my revelry by Shawna's urging me on.

"Out to sea a ways," she instructed. "You will then be able to see the entrance where you should even be able to fly into it if you time it just right!"

I flew over the mountains and past the updrafts then began swooping down towards the ocean. We could now feel the refreshing sea spray peppering our faces, so I began to slow down.

Just as I began this I heard Shawna say, "now turn around Granger, turn around and see for yourself!"

I turned as she asked and was impressed with the sight of a

tremendously large double arched cave mouth that would be easily large enough for me to fly into. I also found it quite beautiful and rather inviting, but as I began to make my way towards the opening to get closer and enter, there was a tremendous explosion of seawater that came upwards and outwards toward us, it was accompanied with an impressive roar that made the whole experience quite imposing.

As I nearly stalled and then hovered in place, Shawna just laughed and informed me, "No one dares even approach the caverns called Blowing Rocks. Many small craft have met their doom trying to enter the mouths of these formidable caverns, as far as I know only I am aware of the secret method of entry."

"Really," I exclaimed. "It seems that it would take a ship or even a dragon that possesses more power than any that I have seen or met in my time."

"Yes my friend, you are right," she confided. "You cannot fight the power of mother Earths mighty seas with power, for she will defeat you always. You must use your intellect and enter with the exactly the right timing; it is the only way!"

"You know this," I queried, "how came you by this secret?"

"When I was very young my aunt and uncle had brought me to this end of the island to fish as there are a large number of the wonderful large red-meat fish here called Tuni. We must have strayed too close to the shore because we ran aground on an unseen rock. Our boat was suffering the heavy pounding of the surf and I was petrified. I would never have survived except for the quick thinking and bravery of my aunt Rea and uncle Selvin; as they wrapped me in the life saving vest before even considering their own safety and the moment that I was secured the boat was torn asunder and we were all washed overboard. None have seen them since and I will always owe to them my life, but I was tossed directly into the mouth of these caverns when right before me a huge wave broke on the rocks in front of the cave as you have seen, but then as the water withdrew and the next swell began to build for a return, I was lifted by the water over the rocks in the front of the cavern and deposited well inside the cave. Once past the rocks at the entrance the cave was far more peaceful, and very large, there is even an assortment of several ledges that one could rest on if the need arose, as it did for me."

"You were trapped in this cavern by the power of the sea," I gasped, "how did you ever find a way out?"

"First, just listen to me and fly directly into the cavern on the left immediately when I tell you to" She instructed me, "get a little closer first."

I tried to be patient and do exactly as she said, as I knew that it was very important. I hovered directly in front of the cave, just out of reach of the tremendous explosions of water that were regularly taking place in front of me.

"Now," she said, "as quickly as you can!"

I dove towards the water in the cave that she had told me about just as the monstrous wave subsided; it seemed to flatten just for our entry. I found it very impressive, "very nice," I said.

"You did that really well my large friend; you cannot overcome the seas power, the secret to entering or leaving this cavern is mastering the timing at the entrance," She explained. "I am glad that you find it so inviting, as this may be the only place that you can safely make a home on the island of Atlantis thanks to the inventions of my father and his friends. I know that they would only feel threatened by you and with the weapons that they possess I do not feel that one even as mighty as yourself would be safe."

"Thank You," I said, "though I have been alive for many of your lifetimes, I have never seen anything like that ray of light we both witnessed today. You could feel its power even at a distance, and I do not feel that it is a natural part of the natural world; I fear that it is a harbinger of evil. It may be taking your people down a path from which there is no return, quite possibly even to their demise. What is there that I can I do to help?"

"I only wish that I knew," she said dismally. "My people have had an inordinate fear of being the victims of conquest for over a hundred years, ever since narrowly defeating warriors that called themselves Alsaruns in a war that was supposed to have lasted for nearly fifty years. They wanted our home and so they just thought that they would take it; ever since then my people have never been trusting of the outside world."

"That is very sad," I said soothingly. "Humans are not all like that."

"Yes, I and many Atlanteans feel that is true, but the politicians that are in control continue to use people's fears to finance the creation of more and more weapons and I fear that it has gotten out of control," she sighed, "I do not know what to do."

"Perhaps if I could talk to him or take him safely to meet some of your more friendly neighbors across the sea," I offered.

"Oh, I don't think so," she squawked. "He would be terrified of you and would not listen or even cooperate. He is even working on an even newer and more powerful weapon that he says uses matter against anti-matter. I do not even understand it, but he says that when he produces it that he will have to be careful to do it in minuscule amounts for he fears that this power could obliterate the entire world if he is not very careful. I fear that his morbid experimentation will be our undoing."

Only now can I appreciate how true her premonition was to become!

"Perhaps we can think of another way to approach him," I proposed.

"We will have to, but right now it looks exceedingly hopeless," she said. "But for now, at least you have a safe place to rest without being found and harassed by my father's solders and the new armaments that he has created for them."

Several weeks passed by without much that we were aware of happening. We just spent our time swimming and dining in our favorite little cove once again, her showing me different interesting and wonderful things about her island home and generally enjoying life; but if it could only have continued so! One of these places, I found particularly interesting, as it was on the lee side of the island so that the trees seemed to have had the chance to grow to exceptionally large sizes. I flew down amongst them and walked into them and was entirely hidden from the outside world (especially the aerial view) by the thick leafy canopy above us. We were enjoying the coolness of the shade when an idea occurred to me. "Would your father come to this place if you asked him to?"

She stared at me and responded, "I am not certain; for he is a very busy man."

"Even for his daughter," I asked?

"Well, I suppose I could try," she said wryly. "After all, I am his "little girl" and his only remaining family; yes he probably would if I asked sweetly enough.

"Tell him that you have someone from afar that he would benefit from meeting," I said, "and I believe that there are some descendants of some old friends that I can convince to come here for a sort of parlay. Perhaps when he sees the kind of people that his neighbors really are he will be less obsessed with death and more interested in having some sort of normal relationship with them, maybe beginning with trading! Is that not that what most humans like to do with one another?"

Looking back now, I realize how naive my thinking was and how little I knew about these particular humans, though I still don't know what I could have done differently!

She told me that she would try to arrange it, but it would most likely take several days to accomplish. I had no alternative, but had to agree.

"In the meantime, I would like to show you something else that I think you will find most extraordinary," she told me in a most intriguing fashion as we again flew on.

"What is it," I asked curiously?

"Oh, it is a surprise, however, as old as you confess to being you may be familiar with her kind" she confided, "though I am told that she is the last remaining of her type left in the world."

"So you are treating me to a very rare meeting," I asked?

"Yes, quite rare," she said, "and her seclusion is very important to her. Only a very small number of my people have ever seen her and know that she exists, by her design and I am certain that her kind has been hiding from your kind for ages. She would never allow you to see her without my attendance."

As she talked to me about her friend that I was about to meet, we walked deeper into the thick growth of forest and it became more difficult for me to maneuver.

"Try to be as quiet as you can be," she instructed. "We do not want to spook her deeper into the forest until she can see me, and believe me we will not see her until she spots and identifies me for she can be as elusive as the morning mist."

So we continued to work our way deeper into the thick jungle. This view of the Atlantean island had eluded me so far and as we passed by

Words of the Piasa

so many different beautiful plants and flowers; unlike any that I had ever seen anywhere else, I inquired what they were called and Shawna told me that they were called the Orchid plants.

"The Orchid is a type of plant that we know to thrive all over the world," she said. "As far as has been discovered though, this forest has more of a variety of them as any place known on our mother earth. That is why this forest has been named Orchid's Nest."

"They are exceedingly beautiful," I told her. "The birds and insects seem to love them also."

"Oh yes," She exclaimed! "Our people also find them useful in many ways. From these Orchid plants we make flavorings for food, oils for paints and perfumes, and even some medicines."

"Medicines," I queried, "they sound very important?"

"Yes," She explained. "That is why we have protected this forest buy law for a very long time; it is not legal for my people to take anything from out of this forest without permit."

We kept making our way through the increasingly thickening dense forest and enjoying the sights that we were being treated to, but at the same time I began to have the strange feeling that we were being watched. We passed many edible looking melons and other fruit even a few of which she told me to try; I found them all very tasty, for fruit. We kept passing small streams and waterfalls that all seemed to be going back the way that we had come. I several times saw large patches of beautiful comfortable looking moss that seemed to be inviting me to lie down and take a nap on it.

When Shawna noticed my interest in it she stopped and warned me, "Not everything is as innocent as it seems in this jungle; that is strangler moss. If you fall down or lay to rest, it can grow around you in but a few moments and once it has you trapped inside it immobilizes and consumes you. This can take days to occur and I hear that it is a horribly slow and painful death. Even beings as large as you would have no chance my friend, the largest patches will even attack you while you are still on the move, and you have seen only the small ones so far. Be most wary of it my friend."

"Thank You, I will," I said.

We continued deeper into the forest, and I thought that the feeling of being watched was indeed becoming ever stronger. We also seemed to be getting somewhat higher up the flanks of the mountain. As we followed the prominence upwards I began to hear the unmistakable sound of the babbling of water; we were approaching a waterfall.

Shawna shushed me saying, "be as quiet as you can be now, for it will not be long now and remember; remain very calm at all times!"

"Yes," I whispered. "You can depend upon me."

We passed through an unusually thick area of trees, trying to part them as quietly as possible and on the opposite side was the most beautiful waterfall that I have ever seen falling majestically down the side of the mountain. It was very tall; easily twelve full lengths of this brown dragon and the canopy of the forest seemed to have opened just for the falls to pass through as it was very thick around the rest of the area. The Orchid plants seemed to find this place very appealing for there were far more of them here than I had seen anywhere else in the forest. Everywhere throughout the entire meadow the mist from the waterfall hung in the air and the sun shining through it made for very beautifully colored rainbow-like fog that gave the place an almost magical feeling and appearance.

It was then that I saw her! Shawna had been walking twenty or thirty cubits ahead of me as I tried my best to follow her as quietly as I could, when suddenly stepping out from behind a very large tree I beheld one of the most beautiful creatures that it has ever been my privilege to behold. You humans called them Unicorns, and my kind has called them many names the most memorable name being Monoceii - the one horned Equis. She had obviously met and captured the gaze of my friend Shawna and seemed to be trying to communicate with her and she was standing in an auspiciously placed sunbeam at the edge of the forest canopy, surrounded by the beautiful flowers that were so plentiful in this forest with a light cloud of the mist from the waterfall floating about her. It was like seeing her in a dream and was truly a memorable sight. She then looked in my direction and seemed to show none of the fear that I thought that I would see, as her kind was mostly regarded as food by dragons throughout most all of history.

Instead I began to hear her voice in my head both friendly and unafraid saying, "You know me not, brown dragon called Granger, but I have known of you for several lunar cycles now since your arrival on our island.

Words of the Piasa

You are very conspicuous being as large as you are and hardly using the powers that we know you to possess in the use of *the Realm*. While I suppose that you have your own reasons for this; yet we have watched you for a good while and can see that you are very different from others of your kind that we have known. You are not such a brute as we have seen in the past from your kind, but actually show a marvelous aspect of kindness that is often exhibited within your behavior."

"I have long realized that I am quite different in many regards than other dragons," I responded.

"Granger and I have become good friends," Shawna said. "You can trust him."

"Yes, this is true," I added.

And immediately the unicorn stated, "This I already know, otherwise I would not have met."

"Granger, my dragon friend, I would like to introduce you to Ursalas; my old and dear friend who happens to be one of the last unicorns," Shawna eloquently introduced us.

"I thought that your kind had long since disappeared," I quietly put forward. "There are even tales of great herds of unicorns entering the realm with great tumult, never to be seen or heard of again and doing so because of sorrow and remorse over the loss of the magic in the world, very hard to understand for some, though I can feel that same sentiment myself at times; however I just feel that I have a role still to fill that can be of help to one and all!"

The Monoceii, or as they are known to the humans; the Unicorn Ursalas gazed into my kaleidoscopic dragons eyes and I felt as though I was the one gazing into the kaleidoscope of colors. I felt that I was entering a trance and could only relax and feel at total comfort in her presence as she quietly stated, "Our hope lies in you brown dragon, this I sense. I do not believe that it will be in the literal measures, but I believe that your future actions will become those which will save our world."

"I cannot see how," I said, "I am no mighty black and cannot believe that any intrigues of mine would have any lasting effect on any who might matter."

Shawna told me differently though, saying, "You can believe Ursalas, it is her special gift to know of what is to come to pass."

Ursalas countered, "Not gift, but a curse, when I sometimes am aware of awful things that are in store for those that I love; yet know that I cannot change anything, try as I may. It leaves a bitter taste and feelings that are most unpleasant; it robs you of your anticipation, your eager desire to see what the future holds turns to uninvited stagnation."

Shawna stepped forward and stroked the unicorns beautiful mane and said, "Come on now, my intuitive friend. Haven't you and I talked about this and decided that there are many possible futures and we are all but in control of only our own?"

"I only know what it is that I feel," Ursalas whinnied.

I spoke slowly to Ursalas, "I can but tell you what a great dragon friend of mine once said to me," I said. "He told me that it was, in fact within our power to guide and shape our destiny, but this can be accomplished only in a natural way. It appears that some of Shawna's people have become unnaturally intrigued with what they call Atlantean Marvels and seem to be achieving wondrous accomplishments that are apparently beyond the point of the wisdom that they seem to have reached, much as their wizards were said to have done many years ago; however the wizards back so long ago were not as fortunate as to have a unicorn and a dragon around to warn them of their folly. If you would hear it, it seems that Shawna and I have the beginnings of a plan."

"Yes, and maybe with your help," Shawna urged. "We will be able to get my father and his associates to realize the unfortunate course that they are steering towards and set things to rights."

"I do not know," said Ursalas! "Humans are so stubborn and conniving. I do not think that a thing that we can do will have any effect on the choices that they will make, or their future."

Shawna held her face on both sides and said to the unicorn, "Were you not the one that told me that hope is the one immeasurable quantity that can change all that it touches?"

"Yes, yes," Ursalas admitted. "But in the short time since, I have seen the Atlanteans create horrible and unnatural contrivances too numerous to mention, always sighting defense. It is lost on me why defending yourself would mean killing in such huge numbers. I am sorry, I feel that they are lost and there is naught that can be done, save enter into the realm with the rest of my kind!"

"But there may be a way," I said attempting to fortify the unicorn.

"We must try to save my people," Shawna pleaded, "Please help us."

"I will help because of the love that I feel for you and the hope that I can sense in your large friend, but I cannot believe that we will be able to sway them from the path that they have ingrained themselves onto; I do not believe that there is any way that we can renew the magic that once dwelled in our world," she repeated, "But I will try."

At the same time that we were meeting Ursalas the unicorn in the forest known as Orchid's Nest, Shawna's father Daryell Ree and a number of his fellow inventors were in the volcanic cone on the extreme other side of the island where they had set up what they had decided was a very special experiment. Their laboratory was over two miles long and they were attempting to collide the smallest bits of matter with one another. In doing this, they hoped to create tiny amounts of what they were calling *Anti-Matter*; as it was Daryell's theory that when matter and anti-matter came into contact with one another that they would annihilate one another in a tremendous burst of energy that he could harness and use as an extremely powerful energy source for a new weapon.

The scientists, as they would now be called, had set up two "safe" observation sites. One about three miles from the site that would control the reaction and another some twenty miles from the site that would measure and record the effects of what transpired from near the mountaintop.

They did not feel that the infinitesimally small amounts that they were dealing with would pose any danger at this range; however they were soon to find otherwise.

Daryell gave the order to initialize the process and it slowly began. Daryell instructed again, "Make certain that you keep up the power to full on the magnetic holding fields."

"Aye Sir, we are most careful with that," His fellow scientist responded.

Daryell listened as the hum began to build over the communication system in the small building in the middle of the compound that was surrounded by the rich tropical jungle which blessed that half of the island. Suddenly he and his assistants saw a blinding light that seemed to instantaneously expand and touch them, blinding several; that was followed a few seconds later by horrendous shock waves and then the sound of a tremendous explosion.

The closer observation post was obliterated with all in it, but although the second was also near fully destroyed there were but two blinded and no one inside was killed.

On the other side of the island where an unusual meeting was taking place between a unicorn, a brown dragon and a young Atlantean girl they were shocked and surprised at the loudness of the explosion and were spurred into immediate action.

"Some new surprise from the scientists," Granger questioned?

"We will return soon Ursalas we must not waste time right now discussing the plan," Shawna said, "Granger you must wait for me at Blowing Rocks. I will find out what happened and make certain that my father is all right."

"Of course Shawna, but first let me take you at least part of the way there to save your long trek through the jungle," I offered.

"Yes, my large friend, that makes perfect sense," She responded, "but then go directly to Blowing Rocks as quickly as you can and I will meet you there as soon as I can!"

"That was an unnaturally powerful explosion," Ursalas sighed. "Your kind is meddling with that which should not be disturbed."

"Yes, my friend and we have a responsibility to act upon it at once," Shawna said. "There may not be as much time as we thought! We are off; please meet us back here at midday tomorrow."

Farewells were exchanged between a human, a unicorn and a dragon and we alighted into the midday sky just as soon as we could. We had just cleared the treetops when we saw it on the other side of the island; a huge mushroom shaped cloud that seemed to be expanding and growing ever taller. We dangerously chose to climb further above the treetops to get a better view and what we saw alarmed us immensely. Where there had once been shoreline, was now a huge crater that in effect had created a new cove large enough to accommodate a large navy of ships, the water rushing in to fill it appeared to have scoured the shore clean of all foliage that had once been there, as it was all now barren rock and we saw none of the people that had obviously been there before, anywhere.

Shawna asked, "Do you see that building on the hill that appears to be only partially damaged?"

"Yes," I told her.

"Set me down about one half league this side of it, as I do not wish for you to come within range of their weapons," She instructed. "Perhaps they will not even see you if we are lucky.

I obeyed and delicately landed her where she had asked, "I will be here to take you back," I said.

"No," She exclaimed, "You are in extreme danger here you must go back to the hideout and I will meet you there later tonight. Please, go there and eat and rest, you will need your strength all too soon, I will be there tonight!"

With that, she was off into the woods towards her father's ruined laboratory.

Left alone, wondering what he should be doing to help his new friends, the large brown dragon was at a loss, so he did as he was asked and made his way back to the cave Shawna had called "Blowing Rocks," although in his entire great expanse of time and life, he could not remember having felt such a dread as he was now feeling, save for when he began to witness the demise of the Amazons. He felt a sickening shudder and was off to do as he had promised his friend Shawna Ree.

~~~~~~~~~~~~~~~~~~~~~~~

Meanwhile, back in the forest which the Atlanteans had named Orchid's Nest, the horned Equis, also known as a unicorn; Ursalas was now arriving at some version of her own plan. It is very possible that she had been changed, somewhat negatively tainted possibly; her once undeniably pure goodness of character changed over the ages by all that she had born witness to. You see, she had lived through the waning of the Magical time, the willing disappearance of most all of her kind into the realm, the horrible black dragons and the many other evils in the world that she loved and now the devious humans and their seeming total lack of respect for the natural world. Yes, she was changed; for she now thought that the meeting that Shawna and her large friend were planning would be the perfect opportunity for her to disappear into the realm with the rest of her kind and take the lot of the Atlantean inventors of "marvels" with her. Yes, she would help and she would take all who would despoil the remaining magic left in her world with her. Her final and most noble act would be to protect her world from the Atlanteans and their horrid "technology."

She finalized her decision; she would help gather the humans for a very special, and fateful meeting, one in which she would take the necessary steps to save her world from those whom would destroy the magic that still remained. The jungle was then bathed in the eerie glow of the realm as she began her travels to make the necessary arrangements; the light that shown when she entered this place had changed markedly in the last lunar cycle also; proof of the ongoing change within her!

～～～～～～～～

Shawna arrived at what was left of the complex that had obviously been quite vast and built for extreme security, however it was now quite different, for the fence that had once surrounded the entire compound had been blown into the forest at the rear of the compound, giving the odd looking appearance of the trees being fenced off in places and a tangled mess of fence and splintered trees in others. Most of the lesser buildings, the utility sheds, the food facilities, the administration buildings and the barracks had been totally obliterated; destroyed to ground level. The main building, where the scientists, who were in control of the experiment, including her father, had been was just a shell, having lost all of its windows, its doors and most of the roof. Even the plants and shrubbery had been laid flat by the shock wave that it was obvious they had suffered even at this extreme range, as were many of the trees within the next few leagues of this area all having been flattened away from the blast point, sometimes beyond where she had been deposited a short time ago by her large friend.

She entered the building and was overjoyed to find her father already beginning the rescue and cleanup efforts and she ran to him and clinched him in a warm and thankful hug, just glad that he was alive. He was glad to see her too, as he had feared for her safety as well, not knowing her exact location, it was extremely obvious that they were very happy for one another's well being.

"What happened," Shawna asked? "I was so worried about you."

"Oh, and I you my child, I am so glad that you are safe," her father responded. "The power of the anti-matter is far greater than we had ever imagined. We must create even stronger magnetic fields to control even the smallest amounts of it."

"It sounds too dangerous father," Shawna pleaded. "Perhaps this is some power that would be better left untapped," She cautioned.

"Yes, my love, it truly is more dangerous than anything as of yet discovered, however if we are not the ones to master it we will surely in time face those that have; they will then become those who covet after the island paradise we have created, just as the conquerors of old and then what hope would we possibly have," he tiredly continued. "I am so close to controlling it; and it is only for the protection of Atlantis and all of her people that I endeavor so earnestly," Daryell said as he trailed off sounding clearly obsessed and overly tired.

"Come father, I will help you regain order here and then we must get home so that you can get some rest, for you appear to need it badly," she said.

The two of them helped the other scientists that had been hurt; several that had been in the control area towards the back of the building tending the controls that were supposed to keep the experiment under control, in some sort of a cruel twist of fate were unscathed except for some cuts, abrasions and a little dirt. While their compatriots that were merely observing the effects had endured a blinding flash of white-hot light that had totally fried the retinas of their eyes to leave them painfully and permanently blind.

She and her father did what they could for his poor blinded associates Shawna contacted the Atlantean Prince Cavetti Reales. She knew full well about her father's wishes to someday wed her to the prince and thought that this was an opportune time to take advantage of his wishes. She called him on the two-way and said, "Cavetti, there has been a horrible explosion at my father's facility at Half-moon Bay, and we need transport."

"Yes, we had heard the explosion and I already have help on the way. Are you well," he said very meekly.

"I am unharmed," she said. "But we do have injured here and my father and I need immediate transport home. He is quite shaken by what has happened and I must get him home to rest at once!"

"I am very pleased that you have not been injured, my future queen and you may rest assured that transport will be there within a few moments, I will not, but always be of service to my future betrothed and the father of not only you, but our glorious Atlantean armaments system as well."

"Try to contain your enthusiasm Cavetti; your plans may be further away than you think," She told him. Her heart did not as of yet belong to another, but she was certain that it would never belong to this man.

"You will come around in time," he whispered bashfully, "you will see. Would you like my assistance with your father?"

"No, we can manage," she said, but then remembered her manners saying, "Thank you."

"Nice, that sounds almost like gratitude," he said, "I am growing on you."

"You are hopeless," She said. "I will see you later."

A few moments later, three hover carts glided silently into place just outside the shell of the formerly magnificent building.

She instructed the leader of the military-type state enforcement officers to take the men who were blinded to the hospital and her, her father and the others to their homes.

He responded, "My orders are to take all of you to the hospital miss Shawna."

"Well your orders were just changed by the future queen," She barked! After all, what good is a prince for a boyfriend if you cannot throw your weight around once and a while? They were all taken to where Shawna had now decreed at once!

Brown dragons are not always the easiest of beings to keep concealed, even when endeavoring with the greatest of effort; this was brought to my attention in a most frightening occurrence on the trip to the cave by the sea where Shawna had asked me to stay for a time. Though I was flying over what I presumed to be sparsely populated areas and was quite low, near treetop level, I was shocked by the sudden appearance of one of the Atlantean flying machines like that which we had recently encountered. It bore down on me from above and behind and for a moment I thought that it meant to ram itself into me, but at the last instant before I would be forced to defend myself or flee, he turned off of his coarse and just passed by me, I suppose for a look. It was not only upsetting, but also interesting, as I could see inside the machine that there was a human male. I could see most of his face (that which was not covered by the mask that he wore) and his eyes showed a grim determination that made me feel a great unease. He whistled by and I at once had an immediate concern for my own well-being, for Shawna had repeatedly warned me of the weapons that her people possessed and I was having a bad feeling that I was close to experiencing one first hand. I quickly dove for the forest canopy; I picked a small opening and ducked below the blanket of leaves. Once below flying became nearly impossible, but I continued to fly and hop to quickly vacate the area where the man had seen me enter the forest, this turned out to be quite imperative, as the Atlantean man and machine returned in only a very few moments intent on my destruction.

    He scoured the beautiful forest with a hot and terrible beam of light that was utterly destructive. The beam sliced through the forest effortlessly; it seemed to mow down and set ablaze everything that it touched; I was being pushed towards the base of the mountain and the quick loss of my protective forest canopy, but just when it seemed as though I did not have a chance and was going to be forced upwards and into what would certainly have been my doom the attack stopped. There was great damage to much of this portion of the forest, as the Atlantean and his flying machine had decimated leagues of the forest in but a few moments and all around me were flames and devastation, the smell of burning vegetation and perhaps even flesh though I was safe, yet sickened by what I had just seen occur. While I knew that all humans were not like this, this man in the Atlantean "marvel" had just exhibited a lack of caring and respect that I thought was not only very callous and repulsive, but quite possibly dangerous to the point that it could be the humans fatal flaw, I decided then that I would attempt to show them, first the flawed ways and then to teach them a better way to live, as I felt then and still do that they are our Mother Earth's true, and only hope.

I had experienced this moving revelation and felt a need to find a way to help the humans, yet I needed to escape the inferno that I had been left surrounded by as the canopy of the dense forest had reached the temperature that it was beginning to burn out of control and it seemed to be closing in upon me. I had to find a clearing and get out quickly and so I retraced my steps back to the clearing from wince I had just come to make good my escape; as soon as I saw the space, I leapt up into the air and flight.

I was shocked at what I saw; the Atlantean had merely tricked me and I had fallen victim to it. He was directly overhead and diving straight for me at a tremendous rate of speed. It was obvious that I was directly in his sights with nowhere to go at the velocity with which he dived towards me; in an instant I saw his face. It appeared that he was enjoying this immensely; his face showed the madness of power, exactly like that of a black dragon; he then fired. There was no other alternative or means of escape; I did the only thing that I could do, I instantly went *between*.

I immediately realized the danger that I had again put myself into, even though I had no choice in the matter this time. I could hear voices that I thought I recognized calling me from all directions, or were they feelings? I was experiencing a horrible feeling of being totally lost with no direction that I needed to go and no desire to find my way back out of this place, as I recognized that therein lays the danger of "The Realm." I lost all since of time; it could have been minutes, hours, days or even longer that I was trapped there, I really had no way of knowing. When suddenly it came to me, I must meet Shawna at Blowing Rocks as I had agreed. This promise is probably what saved me from the dangers of "The Realm" this time, and I can only say that I felt that this should be the last time that I should ever venture to that place, as I fear that my next trip there I may not have the strength to be able to return and I still feel this with all of my being.

The strange light faded and I found myself back inside of the cave at "Blowing Rocks" exhausted; I lay down on the ledge and slept instantly.

This is when Shawna unknowingly began to set into motion the chain of events that was surely the end of the Atlanteans and like so many momentous actions prior and since, it was with the best of intentions in mind that she began. It began the next day with her telling her father about her special friend and his extreme gentleness, but also of his worldly experience. She told him of the other peoples that lived on their world and of the troubles that other people where having, but also of the wonderful and friendly races of men that her large brown friend had told her about. She tried to explain to him that while problems did exist, they were not as bad as he imagined and that his obsession with ever more powerful weapons was not only unneeded, but also very dangerous.

For most of the afternoon they bickered back and forth until finally with all of the charms that a daughter will use upon her father she finally reached the point of his agreement to set up a meeting as she and the Piasa had discussed.

"Father, first I just want you to talk to my large friend Granger," She pleaded.

"You say that it will be safe my child and that may be," Daryell Ree said. He spoke slowly and with great compassion in his voice. "But it would not be the first time in history that a dragon had bewitched and taken advantage of such a one as young as you; I bid you approach this with more caution!"

"Oh father, you cannot understand the uniqueness of this creature unless you are to meet him," she explained. "He has already saved my life on one occasion and I would trust him with it again."

"That sounds similar to many bewitchment stories that I have heard of in the past," he told her.

"Father, you know me better than that," she held his gaze with her own and said. "You are always telling me to be more trusting in people and I am telling you that I know a being with a good and honorable soul and you can trust him. Please believe me father; it is for the good of our people."

"As you wish, my love, although there must be one condition," he said with certain finality that Shawna recognized and understood she had no hope of changing. "The meeting must be held at my lab in the mountaintop."

"But is that not where you have the huge weapon that is powered by the same system that caused the great explosion yesterday," She asked, although she already knew the answer?

"Yes it is," he stated. "But I will not be without any protection."

She did not like it, but she had to agree; and so the meeting was set!

~~~~~~~~~~~~~~~~~~~~~~~~~~~~~~~~~~~~

Those people that had been blessed with the good fortune of knowing a Monoceii; or Unicorn as they are called today would, I think probably agree with me that Unicorns are quite the solitary breed, as they have not only been hunted by dragons, humans and many other creatures that share our mother earth for food consistently ever since time began, but they have had a rather selfish and proud jealousy over whom had stronger magic for as long as I have known of them and I have never known them to become aggressive to the point of violence towards each other, but there have been stories that I have heard... Alas, I am no expert on unicorns other than to say that when I have eaten them, they were very tasty and satisfying. Though it is my opinion that the solitary nature of Ursalas had a major influence on the fate that was to unwind for the Atlantean people for I cannot be certain of the plans or movements of a Monoceii, as my magic is no match for theirs, but I can only put myself in her place and try to let you know what she did from what I do know from the glimpses that I did discover of her magic and the results of which I am familiar of her actions.

Picture a troubled unicorn roaming through the great forest where she and her kind have lived for countless millennia. She is greatly troubled by the direction that the humans have taken and the horrible things that they have the power to and are continuously developing. She is passive by nature and does not want to interfere, but she feels driven to do something. Nonviolent and terribly outnumbered anyway, she had but one weapon; her great magical powers. What would she do? She was greatly troubled, and distressed to see her magical world being replaced by men; to exactly what point I am not certain, but I feel that she influenced Shawna's father in some unknown magical way.

~~~~~~~~~~~~~~~~~~~~~~~~~~~~~~~~~~~~

Meanwhile, back at the cave near the sea called by the Atlanteans "Blowing Rocks" Shawna returned to find her large friend in a grievous state. "What has happened to you my great brown friend," she queried. "Are you not well? You look as though you have seen the very face of death."

Slowly, turning to finally acknowledge her presence, all that I could say was, "That just may be the case my young friend, that just may be that I have sighted the end of us all."

"Tell me what happened," she soothed me as she came to embrace and to stroke my muzzle.

We then sat thusly for the next several hours and I told her of my close call with the Atlantean Flyer and she listened to what I had to say. I told her of the terrible destructive beam of light that the flyer possessed, of all of the forest that had been destroyed in such a short period of time. She listened intently and comforted me as best she could. The thought even flashed in my mind of what a wonderful mother she would make one day; I even told her of the despicable look that the human had on his face right before he had fired upon me.

To this she responded gently, "Yes, I have seen this in my own father whom I dearly love, but fear grievously for. The power that these weapons give them corrupts them in a horrible and I fear irreversible way; for this I apologize for my people."

"There now, it wasn't you," I told her. "We have described the unnatural power of the horrible Black dragons as totally corrupting them with its influence and I can see that it is the same with humans. That is at once both most unfortunate and heartbreaking."

"Yes," she said. "But there is still hope. My father has agreed to the meeting with you; I am sorry though to tell you that he will only agree to have it at a place where he will have a horrifying weapon, as he has heard many awful tales and he now says that he fears dragons greatly."

"It is not something that you have to do," She conceded. "You need only fly away from here, for it is not right to ask you to risk your life to save some humans that you barely even know from destroying each other, I will understand; it is not really your responsibility."

"That is very touching of you," I told her. "But I could not in good conscience ignore what I see about to happen here, for it involves more than just this group of you humans. In fact it involves the safety of every living thing on mother earth and I believe that this is in fact a challenge that I must face, you say that your father is a rational man, can he be trusted at his word of non aggression?"

"Yes, He is an honorable man," She offered. "He will keep his word in all that he says, especially to his loving daughter, but I would not linger for too long if it can be helped."

"You say that I can trust him and that will do for me," I responded. "Let us attend the meeting."

"If you are comfortable with it, it will be tomorrow at the high point of the sun and I will guide you there, but for now let us rest." Shawna said as she nestled herself into the notch of his wing gaining more comfort from this dragon than she could ever remember feeling with any other living being throughout her young life.

And we rested. I must tell you that her listening to me and comforting me on that eve put me more at ease than you can imagine. We both slept like babes with their mothers and awoke the next morning renewed and refreshed, but alas this was not a condition that was to continue.......

At this time, I can only imagine Ursalas strolling through her beloved forest and trying to think of some way to put a stop to the developing *marvels* of the Atlanteans and trying to persuade them to pursue a different direction with their technology. It had to pain her greatly for she had very little experience with humans and could not even begin to imagine any sort of a method with which to influence them. I sometimes feel the similar pain that I know that she must have felt and though I have endured it for an inconceivable time now, I feel that she had strained to the breaking point.

I do know that sometime that evening she made her decision as to what she would do and unfortunately the action that she would finally take; this decision doomed her, and not only the last of the unicorns that I have known, but also the entire Atlantean race of humans. She too was just trying to save "Mother Earth" and those ways of the remaining magic that she had known and while I could feel her magic at work, I knew not what she had done or what steps to take to stop her.

At the lab atop the mountain or "The Peak" as it was called by the population of Atlantis; the supposed benefactors from the protection of the marvels that were created and installed there, the inventor Daryell, or scientist as he would be known today, had gathered a small number of his most trusted assistants. They were very careful to be as cautious as possible, as their leader and as they saw him; their patron had told them to come undetected, so they did as he asked. The name of the lab was a natural fit because the lab sat on a high plateau at the top of the highest of the mounts on the island. What it did not convey about this beautiful and wondrous place though was the numerous caves and grottoes that had been carved in the mount over the millennia by wind, rain and mankind. This too would have an incredibly important bearing on the fate that was to befall the wonderful, creative and prosperous people of Atlantis, for the Monoceii can be most clever at hiding and waiting for the right opportunity and Ursalas was not only very crafty, but she felt a deep motivation to protect the magical world that she had always known. Though in truth, the magical times she had known were now already gone, even though she could not recognize the fact; and that is one of the tragic and melancholy incongruities of this story.

Shawna and I had rested and refreshed ourselves and even had one of our wonderful light breakfasts of fish and fruit. This made the flight to nearly the top of the island seem to take no time at all, and as we flew through the fresh morning air I was beginning to feel as though we might just have a chance to convince the Atlantean scientists of the error in their ways. I was beginning to feel quite positive when Shawna leaned into my ear and told me, "My father may behave strangely at first, he may even threaten you, but it will be only to convey to his associates that he is in control. Please be steadfast in our commitment to bring about this meeting, for I have his word that he will do you no harm," She pleaded, "He always keeps his promises to me, so remain strong!"

"Yes Shawna," I told her. "Just hope that my resolve does not sway when I am looking at that energy beam being pointed at me at such close range. I do not think that I will able to succeed in returning from "The Realm" again."

"You will not be tested my friend," she assured me, "this I promise."

She directed me to alight in the middle of a very large courtyard that looked like it had been hewn out of the solid rock of the top of the mountain. The floor was vast and perfectly flat and we were surrounded on all sides by sheer rock of a most beautiful sort that I believe today is called granite; walls buffed to a marvelous smoothness. On the north side was the peak of the mount that still raised five or six hundred cubits towards the clouds, this was the only direction that you would not be able to see to the horizon once you looked over the rock walls, which for me was very simple.

Spaced around the entire perimeter of the immense hall were strange looking totems; huge, very ornately carved poles that did not seem to be anything like the style that was so obvious on all of the Atlantean peoples other artwork or weapons. Stranger still was that at the top of each of the twelve totems was a beautifully fashioned, from what I can only surmise appeared to be crystal sculpture of a human skull. (10.) Twelve of them in all spaced evenly around the courtyard and they were all facing inward as if watching and waiting. They seemed to possess a strange sort of power that I was not at all familiar with and it felt to me as though they could actually communicate with one another; that gave me an extremely troubled feeling, especially as per the fact that they appeared to be just floating above the totems, held in place by some unknown, invisible power.

I must tell you that I even sensed the surprise in my friend Shawna, she had not known of the scope of all that her father had been involved in and I could tell that she was now most frightened.

Events then began to happen far too quickly for my liking.

On the opposite side of the yard was a tall tower that looked as though it would be utilized as some sort of lookout perch; as we began to look around the compound for someone, the tower began to move; it was rising and revolving at the same time and then the shudders on the top began to open like the petals of a flower. At this time we saw appear as if out of nowhere far above us, a thirteenth Crystal Skull. This one was as large as all of the others combined and seemed to be somehow drawing some type of energy from all of the others and feeding it to what was inside of the great perch that was still slowly revolving before us.

"Stay still," Shawna warned!

The opening metal petals revealed a monstrous gun on the platform at the top of the tower and the two Atlantean "creators" had it aimed directly at me. There was no mistaking the menace of its pulsing clear, lighted barrel!

I remembered the reason that we had come and my small friend's instructions from last night, surprising even myself when I said, "Atlanteans, Daryell, I mean no threat to you and I will do you no harm, I wish only to open your eyes to the possibilities that are waiting for you in that wide outside world.

"I not only want to show you that there is not a need for such powerful weapons as you have been striving to create, but in the possibilities to be taken advantage of in the trading with all of the other peoples of mother earth. You will discover new interests; foods, customs and I know that you could even become more happy and prosperous than you have already proven to me that you are."

This last statement about prosperity seemed to gain their attention somewhat and they seemed to relax the aim on me ever so slightly.

"Father, stop this at once," Shawna exclaimed! "You promised me that no harm would come to my friend."

From an opening on the far wall came a stern warning from Daryell, "The beast shows any signs of hostility and I will kill it immediately, there is no escaping my anti-matter death ray."

"Father, you do not seem yourself and you are frightening me." Shawna spoke quietly but clearly for I believe that she was really troubled by her father's surprising demeanor. "What are these hideous skulls doing in a laboratory and what could they possibly have to do with science?"

"My dear, I do not want to startle you," Daryell tried to sooth his anxious daughter. "But we have come to a very important time in the world's history and the people of Atlantis have been fated to hold a very great place in that record, as for the Crystal Skulls, they were gifts from our benefactors of some many years ago, discovered by myself and my associates in an isolated cave. They have great and mysterious powers that cannot yet be fully understood even by me.

"Yet you would use them as a horrible weapon," Shawna cried!

"No, my dear, they are far more than weapons. They are wonderful tools; they are sources of power and forgotten knowledge. With them, I can transport to other places, know what is happening from afar, process the most difficult calculations. Why I believe that they may even be able to travel through time itself," Daryell exclaimed gleefully.

"I am your daughter, your offspring that you have loved and taught for many years and I am saying to you with all of the respect and love that I can bring to bear and as a product of your own teachings that you are playing a dangerous game and should not be using something that you know so little about to control such a powerful and destructive weapon," Shawna told her father gravely!

"But I am more learned of the crystal skulls than anyone alive, my dear," Daryell boasted.

"But, honored father by your own admission they are still a mystery to you and we have seen the power of the weapon that you are still experimenting with," Shawna pleaded.

By this time I could sense the intense desperation in my friend's voice, but her father Daryell continued to ramble on with his supposed explanation.

"I have been able to use them to harness the power that will enable us to unite the twelve original human tribes into one people, with us as their leaders," Daryell spoke with a dreamlike glaze in his eyes.

"Is that what this is all about father, power," Shawna asked?

"No my dear," He tried to excuse away the obvious. "Do not think that it is for power, nay it is for the good of all. We have seen the other tribes of mankind and those that are not savages are warlike. They would all benefit from our rule; strong, fair and just."

"Justice decided by whom?" I asked, wanting to say more, but restraining myself for the present.

"Why our high counsels of course, we would be the ultimate law," Daryell stated.

"We want only to talk with you," Shawna pleaded.

"You endeavor to conquer the whole of mother earth's peoples," I said. I was quickly dealt a silencing glance from Shawna and got the message to be quiet and wanting to inflame the situation no more, restrained myself of arguing with what I felt was a most unreasonable human.

"Just remember that you would make the perfect test for the most powerful weapon ever developed," Daryell growled.

That is the way in which our meeting began, but we then talked for several hours about the pros and cons of meeting the people outside of Atlantis. Daryell and his followers kept repeating the tale of the warlike people that had come in the past and I countered with the great things that I had already seen humans like him and his people do. I told him of the people that were building the great pyramids in the desert at the shores of the great river, I told of the wonderful people that from whom my friend Ebirius had come and their seafaring skills, I even told him of the strange, yet beautiful and knowledgeable people of the Far East. Yet still he would say that they had learned from and would not forget the past, that it would only be a matter of time until the outsiders would again covet their home like before and once again try to take it by force. He also mentioned that each of the tribes, as he called them would have their own Crystal Skull and that this was how he would know what they were doing and also the means of the delivering of their punishment. I truly did not believe that they were anything more than religious artifacts that the humans were always creating for I had no idea at this time of the genuine power that they possessed. Finally it took just the simplest of compromises offered by his daughter to sway Daryell's opinion, or so it seemed.

She proposed, "Father, let my dragon friend go and return with but two of the people that he describes and you can talk with them to decide if you wish to meet more of their kind; what harm can there be in just two."

"It is only a matter of time until someone finds your island paradise anyway," I offered. "But to solve that problem, I will ask for volunteers and if you are not happy with what you hear you can always keep them here as guests for as long as you deem it necessary."

The inventors talked quietly amongst themselves for a few moments and then Daryell walked towards us and said in a very low voice with great deliberation, "I see no harm in what you request, yet be warned that I do not see much promise in this venture either and were it not for the pleading of my most adored daughter, I would have none of it. So be off with you beast and return in the number of days that you have promised with those with which you would have me hold counsel."

Though as he spoke to me, I could see him looking in the direction of his associates and although I could see no overt sign of any kind, just their exchange of glances made me feel quite ill at ease.

I turned to Shawna and we separated ourselves from her father's group to say our farewells when she said confidently, "That was done very well, I am so happy to have you as a friend. Perhaps there is some hope for us after all."

I was not as comfortable as was she. "Shawna, I feel that all is not as it seems," I told her.

"You need not worry," she said. "My father loves me greatly and will not break his promises to me."

"Yes, but what of his minions," I asked, "can they be trusted?"

"Surely, as he is really the only one that fully understands the magnetic fields; and such is the power of those hideous skulls and what it takes to hold the anti-matter in control that powers the great gun; if they attempt to fire it without the fields being at the proper strength," She told me in an obvious attempt to pacify me, "The result would be cataclysmic I am told. He is the only one that knows how to fire the gun and his promise to me will not be broken, rest assured."

I was far from that, but I gave her a friendly nuzzle and said, "If you say it is so then I believe you. I will return in four or five days with our visitors," I nodded to everyone and alighted into the air for my flight to the lands of other willing humans. As I put Atlantis in the distance I thought of where I would venture to find my volunteers and I thought of what I might say to convince them to come with me, but I never gave an inkling of thought to any other players in the fate of Atlantis. Alas I have only been able to put together the rest of this story from the mental projections that I received from not only my beloved Shawna, but also the magical and mysterious Monoceii Ursalas. This is what I believe must have happened, although no one will ever really know for certain!

The Monoceii Ursalas was not only strong in magic, but also had lived on the island of Atlantis for a very long time and so staying hidden in the caves while she made her way up to quietly espy our meeting was very easy for her to accomplish with no need for the use of her formidable magical powers. She watched us in a rather long and heated discussion, without the benefit of hearing about the promise that Daryell had made to his daughter. We had been rather animated at times in our discussions and Daryell and his daughter had exchanged some cross words after which I was departed. As Ursalas watched from inside one of the caverns in the wall Daryell boarded the great gun platform, purportedly to turn it off. He then did something that the Monoceii did not expect; I know this because my friend Shawna somehow sent me a vision of it happening, it must have been her own desperate way of trying somehow to warn me.

She was not the only one to see this action; it appears as I unmistakably received a vision just a moment later that was definitely from Ursalas. Shawna had merely tried to warn me, but Ursalas did the same only she also took action to stop what she saw as a threat to me and finally to her own way of life.

Thinking that he was about to use the weapon on me she focused her aforementioned formidable magical powers on Daryell and thrust him against his will into the realm.

All that his underlings saw was that their mentor disappeared in the strange light of the realm and all that they could believe that could have happened was that the beast, that horrible dragon that they had just been so noble to have held parley with had stolen their leader with its dreadful magic; they were unaware of the real source of the magic at that time, the Monoceii.

They immediately charged up the podium to the gun.

Shawna screamed, "No, you don't understand. Granger did not do that and you do not understand fully how the weapon's power is controlled.

They ignored her, saying, "We will avenge your father even if you will not!"

They then swung the gun to take aim on the large brown dragon, that even at this long range, as by this time I was nearly over the horizon, was still going to feel the bite of this superb weapon, or so they thought.

They began to power up the gun as they took aim.

The Monoceii Ursalas saw the large skull in the middle increase its otherworldly glow, as it seemed to draw energy from all of the other skulls; she knew then that she must act.

The skulls around the wall began to disappear one by one as the one in the middle growled with an ultra-low vibration that could be felt even more than heard. As the growling increased so too did the reverberating power of the largest skull and hence to the gun that it was feeding the unearthly power to.

Just as it seemed that the powerful vibrations would surely tear her to pieces, the unicorn acted.

She leapt into the air, seeming to stand on an invisible ledge above and in front of the six who would kill the dragon from afar. She seemed to brace herself for a leap even in mid-air and let loose the kind of searing cry that I felt could only have come from a being of far greater fierceness than I was aware that she could have ever possessed; It was terrifying even as it was heard from over the horizon.

She drove all six of the remaining minions of the power-mad inventor Daryell screaming into the same fate as befell their master; the eternal coldness and calamity of the realm. She was doing what she knew to be right, to save her friends and preserve her way of life. Her intentions were purely good, even heroic some would say. If only the good that she had intended would have been what had transpired, the fate of the Atlanteans could have been ever so different; but alas, it did not happen so.

As the large brown dragon labored carefully and eloquently to enlighten the young boy Nathan with the story of the mistakes, the history and the hope of his kind; which that he was hoping the boy could somehow convey to his people so that their knowledge and actions could save their beloved world. There were two others that were concerned with nothing more than "killing the beast for sport" and the trophy, perceived fame and riches that they believed would soon be theirs as a result. They inched slowly through the jagged rocks on the floor of the cave in near total darkness save a tiny penlight, as they did not want to alert the dragon of their presence until they had it in the sights of their guns.

Ursalas; the last known unicorn watched her handiwork with a good deal of distain, as she did not ever wish to ever harm other living beings.

Words of the Piasa

That was not her way and though she was momentarily revolted by what she had done she instantly realized that she was still in mortal danger. The last skull had grown enormous and the vibrations were tearing through her to the depth of her very bones, but it then disappeared, leaving behind the gun that was near exploding with power from the skulls that were there just moments before.

It then did just that; an explosion like none ever seen before or since shook the entire firmament of our world, even the powerful atomic bombs that the humans make today pale in comparison to this blast. Ursalas, Shawna and the entire island of Atlantis were vaporized instantly, along with all of the people and the thousands of leagues of ocean that had been surrounding it.

Being just over the horizon is what must have saved this Piasa, but even at that extreme number of leagues away and out of the line of sight from the event I was knocked tumbling from the air, I fell into the sea and felt all of the waters being pulled back towards where Atlantis, or to where it had once been anyway, to replace the water that had been destroyed. This was when I felt the deepest fear, as I was a prisoner of this torrent of water and it seemed to be feeding into nothingness. How long this lasted, this I cannot say, but after what seemed a great time it began to slow and I was able once again to reach the surface.

For what length of time I am unsure, but I rested on the ocean and tried mightily to gather my strength. Looking back though, it could have been quite a long while, for as I rested there the sea calmed greatly. When I was able, I once again took to the air to try to find any survivors; though I flew back and forth sometimes covering the same areas repeatedly seriously testing the limits of my strength, searching, searching and in the end finding absolutely nothing.

Atlantis and her beautiful architecture, mountains, forests, artwork, orchids and even the technology that had finally become her undoing; Shawna my most special friend among them, Ursalas the last known unicorn, they were all gone, gone forever! They had made an incredible mistake that had provided to them no telltale signs or warnings; they had developed what they referred to as marvels, known today as <u>technology</u> *at such an incredibly rapid pace that it had overtaken and passed their ability to draw on the wisdom that was needed to control that which they had* created. *The cost was their ruin and the total disappearance of all of their kind.*

I felt that my strength was nearly gone, but still I searched throughout the day and night somehow, someway. I finally must have come to the decision to save myself and flew west towards what would become my new home, towards the home of those that would become my new friends and away from the pain and devastation that I felt in this place.

When a dragon has endured a great calamitous event; an event that stresses and uses him nearly to the point of death they can enter a dreadfully deep sleep, something closely akin to what you humans call coma, yet for dragons it is immeasurably longer. It can last for tens, hundreds even thousands of your years, many a human lifetime and this is what happened to Granger the brown dragon now, the pain of knowing and losing his second great human friend was nearly too much for the mighty beast, but his ancient recuperative powers were very great indeed; he arrived near a bluff that overlooked great river to where the forest ended and the great plains began and there he lie down taking the shape of a knoll and slept for a very, very long time.

Now it surely is a point of great debate in certain of your human circles, and most would not presume to confess that they know the reason why it happens, but when some beings have what they consider to be a close call with death (weather true or not) it will sometimes produce a drastic change in their behavior and their priorities in life which they formerly considered important. I believe that your kind would call it an evolution in morals. This is what can be said I suppose that happened to one of the last of his kind, as you will surely realize as this tale continues. This, I believe is when the Piasa made the decision that he would make every attempt to save the humans from the cataclysms that he knew they could bring upon themselves, for he knew that in so doing, he would be saving not only them, but himself and the entire remainder of the world which he loved.

The Nastazi – Today known as the Cahokians; of the Midwest Approximately 1000 A.D.

As it came to pass, after many ages, perhaps thousands of Mankind's years, in a part of the world allegedly newly discovered by certain humans from the East, nearly in the middle of a land now called North America; there lived a group of humans that called themselves the Nastazi. It was said by some that their name translated to "people who follow the soul of Mother Earth."

I actually can say that it is a very appropriate meaning, for never have I seen a people more devoted to the renewing and the maintenance of our beloved home. This was a more ancient time, before the coming of the white men who later arrived from afar. They had existed even before the great and powerful Aztecs unified nearly the entire land on this side of the great seas under their powerful rule. There were many more game animals for their hunters to hunt, the plains teamed with deer, antelope and the great Bison that provided so much for so many for so long a time. The skies were filled with geese, ducks and pigeons, fat and easy to kill. They had also began to replant some of the better tasting and easier to grow plants they enjoyed eating, for this meant that they no longer had to roam the countryside searching for food as their ancestors did; it could be said that their life was bountiful and good.

This part of the country was not only unusually fertile and blessed with an abundance of game, but it was very beautiful, it was known even then, as it is now, as the bottoms. It is actually the flood plain of this mighty river that seems as though it drains nearly all of the land. There were miles and miles of green rolling hills with thick verdant forest starting in the eastern part of their land at the cliffs and expanding north and east along the river valleys towards the mountains that soar skyward much further to the east; and to the west were beautiful grassy plains that were filled with the great Bison and many more prey animals even as far as the great canyon far to the west that would one day be called the Grand Canyon. The Nastazi had a wonderful Eden like world to live in and they had spread far and wide throughout it for many generations, until after many years of plenty the areas that they occupied to the west began to experience a drought; not any ordinary drought as this was a drought that lasted many generations and so, collectively they decided to move into the eastern part of their realm.

The Nastazi had chosen to live on the rising sun side of the great river plain found in the east of their land; close to but not above the river cliff, for above the cliffs the thick forest began in earnest and in the heavy forest lived the many animals that shared the bounty of this lovely place. Some; the panther, the wolverine and the bear could be very dangerous, especially a hungry bear! The medicine men even told of the soul of a great creature that existed in the woods; one that their ancestors had previously called Norander which meant, "Thunder lizard."

There have been tales of this beast existing not only with the Nastazi, but with numerous cultures all across the world, but though people may hand down the story there are not usually many living people remaining that had actually seen it themselves; in recent human lifetimes it has been called Piasa, or dragon or even Quetzalcoatl in Mexico, but is known by many other names as well.

The Nastazi people over the years had built a great complex of mounds; for burial chambers only in the beginning, but as they discovered the usefulness of these constructions they began to utilize them in many different ways. They built some for defense, even though they usually had no known enemies because of their widespread trading practices. They had managed to make many numbers of friend's even great distances away. It was said that the Nastazi even traded with the great civilization that was said to live in the next land many moons travel to the south called the Mayans. The Nastazi enjoyed a wealth of wonderful edible plant seeds that their friends the Mayans always had a desire for and were always anxious to discover what new delicacies they would encounter; while at the same time it was quite similar for the Nastazi at the other end of the trade route as they cherished the tomatoes, peppers and new varieties of corn that the Mayans had been known to send their way. Mainly though both of the peoples enjoyed trading the wonderful gemstones that could be obtained from one another's part of the world; the Nastazi would send their turquoise, obsidian and opal to the Mayans in return for rubies and diamonds, with occasional sheets of silver on the better trips. They would even have gatherings in the spring and fall to exchange their latest ideas about hunting, clothes production, food storage and even warfare. Although in this, the Nastazi had very little to say, for they did not deem provident to exchange secrets as those and they had not had any real enemies for many years, as this land had become a paradise with enough for all; at least for now!

With this pleasant environment it seemed that there were no enemies or dangers to upset the peace, but as so often in life this would not be fully realized as absolutely true!

To the east of the settlement, even beyond the many mounds that were built by their people played several small Nastazi boys, they had ventured all the way to the tree line above the bluff, not obeying the warnings of their elders that had told them of the dangers that lurked in the woods and of the mysteries that they were not yet ready to face; as with young boys of their age then and even now, they had been told this many, many times. Still, this was part of the excitement that the woods held for them and they, as young boys will do, came here often. This would be a very different day from all of the other playtimes though; and they would it be made aware of it very soon!

~~~~~~~~~~~~~~~~~

Still deeper into the woods leaving her cubs in the safety of her den where they obediently waited for her to finish her hungry search for the first real meal of the spring was a very hungry mother bear. She was famished after her long winter sleep, the birthing and constant feeding of her two new cubs and the greens and young bark around her den had only tempted her and made her ever more ravenous, even the mound of termites that she had found along the way, while tasty only seemed to make her hunger worse. What she needed was meat, and the more she found, the better!

She slowly prowled through the thick forest, very quietly as she was ever so capable of doing, just as she was very capable of charging headlong through the trees crushing everything in her way, faster than most any animal in the forest, especially the humans, when it suited her. But for now, she was absolutely silent and she sniffed the air for that which she really wanted, warm, fresh meat. She now came upon the tracks of a deer; this perked her attention significantly, even though they seemed several days old; she followed them knowing that something would soon turn up soon, it always did.

Not far away, but fortuitously downwind from the Shush, as she was called by the Nastazi, you know her as the Grizzly I have learned; three young boys played at games that were thought to someday turn them into great warriors. They took turns stalking one another, climbing over and under logs, boulders and many other sorts of obstacles that they thought to encounter in their future that they hoped to soon grow into. They practiced with their bows and arrows shooting the huge pinecones leftover from last winter's bloom and they were getting very good, but their arms and bows had not yet grown to the power that they hoped to someday achieve when they would carry the large bows as their fathers did. Still they continued their play, unaware of anything out of the ordinary; the woods that surrounded them provided excitement and new experiences, but this same forest could also contain that which would be the termination of their young lives.

Shush drew silently nearer!

The Nastazi women were having an unusually placid day, as the gathering had been very good for the week and they were not really into the season of the growth of plants to turn into baskets yet. They had the opportunity to take advantage one of the wonderful pools that had been constructed over the years to be used as a community bath. They combined swimming, bathing and caring for their hair into a public rite that was not only very useful, but it made for the development of many close friendships. They were enjoying this seldom arising pleasure when Naomi, the mother of Tecumseh, one of the boys playing in the woods realized that she had not seen her son at all that morning since he had left with his father to begin his practice with his bow. She became troubled enough to not only enquire to one of the elder women Zendla, "Have you seen Tecumseh lately, he was with Noran and Cherniko and I do not see any of them.

"Yes," Zendla answered. "I saw the three of them this morning headed towards the cliffs and it appeared that they had mischief on their minds. Naomi heard this and her face grew grim as she looked upwards towards the top of the bluff where her boy had been known to venture in the past.

"What will it take to make them listen?" Naomi murmured as she began to scan the village for her husband.

Shush followed her nose along old paths that she had traveled year after year; she had seen the increase of the humans, just beyond the woods. She knew that she must avoid the homes that they had made for themselves atop of the mounds that they had so laboriously built throughout the river bottom lands, as she knew that it was best to stay away from their hunting parties with their weapons that could do harm to her that no other animal existing could achieve, save maybe the large male bison further west in the plains beyond the great river. She kept towards the river and the clearings that occurred there as her intuition told her that something would turn up in this direction. She satisfied her great hunger with this method each and every spring, and would again this season, of this she was certain.

The bear moved incredibly quietly through the forest for such a large animal. While she possessed the power to rip logs apart with her huge sharp claws, down large trees or upend gigantic boulders in her pursuits, she was now ambling through the woods as silently as any small mouse. The Shush continued to follow the old deer tracks, confident that she would find the animal that the prints belonged to or perhaps something even easier and tastier.

Suddenly, her nose perked up; she smelled something that she could not quite recognize yet, but she knew that she would like it, for it had a sweet smell. It was becoming stronger the closer to the edge of the woods that she came, yes she knew this scent; it was the smell of humans, several of them and young. Her mouth began to water markedly, as she prowled towards the inviting scent.

The boys were entirely unaware of the inescapable danger that was drawing ever nearer!

There are very few things that will rouse a dormant dragon, possibly a large earthquake or volcanic eruption, some such calamitous event as that, or even the thaw after one of the great cold periods. However, dragons are known to be very mystical creatures and their powers enable them to be absolutely aware of the entire world around them; even when entirely and fully asleep, though they are not entirely aware of all as it happens, they have known through the ages that it is so and they have become proud of the fact that it is often themselves that will right a wrong that is being done against our world or even some of it's more innocent beings. This was an especially strong trait within this dragon that had been dormant for so many years, shaped as a knoll atop these cliffs.

The boys were really having fun and felt as though they were really growing into their adult warrior's role, as they approached their thirteenth years they seemed to be growing more and more proficient with their bows and arrows. They continued their horseplay and roughhousing as they continued to climb up the hills. They were going to the top, to their familiar area that they often played at, where the knoll was topped by a huge long mound that may have been built by their ancestors for defense, or may have just occurred naturally as it did look somewhat like some sort of large animal. In any case they liked to pretend that it was their fort and they liked to play there often. Nearing the crest of the peak where they would climb out in front of their mound, they all began to feel a horrible and undeniable apprehension.

They all looked around only to find everything the same as it always was and tried to remain calm as they began to climb upon the end of the fort closest to where they had just topped the bluff; but they could all feel that there was something dreadfully wrong!

Naomi slowly realized that she must locate her inquisitive son and that his curious manner would someday put him in real danger and she was afraid that this might just be the day; for she had a sudden deep and uneasy premonition. She sent word with one of the younger girls to ask for her husband to join her and hurried towards the cliffs.

The mighty dragon did not really know what it was, but something was beginning to stir him after several millennia of dormancy, he did not yet fully recognize its source, but felt the now irresistible draw, it was unmistakable his protection was needed. He began to rouse!

The bear was overjoyed, what could be better; the young humans were not only defenseless against her, but would not be strong enough even to hurt her with any of their weapons and could not ever hope to outrun her; besides she remembered their taste as being superb. Just as she entered the clearing she saw the three heads stick up above the rise that they were standing behind, she could no longer restrain her excitement; she stood fully erect on her hind legs and let out a hideous roar. She relished in watching the terror in their reaction, for she knew that they would be aware that they had absolutely no chance. Her roar again pierced the peaceful forest in a most horrifying way.

The boys saw the beast the instant before they heard the hideous growl, it stood as tall as any two of their fathers standing atop one another. As the growl subsided the monster looked directly at them and began a leisurely trot towards them. She meant to have them as her next meal, this they knew. They had no chance against a beast so large. They all looked at each other, Tecumseh bravely acted instantly and he notched an arrow and said, "Down the cliff as fast as you can go, I will buy you whatever time I can!"

They all just stared at each other and the bear, Tecumseh said, "Go!" With that Cherniko and Noran instantly dove over the side of the cliff. As his friends slid down as quickly as they could in an attempt to reach safety, Tecumseh turned and faced the most terrifying sight he had ever seen, that of a huge charging Grizzly bear, intent on killing and eating this young Nastazi boy. He turned and faced the charging bear with the grim look of a Nastazi warrior, drew his bow, but knew deep in his heart that he had no chance. He let his arrow fly and it flew straight and true where it hit the tensed muscles in her shoulder that were padded by the thick fur of winter and glanced harmlessly off; not even slowing her to glance at where the missile may have hit.

The great bear that the Nastazi called Shush was known by all to be the most formidable and powerful beast in the land, for none could match her power and but few could match her speed, this she was herself certain and her gate towards the young Indian boy showed it. She grew ever closer and could now see his face clearly, his small bow was drawn again, but Shush feared it not and her mouth watered ever more as she imagined the taste of his warm blood and flesh that she was now just about to enjoy.

Then suddenly the ground began to shake violently. This slowed the huge bear as she thought that it was a shaking of the firmament of the earth, as she had experienced this before and new that it could be dangerous at times, until the mound between her and the young boy bulged and began to crumble. The sight that she saw stopped her cold in her tracks for bursting forth from below the ground was a sight that she had never seen; it was a huge beast, dwarfing even herself in size. As it shook the earth from its body she could see that its gigantic head held sinister looking eyes that stared at her with a bitter malevolence, great horns on its skull that were extremely fearsome and long, huge sharp looking teeth that could surly do her great damage, even possibly kill, but the bear had never been challenged and did not know anything about retreat or backing away from a fight. Though she was impressed by the dragon and even felt fear (though she could not initially recognize this new feeling) as she had always triumphed over all that she had faced and new nothing but; she howled another horrific roar and renewed her charge towards the small Indian man child.

While a dragon may not perhaps be up to his usual form when first being awakened after several millennia of dormancy, there are still very few creatures that could hope to stand against the fierceness of a mature brown dragon and Shush was no exception. All of her years of being the top predator in the forest with nothing to fear came to an abrupt end with the wide swipe of the dragon's forearm and inexorable slicing of her entire body by the razor sharp talons of the dragon.

The young boy had watched the entire episode without even the release of his second arrow and stood petrified before the huge dragon with his terror growing even deeper now, thinking that he was sure to be next in line for the killing he had heard usually accompanied an encounter with this malevolent magical being, but in just a few moments he thought that he had now begun to feel something very different, or did he?

Then suddenly the dragon turned towards him with what he thought could have only been described as an unmistakable look of kindness and somehow spoke to his mind saying, "Go back to your home now little one, you are now safe." Hearing this, Tecumseh turned and began to traverse down the cliff as quickly as his two friends had just done, turning to look just long enough to see the immense dragon begin to hungrily devour the carcass of the bear which he had just dispatched.

His timely life-saving appearance was the first time that Tecumseh was to ever see the dragon that had been called by others Granger, but it was destined surely not to be the last. You see, there is a magical and unexplainable occurrence that takes place when a human life is saved by dragon-kind; they are bonded spiritually, heart and soul. The same will happen if a dragon egg hatches in the presence of a fitting human, they will bond, sharing a portion of the same consciousness, inseparable and permanently. This is what unexpectedly took place in the year later humans later measured as 1017 A.D. in the area of land later to be known as the Mississippi Bottoms, or Cahokia, Illinois.

The boy, after that day was not only warned, but also watched as he was scolded not to return to the forest, as his mother was at the bottom of the cliff when Tecumseh finally worked his way down, she not only had discovered from his friends the grave danger that her son was in, but had also alerted his father who quickly appeared behind her. Their love and attentiveness as good parents made it much more difficult to see his dragon friend at first as Tecumseh loved and respected both his mother and his father and knew that they would feel the Piasa was a grave danger. They did make it much more complicated, though he was still was able to accomplish this feat with certain regularity. This began many years of dialog and an exceptional two-way learning experience for both, albeit filled with newly recognized sadness and emptiness in the end for the one who remained.

~~~~~~~~~~~~~~~

The dragon was easy to find for Tecumseh, he just closed his eyes and he could see through the dragon's eyes and discern where he was located. If he did not recognize the area, he could still tell what direction and approximately how far away his soul mate happened to be. The dragon always knew right where the boy was at all times, and was usually far closer to him than he would have ever suspected, for he could be a master of camouflage. Not only could he change his body color markedly to suit his needs, but also over the many centuries that he had lived on this wonderful world, he had mastered many tricks to be used in hiding your appearance; an ability very important in hunting when you stood nearly forty cubits in height, such as shaping his body into unusual contortions or being able to be absolutely motionless for days, weeks or even months if the need arose. He found that he needed to often perform these feats, so as not to be detected by the Nastazi adults, for they did not seem to be near as understanding as the children were towards him. In fact, surprisingly it was they who were the first to show fear when they would happen to catch sight of a dragon, you would have suspected that it would have been the opposite. They being larger, faster, stronger and even having some very efficient weapons, but the children usually seemed happy to make my acquaintance, even to the point of wonder. So out of love and respect for not only the children, but also all of the humans I usually remained hidden, thereby not unleashing the myriad of problems that I knew could result.

The few times that the elders did chance to observe me I will tell you about in time, but for now let me just say that for the time being, I decided to be a hidden benefactor of the Nastazi people. They had already began to call me by the name of Piasa- the winged serpent which is the human name that I have now grown most accustomed to.

~~~~~~~~~~~~~~~

Nathan told Granger that he had heard many tales of the Piasa and his well-meant dealings with the former inhabitants of this area, but never thought that he would be so honored to meet him, as he squirmed a little and became even more comfortable in the dragons folded wing.

Further out into the cavern, there approached steadily two drunken, misguided men who crept ever closer with their powerful weapons and their malicious intent.

~~~~~~

Meanwhile, it appears that Danny and Bill had undergone a extraordinarily altering event in their life that day and they were both just beginning to realize how profoundly that the kindness showed them by the dragon had touched and changed them, for they both now felt the goodness that had been awakened within them growing and knew that there would be much good that they could make themselves a part of; they had seen the men prowl into the cave with their high- powered rifles and sensed what they should do, but they were so very afraid. They were even beginning to realize that it was fear that they had felt for their entire young lives that had been fueling their unnaturally evil behavior, but at this point they knew not what to do, or how to face it!

~~~~~~

Only a few days past the incident with the bear, Tecumseh and his friend Noran were in his canoe fishing in one of the very large horseshoe lakes that was formed in this part of the bottom lands, as his people called this part of the countryside. He was trying to abide as best he could by the rules and boundaries that his father had given him, yet he wanted so to see his new friend badly. While he tried to plan a way to make this happen he was catching the tasty whiskered fish that so densely populated the lakes and rivers of his homeland, fishing was very good today and it could not hurt to sooth his mothers feelings somewhat, though his heart ached to find the dragon.

Their canoe drifted with the wind and the occasional pulling of the more hefty fish, when there appeared no more than a boat length away a huge log that seemed to be pushed by a currant; but they were in a small horseshoe lake; not a body of water that could ever really have a current!

Suddenly a heavily scaled and pointed tail popped up at the stern of the canoe and the huge frightening, yet to him friendly head of a dragon exposed itself at the bow, easily surrounding the small boat. His partner Noran was immediately terrified, but Tecumseh just began to giggle quietly.

Noran did not understand the casual way that his friend was treating their doom, but Tecumseh explained, "This is my new friend Noran. He is called Granger, he is dragon-kind, but he is truly a friend to man."

"Granger, this is my life-long friend Noran," Tecumseh said. "I am certain that he would like to be your friend also." Noran nodded his head in a welcoming gesture, but kept his eyes on the dragon in a very wary manner.

The dragon is not known for humor, but if it were; what followed could be considered a humorous snort as he said, "Fear not young human, no harm will ever come to you from me, I have made the decision to help your kind for I feel that it is with you that all of our futures lie."

Noran and Tecumseh exchanged puzzled looks, but they both smiled and Tecumseh reached out for the neck of his new friend, as they took part in the first of a lifetime of embraces the dragon noticed the whiskerfish on the branch at the bottom of the canoe. Tecumseh saw him take notice and asked, "Would you like a few, they are very tasty."

"Oh yes," the dragon replied. "But those are awfully small for one of my size and I am certain that you are gathering them for your family, besides in these waters there are far larger of those sorts of fish and they are quite easy for me to gather. If you would like to have a grand feeding of your people, then I will leave one on the shore for you yonder, as it would probably be too much for your craft to endure. As he told us he motioned towards where we had built our fish-trapping pond, a sign that he had indeed been watching us. He must have seen in our faces how much that we appreciated the idea for he said, "I will have you a pleasant surprise there on the shore for you very soon." With that he turned to view what was approaching in the lake and quietly disappeared beneath the waves.

Just then as we had already been talking about taking a swim in the lake with our new friend and we were close to jumping into the water, we saw Noran's father's canoe come quickly around the bend of the lake. He and his fishing partner were both large men and propelled their craft through the calm waters very quickly, but the grand dragon had just slipped quietly into the water, supposedly out of sight of the adult Nastazi warriors, or so it seemed for the moment.

The brightly painted and decorated canoe of Himreal, Noran's father drifted silently up beside them, "Chonaka, did you see what the boys had near their boat?" Said Himreal; with what the boys felt was entirely too much craftiness for either of their liking.

Tecumseh immediately replied, "Oh, thank to the great spirit that you saw it too, that was the biggest whiskerfish that I think I have ever seen."

"Yes, it is too bad that you lost it, it was very large," Himreal responded. "Strange, you neither seem very upset about losing such a prized catch."

Noran just stared pitiably at his father, not knowing what to say, when Tecumseh hurriedly interjected, "Honored Himreal, that is not our first encounter with this monster fish and we have made a vow to one another that we will catch it, and soon."

"Humph," Chonaka guffawed! "Watch that you are not the ones whom are being caught."

"Heed his words little ones," Himreal said in a rather strange fashion, seeming to say more than the words that he actually spoke, "The large monsters in these waters can surprise even the most wary; you must take great care that you are not the ones whom are trapped by your actions."

As he turned and paddled off towards the village landing, Himreal looked over his shoulder and said, "Do not worry Tecumseh; I will let your father know that you are in the lake and not out of the boundaries that he has set for you, behaving yourself, is that not correct?" He ended his statement in a questioning manner and paddled off, slowly.

Noran whispered urgently, "They saw the beast we are bound for great trouble and the possible use of my father's bow on my backside."

Tecumseh just began to shake his head no when the canoe was uplifted nearly half of the height of one of the young men, though not a dangerous wave; it was enough to push them towards their home landing. They were quick to get the message given by their new friend, and they promptly began the short paddle home. They were curious

Words of the Piasa

as they made their way towards their village landing, as to what had happened to the huge dragon that they were just in the middle of chatting with; how could a being of that size disappear so completely, so easily and so quickly?

They wondered about what they had just seen all of the way back to their camp, but upon their arrival it became totally clear to them what had occurred, as there on the village launch beach, hidden from the view of those on land was a huge whiskerfish, larger than either of the boys, clinging to his last moments of life. Clearly the dragon was attempting to be a supporter of the boys, and they would surely be thought of highly by the people of their village for providing so much food for so many; they would merely need to complete the charade.

They struggled for a few moments to try and pull the whiskerfish into their beached canoe, but simply succeeded in attracting the attention of some of the men who were bringing some of the Buffalo fish that they had captured in the nearby fish traps that were always regularly tended. They began to walk towards the two young men and call out to them wondering if they needed some help. Thinking quickly Tecumseh passed the hemp rope that already held the rest of the days catch through the giant fishes mouth up to the branch at its base, as the rest of his catch disappeared inside the giant maw the boys fashioned a knot connection through the gill to drag their prize the rest of the way into shore, giving the appearance that they had hauled it in from the lake.

The men tending the traps were the first to arrive and began hooting and hollering in congratulations when they spied the tremendous fish that their young warriors had just brought home to the village; they were soon joined by many others that included both Noran's and Tecumseh's fathers. While the rest of the men present busied themselves with praise towards the young men and much shouting and backslapping, their fathers stayed back towards the back of the crowd and seemed to be talking to one another in a rather anxious manner. This was observed by both boys and caused them a good amount of concern, for they did not want to lie to their fathers, but neither thought that their parents would understand about their huge new friend as of yet.

After a short time the crowd was successful in bringing the fantastic catch into the village and with this the boys and their fathers were once again reunited. Kurlhii Osuwage, Tecumseh's father and his friend

Himreal were waiting for their sons at the presentation mound; a place of great honor where the boys would offer the enormous fish to the village shaman for the use and good of the people of their village. This was the greatest honor that had ever befallen their two young boys and they were very proud, yet at the same time you could see much concern in their faces for something was definitely bothering both fathers about this day's events.

Kurlhii began by telling them both how proud they were of both of the boys, "Tecumseh and Noran, you have made us very proud of you with this great feat that could not have been matched by most any other two of the men in the village, and the making it of a gift to your people." Himreal nodded and Kurlhii continued, "We are your fathers and you are both treasures to us and the future of our families so please try to understand how serious we are as we try to point out the dangers of our world that you have not lived within for long enough as of yet to learn of entirely."

The young warriors looked at each other and looked back at their fathers and tried to look as innocent as possible, though they could fully sense the skepticism that both of their fathers now displayed.

Himreal grasped the shoulders of Noran and looked into his eyes with a deep compassion and said, "My eyes are still very good and what I have seen is spoken of in the legends passed down by our forbearers for many, many generations."

Tecumseh asked, "What is it that you think you have seen?"

"Do not speak so to this Nastazi warrior and my friend that has seen so many more seasons than you my son," Kurlhii spoke very sternly to Tecumseh as he took several steps forward to stand directly in front of his beloved son.

Himreal looked solemnly at both of the young men and went on; the beast that I have seen you with is familiar to our people, they may not have been seen for many ages, but much is known about them."

He had gotten their attention now and they listened intently.

Himreal continued, "They are magical beasts that are famous for not only their ferocity, beauty and strength, but their deceptiveness. They are known to alter the truth to whatever version serves their needs and young boys and girls are said to be especially susceptible to the enchantments that these beasts will concoct. We do not want you to fall prey to something that is so far beyond your experience for lack of a warning."

The boys just shook their heads in agreement.

"The beast is known as PIASA or THUNDERBIRD and he is said to be able to rise from the dead and that they can bring upon the people great storms and even the destroying cone winds. It is said that they will devour any animal that they are near when they are hungry and that they have a fondness for human meat." He gestured towards the rolling hills across the river and said, "They have been said to have breathed fire onto the Great Plains beyond the river and made that fire consume all that lays in that direction up unto the mountains many leagues to the west, killing many of our ancestors." He gazed at the boys to see if they were grasping the importance of what he said and then as he looked back at Kurlhii he told them, "They cannot be trusted!"

Tecumseh and Noran were touched deeply by the pleading of their fathers and were nearly in tears but did not really admit to anything. They merely said that the fears felt by both of their fathers were totally unfounded and that they were always very careful with any creature that they met since the encounter with the Shush.

"The Shush that had disappeared when we arrived to check later that morning, save the huge stain of blood on the ground," Kurlhii exclaimed!

The entire episode left a very uneasy feeling with the men, but they felt the boys could be protected for the most part, you see, though they thought that they had recognized what they had seen, they had not really gotten a good look at the Piasa as of yet, however that viewing would come soon enough!

That evening was a joyous time in the Nastazi village and there was much feasting and celebration. The two young warriors had instantly gained a great deal of notoriety, celebrity and honor. Their feat was being celebrated with a wonderful variety of foods that the people usually only utilized on the most special of occasions. The whiskerfish was prepared marinated and roasted, fried in patties with the wonderful spicy roots that grew in this area and even in a tasty stew made with the peppers and new red vine fruits from far away to the south. They also enjoyed sweets, dried berries squashes and special maize dishes that were normally only seen on the most honored of occasions; which for the most part is what this had now actually become.

As the feasting began to give way to dancing, games of chance played by the adult men and gossip enjoyed by most of the women, Tecumseh was approached by his childhood female friend Billigana, whose name meant "True Morning Light" and was obviously enthralled by the young man. She gathered very close to him and told him, "I heard about your bravery this morning capturing that monster fish."

As she swooned staring into his eyes he merely said, "It was not as difficult as some may think."

"So I gathered this evening when I eavesdropped on the men as they talked of what they think that you have discovered," She said as she gathered herself ever closer. "That just makes you even braver in my eyes, Tecumseh."

So began the "puppy love" of Billigana and Tecumseh; a bond that soon grew into truly one of the deepest and purest loves that our world has ever known, at least from this dragon's perspective. She was certain that her man had seen what her people had referred to as the Piasa, even while never having seen it herself; this was the depth at which she empathized with her future lover and soul mate even at such a young age as her current ten passes of the seasons.

"Noran's father has let it be known among the men, that he has again seen the great thunderbird of our ancestor's lore, the Piasa and that it was with you that he had spied it. He has been telling of the many atrocities that it has been accused of and of the enchantments that it is said to possess, though I do not believe that you could befriend something that was indeed as terrible as they say it is; you could not be so fooled. Could you," She pleaded?

"Oh no, Billigana," He answered. "The beast is not as they say at all. He saved me from a certain ending of my life as the spring breakfast of a very hungry and ill-tempered Shush just over one moon past and I know nothing of what has been done in the past, but you can see what he has done today; no I would have to call the Piasa my friend and would protect him from the wrath of our fathers and their bows."

"When you say that it is safe, then it is safe my future husband," she stated as a simple matter of fact.

Tecumseh blushed slightly and said, "Do not speak so young one, you are but a child and I am far from marriage."

"But it will be so in time, you shall see," she whispered softly.

As he shoved her back towards the village and told her to go back home to her mother and grow some more, he could hear her pleading and chattering with him to "show her his big friend" and "would he come to see her tomorrow" he knew that his future would be overflowing with that particular little women and he smiled thinking that it may not be at all that bad.

As for Billigana; she was convinced of it, they shared a common destiny; of this she was certain!

The next day awoke as a foggy and overcast day that many would chosen to stay inside and enjoy staying dry by a warm fire, but not Tecumseh, he was awake before dawn and out of the longhouse before his father or mother had stirred. He left the usual sign, an arrow through a net ring, the sign that he was fishing pointed at the same horseshoe lake that he had such success on the previous day, although he was not being entirely honest, as he took his canoe to the hidden point and began to head off towards the place in the cliffs where he had first seen the great dragon, something told him that there was more to discover about his large friend in that area. As he approached the cliffs through the only patch of woods left between his this side of his village and the cliffs, he saw the unmistakable pixy-like head of Billigana stick out over a stout bush.

"What are you doing here?" He asked with feigned irritation; though he was actually somewhat expecting her to be there.

"I want to go with you," she responded warmly, melting his mock wrath with her lovely smile.

"It is too dangerous for children." He said firmly, assuming a very mature posture for someone just two and a half seasons her senior and just realizing the changes that were to make him a man.

"I know that you will protect me," She said decisively, "Always!"

"How can you be so sure," Tecumseh asked?

"I just know," she said.

With that, they hugged a long lasting hug of deep love and affection and then they explored their first kiss. It was warm, tender and full of passion; though they did not make love at this time, that would come later, but somehow they now made a deep soul to soul connection. Soon they would give one another the gift of physical love, from that virtuous moment on, they knew they were meant to be together forever and bonded in a love that would not change for the rest of both their lives.

They gazed into each other's eyes and absorbed the goodness of the moment for a time, both knowing the absolute truth that they had both just realized and letting it sink into their young hearts when Tecumseh said, "Come with me, I want you to meet a very special friend."

"Kai," She answered with her peoples universally accepted word of agreement!

They grasped one another's hands and started up the cliff, as they crested the top and could see that the recent rains which had been occurring had brought a wonderful new beginning of life to the forest, the cold of winter was over and the lush mid-western spring had begun to arrive. By this time of the morning the early fog had started clearing and everywhere you looked was seen new growth on all of the plants and trees, many wonderful and diverse grasses bursting forth from the ground and wild-flowers everywhere. They could barely contain their newfound joy and just began running through the meadow embracing how wonderful their lives had suddenly become. At the high end of the clearing in an especially dense growth of beautiful purple and yellow flowers they just rolled into each other's arms onto the ground, not having a care in the world.

They lay on their backs talking and gazing dreamily into the sky for what could have been minutes or even hours, they just didn't know. They only knew that this was their time and spending it together was precious and it was all that they wanted to do. After a time though Billigana turned and looked into her loves eyes and asked, "Is your friend the Piasa not about today?"

"I am not sure," Tecumseh responded. "I feel as though he keeps an eye on us very well and he is around probably more often than we think.

"Perhaps he does not wish to be seen by me or any of the others," she offered.

"Yes, perhaps," Tecumseh agreed. "Though I would bet that he is around here somewhere, for I feel that he is close."

They both stood and began looking around, again admiring the wonderful meadow that they had happened upon, he searching into the woods with his sharp, young eyes and she beginning to wander and pick some of the wild-flowers. She was traveling back in the direction that they had come as he drifted into the edge of the woods, but a quick check on each other and a wave exchanged was enough to reassure both that all was well. Their bond was already very strong indeed.

Tecumseh heard something, but could not discern where it had come from; was it ahead of him in the woods or in the meadow behind him? He thought it must be his dragon friend making his way towards them and he started back towards Billigana.

Meanwhile, Billigana had been ambling towards the place where they climbed up the cliff through all of the wonderful flowers when she was startled that she nearly stepped upon two sleeping baby Digis (the Nastazi word for panther.) She looked closely at them as they began to wake and make their cute little meow calls and she could not help but think to herself how precious that they appeared. They looked so cute and cuddly that she was tempted to take them to her village as part of her family, but her parents had taught her far better than that. She knew that baby animals in the forest most often had a mother nearby and the protection of that mother could be very dangerous for anyone that was around those babies. She began to experience a definite hint of fear!

She rose to call for Tecumseh and when she turned she was frozen by that very fear she had suspected, the mother Digis was there, not two body lengths from her looking directly into her young anxious eyes. The huge cat was staring at her maliciously with a low, menacing and very hostile growl.

Billigana stepped away from the cubs and tried to speak soothingly to the large, wild, and ever so powerful animal, "Be easy mother cat, I mean no harm to your babies!"

The angry feline was not swayed by any sympathy; it was not an emotion that was known to her kind. She began a far louder and more ominous call evidently about to pounce on the little girl and end her short life, when from behind was heard a chilling war cry; that of a Nastazi warrior!

Young Tecumseh had arrived to protect his love, "Neehaiee," He screamed again, "Be gone Digis!"

The foreboding animal turned and confronted her new adversary with very little if any concern and after a short moment turned back around to face the other small human that was threatening her cubs; she tensed to make the fatal pounce.

"Digis, Ignore me at your peril! Take your young and be gone or you will feel the sting of my arrows," Tecumseh howled. He did not want to shoot, as Billigana was directly behind the menacing cat, but felt he would soon be obligated to take the dreadful chance.

The panther turned back towards the brave Indian lad and gave him her undivided attention, as loathsome as it was; she now turned her growls towards him and began her approach.

He was about to release his arrow at his adversary, dangerous as it was to his young love across the clearing when all heard a tremendous calamity in the treetops from deeper in the woods. It grew ever louder and after but a few moments all could see above them the shape of what can only be described as an awe-inspiring sight.

A dragon on the wing is not only exceedingly terrifying, but also very beautiful, the majesty of its huge wings, the multi-faceted colors of his eyes, even the fierceness of its face and claws is something that few can turn away from or view with anything but wonder and the big cat was no exception, she watched as the huge dragon alighted upon the ground within easy reach of, yet being very careful not to harm her little ones.

After several posturing growls that appeared to mean nothing to the great winged beast before her, the fear provoking growls wilted under the stern gaze of the dragon into simpering purrs. It could not be understood by the humans what communication transpired between the two great beasts, but the dragon seemed to be giving the Digis a warning and along with that another chance at life with her young. The panther cringed, hurriedly picked up her cubs by the scruffs of their necks and disappeared into the woods.

The two young people wasted no time at all in reuniting and holding each other in relief, but after an appreciative squeeze and a whispered, "I told you that you would always be there to save me," accompanied by a light kiss, she danced away and quickly approached the great dragon.

When she was directly under his head (which towered over her ten times her height) she laid her hands on his great claws with absolutely no fear at all and said to the dragon in her most formal Nastazi tone, "So you are the great Piasa that my people have spoken and sang of for generations. They did not exaggerate; you are as large and wondrous as they have said. Is all that they say about you true?"

"That depends, small female," The mighty dragon said wryly.

"I am sorry, both of you," Tecumseh apologized. "Granger, grand and powerful dragon, this is my woman of promise, my future bride Billigana, or as her name means "true, morning light." We have not been promised by our families as of yet, but by each other. We have bonded much the same as you and I my dragon friend and I hope that you will love her as you do me and that we will have a wondrous future together."

As Tecumseh talked Billigana gazed up into the dragons multi-colored eyes and the dragon drew ever closer to the young maiden. What Tecumseh was seeing before his very eyes was the bonding of his dragon friend and his woman for the act of saving her life from the Digis had created the magical process between those two, just as it had with him and Granger several moons ago and it felt most extraordinary.

Then, as though waking from a dream Billigana blurted out, "None of the evil they say is true about you!"

"What is it that they say child," responded the wondrous beast.

"They say that you are conniving and evil and that you eat our people's children," She went on. "I know that you are not capable of those things you are too good hearted. Why look at the Digis family, you did not even kill or eat them even though you are very capable of doing so, instead you freed them to learn of different ways and continue their lives. You are nothing like what our people have said about you for so long!"

"True," Tecumseh interjected.

"True enough of me I suppose, but there were once many of my kind and even now others may be found if one knows where to look," The dragon responded. I might add that we dragon kind live for many of your human lifetimes and can sleep for longer than you can even imagine, only to awaken to the same world inhabited by many different creatures. There have been and are even now many different tribes of your peoples and they are very different from each other even as we dragons are. Suffice to say that many stories can be told of my kind, some true and some not, yet they most likely had nothing to do with me in particular, for there exist in this wonderful world many beings, some are very malevolent, but some are full of kindness. This can be said of all types of beings, including and especially your humankind.

"But enough talk," the large dragon stated. "We must make our first day of meeting a joyful one!"

"Oh, it has been unforgettable up to this point, my large brown friend," Billigana said genuinely. "How can I have improved on meeting my loves mountainous friend that happens to be a dragon that also is able to talk to me as a friend?"

Although being still early in their relationship, the young Nastazi boy was already becoming quite adept at gauging the Piasa's moods at sometimes even what he was thinking and this was one of the first times that he let the Piasa know it.

"What mischief do you have on your mind," Tecumseh asked Granger? "I can feel your stirring heart; I am beginning to become attuned to your moods."

The great dragon's eyes glimmered kaleidoscopically as he slowly lowered his head down until it was directly across from where the young Indian maiden sat on a fallen tree trunk and asked through what can only be known as a dragon smile, "Would you like to fly with us Billi?"

This not only shocked, but thoroughly delighted her and Tecumseh. Firstly, she had never been referred to as Billi, but the shortened form of her name was quite pleasant sounding and was relished by all who would later hear it and was how she was called by most from that moment on. The real shock though was being asked to fly, for this was something that she never even considered and she was feeling a mixture of fear and excitement, not certain of what she should say. She looked over to Tecumseh for some kind of sign of what she might do.

It appeared that he was as confused as she was. He looked back at her and then at the face of his huge friend, who appeared to be smiling and then back at her and said, "I have never flown."

"I believe that you would enjoy it," the dragon interjected.

"I suppose that we would like to," Tecumseh acknowledged.

"Oh, it sounds like fun," Billi exclaimed!

With that the dragon laid down as flat as he could and they climbed upon his back up between his enormous wings, where they settled onto the back of his neck, first Billi and Tecumseh behind her holding as well as he could to the thick scales on the dragons base of his neck, just before his wings where the scales were somewhat looser as they would cover his stretching hide on occasion at this point on his massive bulk.

"Gain your greatest comfort and do not concern yourselves with falling, for if you slip have no fear, I will catch you," he comforted them.

With the feeling of their last bit of fidgeting for the perfect fit, he was off. He leapt into the sky as easily as the wind blows the fluffy seed of a dogwood and with what seemed like but only a few strokes of his mighty wings they achieved a great altitude in the sky. Though they could see that he was careful to fly away from their village, towards the rising of the sun and over the woodlands which they had not as of yet ventured very far into in their short lives due to the stern warnings and rules of their parents and their excitement continued growing by the moment.

As the wind rushed by them, making it nearly impossible for them to hear each other talk the dragon kept comforting them by saying soothing things to them in their mind. They never ceased to find this aspect of their life with the dragon amazing. They were told about wonderful hunting grounds that their fathers visited and shown where they were at, the interesting plants and waters that they could find further towards the rising sun, about the great river that emptied into the mighty river that their home was near and upon reaching it they began to follow; and about many of the other beings that they would find in that direction, including more of human kind quite different from themselves.

Tecumseh and Billi marveled at the wondrous sights that they had gotten the privilege of seeing. They saw thick rolling hills that appeared larger than any they had ever seen, tall waterfalls filling the valleys around them with mist and flat-topped mountains that appeared to consist of one huge boulder.

As they continued the graceful flight up the broad river they saw that the terrain was slowly changing, from the flat river basin they had come over the cliffs that they were so familiar with by their home, through thickly wooded forest as far as the eye could see and now they saw no longer just individual mountain peaks poking above the canopy, but chains of mountains bunched together with many streams and waterfalls feeding into the vast river. Also visible was a huge variety of game animals amazingly easily seen from their vantage point. Both of the young people wondered if this would be one of the places that their fathers came to hunt as they saw antelope, wild hogs, coyote and even bear. Then they spied something that was totally unexpected, they saw people unlike any that they had seen before, they were horrid, fierce-looking people who looked as though they had no care or regard for one another or even their homes. As the dragon's flight took them ever closer it was obvious that these people did not grow any of the plant foods that the Nastazi prized so highly, at least none could be seen anywhere around their dwellings. The men that could be seen all appeared to be painted upon most of their bodies with aggressive looking markings and embellishments that looked as though they were intended to cause fear in someone who would oppose them. They indeed looked like a very violent and warlike people; as you could even see it in the way that they treated their women. Also it was apparent that these people had in their midst a small group of what could only be slaves, obvious from the bindings on their hands and feet and the occasional beatings that they were suffering.

"That is the practice you humans pursue that I find most appalling," The Dragon murmured.

"Slaves," Billigana exclaimed as she nudged Tecumseh who had not yet noticed!

Tecumseh looked towards where she nodded and was sickened to the core of his soul.

Why their friend had brought them to see these horrible people they did not know, but Tecumseh and Billi would not soon forget this sight. As they made one more pass just slightly lower something unfortunate happened. It seemed that one of the strange and curious warriors below happened to look upwards and spot them. Even though no harm was being done by the dragon and his two young friends the warrior let out a loud and challenging cry, he immediately loosed an arrow towards them and began to load another. Though they were still out of range and could easily escape the onslaught, it was not certain from where his fellows would soon be firing from and so they made a long sweeping turn to put the sun at their backs and began the return trip towards their home.

"Those humans are as different from you as the blacks and other dragons that I will soon tell you of are from me and therein lies a great lesson that you must learn." With that they began the return flight towards the village nestled within the mounds that lay in the flood plain of the great river that would later be known as Cahokia.

Billi and Tecumseh thoroughly enjoyed this first of many flights that they would enjoy with their large, inspirational friend. They began to understand that he really was attempting to explain, or teach them more about their land and the different beings that occupied it. They tried to listen and take in everything that was said, but the dragon had so much to say, he seemed so intelligent and knowledgeable about all of the ways of the world. Billi was growing ever closer to the dragon and was the first to ask him, "What is it that you are trying to save us from my knowledgeable old friend?"

"Young woman," Granger responded. "I must be as truthful as I can be with the both of you. What I try to protect you from is yourselves."

Tecumseh was thoroughly stunned with surprise, "Our people are good people and more prosperous than most, we live in harmony with the land and care not for war as do some that we have seen, what is it that you mean?"

"I do not understand either," Billi chimed in.

The dragon continued, "I have been trying to show you that you are not the only humans that occupy this grand countryside, there are many others, some that you have seen, some you will never meet and others that you may only hear about, but let me give you this warning. Humans have come and gone many times on our "Mother Earth" and have all found ways to either exterminate themselves completely or just vanish. I would not want the same to become of your good people for they are fine and honorable with good spirits, but alas I have seen other such goodness fall away before.

"What is there that we can be doing wrong or what evil must we protect ourselves from," Billi asked mournfully?

"That I do not yet know, for your people do not experiment with that that I have observed destroy the other cultures that I speak of and I dare not tell you what these are for fear that you may discover that which would become your own downfall," he tried to explain. "However we shall search for the problem together and when we have discovered it we will alert your people so that they may act."

"Are you certain that you do not worry for naught, my large friend?" Tecumseh offered.

"Yes," Billi said, "we are supposed to be envied by all of the tribes in the land." She said dismissively, "The Nastazi have made a wonderful home here in the bottoms."

The dragon sighed, "Alas, girl that may be the problem, only time will tell."

Finally they arrived back very close to their village and the great brown once again flew very close to the treetops so as not to be seen and deposited the two back to where he had met them.

This began years of exploratory flights, adventures and lessons taught and learned by all of the three.

They made their way quickly down the cliff and back to the village where Tecumseh's father and mother popped out of the thick growth by the lake to meet them. This made the two of them rather uncomfortable, as it was now late afternoon and they had been gone since before dawn; however the concern of the parents had nothing to do with the Piasa, but fear of the possible experimentation with their bodies that all parents seemed to obsess about. They were both relieved by this, for both knew that they would have plenty of time for that in the future, but for now this meant that the dragon had not been the main concern.

They were spoken to by their parents and warned not to throw away what remained of their childhood, "For the responsibilities of being a parent will override all in your life," They were told!

Billi and Tecumseh could not agree more and tried to assure both pairs of parents that this was absolutely how they felt about the physical relationship also, although they did not think they were believed fully. They felt a closeness that would grow stronger year after year and were in no hurry for anything too physical as of yet for they were both certain that they would have a lifetime to spend together.

So began the many meetings and great adventures that they were to enjoy with the Piasa as he was called by the Nastazi people, and all was considered part of the ongoing education of the humans by the ancient dragon.

They experienced in the months and years that followed, flights to see many beautiful sights and more than a few real oddities. One flight took them to what the dragon called the sunset coast to see cliffs higher than they had ever seen that dropped into a body of water so vast that all that could be seen from horizon to horizon was that water, it was as if the entire world was made of water and their land that they thought so immense was but a small afterthought. When Billi expressed this to the scholarly dragon he schooled her somewhat saying, "That is for the most part true, although there is far more land than you could ever imagine."

One day they partook of an especially long flight that carried them over chains of mountains larger than any that they had ever yet seen to a land that was lush and luxuriantly green scored with multitudes of valleys, rivers and streams coming from out of the great mountain chain behind that which was now behind them. Now could be seen small groups of human kind in numerous small villages along the way and as they continued just a short way beyond the coast they came upon several rocky islands that seemed to be crawling with large beasts that were easily the size of the bison that they would sometimes see on the plains, but instead of legs these had huge flippers obviously for swimming in the sea. Not only were these beasts huge, but some had enormous tusks and they looked like very powerful fighters though as they flew more closely to them they scattered into the waters.

They thought that they could feel the dragon chuckle.

"Why do you laugh friend," Tecumseh asked?

"They seek escape from me for I will sometimes come to this place to feed," he continued to chuckle, "But I do not desire to feed on them this day; they are safe from me, though there are those that would use them for food in the waters also."

As he finished his statement we saw not far below us a gigantic grey fish with very large, sharp-looking teeth come near fully out of the water attacking and nearly biting one of the smaller females of the wondrous animals in half and dropping back down into the bloody water with its easily won meal. It was most shocking and Billi even seemed sickened by it.

"Do not think less of the toothfish," Granger told her soothingly. "He does what he must to survive. One day his body will feed the fish that will then feed the Sea lions, that is our world in balance and that is nature. Some care not about what it takes to live within this balance and that is very unfortunate, for it is far easier to upset this very important harmony than most would know and the results of its demise can be most dreadful. I will show you an example so that you may teach and instill this knowledge unto your wonderful people, convincing them to listen may not be easy, but believe me when I tell you that it is of the utmost importance.

"Can you accompany me tomorrow for the entire day," The dragon queried?

"We shall have to check with our parents," Billi stated. "Tomorrow is a trading day in our village. The representatives of our renowned southern trading partners, the Mayans are scheduled to arrive tonight and the day has been set aside for trading. I believe that our parents expect us to be there."

"Yes," Tecumseh added. "Our people place a great value on treating our trading partners with the proper respect, and it would show disrespect for us not to be present, besides they have beautiful gemstones that cannot be found elsewhere that I might be able to trade for to give to my lady," He squeezed Billi as he gazed into her beautiful green eyes.

You really could see the beginning of a very fine looking female in young Billigana. She was obviously going to be tall for a girl and she had wonderful long silky, straight brown hair that had many highlights from the many hours she spent in the sun. She was tall and slender, but not skinny for you could already spot a very pleasant roundness to her rear and ample breasts that were very evident for one of her young age of only now twelve full seasons. Both of these attributes, I noticed that Tecumseh and many other human men found quite attractive and would further develop as this young child grew into a woman.

"That is very interesting," Exclaimed the Piasa excitedly! "I should very much like to observe this day.'

This was the first that these two humans had seen the indelible curiosity of this large dragon that had become their friend. They were touched with an instant and contagious excitement that fed the dragons desire to take part in the day.

"What do you have in mind," Tecumseh asked?

"And what would you have us do," Billi added in an all too devious tone.

"Well, how does this sound," The dragon asked? "They have seen a great increase in their harvest from their game traps as of late have they not."

"Yes, that is true," stated Tecumseh. "But they know not that you had nearly all to do with it, they trust only to the great spirits and believe that they have made them happy for now."

"My kind was once worshipped by humans as great spirits of the land, responsible for all good and bad that would befall men," The Piasa explained. "Perhaps it is not too far from the truth for some, for my kind is responsible for many deeds both great and horrible. Can you not convince them that you have discovered the Piasa and that he has become your friend?"

"I am not so sure that our people would be able to accept that," Tecumseh told him earnestly. "But even so, what of the Mayans they come from far away and we do not know of their experience with mystical beings such as you. We are not sure how either would react; it may not be very well accepted," Billi reasoned.

"Perhaps this old worm has a way," The dragon offered.

The young humans immediately grew more excited. They both wanted to ask, but Billi formed the question, "What do you have in mind?"

"Well, they are here to trade, right," The dragon stated as a plan formed in his mind, "Why not let me show them something that they will surely want."

"What can that be," asked Tecumseh. "They are very wealthy and already have so much."

"I could give them many of the things that humans seem to covet, the yellow, red, clear purple and blue gemstones that are so popular with your kind, but I will give these to you for your trading. I could bring to their meeting any game animals that they might desire, but that is not what I think they will really appreciate." The Piasa continued, "I will give them something that not only do I know that they want, but will play into my plans by building a trust between us; I will offer them the power of flight!"

"What do you mean Granger," Billi asked?

"You do not plan on taking all of them upon your back, do you, Tecumseh asked?

"Oh no, they are too many," The dragon explained. "Except for perhaps at first, no I will show them something that I have witnessed in other faraway lands at earlier times. I will show them how to weave a cloth that is far lighter and stronger than the wonderful soft garments that you sometimes wear, and I will show them how to treat it so that it will hold the warm air of your fires and fill a sack of this cloth that will carry a basket that is able to hold many humans. It has been done before by others like you and used much to their benefit. If you two can just convince them that I have this gift to offer so that they will allow me to be present at their meetings, it will benefit us all."

Billi and Tecumseh stared at each other for several moments not really knowing how their people would react or what even they really thought of the idea, but then they both began to slowly gain smiles until they were near bursting with enthusiasm. They both approached their large friend stroking and patting him and Tecumseh said, "Friend that idea just might work!"

Billi was thrilled, but wondered about the practicality of a demonstration the next day and asked, "How can we show this to our people tomorrow for we have none of this wondrous cloth of which you speak?"

"Yes," Tecumseh added, "Weaving cloth takes much time."

"Yes, though I have a solution for that," said the Piasa. "We will need to fly a short way to the caverns that I sometimes call my home. There I have a good amount of the cloth that was given to me by some former friends that I once knew who were also considered to be among those thought to be very friendly humans, although they lived far away from your homelands here."

This was of coarse a reference to the people that live in the extreme southern mountains of what is called today the South American continent now known as the Incas. They had this cloth and technology currently, but did not share it with the Mayans as they considered the

Mayans a very war-like people (which was only really true of but a few of the many tribes of Mayans that shared mostly the same culture in the vast area of what would soon be known as Central America and the Yucatan). The Incas as a matter of fact had used this floating bags or hot air balloons as they would later be called on many occasions to give warning of advancing parties of the war-like Mayans or other tribes of their enemies. It is also believed that this could have been the method used to create the huge pictures and lines on the plains of Nazca located in modern day Peru, see (11.)

"You have other friends like us," Billi asked?

"Well, I would not say that they are so much like you for I feel that you and your kind will soon be found to be very different, we shall see soon enough. They could not overcome the inborn fear that they had long held for my kind; my hope is that yours will be able to move past it." The dragon said hopefully with this gift that I plan to give to them; it is a tool that the people that I speak of have made that enables them to ride the winds of the sky, but I have kept it in safe keeping at one of my favorite dwellings for a great length of time.

"Well then we must go and get it," Tecumseh said with new initiative, "The afternoon is passing." With that the young Nastazi's climbed aboard as though they had been dragon's rider for years and they were all soon off into the dazzling blue sky.

The Piasa flew high and fast as he appeared to want to make good time and in a short time he was obviously following a river that would later empty into the great river that they made their home upon. He followed it upstream for a short time and came down to a very soft landing in front of a large, dark grotto that appeared to go on for quite a long distance deep into the earth.

"This is one of my favorite homes," stated the Piasa. "I call it Cool Grotto, as it is always comfortably cool inside, but never cold. (It is known today as Meramec Caverns). (12.)

"I can see well in the darkness inside, however you may want to make one of your torches. You need not worry about the foul explosive gases that sometimes infect these caves as the air in here is sweet and clean, that is another of the reasons that I enjoy it so.

Billi and Tecumseh made several torches from some readily available pitch-plant that grew not too far from the cave entrance. He lit one and

Billi and he followed the dragon into his lair. It was not only enormous, but breathtakingly beautiful. Rocks of all shapes and sizes seemed to be growing both up from the floor and down from the ceiling, they saw what looked like huge bubbles of solid rock that had hardened into what looked like giant clusters of multi-colored grapes as big around as the red-meat melons that they enjoyed so in the summer. They saw wavy sheets of glittering color as water dripped slowly down a rippled wall into streams that were everywhere inside of the caverns.

They bent down to enjoy a drink of the water when they saw that their friend was doing the same and beheld the water was inhabited by what appeared to be blind fish. They apparently did not need to see as they had no light to see by; they did not taste them now, but made a mental note to do so, as they looked nearly like the sweet trout that they would sometimes catch in the hills to the north of their homes. The water was very cool and oh so sweet, possibly the best that either of them had ever tasted.

Tecumseh turned and looked up to his friend and said, "This is truly a wonderful place; I can see why you have chosen it. Is this where you sleep for the ages that you speak of?

"Oh no, my friend those places are many, the most recent being right where I first encountered you and that malicious Shush," Granger continued. "Follow me a little further and I will show you where I do often choose to rest."

They continued traversing the corridor until it tapered down to where the pathway narrowed enough to make it a rather tight fit for the large dragon, but he managed to squeeze himself through it easily. Tecumseh and Billi followed through the opening and came out from behind the Piasa to behold a grand cavern even more enormous and beautiful than the previous wondrous grotto that they had been privileged to have viewed; it was ten times the size of the previous room and breathtakingly beautiful. There was an entire wall on one side that looked very much like the colorful tapestries that some humans were so fond of putting upon the walls of their palaces and important buildings for decoration, except that it was so very much larger and it had occurred naturally, formed out of rock over many millennia. Also different in this part of the caverns was that there was now some faint light; it seemed to be coming from directly overhead through what appeared to be several enormous deposits of clear crystallized rocks, most likely what is today called quartz. Throughout the entire chamber were many wonderful examples of natural beauty that they had never seen before, stalactites dripping from the walls and ceilings no thicker than the strings that their people produced from the sinew of the bison that they harvested, others as thick around as the hugest trees. Some parts of the floor were as smooth as still water and as slippery as ice and others had an almost bubbly texture, while yet others were entirely covered with sharp spines coming up out of the floor, these they were warned by their friend about in time to avoid any potential problems. Everywhere that they looked they saw beauty, and then in one far-off corner they saw it.

One of the signs about the Piasa that their parents had described to them, a Dragons hoard, they had heard from countless tales told them by their people about how the Piasa had a cave where they always kept their hoard of treasures that they had stolen from people over the years.

"That is yours," said Billi, "your hoard."

"I have heard of the Piasa having treasure," Tecumseh exclaimed!

The dragon emitted a grumbling guffaw and said somewhat humorously, "I cannot say that all is treasure, but it is a collection of items that I have accumulated over the centuries that are important to me."

"It is not true what they say about you stealing these things is it," Billi asked?

"Oh no, that is not in my nature," Granger answered. "Most were given to me, several I have found and I even took a few from the dead after some of the many battles that your kind has the unfortunate propensity towards involving themselves within; others are cloths and things that humans thought that I would find useful, many are jewels as I collect them for their beauty, some I believe are meant as tools and some can be called both tool and weapon; some of these latter mentioned I have found can at times be especially dangerous.

Tecumseh and Billi were in awe, they wanted to inspect and to touch everything, for here in front of them were treasures from so many places and so many times the implications made them squirm with desire, even a strange sort of lust. It was quite unexpected and even somewhat unnerving, as they had never before felt this type of repulsive temptation in their young lives; however they did immediately recognize it for the greed it really was and nobly subdued the wretched feelings.

The Dragon saw this and immediately said, "The cloth that we have come for is over in that corner yonder, you will have every opportunity to gaze at these things sometime later."

The two young humans rather recognized that the Piasa was attempting to protect them from themselves; from the human weakness of greed, for they felt it too strongly, this they knew! Tecumseh scrambled over golden lances, bejeweled shields and the like, to finally gain over everything that had been in his way to the top of the pile in a somewhat reverent place in the corner of all that was there; the cloth folded carefully upon a smooth rock shelf. It was absolutely dry; the Piasa had taken exceptional care of this over the years for its being merely a cloth.

"You seem to value this cloth greatly my friend," Tecumseh commented.

"Yes, I rather thought that someday it would have great value to someone," The Dragon stated. "Perhaps soon we shall see if I was indeed correct."

"True enough," Tecumseh agreed. He began to climb his way back over the path he had come when suddenly his eyes caught a glimpse of something that he had not seen before. Over to his right, far out of his reach on a short pillar was what looked like the skull of a man, it was carven from what looked to be pure crystal. It seemed to radiate with its own inner light. As he started to inch toward it to get a better look Billi asked, "What is it Tecumseh, where are you going?"

Granger then spoke with great authority, "Come now, the afternoon is nearing its end. You will have plenty of time later on to gaze at my collection!"

Tecumseh could not argue the point, it was getting late and so he made haste to rejoin Billi and the dragon, but as they made their way from the cave Tecumseh could not restrain his curiosity. "What is it," He asked of his primordial dragon friend.

"What do you speak of," The Piasa answered back. "There is much inside of my domicile that can be of interest."

Words of the Piasa

"You know what it was which I saw; the skull," he stated the dread obvious in his voice."

"Yes, I was afraid of that; this is one of the tools that are also a weapon that I had tried to warn you of; it is very dangerous and must be studied for many seasons before one can attempt its use. Even when you are quite knowledgeable about its use, it is still very dangerous. I happened to rediscover it a very long time after I had witnessed its ferocious power first hand; when it had a part in destroying some very unique and interesting people. In time I will teach you of all which I know of it, but for now we must go back to your village, as we have more pressing matters at hand.

"He is right Tecumseh," Billi said.

"I suppose," Tecumseh agreed. "But Billi you should have seen it, a human skull carved from pure crystal. It glowed with an inner light, as though it possessed some unknown magical power. I could see that it is capable of many great things."

"In time my young friend, all in good time," The Piasa said peacefully. "You will see all that I can show you in time, but for now you must learn the lesson of patience."

Tecumseh and Billi held each other and gazed deeply into one another's eyes, they resigned themselves to the fact that this was the truth and turned to face their friend and said, "We can sense the truth that you speak with to us, as if you know what it is that our future actually holds."

"I know not the future, but I can help to guide you away from the mistakes that others of your kind have made, if you will but listen; now let us go," the dragon urged them.

They climbed aboard his mighty back and were soon in the sky making quick time under the power of the expansive wings of the Piasa as they flew back to their village holding the cloth that the Piasa had held in such high regard for so long a time.

~~~~~~~~~~~~~~~~~~~~

At about the same time just several leagues to the south and west of the Nastazi village, the Mayan traders had arrived at the ferry point which the Nastazi maintained on the great river. During the spring and summer of every year the Grand River would begin to overflow its banks and this year was no different and they had been forced to move the crossing point to higher ground that was several leagues further inland. While this was an inconvenience it was nowhere near as bad as it could at times become, for many of the elders told of times when the entire village was under water except for the highest of the mounds and the water lapped upon the walls of the facing cliffs for weeks at a time. The younger of the Nastazi's had not seen this but they could see the scars left on the face of the cliffs for miles, upon one of these barren scrapings is the spot where later indigenous people would later immortalize the Piasa with a grand mural that took several seasons to complete and told the story of the dragon a in sometime not altogether positive light, it existed there for many lifetimes; for continuing generations to observe and to learn from.

As the Mayans waited for the Nastazi guides to arrive from across the river they discussed among themselves some of what they hoped to achieve during their visit with the Nastazi, the second in command, a man that was not very tall, for no Maya was very tall, but very powerfully built studied a list that they had brought with them as he approached his commander. Both were dressed in highly decorated ceremonial clothes and carrying ornately adorned weapons, though obviously meant to mainly impress, they also looked as though they could be quite dangerous if actually utilized in a fight. The commander was a man known as Oaxintaal and his approaching second in command was called Hure' Tan. They both could be recognized as men of great importance and they were accompanied by thirty or more very able looking Mayan soldiers each carrying a war club, shield and a bow. They also all seemed to be wearing a sort of interlocking small-linked mail that looked very effective in fending off enemy blows or even arrows from afar that was made not of metal, but of very small and amazingly hard shells which were overlapping one another.

They were also followed by a good number of what appeared to be slaves for some of the Mayan people prided themselves in the number of their enemies that they had defeated and enslaved, some of these were for just a season or two as punishment for some wrong done to the Mayan owner, others who were enslaved for a certain number of seasons to repay a debt or bet and even others that had been captured in war that would most likely spend the rest of their lives in captivity;

not all Mayans practiced slavery, but these traders depended upon it, as many of the rest of their kind did.

Hure' Tan approached his commander Oaxintaal and stated, "My Lord, if we are to return with significant amounts of the items that we have listed, we will need to obtain quite a few more slaves, the burning black rocks are a great marvel to return with, however they greatly add to the load and make it necessary the build a larger number of canoes for transport."

Oaxintaal spoke softly saying, "We shall not proceed imprudently, we will return with only the hardest and longest burning of the black rocks so as to assure room for the more valuable metals, seeds and gems; however if we are discreet about it a few young Nastazi slaves would surely add to the glory of our return, not to mention our profit. Especially if they were a number of their appealing young females, for they are surely as pleasing to the touch as they are to the eye, yes!"

"Without doubt, your plan becomes more promising by the minute," Hure'Tan affirmed. "Tell me what you would have me do and it will be done my Lord."

"For now we will bide our time and trade as we have told them we have come to do, it is best if they not realize our surprise until we are already gone, for they are many; and more formidable than even they know," Oaxintaal stated. "Be patient for now my fierce comrade, the time for action will arrive soon enough!"

With that discussion behind them they gathered their party and boarded the Platform boats that the Nastazi had so amicably provided and they were absolutely correct about their hosts, the Nastazi were very open and friendly people that desired to have many trading partners, but they had shown in the past and even in ancient times before this generation that they were slow to anger, but once that they felt they had been wronged they became a fierce and unforgiving enemy capable of extremely vicious warfare. They felt however that they had now grown as a people beyond such barbarism, although they would soon be surprised to discover otherwise!

Now, at this time there were also other peoples active in this great land, the Pawnee lived in the lands far to the northeast of the bottoms;

that wonderful, fertile land between the great rivers that they and their forefathers had coveted for generations and although the Pawnee were a very warlike peoples who prided themselves on their battle skills they had never been able to take any of the Nastazi's homeland away from them, as a matter of fact the last time that they had attempted it they were so soundly defeated that they had been driven many leagues farther north into much more cold and inhospitable lands. For several generations now they had been regrouping; even creeping closer for the last twenty seasons and had only just begun to develop designs on the Nastazi lands once again during the last two seasons. Just a short time before something had happened that they discerned as something of an omen; during the guide-dance for war that they had began performing again a short time ago, many of the braves were said to have seen the Piasa, and it had been seen as guiding them towards the lands of their old nemesis, the Nastazi. Surely this was a sign to make war on the old enemy who's years of peace had surely made them grow soft and had to be ripe now for the picking, at least this is what their warrior-chief was telling them; often with his administration of the thick tea he made from the horn-flower (known today as Bella-Donna) that grew indigenously in this region. He had his warriors partake of this strong hallucinogen often, especially just before any battle and combined with what he was saying about their enemies he had driven them into an incredible frenzy of misguided hatred.

Towards the end of the ceremony their leader, a self-possessed and purely selfish man named Zauhn felt that he should give his men something to dwell on during the coming deep sleep, for you see one of the side effects of the drug, besides incredible strength and misguided fearlessness was that when it wore off you would sleep like a babe, sometimes even for days. He told them, "With this moon we will take the homelands promised to us by our forefathers. We will take it from our fat, soft enemies whom have forgotten the ways of the warrior and we will enslave their women and children, but moreover we will take our rightful place in the middle of our great lands to expand and impose our ways over all who may dwell there."

Shortly afterwards the melee broke up as the men went their separate ways; some to assault slaves, some to treat their own women poorly, but all were in a deep drug-induced sleep within the next several hours.

Regrettably for them though, their leader had not even bothered to investigate his enemies strengths and weaknesses, a horrendous military blunder in any of the human ages.

The dragon landed gently in the clearing where they usually met, one in the same as where he had rescued Tecumseh from the hungry bear, at near dusk. They used this spot for its convenience as it was close enough to the village to walk back in a short time yet their approach could be hidden from view by the tall trees upon the bluffs. Billi and Tecumseh gathered the cloth and took it to hide until the gathering tomorrow.

"Just call me when you would like me to make my appearance, I will hear you," Granger said.

"I am sure that you will my intriguing brown friend, I just do not know how you do it," Tecumseh said playfully.

"Look, the Mayans must be arriving," Billi exclaimed, pointing down past the village, "There are more of them than I was expecting," she added.

"Undoubtedly they brought many slaves with them to carry back all that they hope to swindle us out of," Tecumseh said wryly. "My father has warned me of these traders and their devious practices, be warned as well!"

"They enslave people," Billigana said, extremely repulsed.

"They are not the only of your kind that still practice this horrible behavior," The dragon stated, "A definite sign of barbaric behavior, one of the sure signs that they cannot be trusted; you must be careful in your dealings with them."

"But they are so very different and from so far away, I believe that interacting with them will be exciting," Billi said in a rather flirtatious manner.

"I have heard that the lands where they live are the homes of cannibals, several different tribes of them," Tecumseh said harshly. "I am certain that you do not wish to become a gift of an interesting new food from afar to some of the Mayans neighbors."

"Yes," said the Piasa. "Please stay where we can easily make contact with you while they are here, as I think it will be much safer."

"Oh, I will," The young lady squealed. "But how could any threaten someone protected by the bravest of warriors and the fiercest of dragons, I feel very safe with you two watching over me."

With that and the promise to meet again in the new day they parted for the evening. Tecumseh and Billi quietly made their way back to the middle of the village where it had become especially easy to blend back into the midst of all of the peoples of the excited Nastazi village, for the Mayan party was just arriving at the other side of the vast village and there were huge throngs of people surging towards their arrival from all directions.

The Nastazi welcomed their guests audaciously, with maidens dressed in the most splendid of costumes showering the arrivals with flower petals, colored torches and fires of all different hues, burning herbs that offered an abundance of wonderful aromas and huge exploding signal fires burning atop all of the major mounds of the central plaza and the Midwestern spring evening could not have been any more pleasurable with its mild temperature gentle breezes and the aroma of freshly blooming honeysuckle wafting through the evening air.

The Mayans were led in the most ceremonious of manners down the full length of the main avenue to the king's mound, where Kharzin Atol, the Nastazi king awaited them. He was not in his customary place of reverence atop the mammoth pyramid, but at the base platform to show his guests as much respect as his station would allow. This was meant to show the utmost of esteem to his visitors, but I fear it was taken as a sign of weakness instead; though all of the humans involved in this saga would find out shortly that all is not ever as it appears.

Tecumseh and Billigana tried to achieve just a short moment of their parents time to attempt to tell them of their intentions tomorrow and of the new and inspirational new friendship that they had developed. Then, if they were successful to that point they would give them the message of what their new friend was ready to offer the Nastazi and their trading contacts. Unfortunately their parents were people of very high regard within the village and they were finding this simple task extremely difficult, as the two mothers had been assigned to orchestrating the feast that was to follow in a short time and could not be located in any of the locations that the young couple had tried and their fathers stood in an honor guard for the king and could not at this time be disturbed.

They decided to just make sure that their fathers had seen them and continue the ongoing search for their mothers. That is when fortune, as it will, took a strange twist.

Nanuma was a Nastazi elder that was very well loved by all in the village. She also happened to have been his caregiver when Tecumseh was but a young boy. They stopped and began to talk to her about the problem that they had encountered and tried to explain to her that it was vital that they speak with their parents as soon as was possible.

"Why is it so important that you speak with them at this moment, do you not live under the same roof as they," She asked?

"We are trying to arrange a most unusual meeting, between our new and special friend and our people," Billi said.

"You have begun a relationship with the Piasa," Nanuma whispered as fact, what she already knew in her heart!

"How do you know this," Billi asked in shock?

"It is true, is it not," She asked as her eyes bore into Tecumseh knowing he could not lie to her?

"Yes, it is," Tecumseh confessed, "How did you know?"

"I have seen the signs before and it has always come to a very tragic end. This I know as I am the only person in our village that has any real experience in this matter," She pleaded. "Both my promised man and the Piasa disappeared, never to be seen again and it left me hurting me greatly, as it still does to this day! Why do you suppose that I have never married after all of these seasons?"

"The Piasa is not evil as all state; he says that he is one of a race of many that once existed and he has shown us nothing but goodness," Billi said.

"Oh of this I have no doubt," Nanuma explained. "I would have sensed the evil in a Piasa that was near, even after so long a time had passed since my relationship with one."

"You knew a Piasa also," Tecumseh asked gently, in an attempt at being most careful not to tread on hurt that she may have incurred early in her long life?

"Oh, yes I did, however only indirectly, for it was mainly realized through the relationship that my love, Tonnel had developed with him, for the Piasa that we knew was not at all forthcoming, as the adults all attacked him immediately any time that he was spotted," Nanuma explained.

Billi replied quite calmly for her age and considering the excitement that she was feeling, "Yes, we know that we will need to get by many of the fears that our people now possess."

"This will not be easy my child, the fears that your people hold for the Piasa are old and perceived to be well founded," Nanuma said calmly. "When I was young, we were told many stories of the Piasa that took people from our villages or from the forest for not only foods, but merely to torture them, making them suffer for their tainted enjoyment, you will not have an easy time of it."

"Will you help us," Billi pleaded?

"It is for the good of our people," Tecumseh added.

"I must first meet your Piasa friend, but you make it sound as though the one that you have become connected with may not be quite the same as the one I have known, they can be undeniably charming creatures but must earn their trust the same as any other being," She said quietly. "Let us go to meet with him at once, as we need to formulate a plan if you wish for success."

"Yes," Tecumseh said. "He is a wonderful creature, it is true; not only is he kind and protective of us, but he is very knowing of the ways of the world, of its people, customs, creatures, forces and the like. Most amazing of all is that he wants to help us for he says that we are the world's future."

"He is as good as he sounds Nanuma, you can feel his compassion for us, you will see," Billi pleaded.

"We shall see my young ones, you make it sound inviting, but we must take it one step at a time," Nanuma stated firmly. "First I must meet the Piasa and then we must convince the people to give an audience, and it will not be easy."

Saying that, Nanuma continued up the pathway towards the bluffs that her two young friends had begun towards; when they both hesitated she turned around and promptly asked, "Are you coming?"

~~~~~~~~~~~~~~~~

This dragon cannot always be certain, but at this time Granger felt as though the kinship he had developed with Tecumseh and Billigana had somehow grown stronger, for he knew that he must move now to meet them, and so he began to make his way towards the edge of the forest. As he grew close to where the canopy ended and his head began to clear the tops of the trees, his sharp eyes could begin to see the strangers that had come into the Nastazi village. It was easy to espy the humans that were the leaders of the group from the ceremonious attire. The bright colors, the highly polished weapons and all of the jewels, it was obvious that they thought very highly of themselves. Then, just a short distance away he saw something that revolted him; the poorly dressed group towards the back of the procession was obviously slaves. He could see the shackles and the defeated looks upon their faces and from their treatment there was no mistaking it.

They have so much to learn the Piasa pondered, how will I be able to reach them?

His revelry was interrupted by his sensing the humans that he had bonded with were headed in this direction; he proceeded down towards the pathway up the cliff, waiting laying low in the brush.

The strange war-loving people that the Nastazi had defeated so many years ago; but were now having new designs on the Nastazi homeland would later become known as the Pawnee and for hundreds of years they would be known as a fierce warmongering people that were the scourge of all that came into contact with them, but at this time they were still a small tribe with unfortunately a most negative manner of dealing with all cultures whom they coexisted with.

Their leader Zauhn had convinced his people that it was now time to take back the lands that he affirmed the Nastazi had stolen from them years ago and they were on the move to accomplish this. Although their force was not as huge as the Nastazi who were entertaining the visiting Mayans, it was formidable none the less. Slightly more than eight hundred abnormally motivated braves traveled quickly and quietly in a huge fleet of canoes, down the great river that poured from the foothills that had been their latest home to join with the mighty river that was the heart and soul of the Nastazi homeland.

They arrived at the village that in time would be referred to as Cahokia on the eve of the second day, and there was a great festivity in progress; this is when it occurred to Zauhn that they had been blessed with good fortune. What better time to attack an enemy other than during a time of festival when he could be caught totally unawares.

The procession down the central boulevard had reached its destination; the grand pyramid in the center of the village and that is where nearly all of the people of the two trading tribes were gathered, the great part of the Nastazi and all of their visiting Mayan friends.

Committing a mistake that may well have been reached out of the years of peace they had enjoyed, the Nastazi had posted no real guards to speak of, as they had been caught up in the events of the evening and the promise of the coming days of trading. The only guards that were to be seen were the personal bodyguards of the king, yet the Nastazi were known to react quickly to any challenge and to always have arms to bear station closely by.

The Pawnee knew about their enemy's capability in battle and were going to be careful not to let this golden opportunity slip by unexploited. They had silently beached their watercraft and stole inland undetected where they stealthily formed a crescent around their unaware adversaries, a crescent bristling with arrows, spears and viciously pointed war-clubs.

Zauhn was very pleased with himself, he had achieved total surprise. His enemy, although they out-numbered his men ten to one, or even better were surrounded and unarmed for the most part. His warriors had been chewing and smoking Ka-nick Anick for the last several hours, making them impervious to pain; all of the signs appeared as though they could not have been any more fortunate. This was going to be a slaughter; he could feel it in his soul.

He gave the signal and his malevolent faction began to make its final advance.

The procession of visiting Mayans and Nastazi community leaders had arrived at the Grand Pyramid in the center of the town of Nakokia with great style and aplomb. They were taking part in the cementing of a trading union that had already existed for many generations and with the agreements that would take place within this next week would be designed to last for many more they believed, while the king of the

Nastazi stood upon his royal platform and began to welcome his guests flamboyantly and with much of the royal style with which he always conducted himself.

"We welcome our old Mayan friends and wish them continued health and prosperity. With the *bighorn medicine wheels* (13.) for guidance that our two peoples have placed through time and the network of roadways that have been completed where land travel is necessary, both of our peoples have long committed to the continued friendship and prosperity that we have established between our cultures," King Kharzin Atol of the Nastazi said ceremoniously; but before he was able to continue his flamboyant speech he was silenced by the buzzing of an arrow that buried itself deep into his heart; the attack had begun!

The Pawnee rained down arrows upon the unsuspecting revelers at a tremendous rate in the first few seconds of the attack. Totally surprised at first, the Nastazi and their guests seemed to have nowhere to go and were taking grievous losses, but after only a few moments they began to take cover and once again get their wits about them and the Mayans, ever the surviving adventurers immediately looped around behind the great pyramid and began to unpack their long range weapons. The Nastazi kings bodyguards bravely threw themselves headlong into the assault upon their foe even though they were equipped with few bows on such a night as this, they charged into the Pawnee anyway and were engaged in bitter combat within only a few moments even though armed with only light mainly ceremonial weapons.

Even as lightly armed though as they were, they were still quite formidable warriors as they had trained intensely for all of their lives for this most glorious of positions; however what they now faced was most unnerving. They would strike down these Pawnee with an obviously fatal blow, disemboweling, the loss of a limb or even a wicked head wound and the drug demented Pawnee would continue to advance upon them, as if possessed by demons. It was terribly unnerving, but the Nastazi were brave souls and continued to protect their village and its people. It was not going well though for the Nastazi Kings Guard at this time and they were in real danger of being overwhelmed.

This is when the Mayans began to unleash a weapon that was not in use in this area of the world, it was a long spear with a razor sharp copper point that was thrown with the assistance of a throwing sling that increased the velocity and range tremendously and the Mayans were very accurate with them.(now known as the Atlatl) For a short time they made a good account of themselves, but the Pawnee had to be killed outright in order to stop them as wound did little to even slow them down. They also showed absolutely no fear, upon seeing their comrades impaled with the terrible weapons it merely enflamed their bloodlust to an even higher plateau.

However the Nastazi were also regrouping and more of their men were beginning to gain real weapons and join into the battle, but the surprise had been complete and many were dying; including Tecumseh's father who was taken by an arrow from a Pawnee whom he had just wrestled to the ground and stabbed what would have normally been a mortal wound, but the Pawnee to the Nastazi's mortal surprise turned with other worldly strength and shoved an arrow from his quiver through Kurlhii's neck. He died with a fully astonished look on his pained face and it did not look good for the fair, mound building people of the great river bottoms at this time!

Tecumseh and Billi had gained the top of the bluff when they began to hear the great turmoil that had begun in their village behind them and they turned to see a sight that shocked and terrified them. Their village was under attack by what was as of yet an unseen; but appeared to be an enormous army of enemies. This is something that neither of them had ever seen, though they had heard of and trained for it even in their young lives, though they had not expected to ever see it; however there was no way to change it, war was now upon them.

A moment later they were startled by a huge presence behind them; it was the Piasa.

He spoke quietly, "This is something else that your kind takes part in that is inexplicable to me. They all watched in horror for a few moments not understanding what could possess people to be so horrid to one another, to kill on such a massive scale is beyond comprehension.

Billi looked up to the dragon, her beautiful eyes filled with pain, spilling from her heart with her hurtful gaze. "What is there that we can we do," She pleaded?

The Piasa suddenly spoke, "This must stop, climb up for I am going to put an end to this now."

He then did something that they did not expect; he flew not towards the battle, but towards the black hills north of the village where the Nastazi gathered the rocks that burned. There he swooped down and landed for a mere moment and devoured quite a few of the large black stones. When he finished he immediately took flight again towards the melee that was occurring, chewing and stomach rumbling all the way. He flew with his agitated crew over the outlying smaller mounds towards the middle of the village to where the horrid turmoil was still underway. They could see the Nastazi and Mayan warriors beginning to regroup, but still obviously getting the worse of the fight and taking very heavy losses. He then flew down low, dangerously close to, or possibly even within the range of the Pawnee arrows. He could now see that they had formed a giant half moon in order to herd their enemies into the fiendish killing zone that they had intentionally created. Unbeknownst to them however, was the fact that from above this made them a very easy target themselves and so he dived even lower and dramatically increased his speed, but what was remarkable was that he began belching a torrent of flame at the Pawnee who for the most part were still separated from their victims just shooting arrows from afar. He traversed the crescent that had been their offensive strategy and now became their undoing up and down torching numerous Pawnee as they came within his reach. This had an effect that the fighting of other men had not been able to generate; the combination of the sight of the massive dragon claws open, wings outstretched and spitting fire at them threw the attacking Pawnee into a sudden and indescribable panic. They all suddenly and completely quit the fight and began a reckless stampede back towards the canoes that they had left at the bank of the great river. They had lost nearly two thirds of their men in just a few short moments between the courageous fighting of the defenders and the onslaught of the mighty beast that had allied himself with those whom they had attacked. Nastazi and the Mayans then changed places with the Pawnee; the attackers had now become the attacked as the Nastazi and Mayan forces were now pursuing them.

The dragon flew once more around the place of battle, but then landed between the antagonists stating, "Stop your pursuit at once!"

"They have attacked our home and killed our people," shouted one of the officers that were leading the pursuit. "They must pay with their lives."

"It is true, they have wronged you dearly and they have already paid a heavy price," The dragon stated persuasively, "Though if you exterminate them now you are no better than they."

"They killed our people for no reason, they should be exterminated," One of the incensed Nastazi bellowed.

"You must force yourselves to grow now, you must let them go," The dragon said forcefully.

"We will not, we have lost friends and family," the officer stammered.

"You must," The Piasa said calmly, "Or risk the wrath of the Piasa!" The dragon said in a sweetly malevolent voice that was surely intended to intimidate as he stared in a terrifying glare that none desired to test.

The pursuit then at once came to an end and the remaining Pawnee again gained their boats and headed back for the long and solemn trip back up the large rivers to their home, beaten severely, but at least still alive and yes, now without the inciting fervor of the power-crazed Zauhn and two thirds of their warriors. He had been among the first to feel the wrath of the dragons fire and would become known as somewhat of a martyr because of this for a time.

The Pawnee in later years would regroup and be the scourge of this entire area, not able to get along with any of the tribes of the many nations that would later inhabit this land, even the white men that would soon begin to arrive in huge numbers, though it would be many seasons until they were able to threaten anyone again.

Now the business at hand was for the humans that the Piasa had just saved to become acquainted with a beast that most had never seen, only heard of through the stories passed down generation after generation. Most of the stories that were passed down about the enchanted (or so they said) beast were not very apt to promote good will, as they usually had something to do with being eaten by or otherwise wronged by the beast and so the present situation did not appear very promising for the moment.

That is when Nanuma made her most opportune appearance; the

old woman gained the attention of the Nastazi and Mayans that had been fighting in defense of all in the village. She, for a moment thought that it may have been too late, for she saw before her that the throng of warriors that had just been the beneficiaries of the timely appearance of this ancient and magical beast now seemed to be showing a newfound fear and mistrust of their benefactor. Even with the children on the behemoths back and the obvious protection that he had just bestowed upon everyone present; there were the warriors that had begun to surround the beast and make ready to aim their weapons.

One of the Mayans that had unpacked and now manned a giant crossbow had it pointed at the breast of the Piasa screaming, "Jump and save yourselves children, we will deal with the monster."

Nanuma interrupted, "No, no you must not, for this creature is not as you perceive him."

Tecumseh stated, "Can you not see the Piasa is our friend, has he not just proven that."

"He is a fierce man killer and breathes fire; he is of the black magic," a Mayan yelled.

"Do not fear him just because you do not understand him, he is our friend," Billi cried!

Nanuma quickly interjected, "I have known his kind before; you have nothing to fear I tell you. He will do us no harm; let us communicate with him for a time as he has saved many of both our people on this day; we owe him at least that."

The Nastazi had lost their king and many of the leading citizens, including Tecumseh's father. The medicine man was old and of failing strength, so fortunately was not present at this time. Certainly, new voices would need to be sounded to fill the void in the leadership that they now faced and it surprised many who came forward and spoke rationally in this time of chaos to offer a new insight into their newly changed lives. Many but not all; Tecumseh was not shocked at all when his mother Naomi spoke up to calm the crowd and convince them to accept the Piasa as a friend, just as his son had. "Listen brothers and sisters," she pleaded. "Listen to Nanuma, she who has lived with this kind as a young girl I have been told. Listen to my son and his young bride to be for they speak the truth, the Piasa is our friend, and he has just proven it, before your eyes for all present to see!"

"Listen to her," Nanuma said. "The beast offers us the hope of a new device that can help us immensely."

"The beast does nothing, but spit fire, kills and eats our young," Someone screamed from the crowd. "What has he for us and how can he tell us of it," issued a screaming voice bellowing from elsewhere deep within the throng.

The dragon finally spoke quietly and calmly, "You have all heard of me though few know me at all; I am not as your stories of old have stated. I am of a race that once existed of my kind that lived worldwide and prospered for ages, though I may now possibly be the very last of my kind. Like humans, there were many different types of my kind, those that you refer to as Piasa and also like you, some of us were good and unfortunately some were very evil. Though I am here to help you, I want to teach you of and protect you from the actions that others of your type have unfortunately found to make their peoples disappear and cost them their lives and cultures; I want to do this because I feel that your fate is connected to the fate of "Mother Earth." I share this world with you and although I am very old, I do not yet tire of the wonder of the life that I have been blessed with in this place. I would show you things that I feel may help you and try to teach you to stay clear of the mistakes that others of your kind have made, if only you will allow me the honor of doing so.

In this way the relationship between the Piasa and the people of the great rivers bottoms began and in the coming days the dragon spoke to all that would listen, he gave them the huge amount of the wonderful light cloth that be had brought from his keep and explained to them the manner in which it was made so that they were able to make even more. He gave them the seeds to grow the fluffy white balls on the plants that one of the cloths was made from and showed the types of caterpillars that could be raised that produced that fiber from which the finer smooth cloth was derived, with the good fortune that the needed trees were already present. He also took great pains to explain to them how to make the large bags that it took that were attached to the baskets in which the people were held so that they could travel into the sky in the hot air bags; all of these were skills that the people were shown by the dragon and seized with a great deal of enthusiasm.

Then the day came, after several attempts and a great deal of assistance from Billi and Tecumseh when they finally fabricated a frame that could properly harness the hot air coming from their fires to fill the bag, as all of their preparations were now complete. It was a glorious sight to see when the bag began to fill with the heated air and float above everyone, everybody responded with a magnificent, roaring cheer.

Billigana and Tecumseh, having been of such great help were treated to the first controlled flight. They rose a good distance above the crowd that was gathered beneath them and were once again astounded at the beauty of their land and the great distances that they could now see, whether on the back of the dragon or in the basket of the floating bag, when they looked down upon their world from above it always took their breath away in amazement. They were flying on the tether of a long rope so at the first sign that the air in the bag was beginning to cool and their altitude drop, they were immediately pulled back in, though in the months that followed they would even devise a way to safely place a raised pot of fire in the top of the basket to enable far longer flights; they could only wonder just what catastrophe could have happened to harm a people so skilled that they had created such a marvelous devise as this.

As they returned to the ground they were greeted by several of the Mayans that had come to their village to trade.

Hure' Tan approached Tecumseh and Billi and said quietly to them, "My leader Oaxintaal has requested that you meet with us in private, as he believes that you show more promise than most of your village and would like to invite you to trading that he feels will be of great benefit for us all."

"What have we that you want to trade for so badly," Billi asked suspiciously?

"Many things you have and many that we have that would be of interest to you, but let us be discreet. Join myself and my leader at a more secure location so that we may barter," Hure' Tan said as he motioned towards Oaxintaal, smiling at them from the edge of the crowd.

"We trade with our people present, it is our way," Tecumseh stated firmly.

"Hure' Tan countered with a quick gesture to Oaxintaal and he immediately approached with a small leather pouch that he deftly opened to show Billi and then Tecumseh. The pouch was filled with very large blue sapphires, the Mayans called them stones of the blue fire or Cobaltons.

As Oaxintaal showed her the stones Tecumseh could see Billi's eyes alight with desire and he heard Oaxintaal tell her, "We have only these, not enough to trade with everyone."

Tecumseh had not seen this look on Billi's face before and it made him feel as though he would like to perhaps trade for these stones so that he would be able to give his beloved something that she would treasure to show a sign of his great and undying love for her at the time of their wedding. "We are interested," He said. "Where shall we go to talk?"

"Come with us to our quarters, we shall have privacy there," Oaxintaal murmured.

Billigana and Tecumseh walked off, following the Mayans to the opposite side of the village to where the Mayans had been provided the private encampment that they had requested.

From the ridge on the other side of the town, the Piasa watched with a growing feeling of unrest; his intuition toward these Mayans was not feeling at all positive at this moment, but they had fought at the side of the Nastazi as allies and so he would have to wait and see.

Naomi and Nanuma had been busy at the river's edge gathering some of the medicinal herbs that grew only in the very moist environment that was found there. They needed many of them to treat the numerous wounds that still bothered the warriors who were injured in the battle not so many days ago. Naomi had lost her husband, Tecumseh's father and was morning very heavily, although she was a woman that knew her duty and understood that she must help the living were she could. She knew also that Tecumseh loved his father and would miss him; but as a young Nastazi warrior coming of age he should be allowed to mourn in his own private way, which he was she was certain, but for now he was caught up in a story that was playing out involving the Piasa and her people; she knew that there would be a mystical and very important happenings within this saga and that she must try not to interfere and allow fate to take its natural course. Her heart felt a barren wasteland, but she knew that she must go on. She prayed to the Wakan Tanka;

their great spirit to give her strength and guidance to help her son and her people through the trying times that she knew were now upon them.

The Mayans led the two young Nastazi's into the longhouse that they had been furnished by their hosts for them to dwell within during the trading visit. From the outside it appeared like any Nastazi longhouse that you would see within the village, but inside it changed drastically, for the Mayans definitely had very different customs from the Nastazi. They had the walls heavily draped with tapestries that seemed to not only serve as artwork with outstanding visual appeal but also seemed to have another hidden purpose; while they would be considered masterworks of art by peoples of any age, it was obvious that they also absorbed nearly all sound for right outside the entrance nothing could be heard, however upon entering you could hear the screams of one of the female slave being assaulted and beaten. It was very discomforting, but with a short nearly imperceptible signal from Oaxintaal it stopped immediately.

Tecumseh was feeling rather suspicious about the motives of the Mayans, but his father and most of the elders had been telling him for all of his life about the wonders of their guests and the great advancements that they were responsible for, so he tried to calm his doubts as best that he could. He just supposed that it was his relationship with the dragon that had piqued the trader's interest.

Billi started the conversation saying, "Our people do not keep slaves. We feel that it is very wrong, especially if they must suffer at their holder's hands!"

Oaxintaal was quick to explain, "There confinement is not as barbaric as it appears my princess, they will serve us for only so long as until they serve the time of the punishment that they have earned, for they were captured in a skirmish that was begun by their own people making war on our sovereign nation for material gain. Instead of killing them, we are making them serve us for several seasons as they are needed for the trading trips and surely prefer hard work to the alternative of having been killed in battle. In any case after several seasons they will once again regain their freedom, having learned the lesson of never attacking their Mayan neighbors again."

With that statement Billi saw one of the slaves almost imperceptibly roll her eyes, but Billi chose to keep it to herself for the moment.

Tecumseh added to his loves concern, "They are still humans and should be treated as such."

"Believe me," Oaxintaal added. "Any punishment that we dole out is always deserved, we are not barbarians."

Tecumseh somehow did not find that statement to ring as totally true.

"Let us discuss what it is that we came for," Oaxintaal slid away from the subject that he obviously no longer wanted to keep explaining himself. "We want to trade for the secret of controlling the beast, we have seen you with him and it is obvious that he does as you instruct him."

Billi was the first to react; as her laughter was spontaneous and profuse.

Tecumseh merely shook his head no. When Billigana regained her composure she informed the Mayans, "He cannot control the Piasa; no one can. We are his friends and as his friends would never consider trading for him, no matter how wonderful your jewels may appear."

"That is unfortunate," Oaxintaal stated slyly, as he once again poured the huge, beautiful stones into clear view. "We imagined that we might have conducted a mutually beneficial trade and imagine that the beast would also enjoy the game filled jungles of our homeland."

Tecumseh said, "The Piasa makes his own decisions about where and with whom he wants to go. You may invite him yourself if you desire, but I do not think he wants to leave this land at this time."

"Perhaps we have other items that might be of interest to you?" Billi attempted to continue the trading session, "Maybe you can use the hard, black and beautiful Obsidian stone that we can acquire for you; it is a fine medium for the jewels and weapons that you seem to admire so well and nothing can be fashioned any sharper than it.

"Or maybe we can show you where to mine great amounts of salt for your cooking and preserving, "Tecumseh pointed out.

Oaxintaal then responded oddly saying, "Not those items, but perhaps we can speak again before we depart. We would at least like to memorialize our condolences to you upon the untimely loss of your father and so many of your people with some commemorative marker."

"Yes perhaps," Tecumseh stated, truly wanting to honor the memory of his great father, but not knowing why these people that did not even know him would show any interest.

Tecumseh and Billi both did not understand, they could see that the Mayans did not desire what they had to trade, yet they wanted to see them again before they left; it seemed quite strange.

Hure' Tan escorted them back exactly the way that they had come and hurriedly directed them outside once more, upon exiting the longhouse he said his farewells and they were off.

Upon re-entering the longhouse Oaxintaal looked into his eyes and said, "They will be perfect."

"Yes, perfect breeding slaves to produce more of their kind and more wealth for us." Hure' Tan said, as he uttered a sinister predatory laugh.

"We still may have to deal with the beast," Oaxintaal murmured. "But we have dealt with its kind in the past; indeed many of the animals that live in our jungles would be called monsters or worshiped by these heathens. It will be a great relief to return to our own civilized people and perhaps we can discover their great Piasa's lair, they are known to keep hoards of greatly valued treasures it is said. The trading is going as well as planned, we will need only a few more days and then we can depart when the first opportunity arises."

The two then clapped one another on the back in agreement and found their way to the back of the longhouse and their favorites of the female slaves where they beckoned this day's choices and the young women reluctantly followed them back into their chambers.

Billi and Tecumseh were slow to walk back to their part of the village, as they were rather confused about the intentions of the Mayans as they had proven to be people of a strangely contradicting nature. Their elders and parents, people that they well respected had told them for years of the greatness and advanced ways of the Mayan people. They had been told of the wonders of their grand buildings and of the fact that they not only spoke to one another, but could draw their words out to be communicated to each other even on their great buildings; and temples that were said to exhibit narratives of their exploits upon their walls. They were even said to know the exact number of days in a year and even a season, yea, they were even said to be able to predict when amazing things such as eclipses would occur in the heavens, and yet they arrived in the Nastazi homeland with a group of people, both men and women, imprisoned as slaves. Something about this did not make sense to the young people of the great river (now known as the Mississippi) bottom lands; unfortunately it would soon become all too clear!

Tecumseh walked Billigana to her longhouse and was surprised to see his mother there in deep conversation with Billi's mother Sha'siang and Nanuma.

Billi began to defend the time that they were arriving home saying, "The sun is not yet below the horizon, mother and I am also protected by my betrothed Tecumseh."

"Do not be concerned my little one," Sha'siang said. "You have done nothing wrong."

"But you all look as if you are ready to scold someone or you must be greatly concerned about something," Tecumseh said.

Nanuma attempted to explain, "You are correct my perceptive young chief, we have a great concern and it is growing with the passing of every moment of time. We have discussed it amongst ourselves and even prayed to the Wakan Tanka, but we cannot decide exactly what it is. We just cannot trust the Mayans, we feel that they are up to something and that they will wrong us; we just do not know exactly what it is."

"Do not trust them and watch them very closely," Nanuma blurted out.

"Yes, be warned," Sha'siang continued. "They are hiding something, this I can feel, or they plan on taking something that we will not choose to trade."

"But they fought at our side against our enemies," Tecumseh exclaimed!

"I think only because they were also threatened," Nanuma stated.

"They seek something as yet unknown and value our comradeship far less than they declare; I can feel it in my soul."

"Perhaps you can ask the Piasa about it," Naomi offered. "It is said that they can see into the minds of all men." She held on to her son's hands and pleaded with her eyes as she spoke, she was troubled by what was happening deeply, that much was obvious.

"Yes, honored mothers; I do not know if my friend can tell what is in a man's mind, but I will ask him if he can help," Tecumseh promised.

They all agreed that it was a good plan of action, Nanuma was especially satisfied, they then said their goodnights and after embracing Billi one last time for the day, Tecumseh had the pleasant opportunity to walk his mother home to their longhouse. The longhouse, though occupied by other families still seemed especially empty to the both of them without Tecumseh's father Kurlhii being there and he was quite happy to be here for his mother at this time of great hurt, for he knew that his mother's pain at the loss of his father had to be worse than his, and his was nearly unbearable. He embraced her all the way home and told her that he would honor his father for the rest of his life.

Naomi was very pleased with and proud of her son, but it could not yet fill the emptiness she felt; as only time itself could finally dull that sort of hurt, but would never make it disappear.

The next morning began rather strangely, for during the night an unusually bad storm had rolled in from the west and the rain was coming down in torrents. Of course no one wanted to be outside in such inclement weather, but Nanuma arrived at the Digis longhouse (the Nastazi often named their longhouses after respected animals from the forest) where Naomi and her son Tecumseh called home, early in the morning with some very strange news. The Mayans were nowhere to be found, nobody in their group was left in the village and it appeared as though they had departed. Every bit of their belongings, the trading goods, their slaves, all gone; they had said absolutely nothing to anyone about their departure and that was extremely odd. Yet another thing that was very unusual was that Tecumseh had not seen the Piasa in over a day and that was also most unusual in that the Piasa had not said a word to him about leaving. He decided that he needed to investigate the strange things that were occurring and told his mother his plan and promised to be careful as she was always want to hear and struck out to find Granger. The route to the bluffs unfortunately did not take him by Billi's home and he would have preferred to check on her and say good morning, but that would have to wait for now; he would be back shortly anyway and meeting with the dragon was important considering the strange things that had been happening this morning. He arrived at the base of the bluffs and began his climb, but when the rain came down like this the bluffs were treacherous and he could see that it might take longer that he had originally considered, he only hoped that his large friend could sense that he was coming and met him shortening his climb; this was not the case!

At the top of the bluffs his dragon-friend had a very peculiar feeling and did not seem to feel his normal connection with his two young human friends; he felt it may be the interference of this horrible weather, but in any case as he was trying to determine exactly what it was, he did not yet notice the approach of his young human friend and it was to prove a most disconcerting lapse.

In her longhouse on the opposite side of the village from Tecumseh's home, Billigana was awakened by a strange noise coming from the wall outside her room. Though she did not immediately know, it was being quietly forced open, suddenly she could feel the freshness of the cold heavy rain coming from outside even though the doors were far from her room on either end of the house. She was at once, extremely frightened.

Tecumseh finally reached the peak of the bluffs, which was extremely difficult as the rain was now pouring harder than this young man had ever seen and the face of the cliff had turned from a muddy quagmire to a slippery, oozing, flowing torrent of mud slowly descending down the trail by which he had to come. If he was not to find the Piasa the trip back down would prove impossible without serious injury or even worse.

Having reached the top he would normally be elated, as Granger was usually very close to this point and normally met him here, however on this morning it appeared as though it was still the middle of the night and he could not see more than a very short distance from himself because of the severe rain and pitch black darkness. To make matters all the worse, he could not hear anything either because of the intensity of the storm. He called several times, but he knew that it was no use; there was just too much noise. The storm also seemed to be growing in intensity, the wind seemed to have redoubled and it was becoming very difficult to stand upright without holding onto something. He moved further into the woods so that he could grab the trunk of a small tree that he would not be blown away for he feared that he was near in the grips of one of the twister-storms that the elders had warned them about for so long. He lunged into a small thicket of trees and grabbed at the base of the strongest one of them that he could see which was within his reach. Just as he was going down headlong into the mud at the roots of his tree he saw it; in a flash of lightning he saw the silhouette of the Piasa. He was sitting quite a distance from where he now lay; his head was cocked to one side as if perplexed over some very troubling problem. Tecumseh saw him, but he did not know how he could communicate with his giant friend in this horrible clamor of violent weather.

Then he realized that he remembered the feeling that had come over him when the dragon and he had first met. The dragon had saved his life and they were bonded, he remembered that feeling and he concentrated on it, he felt it grow and grow. Then he called his friend, "Granger," he called in his mind. The dragon seemed to stir, he called again, "Granger, I am near.... I need you!"

The dragons head rose and the light of his peerless eyes fell directly upon Tecumseh. The boy could see an eerie glow within them that he did not exactly understand, it looked uncomfortably menacing. The dragon approached slowly, constantly staring at the boy with those eyes, which for some would be considered most frightening, never once leaving him.

The dragon finally loomed directly over Tecumseh and the boy felt vaguely uneasy, after all he had known the Piasa for but a small number of moons, and what if the tales about the Piasa told by his elders were true after all?

The dragon slowly leaned down; his maw began to open as he grew ever closer, he said apprehensively, "I feel that Billigana is in extreme danger, we must go to her at once!"

Tecumseh instantly felt both enormous relief and an acute protective rage, however in spite of the horrible wind he rose up to grapple his friend's neck and hold on with all that he was worth for the coming ride. "Why is she in danger, what is wrong," He asked.

"This I do not yet know my young friend," The Piasa answered. "But that she is in danger and needs us now; of this I am certain!"

"Go directly to her home as quickly as you can," Tecumseh shouted!

And they were off directly into the teeth of the storm, but no sooner were they in the air and then they realized that they were in fact encountering one of the infamous twister-storms, for it tossed the huge dragon back the way that he had come as if he were a feather. The fact that Tecumseh was able to hold on was nothing short of miraculous, and the dragon was forced to fly away from the village for a distance in order to avoid being swept up into the storm. He knew though, even with all of the power that he possessed as a dragon, that he was no match for the fury of mother-nature, and there was also the safety of his passenger he needed to consider.

They finally arrived back at the end of their circuitous route at the Nastazi village and it had taken them much longer than they would have liked where they quickly found their way through the darkness and remaining wind and rain to Billigana's longhouse. At first nothing seemed to be amiss, until they approached the front door and herd Billi's mother wailing; Sha'siang sat just inside of the door and was weeping a terribly pained cry.

"My Billigana is gone," She wailed. "They took her through her very wall."

As Tecumseh tried to comfort the hysterical woman the Piasa leaned over to the other side of the structure and saw that there was a large hole that had been cut open in the opposite side of the longhouse. He returned with only a few of his massive steps to tell Tecumseh, "It is very recently damaged; we may still be able to find her and get her back if we are to act quickly."

Tecumseh, as gently as he could, told Sha'siang to go back into the longhouse and wait, and that he would send Nanuma over to be with her, but that they must go to find his beloved Billi at once. She of course complied and blessed them both saying, "Please let no harm come to my baby!"

After a reassuring hug and a short stop at Nanuma's home Tecumseh and Granger were hot in pursuit of the deceitful Mayans that had taken his love, unfortunately they did not have any idea in which direction they might have gone and the storm had wiped out any chance of tracking that they may have had.

They first searched the riverbank where the canoes and the large transport rafts that the Mayan slaves had fabricated had been kept; naturally they were not there any longer. What instantly occurred to both of them was that the Mayans homeland was of coarse down-stream and that it made sense that they would of course head that way, even if it was obvious to anyone who may be tracking them, for as it was, the shape of the horrible storm was bowed and it continued to cover the river downstream for a continuing great distance.

This was most unfortunate for the boy and the dragon, yet they did not dwell on it. They both felt as though she was downstream so that is the direction that they traveled. They could see nothing through the rain clouds and knew that both sides of the great river were heavily forested and so they were careful not to go too great a distance.

Tecumseh informed the dragon, "I know of a place in the river where they will most likely have to stop and possibly have a very difficult time with the larger craft, the river does some very strange things at this point, some portion of it must proceed for a short distance underground as best I can judge. Right past this place the river gets very wide and powerful again. If we are to catch them, it will be there, for they would have had to stop there for a time at least on this wicked night!"

"Yes, I know of this place, it does in fact enter a huge and beautiful grotto that I will show you and your woman in time, but for now we must make haste," the dragon replied and they were off.

Nanuma held Sha'siang in her arms and began in an effort to assuage her horrid fears for the well being of her only daughter; she began to tell her of the encounter that she had with a Piasa when she was a very young girl. "The Piasa is not the terrible beast that so many say, you may believe that when I tell you because I knew one quite well for a short time when I was younger."

"Yes, I have heard of the fate of your young man friend when you were a young girl," Naomi said placing herself down beside the two so that she could also while comforting her friends quite frankly gain an amount of the same for herself. "It is the main cause of my fear and distrust of the monster that has become acquainted my mischievous son," she admitted.

Nanuma caressed Sha'siang ever tighter and told the two of them, "Do not fear what you do not understand my young ladies for things are not always as they seem. I know of the tales told by our people about how the Piasa; that he tricked my Tonnel and he was never seen again; but while he did lose his life and he was the victim of trickery, it was not at the hands of the Piasa."

Naomi stared deeply into her eyes and said, "We have been told by our forefathers that what they say is the truth, who is it that we are we to believe?"

"I would not presume to call your ancestors liars, no far from that, but I can only tell you what has happened to me and you can decide if they were perhaps misguided for yourselves," Nanuma began.

"It was many seasons ago, I was yet to finish my fifteenth year and my Tonnel was in the middle of his sixteenth; we were as your children, young and in love, and seemingly truly meant for each other. It was the end of a particularly harsh winter season and our village was very low on meats and so we had volunteered to go onto the frozen oxbow lake further to the north, the one just north of the chain of rocks in the great river, that one which we call Lake Genesee. We had really just wanted to be together and spend some time alone, but the chiefs gave us leave to go because they really needed the fish that they knew we could harvest there and felt confident in our abilities as ice fishers."

Nanuma allowed time for everyone to adjust and make certain that they were as comfortable as possible and continued, "We had pulled a sled along with us to bring back whatever we may have caught. It was also very comfortable for while we were waiting for the fish to bite! We had brought many warm skins and enough food and water for several days, even though we only planned on being gone until the evening. We had left our village at daybreak and had traveled as quickly as we could all morning, yet we still did not arrive until nearly midday. We stopped and left the sled on the shore and began to search the lake and appraise the thickness of the ice to choose the spot where we would fish.

The winter had been very cold, but the last couple of weeks had become unseasonably warm, so that the choice of locations on which we would set up our camp on the ice was most very important. We did not want the ice too thin to support us and our gear, yet we did not wish to chop through ice that was too thick. Finally we located a spot that we chose as the perfect location and we had set up our camp and began to chip a hole in the ice with the stone tipped ice picking spear that we had brought along with us; it was very heavy and was doing a fine job of eating a hole in the ice; yet it also created a loud, deep vibration that seemed to resonate throughout the entire lake.

We continued for longer than we had estimated that it would take, as the ice had been thicker than we had supposed; but just as we broke through to the frigid water on the other side of the ice, we heard a deep unusual grumble unlike anything that we had ever heard. It seemed to be coming from underneath the ice, and growing ever closer. Suddenly the ice just the other side of where we had put the sled began to groan and bulge up. We were shocked and terrified when suddenly it cracked and burst upwards, followed by a huge green beast that looked very much like the Piasa that Tecumseh has found, the only difference being that ours was green instead of brown and not nearly as large."

Both Naomi and Sha'siang held their mouths agape with excitement as Nanuma continued the recital of her story, "The dragon reared nearly full length out of the water and it was more than the ice that we had been standing on could stand. We heard the continuation of thunderous cracking noises before we could see the splits in the ice that quickly surrounded first our sled and then us and as we watched our sled and our entire amount of supplies slid into the frigid waters of the lake, we grabbed for one another and prepared to be swept into the frozen waters as well. That was when something even more surprising began to happen. Firstly, our sled floated in the water and while that in and of itself should not have been very surprising as it was loaded with skins and bound foodstuffs that would tend to make it float anyway, it almost instantly began to make its way to the shore side of the open water back onto solid ice once again. We watched this happen as we now began to slide on the broken pieces of ice into the frigid water; we thought that we would surely be doomed until something even stranger began to happen. The huge creature instantly began to beat it's wings furiously as it leapt into the air above the broken ice, as it gained the air and actually began to fly right at us it grabbed both of us just as we were about to slip fully into the water. The gentleness with which the giant claws grabbed us and rescued us from a horrible fate was beyond belief, as he tucked us under his massive belly and gently delivered us to the shore and with us deposited there safely he returned and pushed our sled over the ice back to where he had placed us on the shore.

At first it was rather awkward, as we could not really communicate with him at this time, but we did try to express our thanks as best we could and he grunted and made sounds as if he were trying to speak to us also, though we did not understand anything it said at this time we did realize one thing; he had saved our lives intentionally and meant us no harm."

By this time her listeners were enthralled with the story and urged her to continue and as she got up to begin to prepare them a hot brewed drink from the herb leaves that all Nastazi women had great knowledge of; she continued her spellbinding story.

"This is how we came to know our Piasa; he came out of nowhere and saved our lives and while in the beginning it was difficult not being able to speak with each other, but throughout the entire night we sat and attempted to communicate. He soon recited our names and shortly later was able to inform us that he was called Chartil. We could not master speaking to him as quickly, but somehow he deduced that we were trying to harvest fish from the lake and with a few grunts that sounded as though he was trying to tell us something he turned and dove deep into the lake. For quite a time he was gone and we began to think that perhaps we would see him no more when he suddenly burst forth from the water again with his cheeks bulging full of something. He made his way to where we were huddled around a freshly built fire and gently spit the contents of his mouth out near our sled. It was four of the largest fish that I had ever seen, two whiskerfish and two huge fish of some sort that I had never seen. They were far larger than anything that we would have been able to land on our own and we were very glad to have them and when we actually cleaned them at home, they were full of the most delicious eggs that you could ever imagine."

"He seemed to be trying to further communicate with us, but we did not fully understand him. We both felt however, a newfound and incredibly strong bond with this creature and knew that we would be seeing him again soon. We said our farewells for the moment and made our way back to the village where we were received as heroes. The strange new fish was very tasty with easily removed bones for the most part and those that were not as easily removed could be eaten along with the meat, as they were easily chewed. These two along with the huge whiskerfish after being smoked provided most of our people with food for nearly two moons, but to our surprise after we told our people about our benefactor there were few that did not warn us to be wary of the beast. They all said that the Piasa could not be trusted, although few had anything other than old tales that they had been told long ago, as none had actually ever seen the creature themselves. We struggled mightily with this dilemma, for our people warned us of the evil of this creature, yet we knew of and had experienced firsthand his inherent goodness. We both had a strangely perplexed feeling about the whole affair."

"Several days later something happened that somewhat increased the weird feelings that we, as very young people felt at times and were some at times were nearly overwhelmed by, as Tonnel found something during a swim in the great river that was just as strange, if not even more so than that being which we had experienced meeting at Lake Genesee."

"While swimming in a new spot in the river that had been created by unusually high water, Tonnel happened across what he at first thought was a beautifully smooth rock and because of this he struggled to free it from the mud and bring it to shore. This was no easy feat, as it was quite heavy and slippery, though after reaching shore and having the opportunity to clean it off, he was shocked to see what he had actually found. It was a carved human skull, exquisitely shaped and detailed. It was a far better work than he had ever seen with a sharpness and strange beauty that was unlike anything that he or I had yet seen in our young lives, but the most unusual thing about it was that it was totally clear and it seemed to have been shaped from one of the perfectly clear stones, either quartz or diamond, something very hard. This was what so astonished Tonnel, for he knew of no method by which his, or any other peoples that he was aware of had mastered that could carve such stones at all, and definitely not with such magnificent detail as this."

"He wrapped the crystal skull in his deerskin and brought it back to our village," Nanuma stated.

"Later that day he showed it to me and I was instantly gripped with a great and overbearing fear, for I felt there was something evil about the crystal skull, it seemed to have a life force of its own and it seemed to be waiting for the moment that it would be released to spread its own sort of malevolence into our world I felt. I told him on that very day to throw it back into the river that nothing good could come of it, but he said that I was just a frightened little girl and that he wanted to keep it and research its powers. He told me not to worry so much and took it to his home."

"In the days that followed the strange feeling that I had about the weird, mystical things that had been happening to us began to subside somewhat, as we actually began to see the Piasa on occasion and began to realize much more communication with him. We achieved this through secret encounters on distant lakes or places in the forest that our men did not hunt within, as we did not wish it known by our people that we were befriending the Piasa, for we knew how they felt about him, but we thought that we would be able to change their way of thinking in time, or so we initially believed."

"Our encounters with the Piasa took much of our time and turned out to be very rewarding, as not only were we able to begin to further communicate with the dragon, but also bring back quite a lot of large game to feed our people and explain our absence, things then seemed to be progressing very well. However although unnoticed for a while, when he took me home Tonnel would go home and study the crystal skull to try and learn of its ways and unfortunately, it did not take him long to begin to unlock some of the peculiar powers that it possessed which he could take advantage of."

"He came to get me one morning as excited as I had ever seen him and told me that the skull was capable of magic and that he had learned how to use it. He wanted to show me," Nanuma said.

"The thought of him showing me anything that the crystal skull could do truly terrified me and I told him no and reiterated my fears. However he kept telling me to trust him and that everything would be all right and so I finally caved in and agreed to watch him demonstrate the power of the crystal skull, even as frightened as I was feeling towards the monstrous thing."

"He took the skull from his room and we walked quite a way out into the forest into a thick area where nobody could bother us. We sat down in front of a small clearing where we had placed the skull on top of a mound where it was slightly elevated and he began. He seemed to go into some sort of half-sleep or trance and held onto my hand very tightly. That is when a strange vibration began to build as we sat quietly; it quickly increased and was accompanied by the strangest light that I have ever seen, it seemed to flicker, then blink brightly and we were suddenly in a horribly cold and empty place, although it seemed to go on forever and while it seemed to be entirely empty there was also the feeling that there were many, many souls trapped inside this lonely place with you, until with another blink of the strange light we were once again back in the clearing."

"I was shocked to the depths my spirit, I had never experienced anything at all like it before or since and still do not know how it could be possible. Then and there I could feel the terrible danger of the skull and knew then as I do now that it was absolutely evil, yet Tonnel tried to calm me and told me that he would master the use of this marvelous tool that he had been fortunate enough to have found. I begged him not to use it until he had learned more about it that I could feel the danger that lurked as yet untapped within it. After my pleading for most of the evening he agreed to study it further before using it again, he even listened to me about asking the dragon if he knew anything about it, after all the Piasa had been living for many of our lifetimes and could be seen to be very wise. Tonnel calmed me by telling me that he would speak with the dragon about the crystal skull and its powers before again using it."

"Nearly a moon passed, and in that time I barely saw Tonnel at all, and for this he made many excuses, blaming his mother and father saying that they were insisting that he help them at home and perform different time consuming tasks for them, however I knew that it was the crystal skull that was monopolizing his time, I was beside myself I did not know what to do, for when I asked him about it he just told me more of his fabrications designed to appease me, I saw though by now that he was obsessed and did not realize how much the lies he spoke hurt. I felt that I had no one to turn to, so I sought out the Piasa."

"I did not search for long, it was as if he knew that I was troubled and sought me out as I looked for him. He leaned out of a thicket of trees that used to line the base of the bluffs. He was not nearly as large as the Piasa that your daughter and Tecumseh have become acquainted with and hid from our people with far greater ease; "Nana," he called to me and let me see him clearly."

"I told him through a great veil of tears about our finding of the crystal skull and about Tonnel's unhealthy fascination with it. I continued telling him of when Tonnel had demonstrated the thing to me and of the evil and extreme cold that I could feel within the place where he took me."

Nanuma stared deeply at her two friends as she spoke and said unexpectedly, "He agreed fully!"

"We began immediately to search the places where we felt that we might find Tonnel. We knew that we must make him listen to reason, for his sake, and we feared even perhaps for our own."

"He could not be found in any of the places that were familiar to us, so we began to search more obscure locations. Riding on the dragons back was not only thrilling for me when I first took part in it, but it enabled us to cover a good deal of area in a very short time. We decided to go to the other side of the river. There were grottos there that were not known by most people, for the elders considered them to be dangerous, as they were rife with underground streams and said to be inhabited by demons. Our people told many terrifying stories about these caves and painted them with a very sinister aura and I thought to myself that this would be just what Tonnel desired. We arrived at the entrance to the one that Chartil deemed as most likely and easily flew right into the mouth of the cavern. Immediately could be seen the otherworldly light that I recognized at once as the light associated with the skull that I had seen just recently and so I jumped to the ground and we both carefully skirted along the narrow pathway near the edge of the wall to avoid plummeting into the deep, dark waters at the bottom of the chasm which guarded its entrance."

"We both warily made our way further inside until we could see Tonnel clearly. He sat with his back to us facing the Crystal Skull that he had elevated on a natural rock table in the far end of the cave. The cavern was filled with a strange mist and you could feel a weird type of power seething throughout the entire area. I called out to him, "Tonnel, please stop!" Nanuma sighed and continued her story.

"He did not even bother turning to look in my direction," she lamented.

I tried again, "Please my love, listen first to the Piasa, for he knows of these cursed talismans."

Tonnel finally turned and looked in our direction, only stating, "Leave me alone, for I am very close to mastering the magic of the skulls."

"My young friend," the Piasa said calmly. "Many of your kind have spent the better part of their lives trying to master the magic of the skulls, but were not able to even begin to understand the many complexities that they possess. Please let me be rid of it for you, believe me it is your only salvation!"

"No," Tonnel screamed, "I am so very close, do not trouble me!" With that cold exclamation he turned from us and went back to his efforts.

"We had no real chance of reaching him in time, as we would have to travel quite a long way in order to get across the dreadfully deep water barrier that was between us, but this is what we began to attempt in any case. As we began the transit we could see the mist in front of Tonnel start to swirl and then we could begin to see a shape forming within the cloud. It was a man, but he looked like no man from any tribe that I have ever seen, his skin had a strange copper-green hue and he had terrible sharp features. Long spiny looking ridges above his strangely slanted eyes, but what was really disturbing and terrifying about the man was that you could see that he was a being that enjoyed tormenting and doling out pain, for it showed quite obviously in the malevolence of his face."

"The horrid being looked as though he was trying to put some sort of spell on Tonnel and was most certainly manipulating exactly what my man was attempting to perform."

"Suddenly the being began to chant a group of words that were not at all recognizable to me and as he chanted them louder and louder and I could then see terror begin to fill my beloveds face. The chanting grew louder and louder until the sound of it wholly filled the room. Tonnel looked up, but could not tear his gaze away from the horrid being in the vision created by the crystal skull. The dragon saw this and in an attempt to save the young man that he had so recently bonded with, leapt across the fissure to try to break the hold that the vision had now achieved upon him."

"Everything then happened at once; the dragon flew through the air towards the crystal skull, as the vision in the cloud above the skull shrieked its chant to an eerie conclusion and at that same time Tonnel let loose a war cry the likes of which I had never heard from him before. During which the vibrations in the air reached a point that I thought would bring down the walls of the cave. The next instant there was a hideous flash, not of light, but of extreme and bitter - cold darkness as a huge tumult enveloped the entire cavern, with rocks and waters both flying in every direction with deadly force, somehow I remained unscathed in this total darkness and complete chaos that I feared would be the absolute end of me. Though after several moments the light returned, the wind subsided and I was sitting alone, so utterly alone in this horrible cave so very far from home, or so I thought."

"Across the cavern right where the crystal skull had been was a small, sinister looking lark-like bird suspended in the air. Its tiny, evil eyes looked right through me with a contented smile and then in a blink of that same strange light, it disappeared. I have never known what that could have been, Nanuma continued, "But I know from deep within my soul that it was pure evil that I wish to never see again!"

"You see, I have witnessed what a Piasa is really like and while I know there was evil there that day it was not from the dragon. The Piasa lost himself trying to save my Tonnel and probably in some way also saving me, though I do not really know how, I only suspect and I will not forget that I owe the Piasa, Chartil much more than just telling the truth about him and his kind," Nanuma finished.

Naomi and Sha'siang just sat continuing their tears, for the extraordinary feelings that they had been experiencing towards the Piasa had just been confirmed. The dragon had shown love towards a human and even sacrificed himself to attempt to save that one individual man. It was something that Nanuma would never forget and she knew that soon the Piasa Granger would change the way that many felt towards the dragon kind which so many of their people had feared for such a long a time.

~~~~~~~~~~~~~~~~~

Dragons have extremely good eyesight and under even severely adverse conditions can see within situations when most other beings would not stand a chance, yet even they have their limits. After several hours of flight downstream and yes also upstream for they could not discern any recognizable landmarks, they finally realized that nothing could be accomplished in this drenching torrential blackness and so decided to land as close to the strange bend in the great river for which they had searched as they could reckon in this pitch darkness and seek a place of shelter until the conditions improved. They landed on the same side of the river that Tecumseh's village lay on, but obviously leagues farther downstream. They could scarcely find room to land because of the dense forestation and the rising of the river water, but were finally fortunate enough to have happened across a small clearing at the water's edge that was not visible until they were just above where it lie. As they landed they saw that they had indeed been fortunate, for on the side of the clearing away from the river there was a small hill that had a thick stand of old and mighty trees that formed a natural canopy of sorts and offered a rather nice shelter from the wind and most, if not all of the torrential rain. They could rest themselves here and possibly even improve upon their plan that was now indistinct at best.

The human and dragon talked for a while, but could not find any recourse to improve upon their plan; as there was now so much was to be decided by chance. They were not really comfortable with this, but they were going to have to just trust in fate. However as the Piasa had told the young Indian lad, "The pure of heart create their own good fortune!"

The dragon could see the exhaustion in the boys face and demeanor, he comforted him with the covering protection of his massive wings and young Tecumseh slept a deep and much needed sleep.

Early the next morning Tecumseh was awakened with a start, it was just the Piasa gently trying to rouse him, but he was shocked that he had even slept with his love in such serious danger.

"Why did you allow me to sleep dragon," Tecumseh asked testily?

"We could have accomplished nothing my friend; we cannot overcome such ghastly weather as occurred last night," the dragon answered quietly.

"Yes, I suppose you are right," Tecumseh answered ruefully.

"Her captors could not have accomplished much either," said the dragon perceptively.

If only that would hold to be true!

The Mayans were a people who had enjoyed the good fortune to live in one of the richest habitats on all of "Mother Earth" though they did not always recognize the value of the blessings that it contained, as they were always trying to clear and to change it, for it was a vast, rich and dense jungle, they had although over the many years in fact mastered the harvesting and gathering of most all of its riches. Some of these were the meats, skins and oils that could be gathered from some of the incredible animals that were found only there and nowhere else; which included snakes that were longer than five men standing end to end with the girth of three men side by side. Living in their jungles there were giant sloths which stood taller than two men and had dagger-like claws half as long as a man's arm. They happened to be plant eaters, but when aroused to anger had been known to destroy entire villages and kill many people. In their rivers were the great swimming beasts that were said to be as large as this dragon. The Mayans even had in their jungles, spiders that were larger than a man's head, these they had even learned to capture alive in order to keep them fresh for later use as food. In short, they had learned to master many of the very formidable animals in this great forest of theirs, and so they had a great deal of experience in such matters.

With the possession of all of this experience they had a plan for the Piasa also; they had already observed that the dragon had feelings for the young Nastazi boy and girl; this is why they had taken the first step of their plan; they had captured the girl for she would be the bait that they would use in the trap to capture the boy as well. Once they had both of the Nastazi youths, they would be used as hostages in order to find the whereabouts of the dragons lair, for dragons always had one, after all this was not the first of these beasts that the Mayans had encountered. If all went well the dragon would have to show his lair and Oaxintaal, Hure'tan and company would return with riches undreamt of by their peers; additionally they would return with another breeding pair of slaves to add to all of the riches they were already returning with. Either way, they would kill the dragon; it was the only way that the beast could be dealt with in order for their plans to succeed they felt, for after they had taken what they would from its lair, it could only have become a growing problem. They had developed the knowledge and the weapons over the many generations of their people's existence to deal with the largest and most deadly of the world's creatures and they had brought these with them; weapons that had already been proven, the most formidable being the huge crossbows that they had so quickly deployed in the battle with the attackers of the Nastazi village, they were expert with the great weapons and could load, aim and fire them with an almost supernatural efficiency.

These had already been seen, but it was the weapons that had not been shown that would be so much more dangerous to a dragon for they had also an unbelievable level of expertise with long range arrows and darts that they had treated with a deadly poison made from rare orchids and skins of rare frogs and such that were found only deep in the magnificent jungle which they called home.

They dealt with large prey on a regular basis and did not feel challenged in any way by this Piasa as it was called, especially with the ambush that they had planned, it would either agree to show them its lair and prolong the inevitable or die instantly and furnish them a wonderful trophy and a pair of new breeder-slaves, either was acceptable to the Mayan villains; in either case, their riches and fame have already grown immensely upon their arrival back in their homeland!

They had chosen the place of the ambush well for they had stopped before the rain had become too very bad in this area. They had chosen a location on the opposite side of the river where the terrain was much more undulating. They were in the closed end of a glade of thick underbrush that was protected on three sides by steep hills and the only real entry was to come in from the river side, and then proceed up the dale. This would expose the dragon and his young cohort to a cross-fire from three of the remarkable crossbows and untold number of poisoned arrows and darts. They had built a cage and placed it atop a mound at the end of the dell that they would occupy, in this cage they would place their young Nastazi girl as the bait for all to see.

While they planned for the Piasa and young Nastazi warrior after the trap was prepared to Oaxintaal's satisfaction Hure'Tan began to stare lecherously at fair Billigana and as he took her into the area where she was to be held captive he continuously helped himself to overly familiar touches, uninvited and truly unwanted squeezes of her private parts that Billi could do nothing to stop save yell at him and suffer the punishment that he chose to impose upon her in reply. They had her thoroughly bound hand and foot; she was barely clothed and totally at their mercy. "Please let Tecumseh and the Piasa find me," She thought to herself for she knew that they would now be in the process of searching for her once they had discovered that she was missing, she concentrated for all that she was worth in attempting to contact the Piasa and her love by picturing them within her mind.

Oaxintaal saw Hure'Tan and his lewd interest in the immature Nastazi female. He only chuckled and said, "You have always had a taste for the young pink meat. You must keep yourself under control for now, my lustful friend. There will be plenty of time after we have finished her would be saviors for all of us to do as we will with the child. I admit, I will want to teach her to be of service to me for a time also, but for now we must remain vigilant for her rescuers; as they could arrive at any time. When the rain begins to slacken put her back into the cage, but for now give her some water and something to keep her nourished, we do not want her to become too slender now do we."

"No, we do not want that," Hure'Tan chuckled. "In fact I will have the slaves give her a little something that will begin to plump her up in the right places." He said as he leered at her and roughly and threw some skins on her as he dragged her towards the cage, squeezing her hindquarters and other private places as every opportunity presented itself.

As they climbed the small hill to the spot where the cage had been placed and left the cover of the trees the rain began to pelt both of them mercilessly. Billi turned and faced the malicious Mayan and told him sternly, "My Tecumseh will make you and your obnoxious rogues pay for what you have done; you underestimate my man and you will feel the power of his wrath."

For this defiance, she got backhanded quite hard and thrown into the cage. As one of the slave girls arrived with some of their rolled hand held foodstuffs that their race was known for, Billigana could see the empathy in her face, for she had obviously suffered at the hands of this one as well. As she accepted the food and whispered thanks Hure'Tan growled, "I will enjoy killing the boy in front of you so that you can learn the importance of obedience and I will show him such pain that he will gladly offer you just for me to kill him to end his torment. After we have dealt with the beast, I will turn my attention back to you and turn you into my own personal plaything; that is until you grow too old for my desires of course." He walked back down the way that they had come laughing the most sinister laugh that Billi had ever heard.

She shivered, not only from the cold rain, but what if this ugly man was to become right? What would she do if Tecumseh and Granger did not find her? She saw the hopelessness in the slave's eyes, she could not go on living as this horrid mans sex-slave or without her beloved Tecumseh. If she was not rescued she would have to kill herself; there was no other way. She sat down in the pouring rain locked inside this stout wooden cage far from her home and cried a long and futile cry of desperation, for she was beginning to feel that there was indeed no hope. Although at this time her salvation was now much closer than she knew, but right now the poor child had no way of knowing.

The young Nastazi girl had been trying for some time to reach the dragon and her man with the little understood and fairly new link of their minds that the life-saving event at their first meeting had created, she was trying but just did not yet understand exactly how it worked and to this point had been unable to achieve contact. However, when her emotion changed and she began her deeply troubled and emotional sobbing something happened within the perception of both man and dragon. They both immediately knew that Billi was not only in trouble, but now had a very good idea just exactly where she was located.

They dove into the ever-deepening rain and crossed the river flying directly to the area and very quickly, so they covered a good distance of ground in a very short time. When they grew close, they slowed and flew as close to the ground as they could, for they definitely expected an ambush. The problem was to extricate Billigana from the Mayans clutches without falling prey to what they knew the villains had to have planned.

A short distance from where they knew that Billi was being kept they landed on the ground very close to the riverbank.

Tecumseh offered a plan, "Granger, my great and wise Piasa friend, this next part of our exploit is something that one of your great stature cannot negotiate because of obvious physical complications." He then produced a rope from around his waist that he tied to the one that already encircled his huge friend's neck. It then reached nearly the length of the dragon's tail or in flight would be able to hang down a good distance so that the young man could grab it and use it to mount the dragon without the Piasa having to land.

Dragon and man understood each other instantly.

"I will creep into their camp and locate Billi, it may not be easy, but trust me, I will find her. That is when I will need a distraction."

"I do not like this, my young friend," Granger scowled. "You will be in the middle of one of the most ruthless troupes of warriors that I have ever seen, it will not be safe at all, you could easily be killed."

"This is something that I must risk my friend for she is my true love and I must save her," Tecumseh argued. "Besides, they will be looking for you. With the right amount of distraction, they will not even know that I have been in their camp, until they see that their prisoner is gone."

"What is it that you have in mind," The Piasa asked?

"Well, do you remember before the attack on my village when my father was killed," Tecumseh began?

"Yes," Granger answered. "The black rocks, you want me to breath fire into their camp!"

"Perhaps not into their camp, that would be too close," Tecumseh said with a devilish smile. "But perhaps around it, we will make them wonder just who can bring fire from out of rain, no! This plan is beginning to sound as though it may have merit," the dragon said, "What more?"

Tecumseh elaborated, "Make it seem at first that their little gorge is surrounded with fire, but next try coming closer to the top peaks away from the valley for they will be expecting you to approach from the river and their weapons are very fearsome, they could do great harm even to you. We must deceive these Mayans for we cannot over power them."

"In this situation I agree," the dragon acknowledged.

"When you are close to the top of the ridge you must make it appear that you are advancing towards them, but be careful to stay behind the hills. The crossbows that they have are very deadly, but in the beginning they should be aimed away from you towards the river. As you distract them towards the hills at the other end of the valley, I will make my way into the camp from the river. It will not take me long to effect the release of my love, of that I am certain.

When I have her, I will quickly find someplace that is as safe as possible and then I will summon you. Just remember to stay out of reach of those terrible crossbows and remember to protect your eyes; the Mayans are most accomplished archers and have deadly poisons in their possession.

"And you remember that it would take only a small nick of your soft human skin from one of the arrows that they have dipped in their poisons to cause your untimely end," the Piasa stated selflessly.

After this short moment of mutual affection they looked at each other with agreement that could be seen in both of their faces, and the acknowledgement that they had an important job to do!

"Good luck," Tecumseh wished his powerful friend.

"Be careful," the Piasa added.

With that they both took the steps towards the actions to save their dearly loved Billigana.

The Piasa had longer to fly this time to find the black rocks, but when the need arose he could travel through the air with great speed and though it was a far greater distance on this occasion, he made it in only a few extra minutes. Once there he gave the appearance that he was in fact feasting on the wretched looking shiny black rocks and once he had his fill he began the trip back to the other side of the river as quickly as he could.

Meanwhile, his partner was sneaking into the small boxed valley as quietly with all of the stealth which he could muster and his luck was still holding in that the rain continued to fall pretty heavily, although you could feel that it was beginning to lighten and so he knew that he had to hurry.

Billi was as miserable as she had ever felt, she could feel nothing from either Tecumseh or the Piasa and for all that she was aware, they might never find her, they may even be dead for all that she knew. That imagined possibility was nearly unbearable; she had been shivering for quite a while now just sitting in the cold blanketing rain, but now it seemed to be growing much worse. She felt as though she would not last much longer anyway and that she should perhaps just let go and expire.

Suddenly she felt something hit her shoulder, perhaps a small rock or twig, it was nothing. Then it happened again, she raised her eyes to see what it was.

Tecumseh had been attempting to be as silent as possible and this took even more time, time that he did not feel he possessed. He came across the first sentry not very far from the river and easily outflanked him towards the middle of the dell. However, in so doing he had come to where the cover was much sparser and he felt that the rain was lightening far too much for his needs and so he tried to arch around back behind the first guard that he had passed to regain the woods; that is when he saw the next group. They numbered four men at arms all holding long spears and wearing bows hanging across their shoulders with quivers full of arrows upon their backs. They did not look at all amused with the task of standing guard out here in the rain while the others had the sanctuary of the huge trees. What made it so painful is that he could now see a cage upon a mound not far off behind the soldiers and it looked as though his love was tumbled down in a lump on the floor. No telling if she was injured or even alive. He would have to do something about these four, quickly and quietly!

He saw all around him on the ground the wonderful round river rocks that he had used for fun and hunting for all of his boyhood days. Now, as he was becoming a man and growing into that warrior he had always trained to be they were about to turn into a formidable weapon.

He thought for a moment about the task at hand. Killing or rendering four warriors senseless, while not inconceivable would probably take a good deal of luck. No, in this instance he felt that some misdirection would be more appropriate. He tossed two of the stones over the heads of his opponents into the deeper part of the woods, where they fell one after the other very quickly and achieved exactly what he had wanted, they sounded just like quick, muffled footsteps.

One of the four immediately looked up the others all caught his attention and were aroused to attentiveness themselves.

His ploy appeared to be working, Tecumseh carefully let fly two more stones and they landed in even thicker brush somewhat further away and the effect could not have been better. This time the sound seemed as though it was made by someone attempting to be as quiet as possible.

The first to notice signed to the others to encircle the point where the sound had just come from and as all great warriors did, they immediately began to close for the kill. This took all of them off a good distance from Tecumseh, for the moment anyway and he quickly took advantage of his good fortune. He swept around in the opposite direction in order to put as much distance as he possibly could between himself and the four warriors. Being very quiet and careful not to expose himself in any direction he approached to within a short distance from the cage that held his love. He did not dare arouse her captors and so he took advantage of his trusty river rocks again, this time he chose them much smaller and began to lightly toss them at her shoulder and back.

The first few tries had no effect; he worried what they could have done to his precious Billi though he persisted; perhaps she was asleep or even drugged. He continued his attempts as his anxiety continuously increased. After striking her for what he felt was more than enough times to gain her attention and the panic in him was about to reach his breaking point, she raised her head and looked out towards him; their eyes caught one another instantly. She was so happy and relieved; she had known that her Tecumseh would find her. He was so glad that she was not harmed. Their eyes burned together towards each other as if in a caressing of souls.

Tecumseh raised his finger to his lips for her silence and she of coarse obeyed, she knew that her man would be able to save her from this awful plight in which she had found herself; she waited intently.

Tecumseh tried to remember all that his father had taught him about stealth and "the quiet walk of the warrior" as he gained access to the cage that held his woman. He reached the door only to find it locked with a devise such as he had never seen before, it was a strange stone puzzle box type artifact that looped around the wooden bars effectively locking them into place and keeping him from opening the door. His dread began to really rise now, as the rain began to really decrease. He thought quickly and once again his river rocks came forward to his rescue, he quickly searched around to find one that was the right shape; although this would have been far easier closer to the river he increased his vigilance and he finally found the right stone.

Just then he heard the four disgruntled soldiers coming back from the empty pursuit that they had just been falsely persuaded to take part in and they were aching for a fight, the rain had nearly stopped and Tecumseh would have to make a good deal of noise to open this cage it appeared. The situation had gotten very bad, where was the Piasa, he could really use his help right now he thought.

Then Tecumseh heard behind him, what must have been the main party of the Mayans coming down from the cover of the trees and noisily heading in this direction. They sounded absolutely giddy and why not, everything had been going according to their plan.

Granger, or as he is known today, the Piasa was nearly back to where he had left the adolescent Nastazi prince when he began to sense that all was not right with his young charge. He could feel the turmoil that his friend was experiencing and knew that something must be done soon to salvage the situation. He increased his speed as much as he dare.

Billi could see her captors working their way back down the trail from under the protection of the trees and coming in their direction. She whispered, "Tecumseh, the Mayans return!"

"Yes, my love," He answered quietly. "I have been trying to use all of the time that I can, in order for our plan to come to fruition, but it seems as though my partner is somehow delayed. We will have to succeed at this on our own; be ready to move when I give the sign as our only chance is to escape down to the river." He raised the large wedge shaped river rock that he had found and brought it down with tremendous force.

With a raucous crack the lock was split off of the bars of the cage and Billi dropped into Tecumseh's waiting arms. A quick, affectionate squeeze was all that they had the time for and they bolted into the woods behind the cage. The four angry warriors were right behind them in hot pursuit and Oaxintaal, Hure'Tan and the rest of the Mayan party closed in from the further behind.

The juvenile Nastazi's were very quick and agile in the woods, but unfortunately could not keep ahead of the trained adult warriors that now pursued them, it seemed to be only a matter of time until they would be captured and have to endure the kind of death that the Mayans had promised them just a short time ago. The situation looked incredibly desperate for the young Nastazi couple.

Suddenly the woods in front of them seemed to erupt into flames, stopping Billi in her tracks. "No, keep running," Tecumseh urged! "Run towards the river, this is the plan," as he gave her a vigorous shove.

At the same time fires seemed to be erupting all around them; Oaxintaal screamed, "The monster is upon us, man the weapons, turn the great crossbows upon him, aim the poison darts at his eyes." The Mayan commander seemed to relish in the untold amounts of death that were at his command.

While the Mayans attempted bring their great weapons to bear again, more fires alighted all around them until it seemed they were totally encircled. This was very upsetting to the Mayans, though they tried not to show it; as they knew that the ground was fully saturated with water, they were mightily unnerved by this as they were now surrounded by growing fires and still no sign of the Piasa could be seen, yet they feared knew that only he could have caused this growing turmoil with which they found they were now surrounded.

Billi and Tecumseh continued to run, but after a short pause the four maddened warriors continued also; they had in fact gained sight of the two Nastazi youths and had raised their spears to take aim to skewer their prey when an ominous dark shape descended from out of the dark clouds. As they looked upwards the shape defined itself and grew closer at an incredibly fast pace; the dragon then landed menacingly between the Mayan warriors and the Nastazi couple under his protection.

The Piasa turned and looked at the two, then stared at Tecumseh saying forcefully, "Stick to the plan!" Then he turned back around to face his attackers.

The four Mayans at first thought of waiting for reinforcements when they saw the dragon standing so majestically before them for in the land from whence they had come they had seen many large and impressive beasts of all sorts; great huge snakes that devoured men whole, the mighty spotted and black cats that some even worshipped, even gigantic birds that owned a wingspan longer than two men, yes they had seen wondrous and imposing creatures, they had even seen what they thought had been this type of beast at a distance, but nothing had prepared them for what was standing before them now.

Standing imposingly before them was a creature that they had heard of for all of their lives in legends. He was larger than any creature that they had ever seen; seven to eight spear lengths in height, hunched over in a really menacing stance with his wings fully spread as if about to either take flight or perhaps cause a hurricane-like wind to descend upon them. He stared at them with a loathing malevolence that was unmistakably based in the desire to cause great suffering and death; also there were still thin wisps of thick, black smoke exiting from his nostrils and the hideous, dagger-toothed cavernous maw. What now stood before them terrified them like nothing that they had ever seen, but being the highly trained and well stationed Mayan warriors that they were, they controlled their fears and attacked in any case.

Acting as one, due no doubt to their years of intensive training, they all let their razor sharp Atlatl javelins fly within no more than one second of each another and they whistled through the air with an unexpectedly high velocity.

The Piasa reacted quickly; he stayed standing upright and tensed for the hit, yet at the same time he gave a mighty stroke of his enormous wings. This instant turbulence had immediate effect on the spears; two flew harmlessly over the dragon and the other two that had been thrown much truer unfortunately hit right where they had been intended; they whizzed the last short distance through the air and slammed directly into the massive chest of the Piasa, where they splintered into a cascade of wooden splinters and fell harmlessly to the ground.

This was what really let the Mayans see the hopelessness of their situation and the years of training and bravery that they had felt just moments ago was now all but gone. They turned and ran for their lives as a monster worse than they had ever imagined leaned towards them with obvious ill intent.

Still they showed great resolve, or perhaps it was the well earned dread of their leaders Oaxintaal and Hure'Tan whom they had witnessed kill fellow warriors for alleged cowardice or disobedience. In any case they turned, once again held their ground and began to nock up the poison arrows in their powerful bows. Behind them the rest of the Mayan force struggled to finish the re-aiming of the giant crossbows that they intended for the demise of the Piasa.

Time seemed to slow down, as the dragon tensed for what they thought would surely be the jump towards them for his attack, the massive crossbows aimed at the dragon were finally ready to fire. The tension in the air was thick and palpable, and then it all seemed to happen. The great crossbows cracked powerfully with the release of the gigantic bolts that they threw, the dragon leapt, not ahead in attack, but straight up with the Nastazi youngsters tied into the rope upon his back and powerful wing thrusts that enabled them to climb rapidly into the cloud-filled sky. Though the sky around where they had just been was filled with the arrows from the Mayan archers, they had instantly risen straight up into safety; but with one more pass back towards the gigantic crossbows for a parting gift of a fireball for each.

After making one last wide, soaring, slow turn keeping quite the ways out of range of the Mayans, but just within enough distance to see that the marauders were in fact heading back the way that they had come, they began the trip back towards their village in the bountiful bottoms of the great river. They were once again together, safe and did not expect to see the Mayan expedition that had been so loathsome and cruel to them again anytime ever again.

It would be the beginning of a wonderful, prosperous and peaceful time for the Nastazi. They would now be able to mourn their losses, and rebuild their lives. It was also the time that the people would come to know of the goodness of the Piasa, a time in which they would learn the truth to the rumors that they had learned about this wonderful mystical being.

As Billi and Tecumseh watched the Mayans disappear behind them with a profound feeling of relief filling their hearts and their close friend, the mighty Piasa Granger the Brown stirred the air with quiet strokes of his powerful wings and they covered the distance back to their village in a remarkably short time. Even so, by the time that they arrived back home the dragon had to land very carefully, as both of his passengers had fallen into a deep slumber enabled by the extreme security and accompanying exhaustion that they both now felt. The dragon knelt down as he landed and carefully slid the two down his neck to the soft ground just outside of the village. This slight jostling was all that it took to awaken them in the most pleasant of ways and they stood up and got their bearings to great relief; for they were once again home!

~~~~~~~~~~~~~~~~~

Nanuma walked out of the brush at almost the same instant that they landed, her eyes and the dragons locked in a mutually respectful gaze and her face glowed with a warm, knowing smile. "I felt that you would not fail," She told them. "The loving bond that you feel for one another is palpable and strong, the growth of such in the whole of our kind would be most beneficial for all."

Billigana and Tecumseh gathered themselves for the walk to Billi's home; the exhaustion obvious in their strained adolescent faces. They both looked up at the dragon that had become such a dear friend and asked nearly in unison, "Will we see you in the morning?"

"Yes," The Piasa assured them both, "You will see me tomorrow morning and any time afterward that you desire for we are bonded; our lives are joined for the mutual benefit of all. We will begin in the morning the teachings that I would bestow upon you and your kind for I feel that there is to come a time when your kind will decide the fate of our world and all who dwell here, myself included. It is important that I warn you about the traps and pitfalls that your kind has succumbed to over the ages and of the importance of loyalty, faith and most of all, this thing that you have revealed to me called love."

He evaluated once again his two young adventurers, and gave them a nudge towards their homes and the rest that they needed. Tecumseh scratched him behind the ears where he liked and Billi turned and wrapped her arms around his immense neck and gave him an affectionate hug and they were off for a night of much needed rest; the tremendous rain had promoted new growth everywhere around their village and they were overwhelmed with the comforting feeling of being home.

Nanuma stayed and conversed deeply with the Piasa, as she wanted to get better acquainted with the creature that was so like the one that she had been involved with much earlier in her life so many years ago; that she had indeed such wonderfully fond memories of.

As they both got comfortable and settled to chat, she could feel the warmth and gentleness that seemed to radiate from the very core of his being; this was directly contrary to his fierce and menacing looking appearance. He had already proven the great kindness that he was capable of and though they did not yet know it he was soon to bestow even more profound kindnesses upon her people.

She could not help but continuing to gaze deeply into his eyes, for these eyes seemed to captivate her in some unknown and gratifying way, and then she spoke, "I have known your kind before."

"Yes," Spoke the Piasa, "I remember."

"But I have not ever before seen you," she stated as a matter of fact.

"No, but I remember in any case. You befriended a green that I had become acquainted with over the seasons," the dragon continued. "You knew him as Chartil. As I remember, he was good to have on the hunt and most wise in the avoidance of the blacks."

"Blacks," she questioned?

"Yes, they are the members of my kind that have done most of the terrible things that have been blamed on us throughout time. They are the Black Dragons, pure evil with a great power and an evil, most potent magic. Not something that anyone wants to be around, myself included, though luckily now they have become quite rare or perhaps have even disappeared all together, for I have not seen one in many seasons.

Nanuma continued to dig for information from her new companion she asked, "Why do you bother with us? What have you to gain?"

"I do not exactly know why it started, but as I have stated, I know that there is coming a time when your kind will decide the fate of our world. I know not when it is, or how it will transpire, but I do know that some day it will happen and I want you to be as prepared as you can possibly be, for I know that if you humans can make the correct choices then you will save my world and home. I have been here for many ages and have experienced much of what our world has to offer and so I would teach you what I can and learn from you of the special qualities that you possess if I may.

"What could we possibly teach one so ancient as you," she asked?

"Well, though I know much about the natural world, places like the realm and even some of the hideous machines that you humans are capable of creating and plan on teaching and warning you to avoid the dreadful things that I have discovered you should like to avoid within this world. My kind knows little about what you humans call loyalty, trust or especially love. These are parts of life that have escaped my kind for eternity and I believe that I should make an effort to learn of from you. Our lives, although much simpler have proven to be pitifully empty in comparison to what I perceive yours to be and while we have for many seasons felt that your actions and strange, what you call emotions are frivolous and a waste of time I am now beginning to realize that this is not at all actually true, and so I want to experience what I may of the fullness and richness of the type of life that most of you humans seem to possess."

"Yes friend, I can call you friend can I not," She queried?

"I would find it an honor to be considered your friend," answered the Piasa.

"And I would be honored to be included in your teachings," Nanuma humbly affirmed.

"So began what was to become one of the most important of the human / Piasa relationships that had been known to date as the wise Nanuma would soon offer the insight and patience that was to enable her people to become closer to the dragon-kind than had ever been accomplished in their history. We achieved so much together that I Granger or the Piasa as my human friends knew me; had reached a point to where I believed that they might actually be the answer that I was searching for. They became so in tune with nature and so aware of the repercussions that could occur from the changes that they caused, I felt that we would all finally be safe in the wonderful, natural embrace of our "Mother Earth" but alas, at this time another twist of fate was to intervene and all did not occur as I predicted that it would be."

After several days of much needed rest Billigana, Tecumseh and Nanuma called the brown dragon to meet with them and consult with the remaining village elders, this is when they began to devise a plan that would teach their people and inspire them to listen to and learn from the Piasa; being much rewarded by the benefits that they would receive.

Tecumseh asked his wise old friend, "As you say that there is so much to learn, how will you keep them focused enough to learn it all?"

"Well, needless to say," Counseled the dragon, "I will need as much help as I can get, but I believe that the real answer is that I will provide the spark that will make all of you want to learn as much as can be learned about our wonderful home. I believe that we can, if we cooperate awaken a hunger for knowledge that will be the actual key to the salvation of us all."

"Where shall we start," Nanuma asked?

"I will attempt to seize every ones interest quickly later today for I will show them a method that will enable you to achieve flight, just as the birds or my kind do. The cloth that I have brought you can be easily reproduced and I will show you the skills and tools that you will need to be able to achieve this, for I am aware of how much that you humans covet flight," Granger continued solemnly. "Along with these skills, come responsibilities, the fireboxes in the riding baskets can spread uncontrollable fires, or your sudden appearance in a new location can cause widespread panic or even stampedes of the huge heard animals of the plains. These are things that you must be responsible for and as one of your tasks you must learn to embrace responsibility for your actions, for in the final analysis this is the only action that can truly save you and even myself from the trials that are to come."

"We are a noble people, Granger and we will take your teachings to heart, you can depend on that," Nanuma stated as she stared deeply into the all-seeing eyes of the Piasa.

She spoke the truth, for a dragon knows how to recognize these things in all beings.

Billi wanted to start as soon as possible and she was full of questions, "When can we gather the fibers for that wondrous cloth? Can you teach us to build the tool to make it today? What will the men build the baskets from? Can we gather everyone that is to take part now?

She truly shined with a child's exuberance, which in this old dragon's eye is just exactly what she was, an animated and enthusiastic patron of the wonderful blessing of life in this bountiful land of plenty, living with good kind people that give her a spiritual strength along with the sweetness and innocence that accompanies most all the young. I knew that these two would be the trusted humans that could mainly communicate my dire warnings to the rest of their kind.

And so it began, I first taught the women how to spin the fibers from the pods of the white puffy plant that luckily grew in many areas of their home region into what you now call thread. This and the next step, that I believe that you now call weaving I had to tell them verbally, as my claws are much better suited for hunting than the types of labors that mankind is able to accomplish, however, we succeeded in short order. Nanuma was instantly the leader in this task and within days seemed as though she had done it for all of her life, which in fact as far as the weaving part, she had. She was also a splendid teacher and taught a small army of the young women to make the slender thread to use in the weaving of the cloth.

Tecumseh, wishing to be greatly involved in the undertaking was not left behind; he assembled a group of very energetic young men to braid the needed ropes and construct the large holding baskets that would be needed to attach underneath the bags which were to carry them into flight. It even became something of a good-natured race between the two groups to beat each other in the completions of their parts of the apparatuses. When they had completed the first one I was proud to teach them the proper way to align the baskets so that the flames of the hot fires did not touch the highly flammable cloth and only the superheated air could make its way into the bag, inflating it and lifting it above every ones heads. Upon first seeing this the Nastazi were astounded, having never seen anything of this sort before and most of them wanted to go aloft in the large bulbous looking contrivance, yet they all looked to the Piasa to choose the first crew and no one was surprised when the choice was Nanuma, Billigana and Tecumseh; for after all they had spearheaded the efforts to complete the project; also they all knew that work would continue on the others until they had a good number of them and everyone would soon have their chance to fly as promised.

Things were beginning to become very good in the village again, it was good to belong to the Nastazi peoples, their future was looking better by the minute.

With this wonderful sense of elation over forty of the Nastazi people readied the "bag of hot wind" as it was quickly becoming known and they had the crew of three climb aboard, first Billigana followed by Nanuma and Tecumseh. They would be the first of their people to fly as I stated, other than Billi and Tecumseh's flights with this Piasa of course. As the bag reached its full capacity and was becoming harder and harder to keep secured to the ground by the many people that held the ropes the realization struck Tecumseh; however would they steer this thing?

Just as he was about to verbalize his question to the Piasa and they met each other's gaze, whoosh the people released the ropes and the "bag of hot wind" leapt into the air. The three occupants were taken somewhat by surprise and even though they had thought to be very willing and ready each experienced a moment of extreme trepidation; with this Tecumseh could now see the Piasa's delighted chuckle.

The fear was quickly replaced by wonder as the bag gained altitude and in just a few moments they had climbed enough to enable them to survey nearly all of the lands that they had grown up in; that is when the realization hit them of what an amazingly beautiful day it was and how the bag helped them to more fully appreciate as simple a fact as that. As the bag continued to rise and the cheers of their friends began to fade Nanuma was the first to notice that the dragon had begun to follow them up, flying around them in great, lazy circles he was soon at around the same altitude as the first time flyers. He ventured in more closely and spoke, "The bags are not entirely steerable, but you can achieve some control by taking it higher or lower as at different heights the winds travel in different directions. That is the reason that I had your helpers put the large stones in the bottom of the basket that you are standing within. Also, the hotter that you burn the small fire in the embers pot above your heads, the more hot air will go into the bag giving you more height, of course that will use your fuel more quickly and you will observe that it already will be used quickly enough.

Remember, no hot air and the bag comes back down to the ground, this can leave you stranded in some unwanted situations that you must be very wary about."

As the Piasa finished speaking he began to climb higher, evidently researching the wind currents that he had just spoken of.

As they rose in the bag above the clouds and they could see before them the wondrous panorama of the beautifully blessed land they called home and even beyond, Tecumseh fed the firebox and they continued to rise. They could see their great river snaking off to the south disappearing over the horizon, with its many tributaries joining along the way, surrounding it on both sides were great stands of forest were as of yet untouched by humans and off to the west they beheld fantastic oceans of prairie grass parted only by the trails of the immense herds of the huge wooly beasts that traversed the plains in such great numbers at this time. In the very great distance, towards the end of view, you could see a storm on the horizon that seemed to be making its way in this direction, though its arrival would probably not occur today. Nanuma, Billi and Tecumseh were in breathless awe of this amazing land that they had the good fortune to hold stewardship for their short lives; they smiled at one another a look of harmonious contentment and gazed out over the land in silent reverence.

Suddenly the bag and it's three occupants rocked violently as they began to quickly change directions, what the Piasa had told them about was proving to be true, they now seemed to be headed more towards the North and East nearly the opposite direction that they had been traveling, they were now moving away from the storm they had viewed on the horizon and were now headed towards the mountains they had been shown by the dragon in the first flight they had taken as his passengers; a flight that now seemed to be so very long ago. Their speed was increasing also and they immediately began to become anxious about the return to their village. Just then, appearing from below, surprising them as if he had just appeared out of nowhere the dragon was there with his soothing words, "Do not fret; I will be your wind guide until you have learned the skills for yourselves and if we cannot find favorable winds do not let it bother you, for I will pull you to where you need to go. Just take in the beauty and majesty of this moment and learn how very fortunate that you really are to live in this wondrous place in such a special time and know that I will keep you safe and return you to your home."

And so it was with the ancient brown dragon and the people that he had chosen, not only that first trip but for nearly all of the days that followed in this season and for the many seasons that followed in his relationship with Tecumseh and Billigana.

The dragon also grew very close to Nanuma, as she had known of the kind nature of the Piasa for most of her life and she was enamored with the concept of learning all that this ancient and wondrous being could teach her. She was always the one that would volunteer to gather the people as students for one of his sessions in "teachings of Mother Earth" and always was quite helpful when language problems developed. Overall Granger found her to be a joy and she was definitely one of his favorite humans that he had ever encountered, but unfortunately her fate was not entwined with the Piasa's for as long as his other two previously mentioned friends Billi and Tecumseh.

But for now they all grew very close and enjoyed a mutually beneficial relationship, full of growth and understanding for the next few seasons. The Nastazi loved the benefits that they received from the Piasa and saw the wisdom in what he was teaching them and for his part, the dragon felt that the people were listening and learning well and did indeed show much promise in respecting their place in the world and preserving the balance in the nature that they had now learned they were such a large part of. Things had gone really well for quite some time, but then something that seemed most innocent at the time changed everything.

During one of their many outings in the baskets of hot wind they had the fortune, good, bad or perhaps just a part of fate; to come across a young girl who appeared to be about Billi's age, or perhaps just several years her senior, that was being pursued by what looked like a small force of warriors with a most terrible intent. This day the Piasa had not accompanied them, as they had become quite proficient at the control of the bags and upon seeing the pursuit of the helpless young girl Tecumseh immediately responded, for he knew what he must do. He felt in his heart that he had acquired the expertise to bring the bag down in a position close enough to rescue the young girl. He could only imagine why they were attempting to capture her, but he knew that it could not be good. Besides, they ran in the same direction as the wind which would only make it just that much easier for him and so with Billigana's encouragement he lowered the basket to not only within the range of the pursuers bowshot, but low enough to the point where he was able to lean out of the basket with the help of a rope and scooped her up into his arms and back to the inside of the basket and safety in one swinging motion. Though she was covered in perspiration and beside herself with apparent fear it seemed that she was indeed overcome with emotion and ever so grateful; but the pretty young lady was being much more thankful than Billi was comfortable with seeing.

The gorgeous young girl held Tecumseh tightly and showered him with grateful caresses and kisses, which the young, spoken-for warrior devotedly fended off in deference to his own lovely Billigana who sat puzzling for the moment about the arrow straight route that the young girl had run in her attempted escape. Finally Billi looked back to see her trusted love behaving honorably and was somewhat tickled at the reaction of the young girl whom they had rescued. At that moment the girl seemed to realize the situation she controlled her advances, bowing her head and speaking apologetically.

She spoke in a language that they both surprisingly understood, for it was not unlike the speech of the Mayans, their former trading partners and now possible adversaries, perhaps even a newer dialect. She said, "Thank you so much for saving me from those brutes; they have been plaguing these woods for several moons now and I am certain that you have saved me from a painful life of slavery or even worse. Thank you again I am indebted to you; I owe you my life." She then turned to Billi and added, "I did not understand at first, but can see now that he is your man and I meant no offense."

"I am not offended," Billi stated politely, as she gazed at Tecumseh.

"You were very lucky," said Tecumseh! "Let us take you back to our village where you will be safe for now."

Both of the girls nodded in agreement as Tecumseh tended to the steering of the craft, but neither Tecumseh nor Billigana noticed at the time the strange, yet subtle smirk that could be seen on their new guests face, or the small container tied to her back that contained a strange little bird.

So began the bizarre and sometimes tumultuous relationship that was to touch the lives of all that lived in this great heartland of prosperity and good life in the land that has been known as the "Mississippi Bottoms."

In the days that followed Billigana and Nanuma made every attempt to make their new friend comfortable in the village; they began as soon as the bag hit the ground, discovering the young ladies name to be Angelii. Though she told them her name she seemed very agitated and somewhat fearful still and spoke but a few words. Her new hosts soon noticed this and while they were very careful not to be overly forceful, they did attempt to win over her trust in several subtle ways.

First they tried to achieve some amount of privacy by taking her to Nanuma's long house as soon as Tecumseh began to go about the task of securing the bag. This is when she first began to ask a few questions, "Tecumseh goes to take care of the bag of hot wind?" She asked, and quickly added, "Is he coming back?"

Nanuma was the first to see the look in her eyes; at the time she thought it to be fear and perhaps it was, but not entirely.

Nanuma attempted to sooth her in a way that has been practiced by human women for many ages; she escorted her to the far end of the dwelling and offered her a beautiful crushed buckskin outfit to wear. Angelii's eyes brightened at once and her demeanor changed from that of a frightened woman in a strange land to that of one that could be accepted as a friend and would in turn offer to be a friend to you. With what appeared to be the deepest of conviction she gave thanks all around, for now there had gathered several more of Nanuma's young apprentices all trying to placate and calm their new arrival, and she asked for a place to change.

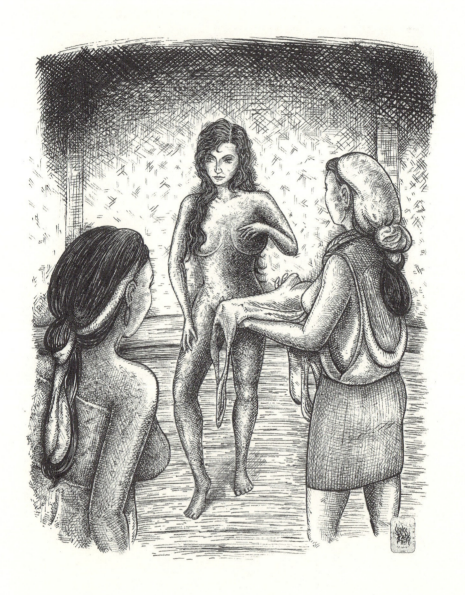

When told by Billi that they would still need to find her some personal quarters and was about to ask her if she wanted to go to Nanuma's room, they were all shocked at the quickness with which she was out of the long baggy and hanging sarong that she had been wearing in favor of the smaller, nicer fitting garment that Nanuma had provided. However for just a few moments Angelii stood there fully nude as if posing with an unusually strange smile on her face. She had a very beautiful body, strong athletic looking legs that were very tan, up to a pert and muscular bottom and slender waist that led up to a pair of very voluptuous, round and full breasts that would turn any mans eye. Then a long lithe and tan neck held a head that was stunningly beautiful with full inviting lips a small button nose, deep emotion-filled aqua eyes that a man (or a woman) could get readily lost in and a thick mane of wavy auburn hair. She looked around the room giving everyone that strange smile and then got dressed much more slowly than was really appropriate.

Once she was dressed it was like a spell had been cast off the people in the room, for everybody began to talk at once offering Angelii quarters, things to eat, and options of what they could endeavor to now do, in all it was a strange spat of chaos that seemed to come from out of nowhere.

Billi though had seen something that Angelii had been very careful to lay down when she had disrobed so quickly before, it was a squat brown tube that looked as if it were meant to carry some of her belongings except that it had holes at both ends that appeared to be breathing holes.

Billi pointed it out on the bench where Angelii had so carefully laid it and asked, "What do you bring that needs to breathe Angelii?"

"Oh, that," she responded. "That is my companion of many years, I call him Elgin. This means, "find my way" in my tongue I was near training him when those brutes tried to capture me.

As she talked she opened the small canister and released the smallest of this type of bird that Billigana or Nanuma had ever seen. The Nastazi knew this bird as Chickwa, in modern times I believe that it is called "Meadow Lark," but never the less it was incredibly small for its type, no larger than a small finch, with extreme luminosity in his light and dark brown colors, but far more intelligent looking than any normal

Chickwa, with piercing red eyes and an ominous ability to speak; before all present it called Angelii by name.

All were taken aback, especially when the bird appeared to talk to the new stranger in some unrecognizable language and she seemed to understand perfectly. The bird appeared to be well taken care of and Angelii comforted him and put him back into the case promising to procure him a home as soon as she could.

Nanuma then spoke, "We knew not that you had brought a pet with you or we would offer what we could, go Tanya," she said as she pointed towards the door, "and bring one of the cages that the lads keep for the yard birds and make our guests welcome.'

Angelii said quickly, "No, there is no need of a cage, as I said we are companions. He needs but a perch next to where I would sleep."

Just as she said that there came a knock at the door and Tecumseh called delightedly, "Have I given you long enough to finish your exchanging of clothing and gossip; may I enter?"

"Hold for a moment Tecumseh," Nanuma said. "We have a flying pet loose that may escape."

Fire flashed momentarily in Angelii's eyes as she restated forcefully, "I told you, he is a companion, not a pet and there is no need of restraint he will stay by me always!"

Nanuma, Billi and the other three girls Tanya, Mandi and Coi were shocked at Angelii's anger over what appeared to be nothing more than a pet and it was obvious in their reaction. Angelii noticed their shock and was quick to appease as she said in an apologetic (and manipulative) tone, "I am sorry for being so protective but my little Elgin and I have been together since I was a small girl; forgive me if I was overzealous in my protection of him."

As they all told her of not needing to apologize, as Tecumseh walked through the door. "Did I miss something," he asked as he gazed around the room at the faces trying to judge what was amiss?

"No, no, just a small misunderstanding over my bird friend," Angelii hurriedly answered. "Everyone has been wonderful, it was entirely my fault!" Then she gazed longingly into Elgin's eyes for entirely too long, but then looked away as the object of the misunderstanding flew up and perched upon her beautiful shoulder, that was now beautifully exposed due to her change in clothing.

Her beauty was not lost on Tecumseh and he caught himself after a moment gazing deeply just taking it in. His woman Billigana was very beautiful too although most who compared the two would probably say that Angelii was much more voluptuous and more blessed in the female areas of anatomy. Tecumseh though caught himself and with the will of knowing that there exists a deeper beauty that is not seen but felt averted his gaze and looked into Billi's relieved eyes smiling a welcoming smile and reached to embrace her.

But the moment had not escaped Nanuma, as there was not ever much that usually did!

She asked curiously, "Speaking of companions, I have not seen the Piasa all day, where has he gone off to?"

Billi looked at Tecumseh knowingly as Tecumseh said, "He has gone to feed. He does not like to feed around the village for he is concerned that it may frighten some of the people, however he will be back in a few days as he likes to enjoy a short nap afterwards."

What luck, Angelii thought; I am already acquiring information about the magical beast without even trying, this may be even easier than we suspected. No one even noticed the short glance exchanged between Angelii and the small bird known as Elgin.

Tecumseh decided to try and do something about the mild uneasiness that he could feel in the room and said, "Why do we not have a wonderful welcome dinner for our new guests, I know that we have fresh whiskerfish in the pens, a new harvest from the gardens and I hear nothing but the best news about Nanuma's new apprentice cooks."

"That sounds wonderful," Nanuma said! "Let us show our new guests how we can treat our friends and make them feel welcome." Saying this she approached Angelii, put her arm around her waist and walked her out the door towards the central longhouse where all of the feasts usually took place, separating her quite a ways from Tecumseh; this was appreciated by Billigana even if it did not obviously show.

The word got around the village about the new guests; actually the talk was mostly about the beautiful young woman and not so much about the bird as of yet. Few could know that both were going to have such an impact on the coming events and it would later be said by many that they were in fact the only cause of the great tragedy that would later become the downfall of the fair Nastazi people, but we are coming to that.

In any case many people, especially young men gathered at the longhouse even before the feast was to begin and before long many of the village's people had filled the gathering house until it had become overly crowded. After engaging many of the young men in very stimulating, at least for them, conversation Angelii approached Nanuma and asked if it would be too much trouble to be shown her quarters, that she had experienced a very trying day and would like to get some rest.

Nanuma responded in an almost motherly fashion, "Of course not, I will take you to your quarters myself immediately."

"Thank You," was all that Angelii said and actually did look very tired.

"Would you like for me to send you a small plate of food," Nanuma asked pleasantly?

"I just want to rest," Angelii said, almost in a snap, but she quickly caught herself and added, "I am sorry I am just very tired, I will eat in the morning."

Nanuma did not question Angelii's choice although she did find it rather impolite in so much as this entire feast was being held in her honor, she just quietly said, "Follow me and I will show you your quarters."

They walked the remainder of the way to the longhouse which happened to be located right next to Nanuma's in silence. They arrived and entered an already lighted dwelling with a small fire going in the fireplace and Nanuma walked her to the end of it where a nice sized, separated room with a light door for privacy awaited her and Nanuma stated, "This will be your room and I hope that it is to your liking." The mature Nastazi woman could not explain it, but she felt that something was amiss with their fair young guest and it gave her an apprehensive and suspicious feeling.

"Thank you so much for your care and understanding," Angelii said; as she flashed her warm smile that had made so many at different times feel a false state of comfort and belief in her. Nanuma however got the strange, uneasy feeling that this warm bright smile was being used as a weapon; and for now she would play along until she could learn what this girl really had in mind.

Words of the Piasa

Closing the door behind her Angelii burst into a sinister laugh that seemed to be shared in some strange way by her small yet aged-looking avian friend; though he was the size of an ordinary meadowlark, he did possess some rather unique qualities not existing in other birds or even any other beings for that matter; for one he had eyes that seemed to see right through you with an unmistakable glare of pure malevolence. Angelii found a space on a small shelf as her laughter began to fade and pointed to it as a possible place of rest for Elgin. He immediately took his place and began to settle in on the shelf when she began to speak coherently once again.

"These people are all so gullible; their nobility that they seem to value so is their biggest weakness. Seizing power here will be far easier than we ever thought possible," Angelii was giddy with confidence in her coming subterfuge.

Elgin on the other hand seemed to be somewhat more pragmatic.

"Angelii, there are steps that we must have taken in order to set our plan into action," The shrewd old bird offered. "We must not lose sight of these steps and our goals."

"As always, you are right my wise old friend," Angelii purred. "Let us set the priorities of our goals once again."

They settled in and began planning; Elgin offering first. "To begin with it is of the utmost importance that you meet their king so that you may begin the use of your "special" wiles upon him."

"Yes," She said. "I just hope that he is not too old, the younger ones that still have some life left in their loins are so much easier to sway and far more enjoyable too," She said as she gave the bird a wry smile.

"Yes, I suppose that you are entitled to your pleasures too," The old bird said as he looked disgustedly at the floor. "Secondly we must begin to convince these people of your healing powers, the more magical that they believe you to be, the easier our tasks will be to perform."

"And lastly," Angelii interjected quickly, "The longer that they are exposed, the more widespread their dependence will become. When they have succeeded in planting the amount that we have decreed, they can come back to this village in time to finish off any who are not under our command. We must guide our agents to this area and instruct them to secretly begin the widespread planting of the Kaav plants into this area in order that we may introduce them to it and its glorious effects," they both looked at one another and again shared a noxious looking grin.

"We must begin with their king," Elgin stressed.

"Tomorrow I will arrange it," Angelii whispered in her most remorseless tone. She then dropped her new clothing to the floor, stared strangely yet longingly at the small, primordial bird and said, "Let us bed."

She slipped gracefully under the soft bed skins provided and was soon followed underneath them by Elgin. She drew up the cover and lay silently for a while, though after just a few minutes the shapes under the skins began to change and the room was filled with a strange purring noise that suggested an intense satisfaction from the bird, the woman or most likely both.

~~~~~~~~~~~~~~~~~

The dinner that was supposed to be in honor of their new guest still continued even though it had now assumed a more subdued theme, and she was still the main topic of interest and conversation. Nanuma returned to find Billigana and Tecumseh retelling the story of her rescue from the band of savages and of all of the good fortune that had befallen her on that day. As she heard what was being said she just mentioned, "Good fortune or a well conceived plan?"

"What do you mean," Billigana asked?

"I am not certain," Nanuma said thoughtfully. "But something is not as it seems with our pretty new friend."

"She has had a very trying day I think that she is just not herself right now," Billi defended their newfound guest. "Let her get some rest and she will once again regain her calm."

"Yes," Tecumseh interjected! "She was nearly captured by that band of brutes that would surely have enslaved and raped her, maybe even worse. Let us forgive her some questionable manners on such a day as this and let her begin fresh again tomorrow morning."

"As you wish my friends," Nanuma said. "It is probably only the suspicious mind of an old woman; at least I hope that it is. Where is the Piasa anyway, I would like him to meet our new friends."

Tecumseh tried in vain to comfort his friend by saying. "Granger will return within the next couple of days and he will meet them and assuage your concerns, you will see."

Nanuma whispered, "That is what I would like to see, especially involving my concerns about that strange little bird with the sinister, piercing eyes."

Tecumseh embraced her to give her as much comfort as he could and was soon joined by Billi.

Several minutes later they were dining on fresh grilled whiskerfish and a wonderful greens salad discussing the introduction of the new guests to their king when to their surprise the king and his entourage walked into the hall.

Trevlon Tankan came from a very old family of Nastazi that had been known for generations for their spiritual pursuits. They had many medicine men and priests within their lineage throughout many generations and it was for this reason that he had been asked to become the Nastazi king after their former king Kharzin Atol had been killed in the attack by the Pawnee several seasons ago. He was a humble man, especially for one of such knowledge and prowess in battle. It was said that he had dispatched more than a dozen Pawnee during the attack that killed king Atol and this without any weapon at all in the beginning! He had been very gracious and attempted to defer to several others including Tecumseh's friend Noran's father, Himreal Gerez.

Himreal also enjoyed a great deal of renown as a warrior, having achieved well-known expertise as one of the greatest archers of all the Nastazi. Though he wanted to help his people in any way that he could he supported the choice of Trevlon Tankan for king because of what he felt was his closeness and understanding of Wakan Tanka or the god spirit as was exhibited by the continued generations of his family that had been devoted to the spirit world, as was shown by his family name. All of the Nastazi approved of his appointment and also loved their new leader for his obvious devotion to his people and the wise decisions that he had already made for the benefit of those people. They not only approved of him, but gave him unwavering support as he had been responsible in the last two seasons for the discovery of a new and very rich source of obsidian that they could use not only in the making of jewelry and weapons, but also a major factor of trade as it was very highly prized by all to whom they offered it. He also had devised a new method for extracting the healing oils from the Echina root, using the power of the sun, for these and numerous other reasons their new king could not have been any more well loved by his people; therein lay the problem.

When a leader is so well liked as the Nastazi king, he enjoyed a great deal of influence over his subjects and it did not take long for Angelii recognize this and begin to find a way to take advantage of this power.

The next morning; after the feast that had been held in her honor; one which she did not attend. The Nastazi's new guest Angelii Zarteen was introduced to the people of the village. While the king and some of his associates were absent due to his responsibilities to his people, his wife the queen was there in his place. Most of the rest of the village were there also and all were very anxious to meet the person that everyone had been speaking so much about, and to see this strange bird that had been rumored to have the ability to speak!

Queen Melanie Takan was also a very beautiful woman; although she was possibly not as outwardly striking as Angelii she would be found by any person to be very attractive. When she and Angelii met face to face there were a few moments of silent evaluation of one another, possibly adversarial appraisal or possibly even some sort of mutual admiration, in any case it did not go unnoticed by Nanuma; something obviously seemed to have passed between the two.

Melanie Takan was no stranger to the ways of what would today be known as politics, she had been raised in a family that could have been called affluent and had seen her share of what it took to lead and influence people. She well knew that the real power was held by popularity; and she also knew that it could be a fleeting and fickle condition. She had been sent by her husband, the king to meet with this new stranger and to make her as comfortable as possible, yet she also had a second task that was equally as, if not even more important; she was to learn as much as she could about their new guests.

This was a task that the queen was very comfortable with, as she had always been able to persuade most to do anything she had wished; she was rather spoiled in this aspect of life and used to getting her own way and experimenting with the situations in life that this sometimes created.

Queen Melanie, leaving her attendants behind, entered the dwelling, approached Angelii and introduced herself pleasantly, "I am Melanie Takan, queen of the Nastazi people. I have been sent by my husband King Trevlon Takan to officially greet you to our village, express our gladness that you were not harmed in the attack upon you yesterday and offer you our help in anything that you may need to become comfortable in our land or even assist you in getting back to your home if this is your wish." The queen made this offer with all of the grace and congeniality that she could possibly gather, giving it her utmost charm with all of the pleasantries which she could bring to bear.

The response shocked her incredibly; "While I appreciate what your hospitality and the timely appearance of Tecumseh and his young lady have done," Angelii snarled, not even mentioning Billigana by name. "The occasion when I Angelii Zarteen actually "needs" something given to her will never arrive."

"I intend no disrespect; we are just offering to open our doors and hearts to you so that you may feel more welcomed," Melanie said, feeling that she was not at all really certain that she meant it.

Angelii saw her opportunity and seized it, "I apologize if I seem aloof or unappreciative, but I am an honored medicine woman with my people and am so used to doing for others that I sometimes forget that sometimes others may want the opportunity to provide for me as well."

Angelii edged very close to her host and whispered again, "My apologies again and thank you for your warm offer," As she spoke, she laid her hand on Melanie's arm and gazed longingly into her eyes.

For a few moments Melanie was captivated as she gazed deeply into those beautiful deep aqua blue eyes, she then tried to shake it off saying, "No need to apologize, I was sent to make you as comfortable as possible and I intend to," But she was absolutely locked into her guests captivating gaze; then with a immense effort she managed to tear herself away.

Melanie seemed somewhat shaken, but tried to regain her composure, as she knew what a queen must do, as she turned around and began walking back to the door of the longhouse she said in a most accommodating tone, "Well, if you can imagine anything that would be in my power to grant, or will please you, all that will be necessary is that you send word, my girls will know where to find me. They will return shortly with some breakfast for you and your bird friend. Where has he gone to, anyway," the queen asked, not seeing the strange bird anywhere in the quarters, for the queen was young and was now growing uneasy with her new guest, even somewhat suspicious.

Angelii answered quickly, "He comes and goes as he pleases, but he will return soon enough." She had actually sent her avian friend to perform a few tasks that were actually the beginning of her plan she would soon apply to her new hosts, the main in the beginning of dealings with their large dragon friend.

Melanie once again offered gracefully, "Later this afternoon I will have time to show you more of our village and some of the surrounding lands, we may even have the good fortune to meet the Piasa. In any case, I will do all I can to please you, I am certain that you will enjoy my hospitality." She paused during her slow, sumptuous walk back to the door for one last almost lustful gaze.

"Yes, I have heard tale of this Piasa and I am looking forwards to the enjoyment of your hospitality," Angelii whispered wickedly.

They parted while exchanging surprisingly hungry, even amorous looks.

Melanie rejoined her companions and they could all see the peculiarity with which she had been affected, they could not exactly tell for certain what it was, but Melanie knew. She felt the heat of a new desire in her loins and even somewhat of a tremble in her normally sure step. She felt afraid that she would do whatever that beautiful stranger asked of her, and it was a new and alarming feeling.

She loved her husband and her people with all of her soul, but felt this love was now extremely threatened; she made a vow to be strong but grew very apprehensive and lonely as she made the return walk back to her husband and her home.

Dragons, being cold blooded have a very different appetite from most other beings. Most are strictly carnivores; however there are those that also enjoy many kinds of fish and even an occasional fruit or vegetable (If they can be found in sufficient quantities). The one fact that is always true with every dragon though, is that once they have reached the point of hunger, they experience a powerful and irresistible impulse to feed and express behavior that may be seen by some humans as frightening. For this reason the Piasa Granger always chose to leave for several days in order to slake his tremendous hunger, which could take as much food as Tecumseh's village would consume in a lunar cycle, then also to take his rest that he so relished after a good meal of several of the fat herd animals that roamed the grassy plains, west beyond the Nastazi village.

This hunt was beginning to be somewhat different than the many hunts that I had enjoyed for seasons as long as could be remembered. The beasts that I searched for had moved further west than I had ever had to travel to find them in the previous occasions, and then when I finally did find a herd, the shock of what I found began to bewilder me in but a few moments; for there were no young to be seen anywhere!

At the moment I felt a certain amount of remorse for the animals that I had grown so accustomed to over the ages. I hoped that it was not a serious problem, as I truly found them most delicious and knew that I was keeping their population healthy and strong by removing the slower animals from the breeding stock. I promised myself to try to find what it was that could be bothering them, I wondered if it could be another dragon or even some other even more voracious predator than myself?

I could see the entire herd flying at the height which I was, as they slowly galloped away when I approached and I did not see any young animals from this season anywhere within sight and so I settled for an adolescent that was not so mature that the meat had began to become tough.

Sailing over the ample countryside that lay beneath my outstretched wings, I was once again reminded of the wonder of my beautiful home world. Horizon to horizon stretched below me plush fields of green grass that nourished and provided homes for so many creatures and as I glided towards the now terrified bison youth I thought to myself of how the humans did not realize that they had nearly as much influence on this world as even the weather and nearly as much power, though they would possibly never come to terms with their power unless I could somehow get them to listen and realize its presence and potential.

The forefather's of these wonderful Nastazi people had begun to grasp the points that I would teach them, but were scattered far and wide from their land to the south and west of here in the beginnings of the great mountains by drought that had lasted many of their lifetimes.

I can only hope that there will be time for my teachings to take hold with these humans, for I believe that their time is running out; and I so want to do what it takes to save this wonderful world. The final dive ended with the young bison changing directions wildly in his attempts to escape, but inevitably succumbing to my outstretched, anxious talons.

I flew with my prey to a small grove of trees that I somehow felt an incredibly inviting attraction towards; so that I could leisurely enjoy my meal I settled comfortably into the shade and as is usually the case with the first animal it disappeared rather quickly, but I grew to like the grove and so after another short, yet successful hunt returned to it with my next bison. As I enjoyed my meal, I noticed a plant that was new to me and I had never seen before that was growing in great abundance throughout the entire grove. I thought that it appeared young and tender and so I decided that I would taste of it. The plant had an interesting bittersweet flavor, not so unlike its pale yellow-green appearance and very faint aroma. I decided that the plant was unique from most others and found that its pungent flavor was very tasty with the bison that I was in the midst of consuming. I decided that more should be discovered about this plant other than just its interesting flavor so as to make certain of its safety, though I continued to devour it in ever growing amounts; if only I had known how accurate that my assumption was!

After several more of the young bison and getting my fill of the interesting new plant that I had discovered I settled in for my customary nap, when I awoke I would be renewed, enriched and rested. I would make my way back to the Nastazi village and my wonderful new friends Tecumseh, Billigana, Nanuma and their families. They were understanding so much of what I was teaching them and had given me such cause for hope I was certain that we were about to break new ground in our relationship towards one another; unfortunately, I had no idea the dire effect that this new vegetation would have on me as I quickly became increasingly very tired.

Then, quite suddenly, the dragon slept!

~~~~~~~~~~~~~~~~~~~~~~~~~~

From its hidden spot in the branches, not so far away the evil little bird watched as the Piasa fell into a coma-like sleep; this had been his wish and he was now most fervently pleased.

The Blightlark observed for a short time more and then was off to other tasks.

~~~~~~~~~~~~~~~~~~~~~~~~~~

Back at the village Billi had managed to get her young man alone and to their favorite picnic spot at the horseshoe lake; this was no easy feat with all of the responsibilities that he had taken as his own since the attack and death of his father, the befriending of the Piasa and all of the requests for help in the teachings that Nanuma always needed and he was so quick to comply with. She was proud of all that he was doing for his people, yet she did not want to share him with yet another. Especially someone for whom she had so little trust and this would be the perfect time to speak to him about how she felt. They had spent the entire morning and early afternoon together here in their "favorite spot" swimming, eating fresh fruit and making love. They were still young for conceiving children, having not yet reached their fifteenth and seventeenth seasons and so Billi was careful to partake of the herb mixture that her aunt had taught her to make that blocked the formation of the eggs that would someday be impregnated by her loves seed, filling her with the gift of motherhood, though the time was quickly approaching when she would no longer block this blessing for in the spring she and Tecumseh planned on becoming man and wife with the nuptial ceremony that was her people's custom.

As they lay entwined in each other's arms Billi Looked up into Tecumseh's eyes and asked, "What do you think of our new guests?"

Tecumseh's eyes began a slight gleam, thinking that he detected a flash of jealousy in his loves demeanor, "Oh she is beautiful yes, but you need not worry. She could never touch me in the way that you can my love."

"That is very wonderful to know my love," Billi responded, "and know this I do. You and I were meant to be, of this I have always been certain," but she continued, "That is not what I mean. She is so mysterious; like she is keeping some secret from us that will do us great harm, and that little bird of hers really frightens me as it is no ordinary bird and I can feel that it is most evil."

"Fear not my love," Tecumseh responded. "It is just a talking bird. We have seen it's like before when traders have their pets perform; do not let it frighten you."

"Well it does frighten me and greatly," Billigana exclaimed as she cuddled even more tightly into his embrace.

Tecumseh squeezed her affectionately and assured her, "I will always be here to protect you; of this you can be certain!"

Billigana thanked him for being her love, their embraces became more amorous and before long they were entwined in passionate lovemaking once again.

Back in the village Nanuma had instructed several of her apprentices to keep an eye on their new guest Angelii; she had even told them to tell her if and when they saw the strange bird again. Nanuma busied herself giving instructions to her students as to how to spin the thread and then how to weave the cloth that they were making for an even larger hot air bag that they felt they would be able to control even more, it was to be triple the size of the others and be lined with many bags of sand to enable them to control the height that they would fly and guide at as well as could be done. Unfortunately, if the winds were just not cooperating you could still not travel in all directions and when this happened all that there was to do was bring it back to the ground and wait for favorable winds or walk back to the village, which was usually the case, fortunately this happened very rarely.

But, even though she tried to busy herself, Nanuma could not help but be preoccupied with the thought of just what the stranger among her people was really up to. Nanuma felt that she had a concealed motive, and just knew that she had no good intents towards her people.

As the afternoon passed and the business of the village took care of itself she saw the day's events unfold. She witnessed King Trevlon Takan and his nubile young wife Melanie walking quickly back to their home, apparently in the very first instance that she had ever seen them having some sort of disagreement. They were so much in love, rather like

Tecumseh and Billigana that it seemed to be very out of place for them to have any kind of unease, but everyone experienced this sometimes, right!

Her students made real progress on the cloth and she was beginning to think that perhaps someday soon these balloons would surely fill the sky and be an incredible sight. She then witnessed Tecumseh escorting Billi back to her mother's house, a practice that would be ending soon, as she knew that the two planned on being wedded early in the next spring. She felt such love for those two and would do anything that she could to make them happy, yet she could not get past the feeling that this new intruder was going to threaten the happiness and well-being of all the Nastazi people and that they would not recognize her deceit, until it was far too late!

Nanuma's vigilance continued, as the sun grew low in the sky and the evening meal that was being prepared in the square was beginning to waft its pleasant aroma throughout this end of the village and this was starting to invite most of the people out into the square, but not Angelii, she was nowhere to be found!

Nanuma motioned to her trusted trainee Leona and she came as beckoned, "Take the initiative and go to our guests dwelling. See if she would join us for dinner, for she must still be in her room. I have seen her nowhere since last evening."

"As you wish," answered Leona.

She was joined by another of her comrades for what I gather to be mutual support as they approached the door there they began to feel a strange fear that they were want to be able to explain. Leona gave the door several loud taps, as was the custom, but they were unanswered. She made another attempt, this time even louder, still no one answered. She looked to Nanuma for direction and Nanuma motioned for her to enter the longhouse. She opened the door easily, as it was not locked in any way; she entered and scanned the interior of the longhouse. It had undergone a tremendous amount of change in the few days that their guest had occupied it. The usual soft forest colors of green, tan and light brown with which it had formerly been decorated with had been replaced with mostly black in different varied shades and dark deep cobalt blue. There was also what looked to be somewhat of a shrine that had been erected in the far end of the longhouse from the main door and in the middle of it was a sapphire the size of a man's head and it seemed to have a strange inner glow not seen in jewels normally. Fear now really took hold of the two adolescent Nastazi girls and they bolted from the dwelling. Nanuma was right outside and quickly asked them what had happened.

"The longhouse is empty Nanuma, and it has grown fearfully strange inside," Leona told her in a scared, quivering voice.

"Our guest is nowhere to be found," Nanuma exclaimed! "That is most strange; she has hardly seen anyone since her arrival three days ago, I must get to the bottom of this peculiar behavior."

At that same instant above the bluff east of the village deep into the forest Angelii sat in conference with what looked to be some of the same group of ruffians that had been pursuing her the day that she had been "rescued" and brought to this village by her new "friends." They spoke in strangely conspiratorial tones.

Angelii said, "Have your men redouble their efforts to get as much of the planting done as possible before this moon is over, we will need much Kaav ready for harvest in a very short time. There are many of these naïve Nastazi's to feed with our control."

One of the warriors that attended the meeting let slip an unfavorable remark, "We have been reduced from warriors to farmers."

Angelii sprang catlike into his face and told him, "You have not yet seen their warriors or weapons and they out number us one hundred to one. You will do battle in the way that I tell you, we will fight with our minds and we will win, and you will do as you are told, do you understand?"

He could only shake his head in disbelief at her physical ability and stammered, "Yes, of course my queen, as you say, now and always!"

"Good, if you will follow my plan dutifully you will be able to enjoy the fruits of a warrior without the bloodshed," she told them. "And if it is the bloodshed that interests you, well then once that we have them on their knees as a conquered people we can arrange that at our leisure, however it may please us."

Another of the men approached her from the side and told her, "We have gathered all of the able bodied warriors that we have, yet that is no more than twelve hundred and twenty, to plant the Kaav properly will take time and we have brought tens of thousands of seeds."

"Time is what we do not have," Angelii stressed. "Forsake sleep, any free time until they are all planted. They must be planted correctly, keep them from the direct rays of the sun and place them where they will benefit from the morning mists, but do it quickly. Our plans depend upon this plant, so get it done!"

"It will be done as you command," was his fearful response.

"Have you arranged what I have told you of," Angelii asked remorselessly?

"Yes, that too will be done as soon as the opportunity presents itself," he answered obediently.

She spoke of an extra large amount of the refined Kaav plant being delivered to her for her initial widespread use that was to include the young queen!

~~~~~~~~~~~~~~~~~~

Several hours later as the sun just began to dip below the horizon Angelii and her small friend reentered the village as calmly as could be and walked towards the middle of the courtyard where the evening meal had just been served.

Nanuma was alerted by several of her girls and a young man that happened to be with them this night. She walked pointedly out to meet with Angelii and make another attempt at offering a friendly hand. She said, "You are just in time for a fresh cooked dinner. We had begun to wonder if you would make it back, as we had not seen you for the entire day."

Angelii had a ready response, "I did not mean for you to worry, I am quite often out and about before first light. I took the opportunity to do some exploring of your beautiful countryside. You have so much to offer here and have done so much with it. I just love the design of your village, especially the pyramids that seem to be everywhere, and the great one in the middle is breathtaking." She knew that some flattery of Nanuma's people would displace her mistrust for the moment for you see Angelii was a master at controlling the way that people would think.

"Yes, thank you. We consider ourselves a very progressive people," Nanuma said.

"You also seem to have deep roots in spirituality," Angelii toyed with her to try to bring out any information that she would unintentionally offer.

"Yes, we are also a very spiritual people," Nanuma said. "Yet some of what you see is defensive in nature, we have disguised most of it, but it is there." She stopped; realizing that she had already said too much.

"Yes, I have seen already how industrious and creative your people can be." Angelii flattered Nanuma's people, trying to continue the line of conversation, "Especially the bags of hot wind, they must be especially useful when it comes to warfare."

"We are not a warring people," Nanuma responded. "They were a recent gift of the Piasa."

"Yes, I have heard many great tales of this mighty being, yet I have never been in its presence." Angelii said coyly, only giving the appearance of half believing in the existence of such a creature.

"You will get your chance soon enough," Nanuma chuckled.

"That is good," Angelii halfheartedly decreed, "I want to meet this being."

"That bodes well," Nanuma murmured, "For I believe that your meeting of him would be a benefit for all."

Suddenly the strange little bird known as Elgin interrupted and broke the strange mood that had befallen everyone with the strange chattering of what sounded to Nanuma like words of a language that she did not know, possibly pre-Mayan or some such dialect thereof that she did not understand.

This bird was very strange looking, in that it looked much like some of the common lark that were so prevalent in this area, yet he was much smaller. No more than half of a hand in height and his markings were very different than any she had ever seen on any other local bird. They began as sharp lateral stripes going down the sides of his head and neck to the fronts of his wings and continuing all the way to the tips of his wings. This was as sharp and intense a brown as she had ever seen on anything and was an extreme contrast to the very light creamy beige that covered the rest of his body. At the peak of his crown of feathers atop his small head was one long and sharp-looking feather that stuck straight back nearly two lengths of his head giving him a sharp, dangerous look. But what really seized your attention were his hideous red eyes, they could look right through you and they bespoke of a great malevolence and death. Looking into the eyes of this strange little bird would chill even the bravest of souls. Nanuma ached for the return of their beloved Piasa for she felt that he would have the answers that she was seeking.

Angelii spoke back to the strange little bird in the same dialect and the little bird quickly flew off. She apologized for the interruption and said, "I seem to have upset Elgin, but he will return."

Nanuma asked, "I have not heard that language before, is it the tongue of your people?"

"Well, in a way it is. It was the ancient language that was spoken by my ancestors," Angelii responded.

"It has the sound of the Mayan tongue," Nanuma said.

"I find it interesting that you know of the Mayans," Angelii quipped.

"Yes, we have had dealings with them in the past," Nanuma told her, not elaborating on just how those dealings recently took place.

"No, my people are far more ancient than the Mayans, yet the language has changed over the millennia and the true form is spoken only by the priests and priestesses of my culture, the rest have simplified the language to a more common form," Angelii explained.

"Yet the little bird speaks it," Nanuma stated inquisitively.

"Oh, do not let Elgin's stature fool you, he is more than he seems and quite ancient," Angelii nearly bragged.

Nanuma had become anxious to find out more of this young woman's intent and had arranged for her to finally meet with the king. "I have a meeting scheduled for you to finally meet with our king, if you would like," she offered.

"Yes, I would like nothing more," the scheming Angelii seized at the opportunity.

"Good, I will take you to his ruling hall, it is not far," Nanuma stated.

"We will not offend him coming at this late hour," she asked with feigned demure?

"No, not on this night," Nanuma explained. "He has been very busy as of late and was gone all day, yet he did want to finally meet you in person."

"And what of the queen," Angelii asked strangely?

Words of the Piasa

"Of that I do not know," Nanuma answered. "When addressing his subjects in his hall he is usually accompanied only by his bodyguards and sometimes not even they accompany his highness, for he is a very formidable man and his hall is in the very heart of our city."

As they approached the hall at the base of the grand pyramid the stranger Angelii mumbled to herself barely audibly, "Formidable, yes perhaps."

They entered the tall doorway and walked down a well lit hallway that had obviously well tended torches spaced every six paces on either side of the corridor that shined with a polished floor and walls painted with stunning murals of the magnificent countryside in the area and the people and animals which occupied it, of the waterfalls and the spectacular chain of rocks that crossed the great river not far from here. Towards the end of the passage they met two very well armed warriors that were obviously clad in their best ceremonial garments though even as well garbed as they were their weapons commanded serious attention. Both carried large bejeweled daggers at their sides, with a short extremely opulently carven bow strapped to their backs and a vicious looking war-clubs resting in their grip that looked as though it was some extremely hard, hand carved wood, studded with pointed stone for the last third of the business end of it and on the very tip was a head of shiny black obsidian carved as an axe blade on one side with a lethal looking flat trident on the other. Both of these men looked as though they had trained their entire life to be a warrior, they were robust, attentive and muscular men that looked as though they were very loyal to the king and truth being said appeared obviously ready to die for their king.

Nanuma nodded to the guards and they let her enter immediately, for they were quite familiar with woman and her popularity with the king. The two women stepped into the interior room.

King Trevlon Takan sat in a plain large chair; where other kings might have a much more elaborate even ornately bejeweled throne. To him it was just the place where he would make decisions that he could to help guide his people and not a place of power, as many that occupied similar stations would proclaim.

Nanuma watched as Angelii looked around the room, she espied many more beautiful paintings and murals of the beauty that this land consisted of, the birds, the plants and trees, multitudes of the wondrous local wildlife. Then she saw in one corner something that really attracted her attention; a box full of the many types of jewels that she supposed this land possessed.

The king could see that they had caught her eye and said, "The jewels of our realm are unfortunately not as plentiful as they are beautiful and even their beauty pails when compared to yours," king Trevlon Takan began charmingly.

"I had heard of the king's stature and his prowess in battle, but I had not been warned of his charisma with the weaker sex," Angelii offered with most utmost demure.

Nanuma could see already that this was going to be a test of wills as they probed one another discreetly for as much as they could discover about the other and she wondered what help she could offer, what there may be that she could say or do to help.

Her unasked question was answered immediately.

The king quietly, yet firmly commanded, "My trusted guards, Nanuma, my close friend and advisor, please leave us for a while, for I would talk to our guest in private please."

Nanuma looked into the eyes of the king and he nodded confidently, the guards looked at one another, the king and his guest; though they thought that they had known their king far better, assumed that the king was about to perhaps enjoy one of the privileges that a king would take advantage of at times, though they did not really know his mind. They all three turned and left, just as they were about to exit the king commanded again, "Shut the door behind you," and then they were gone!

Angelii met the king's eyes with her sparkling smile and said, "I am honored."

"Oh and I am sorry to have put our meeting off for so long," the king replied. "They were wrong about your beauty; you are far lovelier than any has affirmed to me."

She acted as if she was shocked and flattered, but in truth she knew that her beauty was a tactic that she could readily use on this man, who was in fact as formidable looking as she had been told. His strong muscular arms looked as though they were just as accomplished at holding and loving a woman as she had heard that they were in doing battle with his foes. He was a full head taller than her and she was thought to be very tall by a woman's standards, he had broad shoulders and a flat stomach and his head was topped with a mop of wavy brown hair that was not near the dark black color of most of his companions, with the exception of the one whom had brought her here, Tecumseh who also shared the sandy brown and wavy hair of the king.

She stared deeply into his warm brown eyes that not only shined with an intelligence and fierceness of one who was born to lead, but also of a compassion and understanding that she knew that few men possessed. This man would not be easy to fool she thought to herself I may need to alter the way that I had planned on dealing with these people, at least concerning this one.

She began to explore the possibilities anyway, "Your queen is a very lucky woman," She started.

"As I am a very lucky man," the king retorted.

Angelii could sense the devotion in this man to his woman, she knew that this was the sort that would prove very hard to manipulate, but she must try to set the stage in any case.

"Yes, I have known what it is like to feel this way about another," Angelii slowly stated. "Unfortunately the one that I had felt so for is long missing and will probably not ever return" Angelii began her subterfuge.

"I am saddened to hear of your loss," King Trevlon Takan told her with heartfelt empathy.

"Perhaps I will one day feel the pleasure of his return, but until then I have attempted to busy myself with well-being of my people," she continued.

"Yes and how is it that you help your people so," the king responded inquisitively?

Angelii gazed deeply into his eyes with a strange passion that caught the king somewhat off guard; it was not a lustful or physical passion as might be expected from the sight of such a beauty, but what appeared to be a deep concern for well-being, her people's well-being, and especially his.

She said, "I am a healer, I can cure the ill and mend wounds, I have been bestowed a gift from our mother earth that I can help all of those in need of a healers touch."

As she was speaking, Angelii had slowly approached and worked her way until she was standing very close to the king.

He said quietly, "This is a wonderful gift to possess; you have the ability to help many." He told her, as he looked down at her, nearly losing himself in those deep, beautiful blue eyes.

"That is my blessing, the gratitude that I feel from the people that I help fulfills me in a way that nothing else ever has," she told him with the seeming utmost of conviction. She then began to lean upon him, pressing her breasts voluptuously upon his firmly muscled chest.

Somewhat surprised; yet rather pleased by the sensuous touch, the virile young king found himself at a loss for words for just a moment.

Angelii pressed her face into his muscular chest and began to slowly roll her face back and forth. "I am uniquely skilled in the arts of both healing and pleasing," she told him as she finally rested on her knees resting her head against his groin breathing very heavily.

His mind and heart finally regained control over his heated loins as he gently caressed her face and gently lifted her back to her feet saying, "I look forward to the benefits of your gifts and the good that they will bring to my people, yet though they are likely wondrous, they are not needed on this night."

"No, perhaps not on this night, but there may be another time," Angelii said with conviction, "When you have the need, but let me know."

The good and mighty king was confused, but his love for his wife Melanie was well known and solid, but there seemed to be something about this newcomer that was pure and good and magical he felt at this moment, momentarily confused by animal lust. All that he could manage saying was, "We shall see." These surprisingly were not the words of the type of man that he really was he thought, what had happened to the faith which he shared with his wife?

"Yes, we shall see," Angelii exclaimed bitterly! As she slowly walked away she said, "We have other ways in which we can help you king."

King Takan merely responded by the raising of his head and meeting her turned back glance.

"My companion Elgin is gifted in the finding of those jewels that you have seemingly been blessed to find in your land; you can believe me when I tell you that they are here," she quipped as she walked out the door, down the corridor and past Nanuma and the guards out into the night air.

As Angelii walked off into the night, the guards returned to their posts and Nanuma thought for a moment to check with the king, but then decided to let him be, lest he think her to be meddling. She did think, however that things could not have been as forthright as their king was used to, she certainly knew that their visitor was plotting something that was not going to bode well for her people, and this she could feel most certain of.

Back at Billi's longhouse, as Tecumseh finished walking her home, for this he would do each evening until they were wed and they would be able to spend their first moon cycle together in the marriage pyramid as was their people's custom. The pyramids of their people were unlike any found elsewhere; they had smooth stone inside in the hallways and great rooms and great wooden beams to buttress the roofs and entrances, yet the outsides were made of the rich earth and thick sod-grass that grew so heartily here in their homeland and stretching for what seemed forever upon the plains to the west. They were meant to be living mounds with the pyramid structure that was thought to be able to last for nearly all time and it seems that they have been quite successful as they are still found throughout the Midwest of our country even today.

It was said that the newly joined needed that time in order to blend with one another; though Billigana and Tecumseh did not feel that they needed this kind of help to forge their love, as they both knew in their hearts that they were meant for each other for all time; however they were really looking forward to the peaceful and most joyous time it would provide them being alone together.

Billi asked Tecumseh, "What of the girl that we rescued, Angelii? Do you think her forthright?"

"Of this I am not yet certain, my love as I have seen very little of her since we snatched her from the havoc that she had found herself involved within. Though what I hear from my mother and Nanuma is that she seems to be acting very strangely, distraught, or even hiding something. If those two feel that something is amiss, I can only believe that they are correct, but perhaps she just misses the friends and family that she has left behind," he conjectured?

"Or perhaps she has reasons unknown to us for being here," Billigana offered.

Tecumseh looked into his loves eyes and said patiently, but beginning to think that she may still possibly be feeling some jealousy in the way that Angelii had tried to thank him on the day of the rescue, "But we are the ones that brought her here; we saved her from a surely horrible fate."

Billi's eyes grew distant and she whispered quietly, "Or did we?"

He caressed her shoulders to gain her full attention and asked, "What do you mean, you were with me?"

"Remember back upon the day Tecumseh," she said. "The day had hardly any breeze at all; we floated that day at a leisurely pace at best, much of the time traveling in the same direction.

"What is it that you are trying to say," Tecumseh asked?

"Suppose that the entire chase was staged so that we would pick her up in a supposed rescue," she conjectured?

"I don't think so," he answered with a chuckle that was more forced than he had thought it should be.

"Wait; picture it for a moment," She explained. "The entire time that it took us to pick her up, did you see any of them gain on her at all?"

"No now that you mention it, but she was running for her life," Tecumseh stated.

"Yes, maybe," she continued. "But while she appears quite healthy, I was not really impressed with her running speed. She did not appear to cover enough ground; not close to the way that someone like Noran or one of his fleet of foot running comrades does and yet none of those brutes could gain on her at all?"

"Yes, that is curious," he admitted.

She explained further, "Not one time did they threaten her with bowshot, even when you lifted her into the basket, at which time I could see the whites of their eyes clearly. You could have easily hit somebody with your arrows at that range, yet they did not even attempt a shot, even when their prize was being taken away by someone else."

Tecumseh seemed to be deep in thought now and began to find

himself beginning to agree to a point, "You may have something here, this is very strange indeed."

"We must find out what it is that she really wants with us. We must help Nanuma in finding the truth," Billi said guardedly though there was no one there to hear."

"We must investigate in every possible way and I can only hope that we are not being too overly skeptical of one that is in pain and really needs our protection," Tecumseh said.

"If we are not right about this, at least we make the mistake with the protection of our people in mind," Billigana said finally, and with that and a long embrace Tecumseh and Billigana said good night and parted for the evening as per the customs of their people.

～～～～～～～～～～

During the night as the Nastazi slept, their Piasa did as well. The dragon however had been erroneously guided into succumbing into a far deeper sleep than humans were able to understand and it would become the source of great dismay for his Nastazi friends in the coming days.

Everyone slept except Angelii and her strange bird friend Elgin, they communicated in an eerie way that was understood by none save themselves and they seemed to derive an almost intimate pleasure from this fact. Nanuma seemed to be on to something; there was something about these two was very much out of the ordinary and it instilled a fear deep into one's very soul.

Those few that had shared the longhouse that housed their guests had long since fled that abode to eliminate the uneasy feeling that they had in sharing the structure with their guests; though it had done little to help!

The longhouse that contained the new beautiful woman guest and her weird little bird seemed to buzz with an unholy deep humming that no one but these two could find any comfort in.

～～～～～～～～～～

The next morning found many different activities were beginning in the village. Nanuma was teaching a large group of the younger women exactly how to make the fine cloth for the "bags of hot wind" that everybody in the village seemed to now having become preoccupied with while Tecumseh and Billi had once again joined together and were both going to the large horseshoe lake in the north where they would then separate for a short time to be with their different groups, hers was gathering a lush assortment of the wonderful berries that grew around the lake, especially on the north side of where the waterfalls were located. This was one of the places where Billi and Tecumseh had always loved to spend time together to them it was known as "Berry Falls" and was one of their favorite romantic meeting places.

While Billi's group made its way to Berry Falls, Tecumseh led his group to the place on the lake where the fishing canoes were always stored. He had been bestowed the honor of being known as the finest fisherman in the village somewhat unfairly; yet being quite good at locating and catching fish, thanks to his late father's years of teaching, he had accepted and now warmed to the tasks that were involved in holding this title. He was especially adept at finding the large whiskerfish that his people loved to feature so often at their community feasts, and so he showed his comrades where to search and they began to look in earnest for the huge fishes under logs, in under water caves and places of the sort; he even showed his comrades the art that his father had taught him of fishing with only your hand and arm by pushing it back into where the huge whiskerfish preferred to make their homes and although this method of catching them is not without its risks it is still even practiced today in many parts of the Midwest. (It is now known as Noodling.)

They busied themselves canoeing from place to place along the shallows of the lake that was actually closest to the great river that had obviously been the source of this large and fruitful lake at some point in the recent past, for it was no more than fifteen minutes walk due west and when the great floods occurred it was said to once again make this lake a part of the river. That had not happened in Tecumseh's lifetime, but both of his parents and all of the elders had seen it more than once and so warned the young ones of the possibility. The fact that Tecumseh's generation of peers did in fact pay great heed to this type of warning seemed to please the Piasa immensely. Tecumseh had noticed this and had wondered just why this was and meant to ask his friend about it.

As the morning began to grow longer they began to have success as suddenly, having traveled the furthest down the bank Tecumseh's good

Words of the Piasa

friend Noran let out a piercing cry of triumph as he disappeared into the shallow water near the shore, for several moments he was no longer seen and Tecumseh urged his partner in the canoe towards the place where his friend had disappeared with an urgent haste, fearing that something horrible may be happening to his dear friend. As they began to close distance and search the water where Noran had disappeared, the young man and huge whiskerfish came erupting from out of the water, as though they had been spewed forth from the bowels of mother earth herself. He had the huge fish tightly grasped with both hands on the bottom jaw holding it belly to belly so as to avoid the dangerous spines, just the way that they had been shown by their elders; again the Piasa would have been greatly pleased had he been there. Tecumseh again wondered where his friend could be, for he did not normally take this long to feed.

Noran quickly gained control of the large, struggling fish and was soon joined by his comrades in the struggle to wrestle it into the canoe. They all gazed at one another and congratulations were exchanged all around. They took turns splashing and dunking each other and spent the next couple of minutes in a youthful celebration of their success. Finally ready to renew the hunt for more of the large, tasty fish Noran quipped a friendly challenge, "I hope that you fierce young warriors are not going to make me be the lone fisher of the group."

The young man in Tecumseh's canoe Cahtar answered wryly, "We will let you keep this small one and now we will capture a few of decent size."

Noticing that the size of the first fish was nearly the size of the man that caught him, they all enjoyed a long and healthy laugh before they returned to their fishing. The morning had been passing peacefully for the group, as they all spent it doing something that they loved that was also for the benefit of their people. This made life very good; they were truly a blessed people living their lives in the lush green bounty of the land which they called home.

The maidens also shared in the bounty, they had found the berries to be plentiful, plump and ripe and where collecting them in such abundance that they were now even considering drying some for storage for the winter, although it was still very early in the year for that they did not want to miss out on this wonderful opportunity and let this bounty go to waste. They were all full of smiles and playfulness as this chore for the good of the people of the village had become an enjoyable morning out in the fresh air and sunshine of the beautiful countryside that they all loved so very much. They frolicked with each other, tossed berries playfully at one another and even spent time weaving each other necklaces and tiaras from the beautiful green, leafy vines of the berry plants. They truly led lives of bliss and wonder and they all now felt a deep and abiding happiness.

As their harvesting of the ripest of the berries continued and the morning lengthened; so too the search for the most perfect of the berries expanded, the blue berries that were so plentiful were still readily available near the lakeside, but the red berries that were somewhat more tart and desired by many for cooking were growing more thickly further up the slope where the waterfalls cascaded beautifully down the side of the small chain of rocky hills at the head of the lake and more shade naturally occurred from the denseness of the brush. This drew the attention of Mandi, who was always trying her hardest to please Nanuma. She climbed slowly up the face of the falls to gain access to the more abundant red berries growing there. She did not rush, picking and eating the really ripe ones on occasion, but slowly working her way up the rock face that was actually much more jagged and foreboding than it appeared, as the thick growth of the berry bushes upon it greatly softened its appearance, but she had been up these trails on many occasions and felt no apprehension of danger. She climbed over the last rock shelf that jutted severely out from the side of an immense pile of boulders that appeared to have been pushed into place by the hands of some giant at an earlier age and gathered herself atop the flat plateau above to get serious and fill both of her new baskets with the succulent red berries. Down below she could see that her good friends Tanya and Coi had spotted her and they had begun to wave. She returned the gesture, beckoning them to join her. Soon she saw them begin the climb to approach her, knowing that they not only wanted to share in the harvest, but share in the time spent with their good friend for they had all been mostly inseparable from the very youngest of ages, where you would see one of them; so too would you find the other two.

She glowed with happiness as she awaited her two friend's arrival, but she was then surprised by spotting over her shoulder that peculiar little bird that their new visitor prized so highly. It sat (just out of the distance of a well thrown stone) staring at her with those hideous red eyes. It was very small in stature, yet the very presence of the strange little bird filled her heart with dread.

She tried to ignore the menacing little creature and kept on with her harvesting of the wonderful, juicy berries, but as she continued she began to notice the arrival in the area of quite a few of the large black birds that her people tried to keep away from their gardens. They were considered nuisances and thieves and it was better that they were here than down by the village gardens.

She turned around to gain better access to the bush that she was concentrating on at the time and saw behind her hundreds more of the hungry looking black birds. She grew nervous and glanced down the cliff at her approaching friends, and then back up at the huge assembly of angry looking black birds that now had cornered her against the side of the mountain.

Mandi tried to continue her task as best she could when suddenly one of the birds swooped down upon her with outstretched talons, clawing at her face. She dodged its flight and shooed it away with her free arm. She had never had one of these birds attack her or even heard of such an occurrence concerning these birds and so she began to grow very frightened; this was an occurrence that was truly not natural, for these birds had never been aggressive, something about them had changed.

Further down the slope Coi saw the bird swoop down at her friend and said, "That is strange, it looks as though the birds are trying to protect the berries, the do not understand that there are enough for all." They continued up the hill, but now with a slightly increased sense of urgency.

But it was not the same for Mandi for she was now terrified and the peculiar little bird continued to stare right at her with a look that was somehow lustful but at the same time very cruel. It looked at several of the black birds and they all began to dive on Mandi with malicious intent. She again dodged the first one, but the next two both struck her successfully on her soft, exposed neck and head slashing down her cheek dangerously close to her eyes; she was knocked against the boulder next to her and fell crumpled into a pile on the ground.

She then decided that it was now time to defend herself; she unsteadily got up off the ground and quickly searched for some kind of weapon, but the rocks in the area were all too large for her to be able to lift, let alone throw there were no branches save the small, wiry, curly ones from the berry bushes, none that could be used as a club. All that she had to bring to bear was her small knife that most all of the Nastazi girls carried as a needed tool in their daily chores; equipped with only this she stood her ground and began to fight the cruelly influenced birds for her life!

Further down the cliff past Tanya and Coi, Billigana saw up on the side of the mount the birds diving on one of her sisters, she was close enough to them that they would hear her when she screamed to Tanya and Coi, "Can you see what the birds are doing to Mandi?"

Unfortunately, by this time they could not see their friend because of the blockage of the huge boulders between them, but Coi answered, "We saw one that looked like it attacked her, but alas we cannot see her any longer.

Billi quickly urged them on, "She is in need of our help; many now attack her; please get to her side as quickly as is possible."

They increased to running as quickly as they could up the incline, but above the terrible black birds increased their attack attempting to slash poor Tanya's face, neck, hands and especially her eyes. She feared for her life by now and could still see the strange little red-eyed bird stare at her with that peculiar look of desire. Suddenly several of the birds seemed to appear out of nowhere flying up towards her face; she turned to escape their assault and slipped over a ledge, where she dropped to the rocks below, with a sickening thud. She was turned by the fall and landed in a very awkward and twisted position with her head squeezed face down trapped between two huge, flat rocks which were standing on end.

The little bird Elgin saw this, smiled, turned away and the attack was then ended, as he flew off.

After finding and just finishing the capture of the forth huge fish, the peace of the morning was suddenly shattered by the screams for help from Billi's group at the other end of the lake. They were faint and not entirely understood, but it was obvious that they were in need of immediate assistance. Tecumseh, Noran and the others were off instantly; they paddled their canoes at a furious pace and covered the distance in just a short time. The yells had emanated from somewhere near the base of the falls and on the near side could be seen several of the young woman that were assisting his love, but his heart began to sink as his Billi was now nowhere in sight.

Tecumseh sliced furiously through the water and catapulted upon the narrow shoreline, leaping out of the canoe just as it struck the shore, "Where is Billigana," he blurted out? One of the maidens attempted to put him at ease and yelled after him, "She is not in danger." Leona urged as she approached from further up the path where she had just seen Billi run to her sister's aid, "She is trying to help poor Mandi. Please help her as those things would kill her."

Tecumseh wondered what it was that she meant by this cryptic statement. Whom did she mean by "those things?" He approached her and grabbed her to calm her, as she was obviously quite frightened, "Who would kill one of our maidens, what villain would do this to such a peaceful people?"

Leona began to shiver as she answered him, "The black birds, they have become strange as never before. The black birds attacked Mandi further up the side of the mount and have succeeded in throwing her down."

Tecumseh embraced her warmly to calm her and told her, "You are safe and I will stop the birds, stay here with my friends and they will look after you."

Tecumseh turned and began sprinting up the grade; he quickly overtook Tanya and Coi who were approaching the ledge that Mandi had climbed over to gain her spot on the small plateau.

He passed them trying to calm them saying, "I will stop the birds, do not fear."

As he arrived at the ledge and began to ready himself to climb up to onto the plateau where he was told the maiden that was in such dire need of his help awaited; his eyes caught something further along the face of the cliff. It was Billigana, carefully bending over young Mandi who lay crumpled into a cleft of sharp, forbidding-looking boulders and not moving. He immediately feared the worst and was at Billi's side in moments. Together he and Billi carefully began the difficult process of extricating the poor young child from the horrendous plight that she had so innocently become the victim of.

After carefully lifting her out of the horrible, tight cleft in the boulders, they cautiously laid her on the soft ground that was only several steps away to inspect her injuries and stabilize her as best they could. They both stared at the poor girl and then at one another with a piteously soulful look, she looked as though she was injured horribly. They began to do what they could; though they felt it would only be in vain.

~~~~~~~~~~~~

In the village Angelii had been busy with her own intrigues. She had sought out and found King Takan in his armories where he was busy with the duties of a king, inspecting the maintenance and numbers of his weapons of war. She was rather surprised by the number and readiness with which they were maintained; considering the Nastazi prided themselves as such a peaceful and advanced culture. She decided that this is how she would approach the young king, for he was truly very young in her eyes; far younger than herself, although he would never know of it. She offered modestly, "For peoples who speak so highly of your peaceful culture, it appears that you have planned seriously for the possibility of war."

King Trevlon Takan finally looked up from what he was doing; even though he had noticed her several moments before and said with a warm smile, "Not only war, but victory. You see, if one does not learn from the past, then you are doomed to repeat it once again. The Nastazi will never again be driven from their homes or serve a master."

She smiled at him most likely thinking of how she would be the one to make that statement untrue, but continued her ruse saying, "So your people have a past filled with war, do they?"

"We were never an aggressive people, but our songs and legends from ages ago tell of a time when we were surrounded by many enemies that were all jealous of the beautiful cities that we had built into the sides of the cliffs far to the west of our current home village, and coveted the herd animals that we kept at the bases of these mighty fortresses that we called our homes and even of the hanging gardens that we had taught ourselves to tend and make prosper over the ages. They coveted our wells; being too lazy to dig their own and they also constantly kidnapped, raped and killed our people. Never brave enough to confront us as real warriors in a battle, they continued this harassment for many seasons and although we found and killed many of them, we could never find and destroy enough to make them cease. We would have continued until we found them, but during these many seasons accompanied by their harassments we also lacked any substantial rain. Year after year the desert grew drier around us until our wells began to go dry or even worse, become so alkali that the water was no longer healthy for us, or even our plants," he exclaimed.

She shook her head in apparent compassion, but said, "Are you certain that your people did not anger the gods?"

He explained to her, "Our people are always very devout, about asking for permission and giving thanks to the Great Spirit for all that we do in life, besides the Great Spirit that I know is not a vindictive evil power, but a forgiving, loving benefactor."

"So you say," she said shortly. "But I have seen and heard tales from others that do not concur with your innocent views."

"In any case, that is when our legends say that the remnants of our ancient people decided to strike out and leave their homes of so many lifetimes and head off to find a new homeland, though at that time we had become a people divided and so one group headed to the south, where they had heard of great riches from the ground and more mountains running with water than could be counted. Then there was the other group; these which were my ancestors and they decided to come to the east where they had heard of a great river that had many tributaries and wonderful surrounding forests and rich lands. When they arrived on the other side they even decided, in their wisdom to cross the river so that it would be a barrier to any that would follow," King Trevlon Takan seriously expounded, somewhat giving her a shortened history of his people.

She merely looked around the room, in supposed disbelief and shook her head.

"You do not appear to understand our stance on defense, but even over the last few seasons we have experienced attacks from other tribes that desire to either usurp our homes, enslave us or both. Just two seasons past the Pawnee attacked us with no warning, resulting in the death of our most honored king," he told her.

"And putting a younger, more virile king in his place," She said to him, smiling broadly as she approached. "I have told you of my many abilities, are you not ready to taste of them for they are many and I can not only make you feel as wonderful as you have ever felt, but I can help you and your people in many, many other ways."

He held her in his arms for several moments as she leaned upon his heaving chest feeling that he was definitely going to succumb to her charms on this night. She reached up eagerly to his lips with her own full, moist and brightly colored lips. He leaned down and began to part his lips as he drew her to him, but stopped at last and gently pushed her away.

"You would tempt even the strongest of wills with your beauty, but I cannot enjoy this offer; alluring though it is, as my heart belongs to another," he told her, though his eyes burned with the fire of unquenched passion.

She looked at him with the fierce scowl of the rejected; searing in her eyes, yet she was surprisingly cordial and backed away delicately saying, "Affairs of the heart have strange ways of changing. Perhaps we are not meant for each other right now, but who knows what the future may hold. In any case, there are many other ways that I can help your people if you will just let me show you; for I am truly here to help, you shall see in time."

He was taken aback and told her warmly, "Yes, I would be very happy to accept your help if it is actually for the good for my people. Perhaps we can ask Nanuma for a way that you could address her students in some of the morning classes."

"Yes, I would enjoy that," she said. "Or perhaps someone will need some of the incredible healing power of my medicines."

"Yes," He agreed. "You never know when something like that may take place."

"No, you do not," she said with a knowing smile she then turned abruptly and left the armory.

Words of the Piasa

Outside, she resolutely walked a short distance to the back of the main pyramid where the king and queens lavish quarters were located and incredibly just walked right past the guard that was there saying, "I need to speak to the queen at once!"

She walked into the middle entertaining room where the queen sat handling a very beautiful necklace and just began to gaze at her longingly. She and Queen Melanie locked their passionate gazes as Angelii slowly approached the younger, more naïve woman and said, "I am in a position to help all of your people immensely and all that I ask in return is your passion and acceptance of my ways; but none must know of our closeness." As she completed her statement she had finally reached the young queen and began to lightly stoke her hair and face.

"I, I can see that you are very special and want to do whatever I can to help my people," Melanie stammered.

"Have you a place where we will not be disturbed," Angelii said as her hands moved down over Melanie's shoulders and down to her breasts, "I would explain to you and show you much!"

"Yes," the queen said, crackling with the type of passion and desire that she had never felt before. "Yes, follow me through our escape chamber and I will take you to a secret place that I know of where no one will disturb us."

The intrigues of Angelii were beginning to take on their form and she followed the nubile young queen with a strangely hungry smile. She would enjoy this fully, she thought to herself.

As the two exited the great pyramid and walked quickly through the thick forest on the north side of the grand structure one would have been able to see, if they had taken the time to look, that they were being followed by the small bird with the red eyes full of hate, alighting back and forth throughout the tree limbs, watching all that they did with great interest.

~~~~~~~~~~~~~~~~

Far to the west, at the edge of the forest just beyond where the Great Plains began slept a mighty beast known by some as a dragon, by those that knew him more closely as the Piasa and his closest friends as Granger. He had succumbed to an unrecognized and as yet unknown plant and would be sorely missed by all before he awoke from this deep and terrible sleep. Proof once again of the cruelness, that fate could sometimes hold.

Far east of the sleeping dragon, on the other side of the great river, north of the wondrous and often coveted village of peaceful trading peoples known as the Nastazi; there were warriors from another loosely bonded tribe, perhaps not as proud of their ancestry and heritage, if they knew of it at all, doing the plantings of the special plant that their priestess had instructed them to perform. They were expressly forbidden any kind of consumption of this plant at this time, being told that not only was it sacred, but that it was also very poisonous if not processed exactly correctly, as only the high priestess and her little sacred bird had knowledge of and could perform.

The rules did not bother any of them and were obeyed explicitly; and why not for they wanted for nothing, their village to the northwest of this region was one week away upriver, but only two days were needed to come back downstream. Back at their village labored constantly, a large number of slaves that they had captured during the many excursions that the priestess Angelii had led them on. They were closely guarded, but also seemed to be under the control of Angelii's seemingly magical will and always appeared very content just to toil as long as their strength would last which often proved to be of extraordinary lengths of time, at doing whatever her bidding might that day be. They could not understand what the power was that she held over them, but it was very strong indeed.

They however, not realizing the striking similarity with which they also obeyed her every command went about as they had been instructed performing the planting, growing and harvesting the supposedly sacred plant for their beloved priestess, for after all she did provide them with all that they ever needed, food, lodging, slaves and even the health powder that kept all of them so vigorous and strong, she also obviously loved her people as much as she said on so many occasions, trusting them to achieve all that she asked, which was sometimes an incredible amount, leaving them on their own for many days even moon cycles knowing that they would do as she had bade them, seeing no signs of her, only her strange little bird with the glowing red eyes!

Words of the Piasa

~~~~~~~~~~~~~~~~~~~~~~

To the south, just outside of the great Nastazi village that would later be known as Cahokia, the young Nastazi warrior Tecumseh, his mate Billigana, and several of her close friends were attempting to save the life of their sweet and delicate friend that had fallen victim of one of the strangest and most malicious events that any of them had ever witnessed. They had cleaned and taken care of the wounds that they could see on the outside of her petite young body, but their real concern was towards the injuries on the inside that could not be seen. They cooperated as carefully as they could and lifted her to place her limp torso on a hastily prepared litter and began the lengthy process of taking poor Mandi back to the village. Billi now feared that it would take longer than the time which the sweet young girl actually possessed. The long procession slowly made its way back home, holding on to whatever hope that they were able to now muster.

~~~~~~~~~~~~~~~~~~~~~~

In another part of the village; the queen having just experienced her first ever infidelity in a marriage to a man that she knew she had loved even more than life itself; but unfortunately it would certainly not be her last as she was now utterly enchanted with this tantalizing new stranger with what seemed like witchlike lovemaking powers, it was the strangest feeling that she had ever experienced. It was not a love or even an infatuation, but more like a strange form of enslavement, she could not even begin to understand the strange power that Angelii held over her, but it was present and it was very, very powerful and she could no more fight it than stop her own breathing, she needed to feel her touch, to be entwined in her embrace, and she had to be near her as much as was possible. This new tremendously intense feeling could not begin to be denied and it made her feel very, very frightened!

Far deeper into the room just arising from the fresh water cistern, Angelii gazed at Melanie with an imperious, hungry, predatory look as she walked past the disheveled bed of skins where she had just taken so much from the young queen, of both pleasure and will! She stated, "You do as I have told you to do; it will be for the better of all of your people. The Kaav will invigorate all of your people, help with overall health and can even cure the ill, and make certain that you convince your husband, or I will be forced to convince him with my own means and of my own accord."

Melanie looked up to her sheepishly, trying to combat the instant all encompassing, painful jealousy that she felt at that statement, not for her husband's possible infidelity, or even safety, but for the fact that she wanted to share Angelii with no one; not anybody. She answered obediently, "I will convince him for you, men can be easy to sway using the correct methods."

"Yes, they can," Angelii agreed. As she parted, slightly caressing her new conquests upturned face she told her, "Do not fail in my requests."

Melanie overflowed with the effort of trying to please her new lover and insisted, "I will do whatever is necessary to please you my love."

Angelii exhaled deeply, smiled and turned and walked away, she was finished here for now and had other tasks to attend to.

She walked leisurely to her quarters where her coconspirator Elgin met her; she gave him a knowing smirk and asked knowingly, "Has all proceeded as we have planned?"

Elgin sighted her with a somewhat mocking glare saying only, "You know that I have the power to sway all beasts."

"Yes," she said, "and all humans as well!"

Elgin smiled appreciatively as he then told her flatteringly, "You also can be most convincing." After staring at her for several silent moments he added lustily, "My priestess with the heart of fire."

She advanced with a few quick steps, gathered him gently and pressed him to her heart between her most ample bosom saying, "We have important matters to attend to now, but I will await our time together tonight with a longing that you do not know."

As she held him against her warm, voluptuous body that strange faint humming seemed to fill the room, but after only a few moments she lovingly put him down and left the room showing her serious disappointment at the constraints that they currently had on time, as it was most obvious that she desired time spent alone with this strange unfathomable being.

The group of Nastazi's had made their way a great distance, from

Words of the Piasa

the opposite side of the grand horseshoe lake, through the thick forest to the north of the village and were approaching the outskirts marked by several of the smaller pyramids with Billigana leading the way, six of Mandi's closest friends including Tanya and Coi helping to pull the litter and keep it as steady as was possible, with Tecumseh and most of those from his party bringing up the rear.

Suddenly, appearing out of nowhere in front of them stood Angelii, she had appeared so quickly and unexpectedly that she had startled one and all. She was alone and walked as quietly as a stalking mountain lion, to which she not surprisingly also held quite a number of marked similarities.

She was scantily clad in a very snug and short buckskin skirt that was combined with an equally tight blouse that continued up from the waist of the skirt to a most revealing top that barely held the overflow of her round, firm breasts. Both pieces of clothing had the appearance of being some sort of very soft buckskin, but they were of a most unusual color for such a skin as they were deep, dark black, a color that most had never seen on this type of skin before and it even seemed to have a somewhat shimmering quality somehow bestowed into it. This was definitely a woman that was truly in possession of many shocking surprises.

She stood in the middle of the pathway and spoke quietly, yet with an unnerving sort of force asking, "What is the problem, has there been an injury?"

Billi hesitated for a moment, but then told her just what had happened, "No one has ever seen the black birds behave in this way," She concluded, but then added as she stared deeply into Angelii's eyes, "There is most certainly something very strange happening here."

Angelii returned her glare saying, "If something that is not normal is being done here then perhaps I can be of assistance before it becomes too appalling."

"The Piasa will return at any time now," Billi said, only slightly exposing the hope that she surly tried to rally for all.

Angelii stepped towards the stricken Mandi, knelt down and inspected her wounds under Tecumseh's watchful gaze. She looked up into his curious face and said bluntly, "She is very seriously injured, but I believe that I can save her."

Tecumseh leaned into her and spoke quietly so that the others would not hear and said, "Please do not give them false hope, for we all love this girl dearly and can see how serious her injuries actually are."

"I do not speak lightly my friend," She told him in hope of reassuring all present and taking yet another step towards bending them to her will. "I am a high priestess in my tribe and as such have been entrusted with many of the most ancient secrets of healing. I know that I can save her and I would not misguide you and your people and after all, it was you who recently saved me and so it is only fitting that I in return save one of you, or even more if you will allow."

Tecumseh looked at Billi; Billi at poor Mandi and then back with her eyes beseeching to Tecumseh, he turned to Angelii and pleaded with her saying, "If there is anything that you can do to help her, please do it now!"

This was exactly what Angelii had been waiting for!

They all turned their attention back to Mandi, who had turned very pale and could be seen imperceptibly shivering, as though she was attempting to hold onto her very last essence of life that she was able to secure.

The self-proclaimed priestess Angelii was obviously well practiced and moved very quickly about her tasks with dexterous and experienced hands. She first removed a small vial from her pouch and sprinkled the powder into a small cup and added fresh water from her waterskin, immediately she propped the broken maidens head up and forced the contents down her throat; and though Mandi gagged slightly, she kept it down. The declared priestess then mixed a thin salve with the same white powder and shocking everyone, stripped the girl of all that she wore and began to cover every part of her body with the salve, everywhere; head, breast, back, arms, legs, her ears, nostrils, even her private places. When she saw the expressions on the faces of her small crowd, she was quick to tell them that this was a very important step if they were to save the girl. She then put young Mandi's clothes back on her and requested that any with extra clothing or skins to please give them to her that she might wrap the girl as tightly as possible with them so that the medicine had its best chance to work. They all complied with something and in a few moments little Mandi was wrapped up tightly in skins and reeking of the pungent medicine. She finally stood over the young girl and said, "Now we must get her back to her home and let her rest, in a few days the Kaav will have worked its magic!" Only she knew exactly how accurate the statement she had just spoken actually was!

The group tried to be appreciative as they made their way back to their homes; Billi even asked if there was anything that she could do to help Angelii with anything, offering obligingly, "If there is anything that you need from me that will be of help to you in our village, please just ask me."

Angelii just looked at her strangely and said, "No, not now however if the need arises your offer pleases me greatly and I do appreciate that you have made the gesture."

Billi had felt obligated to make the offer to their unfathomable guest because of the caring and medicinal care that she had just exhibited in the attempt to heal her dear friend, but now she had the very uneasy feeling of entrapment as she looked back at Angelii only to see her returning her gaze with a most peculiar, almost hungry gleam in her eyes.

They all once again gathered what was needed and made their way restlessly to Nanuma's quarters; there all were certain that Mandi would be constantly cared for by her mentor and teacher.

Angelii made quite the spectacle of caring for the young injured Mandi and everyone present noticed, even to the point of Nanuma commenting about the care that she was showing.

"It is merely the training that I have been exposed to, I was born and have been raised a priestess of the Makai." She paused and looked around the room, as if judging the reaction and then continued, "I have been raised for my entire life in training to become a priestess for my people. This is not only training of the spiritual nature, but we are taught to be expert in the ways of the healer." She intentionally omitted the thousands of grueling hours that she had taken part in learning all of the deadly arts of killing; of these practices she would be called an expert by any that had seen her exhibit these skills and still actually survived.

She continued with her tale, which although entirely false, was quite convincing, "Just a short time ago, our village was attacked by these horrible people that called themselves Mayans; they appeared surprisingly one night from the south and began killing most of my people. Myself and just a few other women of my age or younger were the only ones to survive and that was only because they had plans to use us as slaves for sex and to bear their many burdens. Had you, Tecumseh and your wonderful partner Billigana not rescued me on the day that I attempted to escape I am certain that I would now be dead like the rest of my clan."

Tanya, Coi and some of the others whom had gathered looked at Angelii with a deep sympathy and tried to reach out to her in comfort and pity for as I have earlier stated she was most expert at the spinning of the spoken web of manipulation.

While the small group on the other side of the bed where Mandi now lay were immersed in a deep emotional discourse, Nanuma, Billi and Tecumseh also embraced each other, attempting to dispel the horrible lost confusion that they now felt and as they stared forlornly into one another's eyes they all whispered and asked one another, "Where can the Piasa be?"

They subtly made their way across the room, away from the object of their unease, the rescued stranger who was the doubtless cause of all their unease, Angelii.

Billi then continued, "We must attempt to reach him with our thoughts. Did you not tell me before that you and he were capable of this?"

Tecumseh responded, "Yes, it has happened before, though I just do not really understand exactly how that it came to pass, or that which created the conditions which caused it to occur."

Nanuma put her hands on his shoulders and said, "You are both linked with your minds, I am not certain just how you would do it, but you must try for only the Piasa can see trough the deceit that I feel is being woven here, you must call him back here to us, and quickly!"

"I will try," was all that the young Nastazi brave said at this time, he and Billi then gathered themselves and said pleasant farewells to all and departed.

The Makai priestess had seen the exchange on the other side of the room and heard the mention yet again of the being called the Piasa. She had learned through the ages that there was indeed such a creature as this and with this she was not pleased. She knew that Elgin had said that the Piasa was under his control and not to worry, but she was not certain that her little shape shifting friend was actually capable of the control of such a beast; she would talk to Elgin about it very soon!

Elgin was so secretive at times that even the wily Angelii would not become aware of his presence for he was inside the very longhouse undetected by all and had heard every word of the conversation between the three Nastazi standing slightly apart from his precious Angelii.

Piasa, he thought to himself, this could only mean trouble for their plans; those beasts had ways of seeing into the best kept secrets and were known to have powerful magic of their own. He must take immediate steps to prevent the beast from being awakened and coming back to this village and interfering, as all of these people and al that they possessed would soon fully belong to Angelii and himself.

There are many ways to kill even the fiercest of beasts he thought to himself, as he began to formulate a plan, while he awaited Angelii, for he desired first before speaking with her to once again use her for some more of her considerable amorous talents, if even for only a few times more!

King Trevlon Takan had come back to his royal quarters, surprised to not find his loving wife waiting for him as was usual, but he quickly learned that she had departed hours ago with the guest of the village, the priestess that called herself Angelii. He had a very strange feeling about his one, but he could not exactly fathom what she was really about, surely he would in time, for he had many eyes and ears. She was very attractive, but he felt sorry for her that she could not understand the loyalty of a true and earnest love; however even though he felt this towards her he would never hurt his sweet Melanie's feelings by being unfaithful he thought privately to himself once again.

Just then Melanie returned from her outing with the priestess, she was behaving rather peculiarly, or so he judged, for she came into the bed chambers but walked across to the other side of the room from him, not the normal deep embrace in one another's arms to which he had grown so accustomed to over these past seasons. He approached her from the other side of their bed and tried to caress her into his arms, but she pulled away saying, "I must talk to you my king." She addressed him in a strangely formal tone that he had never heard her use before and it disturbed him greatly.

"I have just spoken at great lengths to the priestess Angelii," she said as she looked at him coldly. She watched his expression in a strange calculating way and went on, "She has much knowledge that can be very beneficial to the well being of our people."

"Yes," he answered her, "She spoke of this to me and I told her that I would like to see examples if and when the need arises!"

"You must not ignore her talents," She blurted out belligerently towards him!

King Trevlon Takan was shocked; his wife had never before spoken to him thusly. "I do not intend to ignore such talents, but we have not yet had the opportunity to view them, thanks being to the Great Spirit."

Melanie became somewhat more composed and said, "Of course not, I am sorry my love if I was overzealous, it is just that I am so excited at hearing of the wonderful gifts that she can bestow upon our people. Forgive my impudence my love."

Trevlon Takan embraced his wife and held her tight, greatly concerned at the unusual change that had seemed to have come over her. He had known his wife since her earliest of years and had no idea what strange change could have taken place to create such an alteration in her normally loving and caring attitude, but he was certain of only one thing, the stranger Angelii was somehow at the center of the problem. He needed counsel from some of his trusted friends and his family and though he was yet to realize it, he would soon feel as most all of his people already felt; trapped. He too felt what he needed was the counsel of the Piasa. He must discover from Tecumseh when his large friend would return, for he had been gone for such a long time!

~~~~~~

Once Mandi had been cared for Billi and Tecumseh decided not to immediately return to their homes, but instead they chose to travel the short distance to their favorite spot to be alone, it meant climbing up the bluff and walking a little way in the forest until they arrived at the meadow within a clearing of the forest where they first made love. Here they thought that they could remain undisturbed and try to sort out the strange occurrences which they had been confronted with as of late; also they would attempt to clear their minds and see if it was at all possible to communicate with the Piasa; he had always such reliable counsel and they were all in need of that counsel now as never before.

They arrived at the far end of the meadow, near where the clearing began to close into forest once again and both slid down with their backs against a large old Oak tree under which they had enjoyed each other's love for the first time; it was truly a place of reverence for the both of them.

Tecumseh shortly lowered himself down to where he was laying peacefully in Billi's lap and soon the tension of the day's events began to drain away. He looked up into his loves eyes and told her, "You know how much that I love you."

She answered unwaveringly, "Yes, I do."

He continued, "I want to be strong for you and to do the right thing, but I am truly at a loss. I know that I must do something and feel that the girl that we rescued poses great danger to our people, yet I do not know what that danger is or what there is that can be done about it."

Billigana tried to sooth her man saying, "We will find the answers that we need; the Piasa shall surely return soon and if not then we will trust in one another and face our problems together."

Tecumseh looked even more deeply into her eyes and went on painfully, "That also, for all seem to think that I can just call the Piasa and he will come, yet I do not feel that I have any more knowledge as to the contacting of the Piasa as anyone else. I do wish that he were here, he could see through whatever it is that she is planning.

She caressed his head and held it to her breasts and told him, "Just relax for now my love and in a while we will decide what it is that we must do."

She held her Tecumseh as they both drifted off to sleep; it was for both a trusting, loving nap that they equally enjoyed, as they took great pleasure in just laying in each other's arms, enjoying the mutual acceptance and protection and dozing for they had grown to value greatly these refreshing naps that had grown to become so much a part of their loving one another. Unfortunately, the nap on this day was very different, as they were both troubled deeply by dreams that matched and they each seemed to share, dreams of the whole of their people strangely afflicted in a way that neither had ever seen for they all seemed to be walking as if already dead, as if they had become the undead that had been spoken of by the elders in the stories told to the children in order to scare them at festival time. They still knew not what this meant, but both had been affected by quite similar dreams and when they awoke and compared stories were both quite unnerved by the likeness of the experience.

"It has to mean something," Billigana pleaded with her love, "We must try to find the Piasa."

"I know this to be true," Tecumseh said painfully, "But I do not really know how it can be done."

Billi said calmly, "We shall keep trying until we succeed; we will and must find the way."

"I do not even know where to begin," he told her glumly.

She began to direct him calmly, "You successfully called him on at least one other occasion."

"Yes," he responded, "When the mother shush was about to kill me!"

He thought for a few moments and then he said and several other times around the village and the lake, but I was not even really trying and have no idea whether it was I that called him or he just found me, in any case I don't know just what it was that I really took part in, or how to reproduce it."

"Try, first by just picturing your friend the Piasa in your mind," she urged.

He did just that and could actually begin to feel the presence of the large beast that had become such a close friend. He stayed at this for quite a while and even sensed that he could see his friend far away in a lonesome grove of trees sleeping a very deep sleep, a sleep that seemed nearly impossible to awaken from without some sort of as of yet unknown aid.

After a great while and much exertion, he had to stop his efforts for a time to rest, as it seemed to drain him immensely to keep trying to make this communication and receive absolutely no answer. He eased his attempts for a while and explained to Billigana just what he had seen and explained to her what he thought that it meant.

Billi asked, "Is he just napping after a large meal, or might it be something more devious?"

He answered somewhat unsure of himself, "I am not really certain, but he seems to be in some sort of unnaturally deep sleep, I believe that he needs our help as much as we need his."

"That is not well," Billi gasped! "We do not know where he is at."

"No we do not," Tecumseh continued. "We need him and he needs us and it seems that we cannot bring ourselves together."

Billi offered, "Perhaps the solution will be easier than we can now imagine, let us both try to call him with our minds, for he has told me that we are bonded also."

So they both once more attempted to look deep inside themselves and visualize their friend, thus calling out to him and attempting to wake him from the dreadfully deep sleep that he seemed to have somehow succumbed to. Both tried their most earnest and both were able to see their friend; sadly neither was able to rouse him in the slightest, though they kept trying until the sun disappeared from the sky. Saddened, but not beaten they returned home vowing to find a way to reach out to him in some way the next morn.

Billi told her disheartened man as he left her at her mother's longhouse, that the time of their separation at night was coming to a close, but it was still the respectable thing to do for now and they always made every attempt to treat the elder's whom were deserving, with the greatest of respect that one can be shown. As they were about to part she offered one more idea, "Perhaps we can find him with the bags of wind."

"Yes, this is most certainly a way to cover the distance; we just need to find the way which to aim our travels," he answered.

"One thing at a time my love," she comforted him. "We will try again tomorrow."

Back in the comfort of the lodging that the Nastazi had so graciously provided for her, Angelii had just finished washing and was beginning to make herself more comfortable for the evening. It was quite late and most of the rest of the village had retired long ago. She was joined by her odd little bird friend Elgin; he was very agitated and told her, "The youngsters that brought you here have an ally that we have never faced as I told you; a Piasa and they cannot be allowed to interfere."

"Yes, but you told me that he was under your control," Angelii stated as just a matter of fact.

"He slumbers, but I could not kill him though I bade him consume enough of the plant to have killed one thousand of these natives that you wish to overcome," Elgin hissed.

She attempted to calm him, "Stay calm, my lovely little friend, things are progressing even better than we had hoped." She appeared to be in a rather strange, somehow romantic mood.

Elgin continued impatiently, "We must do something about it quickly."

"We will, we will my love," she said softly. "Why perhaps something has already happened to the monster, I have been told that it is long overdue from feeding. Perhaps he has eaten something that that has proven ill for beasts such as himself." She added with a smirk and malevolent chuckle.

"He only sleeps," Elgin again stated testily!

She glided across the room to caress her small little avian wonder and held him delicately to her breast and said in her most alluring voice, "It is nothing that will not wait until the morning, let us take pleasure in the comforting of one another."

The little bird was obviously, by this time swept up in a passion that was not only unusually strong and undeniable, but wholly impure. It was a strange purely sexual type of passion that seemed to be entirely void of the normal love and caring that one might expect; it was a passion that was the result of a purely selfish encounter, one which each of the two cared only for the pleasure that they themselves received, in this instance both partners enjoyed it immensely, but this was entirely coincidental and in no way due to either trying to please the other, it just so happened and they had enjoyed this bizarre relationship for untold ages. Though the partnership that they were involved in could not accurately be called love, it was more of a long lasting partnership of co-conspirators and this suited them quite well. They slid together underneath the soft skins of the bed and the room was permeated with the strange humming and sounds of the writhing of the skins as they twisted and wrapped under the bedclothes as the bird seemed to grow

Words of the Piasa

and change into many different sizes and shapes. It was an unnatural and truly foul relationship, but very strong and they both possessed great skills at the manipulations they had fashioned. The room was once again filled with that seemingly poisonous buzzing sound that all save these two considered most foul.

~~~~~~~~~~~~~~~~

The next morning it seemed as though the entire village had risen before first light. As Billi and Tecumseh quietly made their way through the settlement, with barely enough light as of yet to make the way clear on the way back to their "special place" to once again attempt to raise a response from the Piasa using merely their own thoughts they happened to cross the path of their strange guests and this seemed to surprise Angelii quite a lot, even her bird friend seemed to be taken aback at seeing the two out at this early time of the morning.

"What special purpose could have you two up so early," Angelii asked, in as friendly a tone as possible for being as totally feigned as it was? She then began to smile at them when they did not respond to her query immediately, "Perhaps you two are traveling on a young lover's picnic to some special, secret and far away location."

Tecumseh and Billigana looked at one another wondering if this stranger might have some sort of power to read their minds, as that was indeed exactly what they were about to do, just not exactly for the same impure, lustful reasons that she made it so clear from her tone that she suspected.

Billi acted quickly saying, "We are to be married within two more phases of the moon, but we do need some time to ourselves at times."

"We all need that," Angelii was quick to agree as she shot a knowing glance at the little bird.

Tecumseh grabbed his opportunity and said, "We have seen very little of you since you joined us here in Nakokia, we hope to see you at tonight's evening meal."

"Yes, we would like that for we are making arrangements to speak to your people with the blessing of the king and queen about the benefits of some of the medicines that I can teach your people how to use," Angelii told them. "You should already have been able to see the great healing powers that the Kaav has in the way that it has helped your friend Mandi to recover."

"Yes, it has been truly remarkable so far," Tecumseh answered.

"We cannot thank you enough," Billi offered humbly.

Truthfully, what Angelii was saying had great merit since Mandi was obviously responding very well to the medicine that she was being treated with, it had certainly brought her back from near the door of certain death and she was getting better by the hour, although all of the Nastazi would soon learn that the wonder with which it healed and provided overall health came with an extremely heavy price to pay!

"Then until mealtime," Billi settled courteously, and then added, "I look forward to an interesting dinner tonight and am certain that anything that you are to teach us about herbs and medicines will help us immensely and be very advantageous."

"Yes, I wish only to help where I can," Angelii quipped, while at the same time talking to Billi and Tecumseh yet looking warmly at her little bird with a strange twinkle in her eyes.

Tecumseh said in short farewell, "Until this evening!" Then the two very different couples went their separate ways.

As Billigana and Tecumseh walked towards the thicket of trees that partially covered the path up the side of the bluff that many of the Nastazi frequented to gain access to the high plateau and forest above, Angelii turned and said quietly to her odd little friend Elgin, "This should be your opportunity to find out if they can manage to discover where their friend the Piasa is keeping itself."

"Yes, I suspect you are correct," Elgin stated as a matter of fact. "I suppose they are attempting to communicate with the beast with their minds, or even in dreams. They do not know of the powers that I can wield and I am confident that they are in fact the ones that will show us how to conquer their dragon friend, and when they do I have in mind a number of ways that we can deal with the beast and they will all end the same; with its death."

"And our gaining the ultimate power over his Nastazi friends, giving us a new race of willing slaves to do with as we will," Angelii reveled in her deliciously evil power.

The bird looked at her in a wonderful agreement and at that point you could see what it was that really held these two together for the long time they had shared their sinister partnership. It was not just the strange and impure sexual encounters; they rarely dined together or for that matter had nothing else at all spent in common time. No, it was easy to see now, that which bonded them together was the incredible power that they felt and were able to wield as the masters of an incredibly large number of slaves that they had been able to amass; the life and death, all encompassing power that they enjoyed over their submissive multitudes. Though throughout the ages it has been witnessed by this Piasa and was well known that this kind of power does nothing positive, as exampled by the loathsome black dragons that had been the cause of so much heartache and pain both before and after the humans had arrived; these two were truly examples of the evil that the Piasa now most wanted to change in the world.

The Nastazi would be yet another group under their evil control and the horrible physical slavery that they could empower over beings with their vile plants, drugs and subterfuges, how many more had there been? How could anyone hope to prevent it from happening again? For now these questions would remain unanswered.

～～～～～～～～～～～～～～～

King Trevlon Takan was very puzzled at the way that his lovely bride had begun to behave and was concerned with the possibilities, as the guest Angelii had been very forceful in her attempts at luring the king into infidelity and although he had never seriously considered succumbing to her stirring charms, he also had witnessed in the past the cruel manipulations that could be conceived by the fairer sex in their wiles of romance, or even of more base needs and desires. He would need to keep an ever closer eye on that one, he thought once again to himself.

He turned back towards Melanie and began to attempt to comfort her as best that he could. He asked her, "My love, is there something that is upsetting you, or some way in which I may help you"

She looked up at him in a hurtful way, not speaking, the new pain etched upon her lovely face.

He embraced her in an effort to comfort her with his love.

She drew back again, as if his touch pained her.

The strange and beautiful enslavement that she had succumbed to had a strange poisoning effect on his wife, turning her very cold to him and he was at a loss as to what could be done about it; now seen was the fact that even the king was capable of feeling most utterly alone.

Billigana and Tecumseh had walked solemnly to the spot that normally held such wonderful feelings and memories, yet today they felt only desperation. They were frightened by the lack of communication from the Piasa and becoming distressed and dismayed by the fact that they really needed his help at this time and he was nowhere to be found, additionally they were confused by the many faces of the girl that they had rescued and not understanding her real intentions. Increasingly they had begun to feel less like a young couple about to marry and embark on their lifetime journey together and more like two young children that were in desperate need of help from a sage and knowledgeable friend that they had grown to trust. This friend also was the most powerful being that they had ever come to meet in their young lives and seeing that he was also in some sort of danger they were even more saddened and desperate, but with this their inner strength recognized by the Piasa also shown through for they were also very determined; and so they began another attempt to communicate with the Piasa.

They both lay together; first Tecumseh nodded off into a guided trance, repeating the call for the Piasa over and over again, "Granger, Graaaangerr, Graaaaaanngerrr." Until he finally drifted off to a strange, restless sleep, Billi followed shortly afterwards, mumbling the dragon's name and picturing him in her mind, she had begun sleep also, but seemed to be dreaming immediately, she dreamed that she was flying above the ground much as they had in the "bags of hot wind" that the Piasa had given them the knowledge to construct; only she was flying free with no balloon or dragon to aid her. She was flying to the west and to the north, even towards the great mounts that they had seen on the one trip that they had made beyond the mountains to the western coast, she seemed to travel over the vastness of all of the land, yet still could not find the Piasa.

As she traversed in the dream world she happened be making her way once again back to the north of her country where she was fortunate enough to see a particularly unique mountaintop. (Its distinct shape as a matter of fact would enable it to be used many lifetimes later to be carved into four of the humans most important men and called Mount Rushmore) She seemed to be attracted downwards past the mount to the plains beyond and towards a small grotto of trees where she finally saw her beloved Piasa, he seemed to since her and made attempts to stir, although at this time they proved unsuccessful. She called to him in her dream, "Granger, Piasa please awake, we need you!"

Billi was dreaming very fitfully and began to rouse Tecumseh somewhat though he also seemed in a strange trance, one that left him very open to any impressions sent by the Piasa. They both lie there, not entirely asleep or awake attempting in the only fashion which they knew to reach their friend Granger.

The strange little bird that was Angelii's evil partner was very close and observed all that was going on between the two, he also was endowed with a very useful ability in such instances, as he was able to intrude upon their dreams. He could see what it was that they dreamt even though he was not invited or even known about. With the intrusion upon their dreams, the wicked little bird was as he was in flight within their dreams, especially Tecumseh's. The little bird passed within both of the dreams for a while until he, ancient avian that he was, began to recognize the land beneath his flight, it was where he had left the beast. The unknowing and innocent dreaming of his wonderful human friend Tecumseh was about to expose the fact that the Piasa could now be found by these young slaves to be, perhaps enabling them to assist the monster against those who would finish the dragon for himself and Angelii. They would need to deny the beast any chance of protection from his newfound human friends and in that way expose them all to a fate that no one deserved or could ever endure, the complete dependence on a corrupting drug and total slavery, slavery of the mind, body and soul for the remainder of existence!

Deep within the dream state, the small avian devil Elgin approached the small grove of trees that was just at the edge of the Great Plains that covered this bountiful land and he not only recognized the area, but then fully understood that the Piasa would be at his most vulnerable upon first few moments of awakening. It had been one of the first places where they had begun to sow the Kaav plant and control its growth to strengthen its properties, especially the dependence value that they had noticed it possessed. It was, in fact a great stroke of luck for the evil Angelii and himself, as these were the variety that were far too strong, a fact that they had discovered with the unintentional deaths of many of their former slaves, a fact that they had been very glad to learn of and cared absolutely nothing about the price in human life since they held human life as to be completely worthless, with the possible exception of what they could be forced to do as slaves. The bird approached the grotto of trees and began to recognize a shape; the shape of the dragon that had long ago told him to be gone from this land, the shape of what the humans now called the Piasa, the shape of the one being in this world that Elgin the Blight-lark as the men of old had called him held a real contempt for. The Blight-lark recognized the Piasa was unmoved where he had left him in the hideous drug induced sleep and now knew exactly just when he would be at his most powerless!

As the bird approached ever closer, even within the dream, the Piasa started, something deeply disturbing momentarily jolted the huge Piasa to near wakefulness, shocking the Blight-lark from its intrusive spell, shocking him back to the woods where he spied on the helpless Billigana and Tecumseh, who were likewise shocked from the spell. They awoke both shaken and frightened; both could remember fragments of the episode, fragments that shook them to their souls. They examined their surroundings warily, fearing something that existed which they did not really know or understand; they just surrendered into each other's open arms, trembling. They were certain that something horrible had just happened and that somehow they had unknowingly been part of it.

Back in the village Nanuma was still at Mandi's side nursing her as she had done for so many of her people throughout her days, she would have loved to have taken credit for the astounding recovery that she was now witnessing, but it was far too fast for that, it had been nothing short of miraculous! She had no doubt at all, it was the drugs that they had been given the stricken girl, and it no longer resembled an herb, as it had now been refined into a clear liquid or powder. No, she was certain that the cure could have only come from the Kaav, it was not only very strong, but it began to exhibit other qualities as well, for Mandi had begun to ask for it daily! As the last several days had passed she had appeared to be craving it more and more, the Kaav plant seemed to be gaining some sort of peculiar power over her. Nanuma had never seen anything like this before, she found it very fascinating, but it also provoked a weird fear in her that was unlike any she had never known.

What she did not understand, she had always tried to study, and this is what she now vowed to do, but she was so confused; she desired with all of her heart to meet with the Piasa, where could he have disappeared to? She had begun to feel a deep and all-encompassing fear, of what she was not really certain, but it was an entrapping fear that was like none she had ever felt. She only hoped that her gallant young friends would soon be successful in their attempts to reach the Piasa, for throughout all of the apprehension and even with the tremendous amount of confusion that they all felt now, one thing was certain, they all needed the Piasa now more than ever!

Mandi turned and made an attempt to lift herself from out of the bedclothes, but was quickly intercepted by Nanuma who caressed her as she persuaded her to once again lie quietly saying, "You must not attempt to speed your recovery too much, my little dear."

Only to be answered with a sweet and manipulative side of Mandi that she had never before seen, "The Kaav makes me feel so much better; can I have just a little bit more perhaps?"

~~~~~

Angelii and Elgin were never apart for long and they always just seemed to know where to find each other, this time they met in the deep woods to the north of the village, past the chain of rocks that had been left long ago by the advancing ice sheets, where the forest had become so thick as to make travel for even the animals difficult. They met in a small clearing at the shore of the great river that was easily two days walk by foot, normally from the village. She had come by canoe, as had a large number of their minions the difference being that hers was slave propelled. She and Elgin had come to meet and instruct their mindless hoard about the Piasa where they could find it and the preparations with which they wanted them to prepare for killing it.

Elgin spoke, this was the first time that many had ever heard him speak, save several of the inner circle of Angelii's commanders and most were not only shocked to hear such a small being speak with such power, but all were completely enthralled with the mystical command that he seemed to possess, "The dragon is not like anything that you have ever before encountered; your knives, spears and arrows will do little, save wake him and incur his wrath. We must approach this with great caution and the utmost in careful planning. We can only kill this thing with poison and it must be done just as it is emerging from its internment of his deep, Kaav induced sleep!"

He had all of the humans before him in an unnatural kind of spell, even Angelii seemed entranced to a point, and this was in fact the most probable cause of the astounding sexual effect that he was able to achieve with her, especially considering the vast difference in size and species. However, as inconceivable as it may have been, it existed and was also obviously very powerful!

He continued his instruction, "The beast has some amount of the magical powers that are left in the world and with those it is able to be protected at certain times and we must be aware of these and use them against him. When it sleeps, as it is doing now, the magic becomes very strong and the monster becomes as if made of stone. There is naught that we can do to pierce its mighty hide when he is in this state, however there is still a way to poison the creature."

Elgin slowly gazed across the enraptured crowd making certain of their all consumed attention, even noting the vacant stare exhibited by the powerful woman with whom he had the bizarre, but potent relationship. He continued with his morbid instructions, "We will poison the beast with the smoke of the sacred Kaav plant; I have seen it done before and am certain that it is the only way to successfully kill our nemesis. If it does begin to awaken then we can use our poisoned arrows in the soft spots under its wings and in his eyes. I will take you to where the monster sleeps and you will begin at once, we must not let the thing interfere with our plans!"

Angelii seemed then to stir and looked around with great authority and stated, "Make ready immediately, you now have your orders you must proceed to where the dragons sleeps and kill the monster quickly!"

Her remarks seemed to stir the small throng of warriors into a frenzy and they began to shout and scream many war cries, emboldening themselves to the task to which they were now committed. They seemed to be growing fiercer by the minute and their blood-curdling screams would have struck fear into any opponent that they would have faced, although doubtlessly none had ever had the opportunity to view the Piasa first hand.

Angelii gathered her warrior/slaves to the task at hand and the entire throng followed the lead of the evil little bird across the great river and to the west and north to assault the mighty Piasa; though they were not as ready for this task as they seemed to believe themselves to be and would not achieve exactly what their desired goal was, for they were about to take the steps that would ultimately lead to the destruction of most of the humans in the entirety of what would later be known as Cahokia, leaving the questions that future humans would ask, "Who were these incredible people that built such wondrous mounds and culture? Where could so many have possibly disappeared to?"

Back in the Nastazi village Angelii's work had progressed even in her absence. Tanya and Coi, having witnessed what appeared to have been the miraculous recovery of their friend Mandi had become two of the strongest proponents of the medical use of the Kaav drug. Before Angelii had departed the two were recruited into the ranks of those who were appointed the doing of her bidding, and they were pursuing the task that their new friend Angelii had assigned them with an invigorating vengeance. They were convinced that it would benefit the health and well being of everyone in the village to regularly partake of the mystical Kaav plant with its strangely beneficial qualities; because of this they recruited many of the other young maidens to assist them in this endeavor, after all everyone had seen how it had saved their friend and none could deny its invigorating effect and the feeling of invulnerability that it enabled you to possess; for a short time period anyway!

They had made it their own personal mission to enlist as much help as they could and show the entire population of the Nastazi the blessings of the Kaav plant and as with many impressionable young people, especially those whom had been influenced by such a strong and strangely persuasive individual as Angelii and her funny little bird, they had become absolute zealots in promoting the way of life and the use of the medicines that their new redeemer espoused the use of.

They had listened to Angelii's lectures about the pureness of living and about service to the family that she had been delivering so often in the community hall during the meetings for the production of the cloth for the "wind riders" as the bags of hot wind were now known for this now seemed to be one of the great woman's favorite pastimes; she would come to where most of the young people were hard at work for the good of the whole and commend them for their devotion. She would then not only praise them for their altruism and hard work, but even give of her time and show them how they too could produce the wondrous herbal concoction that had been proven so beneficial and healing. This seeming selflessness had successfully enlisted most of the young people to the promotion of what she called the true way to health and in a very short time had nearly all of them enjoying the daily use of the Kaav herbal mixture which enabled them to all enjoy the remarkable, though not permanent effects of the plant; save just a very few individuals; though one would soon have a change of heart!

~~~~~~~~~~~~~~~~~~~~~~~~~~~~~~

Tecumseh and Billigana had been skeptical from the beginning, for they were not at all comfortable with a medicine with effects that were not at all permanent and had been adamant about abstaining from its use, thinking it the wiser course of action. They noticed also that the king was among those that would not partake of the invigorating concoction, as he had been made very skeptical of all that Angelii had offered after the strange change in his beloved wife Melanie had occurred after her relationship with the new stranger had begun.

He also did not understand how the young woman Angelii could be so wise and knowledgeable for one who appeared to be so young as her and how she could espouse the practice of "clean and pure" living on one hand and propose the use of this strangely invigorating herb on the other; something just did not fit!

~~~~~~~~~~~~~~~~~~~~~~~~~~~~~~

The bird Elgin and Angelii had moved their throng of devotee's many leagues and although they were not yet upon the Piasa, they would most likely arrive in just two more days. The two had been inspiring their warriors into what can only be described as a frenzy of anticipation; they had increased their use of the Kaav powder and been challenging one another with claims of what they would do to kill the beast and as the use of the Kaav and the claims grew, so did the delight of Angelii and Elgin.

Procedures that they had used in the past were in place and it seemed that they had their warriors in the perfect state of mind to deal with this expected appearance of a supposed magical creature; one that they were not about to allow it to interfere with their plans which were again being fulfilled just as they had in the past. Overall, the two felt as though nothing could stop the inevitable attainment of yet another tribe of men under their all-powerful rule, for after all it was the power that they found so gratifying. The power to command one of the throng to cut his own throat and watch as it was done if they so desired; the power to do as you wished to any of the people and not be questioned. This was unnaturally rewarding to both Elgin and Angelii and both had an insatiable taste for it that seemed only to be increasing, not unlike the horribly menacing and truly malevolent black dragons. The evil army, though they had time to spend even as the plans that had been put into place back at the Nastazi village came to fruition, increased their pace in order that they might find and kill the Piasa sooner!

Events were beginning to take on an inertia and power of their own and the entity that might have had a chance at the salvation of the situation was in a drug induced sleep that he would perhaps never be awakened from.

Billi and Tecumseh were very concerned with the strange following that the stranger that they had brought into their midst had begun to enjoy. Unfortunately they had no idea how really bad it was becoming for their people, or what they could in fact do to right the situation, but they knew that they must contact the Piasa and so they were again attempting the light dream state that had seemed to be working before.

Tecumseh told Billigana, "If we are not successful today we must take a wind-rider and go to where I have seen him, I know that I can find him and we must."

"Agreed," Billi answered! "But we seemed to be so close before, I feel that we can reach him this time."

"I shall try again," he said.

Together they lay in their clearing and relaxed in order to attempt to reach the dream state that they knew they must achieve in order to reach their friend the Piasa. They needed to relax and be in a restful state to do this, but they could not help but feel the urgency of their situation. They not only needed their friend, but now they needed to warn him of the bad intent that the stranger Angelii had in store for not only their people, but they felt surely also for him. They had seen the strange small bird watching their attempts at reaching him and felt that they had somehow given away his whereabouts or perhaps something even more important to the enemy, though they knew not what or how.

This time it seemed to take forever, but finally the near-sleep state arrived Tecumseh seemed to leave his body, stretch out and take flight into the beautiful Midwestern sky. He rose above his beautiful village, with its tremendous network of mounds and ceremonial sites, its great wooden halls for the gathering and domiciles of his good people, the crops that they had planted and the practical and even beautiful fish trapping areas that they had constructed next to the horseshoe lake that was at a very recent time, also part of the great river. Then it was over the great river itself and onto the gorgeous and game filled rolling hills that made up the countryside on the western side of the river that would by later people be known as the Ozarks. Still he progressed in the direction that he could feel the attraction of the deep bond that had developed with his friend Granger, the Piasa. Soon he saw the landscape below change entirely, the hills disappeared as did the trees and they were replaced by the endless flat grasses of the unending prairie. As far as the eye could see was a tremendous sea of tall grass, yet he continued to be pulled in the direction of his friend, Northwest towards the black hills that he could not at first see, though he continued to approach unflinchingly, being honest to his feelings and true to his heart he could soon see upon the horizon the outlines of the dark hills that he sought.

He was amazed at the control that he seemed to have in this dream flight, it all seemed so real, the colors of the grass on the prairie below and the waving motion that the wind seemed to caress it with, except for the speed with which he could cover the vast distances which was most astounding. Off to the west he could see the beginnings of another thunderhead that would surly drift his way, as they always did, but ahead of him he was beginning to see a cloud of dust rising into the air from the earth below. He strained to be able to see what was making such a commotion on the ground that it would make something so visible from such a long way off.

He thought for certain that it must be one of the huge herds of the animals that many of the people of the plains utilized for most all of their needs. They called them Tatanka and their lives seemed to totally revolve around this creature and the use of absolutely everything that the animal provided for nearly all of their needs, it seemed to Tecumseh that this was of an extremely narrow focus, especially considering the diversity that his people enjoyed living in the incredible trading center that was his home, for his people were fortunate enough to see and taste items from many faraway and sometimes unknown lands. The time seemed to pass very slowly, but soon he was able to see that it was not the herd of Tatanka that he had expected to see, but a gathering of a hoard of people. No, he was soon able to see that it was not just people, but a large group of warriors and from his limited experience he thought that they looked very much like the Mayans that his people had the bad experience with several seasons ago, just after the attack that had killed the previous king and so many of the elders, including his father. He then noticed that there were those of his own people mixed within the throng and even some of the hated Pawnee that had been fought off several seasons before in the formerly mentioned attack. It made him feel very strange to see this unusual mix, many of which appeared to be his own people and even stranger still that he somehow knew that they were looking for his friend the Piasa, he knew not how, but he knew this to be true and their numbers also seemed to be growing in some manner!

He began to panic; he had to warn Granger about the army of warriors that were headed his way, surely with malevolence in their hearts towards the Piasa. He was in a desperate situation he must warn the Piasa, yet he was not physically there, he was there solely in a dream.

He tried to scream as he grew closer, but even the warriors below did not hear him as he passed overhead. He grew closer to where he knew his friend lay and tried with all of his might and everything that he could muster to reach him with the pleadings of his mind, but nothing would work. He had absolutely no response from his friend, but finally he was able to see him. That is when the dream became very strange, for all of his efforts he could not go down to reach or touch his friend, as he just seemed to float in the air above him and could not receive any kind of response from the Piasa. He just seemed to be suspended there with his situation becoming ever more desperate. He could only estimate that the warriors would be there by the middle of the day tomorrow and what they had planned for his friend would surely be horrific.

He could not even begin to think of what he could do to save his friend, but then like a bolt of lightning it came to him; the wind riders. He must wake and use the hot windbags to come to the rescue of his friend, but he seemed to be a prisoner of this dream and for some reason could not seem to make anything within it change, the turmoil within him continued to grow for he knew not what he could do to escape this horrible condition. The suffering and pain that he felt seemed to be tearing at his heart and was becoming unbearable, he thought that it would burst, his face began to form a terrible grimace and he was so distressed that he began to think that he would surely die!

Billigana had been watching her man intently and had watched upon his face a myriad of expressions, all of which she recognized, for she knew her man like no other. She had sensed his wonder as he had begun his dream and realized the changes that he had been experiencing, until in the last several minutes the look of his face had become more puzzling until she thought that she could see fear on his face and then to her horror she knew that she could see the terror upon her lovers face.

Suddenly he started violently and was instantly wide awake.

"The Piasa is in grave danger," he exclaimed hoarsely. "We must go to him."

"It was only a nightmare my love," Billi consoled.

"No, it was more than a mere dream," he held her shoulders tightly and stared directly into her beautiful green eyes. "It was a vision and I know exactly where our friend is at and since we cannot awaken him then we must go to be at his side and find a way to protect him."

"You are certain," she queried?

"I am as certain as the sunrise, as certain as my never ending love for you and you and only you truly know the certainty of that love, but he is soon to be surrounded by enemies."

She looked at her love with a terrible dread, a feeling of impending horrible doom, a feeling unlike any she had ever felt before.

"It is Angelii and she has with her more warriors than I have ever seen before. Their numbers cover the plains for as far as the eye can see. They are many more than we could ever protect the Piasa from by ourselves and they look as though they are possessed of some sort of madness. They now descend upon the Piasa and will be upon him soon, by tomorrow mid-day for certain."

"So the helpless maiden played us for fools and has designs that we were unaware of," Billi realized, as the reality of the situation was finally making itself known. "But what of all of these warriors, why did she come to us in the strange deceitful manner if all that she would have needed to do was attack with her hoards of crazed warriors?"

"I am not certain of anything yet my love, but I feel that a major part of the huge group that I saw her leading were our own people. This could be why the population of the village has appeared so scant these last few days and a result of her deceitful ways," Tecumseh theorized.

"But she has been with us for such a short time. Yes she has begun to do some good, but what kind of power could she hold over our own people to make them turn against the Piasa, especially to the point of wanting to harm him," Billi said, now very much distressed. She gazed into her mans eyes as he did into hers and suddenly it was very clear, it had been right in front of them for a number of moons now. The Kaav plant; that is why she wanted all to partake of it as often as she did, not only did it make you ignore any ailments and even feel as though you were nearly immortal and possessed of unsurpassed strength, no these were not its main attributes though they at first appeared to be. The main power that the plant possessed was the power to enslave those that used it, the term that would become known in the modern times was addiction; indeed a horrible power to wield!

Simultaneously they whispered to one another, "The Kaav plant."

Billi said to Tecumseh, "We must save any who are not already under its grasp." But Tecumseh was already up and on his way urging her to follow as quickly as she could.

"You travel through the young maidens by the community gathering lodge and I will pass through the woods and down by the lake, warn every one that you can. But do not tarry, we must meet at Nanuma's teaching hall and enlist her students help in preparing the bag of hot wind, for it is our only chance to help Granger, make every haste!" He was off down the cliff and stopped just long enough to spot her in case she tumbled on the way down and then they were off their separate ways.

Billigana was the first to encounter anyone; she came upon a group of young maidens that were gathering the prickly white plant that was spun into the thread that made the strangely light fabric that was used for the bags of hot wind. They were picking it so rapidly that they were actually wasting a good portion of it by leaving it behind; not taking the great care that the Piasa had taught them was needed, they were also laughing and joking, acting as though they had not a care in the world, but what was really strange was that they were all harvesting the fluffy white fibers so quickly that they were oblivious to all of the deep gashes that were being gouged into their hands and did not even realize how much blood that they were tainting their harvest with; she stopped.

Billi tried to explain to them, "The plant that she has you ingesting will make slaves of you all, look at how you are acting. Is this the way that we were taught to harvest the plant for the fine threads?"

Of the dozen girls that were there, only three of them bothered to stop and listen and one of them said just, "No, it makes our lives better." Then when she continued in her frenzy, Billi blurted out, "Do not become slaves to the strangers plant," as she left the group; but she felt in her heart that it was probably too late; for this group anyway.

Upon entering the village she saw several of the stranger's warriors slumped into some of the ornate hammocks that her people loved to make and use for resting. Many cultures admired how large and well made the hammocks that her people produced were and for many generations they had been one of their many goods of trade. The hammocks were extremely comfortable to doze in and were greatly valued for this aspect along with their wonderful workmanship, but these two warriors were in a far deeper sleep than a nap in a hammock. They seemed to be in the throes of what seemed to be one of the effects that accompanied the use of this insidious drug, Kaav. She had witnessed that many of those that had used the drug and stopped ingesting it for a while could not help but fall into a very deep sleep, somewhat like the effects of the drinking of too much of the wine that the elders produced, only far worse. She also noticed as she stole quickly past them that they had sprawled very close to them their bows and the strange blowguns that she had heard of with what looked like the satchels containing the darts that accompanied them. She picked up the blowguns and dart satchels and quickly hid them and the bows in the nearby brush and was quickly on her way.

She continued into the village and witnessed several more terrible examples of the influence of the dreadful plant that she felt certain was infecting her people like some kind of sinister disease. She ran past gourds and many other root vegetables that appeared to have been harvested from the gardens yesterday yet had not been cleaned or cared for in any of the customary ways that were usually performed immediately by the persons that had gathered them, but instead these had been allowed to lay exposed to the sun and weather not far from the walking path that they had been haphazardly tossed beside.

She knew and loved all of the girls that would be involved in this duty and was appalled at the thought of the negative changes brought about by this deceitful woman and her horrendous plant. She was even more concerned though when she came upon the next group of young people that were gathered just outside of the interior of the village near the southern entrance close to the main mound were most of the community functions normally took place. It was a place of worship and considered sacred ground, yet they were all partaking of the strange new drug in different ways that she had not yet seen, some were smoking it which was surprising to Billi, as she had not ever seen it partaken in that way and some were ingesting it in much more personal ways that appeared to be some strange perversion of the loving sex act that her and her man shared out of mutual love and respect; they were defiling sacred ground and thought nothing of it! She was certain that there was no helping of this group of her people either.

Further into the village she was finally rewarded with the occurrence something positive. She stumbled across one of Nanuma's best apprentices; Coi LeSerre seemed to be ambling out from the longhouse next to the shelter where Nanuma was always busy teaching her disciples about the ways of the Piasa that she called the "Truth of living" along with all of the other important skills that she was teaching them. She was dressed only in a long toga-like shawl that barely covered her young body and was torn and bloodied in places and very dirty. She looked as though she had been through a very rough time of it indeed, but you could see the recognition of her friend in her eyes as she approached.

Coi LeSerre grabbed at Billigana and bade her to be silent as she whispered to her, "I tried to stop the use of the dreaded Kaav and I was taken prisoner several nights past for renewed acquaintance with the herb. They have forced themselves upon me and made me consume the herb for the past two days, but I have fooled them; I upchucked much of what they made me consume," she said proudly. But you could see that she had not been entirely successful from the weak shuddering of her small, young, bruised body. She continued weakly, "The evil one has many warriors that have come into our village and they are forcing those of us who will not consume the plant any more to partake against our will, they force much upon us; they have forced so much of the deadly plant upon me in this past morning that I fear that I no longer have control of myself, it makes you crave it so!"

Tecumseh and I are going to help you," Billi looked into the helpless girls eyes supportively and asked, "Where is Nanuma and how many are those of our people that have yet to succumbed to the plant?"

"There are so few of us left and it is about to become even less," she paused and sobbed. "The stranger's warriors are even now in Nanuma's longhouse forcing those that are still pure to partake, it is of no use; they also force upon you far more than just the Kaav," she said feebly.

"Tecumseh is here with me and we can help," Billi said.

"It is no use," Coi LeSerre whimpered, "They are now too great in number and the size of their force continues to grow with time as more of our people are convinced that they need the Kaav so, that they would become this evil woman's slaves. The king gathered his army and attempted to stand, but it was to no avail as they were overwhelmingly outnumbered. The king and his forces did very well not to just be massacred, but he only managed to escape into the woods, only one can help save us now; the Piasa?"

A more pitiful cry for help could not have been heard and Billi was grievously certain that her answer was also just a hollow plea for the help that she knew must come if they were to survive. "We have found the Piasa, he will be here soon," she said, but was also quick to add, "Though we could use your help!"

Coi LeSerre shook her head in agreement, but it was obvious that even this trivial movement took a great effort and while her loyalty would not be in question, her ability to help was a source of real concern.

"What would you have me do my friend? I will help in any way possible," Coi stated bravely.

Billigana looked at her friend thoughtfully for a moment as she weighed her options and said, "Firstly we need to help our sister Nanuma out of the dilemma that she is now in. How many warriors did you say were in the longhouse with them?"

"I saw seven men at arms and four of the maidens from our own people that now swear their allegiance to the wicked stranger and her strange little bird. They are all heavily armed with bows and even the strange blowguns that seem to have a poisoned dart of some kind inside, they are a force too large for you and your Tecumseh, I fear," as she again began to appear very hopeless.

Billi gazed at her and let her now quietly, "Not when you have a plan."

She smiled as she began to speak, "Are there any more of us that you know of that are still loyal to the king?"

"Yes," Coi answered. "But, I believe that they have run to hide in the woods near the fishing camp."

"If I assist you to the main temple can you sound the Gondel for at least one dozen strokes?" Billigana queried, a plan taking shape in her mind. The Gondel was located on the front of the facade of the main temple. It was made of a strange metal that the Nastazi did not understand how to produce, as they did not really ever work with the metals that they sometimes traded for. It was huge, taller than any of their men and was hung on an ornately decorated archway that was even approaching the height of the standing head of the Piasa, yet it could be struck and rung with an ingenious system of ropes and levers from near the main alter and fortunately for them the system required very little strength.

Billi wrestled and dragged the nearly helpless Coi to the main temple in the middle of the village as quickly as she could, but still felt that she was using up time that she could not afford to lose, she hurried along as best as she could.

Coi began to show signs of duress and the effects of being overcome by the drug, she asked, "What about Tecumseh?"

Billi thought to herself, yes I could really use him now, but answered, "He will be along shortly, but for now we must start the plan."

Billi was making tremendous headway, but the sheer size of the main pyramid that she had to travel the entire length of, had cost her a great deal of time. Finally she approached one of the four great cornerstones that had been put at the base of the earthen structure as part of its impressive construction and was about to turn to travel down the front of the temple to the Gondel when from out of nowhere appeared Mandi, standing blocking her way with her hands balled upon her hips defiantly. Mandi was the first of her people to experience the use of the terrible plant that was in fact enslaving her people, this was not good!

Tecumseh was beside himself with grief for the Piasa and was terrified about what was surely about to happen to his huge and glorious, but at this time seemingly helpless friend. He was also filled with a terrible rage towards this woman Angelii that they had opened their hearts to and not only rescued her but made every attempt possible to help her in any way that they could only to be rewarded by her treachery and the attempt, so far very successful, at the enslavement of all his people. He had made his way into the village in a more circuitous manner in order to attempt to locate some of his trusted friends and comrades.

He first traveled around and came up from behind the warriors practice fields, hoping to find King Trevlon Tankan or some of his men at arms. He approached quietly at first, but soon found that this was not necessary as the fields were deserted. This was strange, but not entirely unexpected as they probably had already encountered some of Angelii's brood and might now even consider themselves in a state of war. He ran in his well-trained warrior's gate of silence around to the other side of the village, skirting the parts of the village that were most likely to be occupied. He was dwarfed by even the smaller of the pyramids and mounds that he ran past and he was as careful as he could be to stay entirely out of sight; attempting to stay just on the edge of the woods in order to have an effective method of disappearing quickly if someone should get sight of him.

He traveled to the other side of the village towards the horseshoe lake and the great river, entering the area where the woods grew much more thickly because of the fertile ground from the constant floods of the river and soon came upon the fish camp that was located between the lake and the river on what his people called "the bottoms," in fact the people that occupied this land in more modern times would call the entire area by this name. (The Mississippi Bottoms is a name used for this area even today describing the entire flood plain.) This was a place where he certainly thought that he would be able to find some of his comrades, but the camp like the rest of the village was strangely deserted.

As he searched further he was rewarded with the discovery of many tracks that looked as though they were left by an assembly of men and upon careful inspection he was able to realize that these where in fact the tracks of Nastazi warriors, he could see from some of the clearer prints the locking stitch pattern that his friend Nanuma was so fervent about teaching the young girls in the art of making the moccasins that they all wore. This was a very good piece of information and he knew that he should go immediately to catch up with his fellow Nastazi warriors, but he could not leave Billigana without aid of any kind. The Great Spirit only knew what she had encountered and he must be there if she was in need of him. He would return here as quickly as he could, but for now he must find Billi.

Tecumseh was not aware, but he was being watched from the brush somewhat further on by two young Nastazi warriors that were following their orders very well and just observing, although they had their bows drawn and had targeted Tecumseh for fear of him being one of the Nastazi traitors that they had heard of and even seen for themselves several times. They were honorable Nastazi braves though and followed their orders well; this was a good thing for Tecumseh for it saved him from an untimely end!

The Nastazi queen, Melanie was still near the center of the village and did not realize that she was just about to unknowingly contribute to Billigana's plan to free Nanuma in a way that could not have been more helpful had she planned it that way. She had been totally corrupted by Angelii and her drugs, along with her strange and before now among her people rarely practiced; woman on woman sex with its bizarre newness and fascination, or perhaps it was merely the influence of the drugs, she did not really know. What was certain though was the way that she had torn her once avid loyalty to her husband and only other lover, King Trevlon Takan asunder and made her one of the first and most strongly held of the slaves that Angelii had taken from the Nastazi people. Her husband had recognized her loss to himself and somehow although she could see the furious rage in his eyes; had chosen to spare her even though he knew that she had betrayed him!

The queen had now realized that her husband knew of her unfaithfulness; she did not now understand this type of unconditional love and it bothered Melanie greatly as she sat alone in her chambers just a short distance from the main temple. She simmered in a deep loneliness having been alienated from her husband and now not having seen Angelii for many days, her mood was black and sullen.

Billigana was taken aback and thought surely that she would have to drop young Coi and fight Mandi or even silence her with her knife; for Mandi was most certainly the furthest under the influence of the hideous drugs effects; Billi gently dropped Coi and prepared to pounce.

Mandi could see her reaction and pleaded quietly, "No, my friend, please wait all is not as it seems."

Billi stopped momentarily, uncertain of just what to do, but she listened.

Mandi was quick to explain, "I am not under the spell of the plant any more. I saw what it had done to me and while it was the most difficult thing that I have ever done in my life I have stopped partaking of it."

Words of the Piasa

"What do you mean," Billi asked with the fire of disbelief strong in her tone? "I saw her feed it to you for days."

"Yes," She said. "Without it I probably would have died, but after a short time I could feel that I had become its slave and I could not stand that situation, that is when I vowed to make the change."

"Is that so," Billigana hissed, still not fully believing all of what she was being told?

"Yes, it is true. It took a many days and I do not even know that everyone would be able to accomplish it; but I did. It was very difficult as they kept bringing me more and so I had to hide it on many different occasions. Sometimes the pull of the plant was so strong that I could not even resist and had to have more once again, but slowly I was able to break away from its terrible grip and I feel so much better for it now, though I am still very weak."

Billi began to show her beautiful full and hopeful smile saying, "This is a gift from the Great Spirit, I am so thankful to see that you are back to your old self. Our people are in desperate need of our help now, can you help me to free Nanuma and some of her girls?"

Mandi was overjoyed at the opportunity to be able to help and said, "Yes, anything that I can do for my people and especially you I would be honored."

"Good," Billi said as they gingerly placed Coi at the foot of the alter with instructions to begin to sound the Gondel in just the time that it would take them to get back to Nanuma's longhouse and get into place.

As they raced silently back to the longhouse to take up their place and retrieve the blowguns Billi quickly went over the plan as it was, "We will place ourselves at two of the spy-holes that Nanuma has in the longhouse for her teaching uses and upon my hand signal we will begin to quietly take out the guards with their own blow guns. Then when Coi begins to sound the Gondel we will scream away from the longhouse that the Piasa has returned, repeating it with great joy and conviction convincing those inside that he has indeed returned."

"And when they come outside and realize that there is no Piasa," Mandi asked?

"Just shoot the darts as quickly as you can," Billi said with a hopeful smile. They were both aware that the eleven lives of the prisoners inside; their friends all were now fully held within their hands.

Then something unexpected happened; they hugged one another a deep meaningful and emotional hug for good luck and took up their places. Billi was quick to give the signal, but it was difficult for her to be able to see any way to get a clear shot as the prisoners were in between the rescuers and the captors. Finally Mandi was able to get off a shot and it was right on target, it hit one of their quarries right in the back of the neck, he dropped sinking to his knees almost immediately.

An instant later Billi was able to get off a shot and struck her target squarely in the base of the throat. Luck was with her, as he had his back to his comrades and fell forward although unfortunately with a great deal of noise.

The attention of the leader of the brutes that had imprisoned her good friend and teacher Nanuma had been piqued and he now began to step towards the teacher; his large muscular bulking frame dwarfing that of the little teacher. He was not certain what had dropped two of his men, but he had a feeling that this one was involved in it for he had seen her kind before. He knew that she was a planner; quiet but always thinking, as he took another step towards her looking ever more menacing the closer that he approached. From the corner of his eye he then saw another of his men on the other end of the room slump down onto the floor; his rage began to reach a crescendo just as he was now within reach of the old woman that obviously seemed to be the leader of all these girls. As he reached out to grab her by her full head of hair a loud piercing sound began. The Gondel was being rung for the first time in many moons and for him the very first time that he had ever heard this distinct and most deafening sound, it stopped him in his tracks. Nanuma took this time to move a few steps out of the way, for she had finally realized what had been happening. She had help from outside and they knew of her spy-holes. Only a very few people knew of these "tools of her trade" and she could only guess who it may be, Billigana or Mandi perhaps, but for now she just got out of the way!

As soon as Nanuma had made her move she was rewarded by the sight of the leader of the Sunomayans, for that is what she had heard them call themselves, fall into a heap on to the floor and at the very same instant she began to hear from outside calls of the return of the Piasa.

The calls seemed full of joy and continuous and all seemed to be coming from the direction of the main temple where she thought certain that he would land; oddly though, she had not heard a sound at all from the Piasa and she knew that he was in the habit of loud trumpeting upon his arrival so as not to frighten the people upon his appearance. She saw also that over half of the force that had been holding them was now incapacitated and her and her girls now outnumbered their captors eleven to three; additionally they seemed to be in an awful state of disarray, torn between going out to face this Piasa that they had heard so much about or their duty to maintain the guard over the hostages. They had also gravitated up into the front of the longhouse where it was no longer possible to take a shot at them for their outside rescuers. They were still three very strong, well armed warriors against an old woman and ten young girls.

Fortunately Billi and Nanuma were both of the same minds; Nanuma told the three from across the room. "The Piasa does not take the holding of his friends as prisoners very lightly, if you leave out the front door at once before we begin to scream, you may be able to save yourselves."

They looked at her with definite distrust and then at one another with what could only be described as deep fear and bolted for the front door to attempt their escape. However, waiting for them outside were two Nastazi warrior maidens that dispatched two darts and a crisp blow to the skull dispatching the last three of the captors instantly.

Mandi and Billigana stood over the three for only a moment and were then joined by the group that had been held hostage. Many thanks were exchanged and hugs and caresses of well-being were exchanged; Nanuma was last to appear from out of the longhouse.

Billi; and Mandi too, I thought that it might have been either of you, but to see you both does not surprise me either, she approached and embraced them both.

"So much bad has happened in so short a time," Billi said!

"Yes," Nanuma agreed as Mandi just shook her head in accord.

"How many of our reliable people are still left," Mandi asked?

"How many who are loyal to the Nastazi chief and not to the drug," Billi questioned?

"I feel that there are none left in the village, save Coi who may or may not have lasted. They had her in here all night last night before they brought us in. I am certain that she was filled with the drug. May the Great Spirit protect her from what else they have done to her." Nanuma informed them with revulsion obvious in her voice. "May she be furnished with the strength that she needs," She added.

Billi responded with deep felt compassion, "Yes, we saw her and she looks as though she has had a very rough time of it, but she has a great inner strength as she has proven it by helping us to free all of you."

She asked Mandi quietly, "Can you take several of these girls to the main temple and help her to rejoin us so that we may help her regain her strength?"

"Certainly, my friend; as you say," Mandi proclaimed enthusiastically!

Billigana was somewhat surprised by this incredible show of loyalty, but nobody else was. She asked, "Are there any others that we can count on?"

Nanuma looked very hopeless and stated, "Perhaps one quarter of our women escaped into the woods or were sent by their husbands for safety, but not more than one fifth of our men I fear and they were mostly the elders and the king's personal bodyguard. So very few are left and the Piasa I fear has been killed. These hideous men said that they knew where he was at several days ago and sent a large force to deal with him. The Piasa is very powerful, but what can even he do against so many?"

Billi attempted to comfort her, she said. "The Piasa is not yet perished, he is in a trance and according to Tecumseh it would take much to harm him while he is within this trance. The danger will come when he awakes and we have a plan to assist him if we can enlist your help."

"Anything that I can do, when our people's lives are at stake, the future of all of the Nastazi rests in our hands now," She exclaimed! "What would you have me do I would lay down my own life for my people!"

"Yes, of that I am certain Nanuma," there was no doubt of the loyalty within this woman. "With any luck that will not be necessary. Tecumseh and I are in need of the fastest of the Wind Riders and we need it ready as quickly as possible."

"As you wish," Nanuma spoke as though she was speaking to the new queen; which many of her peers began exactly at this time to respect her as. "But what of Tecumseh, where is he," Nanuma asked?

Billi answered knowingly. "Do not worry my wise old friend he heard the Gondel and I am certain that he will be here shortly."

Just as was spoken so recently by his soul mate, Tecumseh appeared just moments later carefully picking his way down the main causeway towards the temple where they were all gathered. This also now included a stack of prisoners that had been tied in very secure knots and piled in a group upon the steps of the temple. As the group was debating where to keep the prisoners Billi saw her man edging down the road and quickly dropped what she was doing and ran to meet him. They met in the middle of the road surrounded by the magnificent pyramids that their people had built and embraced enjoying a long and ardent kiss, as though they had not seen each other in days, it must have been the feeling of danger that was so palpable at this time.

Tecumseh spoke first, "I am so glad to see you, I worried so for you for much is amiss with our people and I feared greatly for your safety."

"And I yours, my love, but do not worry for me for I will always find a way to return to you," she assured him.

Billigana showed Tecumseh the prisoners and reacquainted him with Nanuma and all of the other friends that she had managed to rejoin and he was very pleasantly surprised, "You seem to have managed very well in my absence." He complimented her as he gave her another welcomed hug.

"Yes, but there is still much to do and we must begin now," Nanuma added as she and half of her girls scurried past in order to get the Wind Rider ready for flight.

Tecumseh and Billi watched their friends quickly disappear around the corner in order to prepare the craft that they would need to succeed in their quest to save their people. Tecumseh said, "I believe that I can find the remnants of our warriors, but I need to go to the Piasa. It is important for us to get a message to the king and his fighters as they are most likely our only chance at reclaiming our village."

"Yes, we will send one of the girls with the message," Nanuma agreed.

"It cannot be just anyone, there must be numerous enemies spread throughout the woods. It must be somebody exceptional, someone that you can trust," he stated firmly.

"I have the perfect lady in mind," Billi said with assurance.

Mandi has already proven herself to be a dependable warrior and most helpful when problems arise," Billi said convincingly.

"But how can she be free from the drug, she was the first to use it," he asked in disbelief.

"She recognized what it was doing to her and fought off the effects and then kept them off with trickery, it was an amazing and resourceful feat. I truly believe that there are few that could have done it," Billigana said in a most approving tone.

"She was always one that I felt held special qualities," Tecumseh agreed with her fully and immediately. "I just hope that she has recovered enough to be able to take part in the physical aspects of the battle that I fear awaits us.'

"This same hope, I hold in my heart for all of us that look ahead to the next period of time that I fear will decide the fate of our people," Billi said softly as she gazed lovingly into her man's eyes.

"You, as always speak the truth my love, these will be trying times, but we will face them together," he told her gently and embraced her with the greatest of love and admiration. "It is time now that we act. Send Mandi to the South side of the "Bottoms" and there she will pick up the trail of what I am certain are our remaining forces under King Trevlon Takan. She must get word to him of the danger that the Piasa is in, but moreover the size of the army that now opposes us and see if he can devise some sort of plan to battle a force that outnumbers us ten to one. Also let him know that we have gone ahead to attempt to revive the Piasa in a wind rider and we shall return as quickly as we can, hopefully with the Piasa."

"I will tell her all, is there anything else," Billi asked?

"Send her with our love and let her know that we hope the Great Spirit watches over her," Tecumseh told her, and added, "And return quickly, as we must make haste."

"Yes, my love," she chirped, as she turned and sped off.

Tecumseh watched her disappear around the corner admiring completely of the woman that she was now becoming, her strengths, her compassion for all of her people, her athletic, nubile and increasingly voluptuous young body and mostly her uncompromising love that he knew she felt for him. He was a very young man, but felt that he had been blessed for life, but he must make time to reverie later for now he had a responsibility to his friend. He must find a way to rouse the Piasa before the hoards of the evil Angelii reached him and did terrible deeds to him, or even kill what might possibly be the very last of the grand and wondrous dragons.

Not far from there, in a deep part of the woods between the great river and the largest of the horseshoe lakes in the region, at the spot that their people called "The Bottoms" waited a force of men that was now the last of what could be called loyal Nastazi warriors. To the man they were exceptionally well trained and this was made quite obvious by their undeniable following of their kings orders not to ever imbibe in the strange new plant that had been introduced by the sensual, but as it had turned out, very malicious Angelii and her evil little bird, called Kaav; while most of their people had succumbed to the deceitful wonders of this as of yet undiscovered plant, these men and for that matter quite a few of the stronger willed women had kept themselves free of the treacherous influences of this promised "wonder drug" and they were the last of the loyal followers who remained loyal to King Trevlon Takan, the last that followed the ways and directives of the Great Spirit that they felt were and continued to be channeled through their king, and they were the last that had not fallen under the addictive powers of the evil conspirators Angelii and her wicked associate who promoted only evil.

They had made a temporary camp that was only a few leagues from their village, but was very easy to defend as it was surrounded by water with only small isthmus's on either end of the area to defend and for that matter since this was some of the thickest woodlands in the entire land they would also be nearly impossible to detect in the first place. Trevlon Takan took no chances though and had sentries and lookouts posted around the entire perimeter of their camp, yet even with his thoroughness of guards and scouting, he had been very surprised at the fact that they had not had even a single encounter with their enemy as of yet, this was most peculiar as it was known that the invaders outnumbered his men ten to one in and around the village and he felt certain that they knew that he and his men had come in this direction, they seemed to be in no hurry at all to enter the final battle for his village, or perhaps there was some other reason.

The reason likely had to do with the person that he was certain had been at the bottom of this, what had now been discovered to be an insidious and well planned plot, a plan that had unfortunately made victims of most of his people, including his beloved wife was already very clear to him. Angelii had used her beauty as a most powerful weapon and it had unfortunately affected most all that he held precious. He could only trust that perhaps there was still some remaining hope that Tecumseh and Billigana were still remaining free, he had thought to himself and perhaps they will bring back the Piasa to help us to make things right. He only stared off into the distance over the water of the great river and slowly closed his eyes and lowered his head as the intense despair tightened ever increasingly around him.

Suddenly one of his young warriors that had been on lookout at the south end of the bottoms came running to him and striving to catch his breath while attempting to speak at the same time saying, "King, I have seen your friend that you spoke to us of; Tecumseh."

The king perked up immediately saying, "Yes and what was his state, how did he appear to you?"

"Well, I believe what you thought of him is true as he appeared to be quite tired," The young scout blurted out that which was obviously very good news to his king.

"Tired was he, I knew that he would resist this horrible and sinister plant," the king Trevlon Takan smiled as he said softly. "He may be tired, but he has the heart of a panther and he will not fail in his mission, "Which direction did you see him go?"

"My King, I only saw him return to the direction of the village, after that he was beyond my sight as you had set limits on how far that you wanted us to venture."

"Yes, my son and you did well to obey, I am certain now that we will see him alight in one of the bags of hot wind shortly," The king mused out loud. "This can only be the best of news for it means that there is still a chance to have the help of the Piasa once again."

He clasped the young man on the back with as hearty and appreciative shake and told him, "Well done; now return to your post and continue with the same vigilance." The king was an honorable man, but not always one that praised those whom he felt were just performing their expected duties, no matter how well or with what vigilance that they performed them. However, he felt now that these had become special times and that possibly even all of their time could possibly now be growing very short; he felt that this was a time that the young man just needed to hear the appreciation from his commander and was glad to bestow it.

He did not fully realize at this time how accurate that this thought actually was.

Something told the king that a great reckoning was about to occur, the warrior within him told him that it was to be a great battle. This was very true, but it was not at all the kind of battle that he was used to fighting, and he did not realize at this point in time how poorly prepared for it that his people really were.

Sadly some effects, once set in motion were quite impossible to stop!

He did not exactly know what to do for he had the nagging feeling of the approach of the unexpected and so he did what he had become comfortable with, he called out new orders, "Redouble the guards and continue producing as many arrows as possible their great numbers may be our only salvation."

His warriors busied themselves with the preparations for the battle that they knew was coming, but they had no idea that the weapons that they were preparing would be useless against the type of foe that they would soon face. Alas, some of them would surely find their salvation and survive through these horrible times, but they would be so very few; and his people, the Nastazi for the most part I am sad to say were already doomed.

Back at the kings quarters in the Nastazi village of Nakokia the queen Melanie was simmering and had transformed into the darkest of moods. She had not seen her husband King Trevlon Takan now for four days and felt assured that he had given up on her and left her to her own methods. "No matter," she murmured to herself, but for an instant she wondered how her deep and unending love of a short time ago for her husband had changed so. How did this strangely tempting experiment in a strange new love become what it had, and how had it cost her so much as it now seemed? She sensed a great longing and felt the memory that she had, until recently had only for her husband and king begin to flicker back to life.

Yet she had a physical aching in her loins to see Angelii again and to spend more time in her embrace, more time experiencing her warm touch, it was the way that she used to feel for her husband, the king, only somehow far stronger and in a way far more primitive. Her thoughts of him once again disappeared.

She was told by Angelii to make certain that the production of the Kaav powder was kept up in order to meet the needs of all that used it. It was very strange the way that it seemed that after a short time you did not just want it for its remarkable effects, but actually did "need" it in order to feel yourself. In fact she was beginning to need it just to prevent the onset of violent sickness, but she did not care for she was Angelii's lover and held in very high regard and this meant that she could have as much as she ever desired, so she decided to fight her anxiety with an especially large dose at this time. The feeling that this much Kaav gave her was reward in itself, she would most certainly be able to handle the waiting under these conditions. She snorted a long line of the Kaav powder and laid back, her whole body beginning to have a wonderful, warm almost sexual tingle. She was in no position to realize it, but the strange little bird had returned and was observing her and he had that sickly, evil look upon his face as if everything that he desired was happening just as he had willed it, though few that he had encountered and had actually survived really knew, that this was for the most part absolutely true so far!

~~~~~~~~~~~~~~~~~~~~~~

Many leagues away only perhaps one half a day's march from the sleeping Piasa Angelii's incessantly growing army had made camp for the evening. They did not camp so much for rest, as her troops all being under the influence of the Kaav plant did not have the same needs for rest as regular warriors may have needed. They camped more for the fact that they needed the advent of daylight to assist them with their search for the dragon-beast that they intended to capture or kill and with that crush all of the remaining hope that the Nastazi had of remaining free. Once again Elgin's plans seemed to be bearing the same fruit as they had so many other times in the past, they would be able to continue their life of taking all from those that they met, until they had no more to give and then move on to the next culture to take all that they had to give and so on and so on. They had enjoyed this lifestyle now for many hundreds of seasons passed and fully felt that she and Elgin were fully entitled to this style of life. All that they encountered was always theirs for the taking, if there was giving to be done then it would be only when she or the strange Elgin willed it and they did not often feel of the giving nature, that was just the misfortune of what they considered the weaker beings who the evil couple felt existed merely to serve them and for no other reason!

She surveyed her troops and motioned towards one of her commanders Laird. He approached forthwith and she posed a question that could not be misunderstood for a direct order that he must have the absolutely correct answer to, "How many head do we now have in camp?"

Laird did not need to search his memory for long, as he knew that this was something that he was expected to know and he was aware of the penalty for ignorance of facts that the queen expected you to be aware of, "The last count this morning had us at forty legions and fifty six heads (40,056 in modern terms.)

Angelii shook her head in obvious satisfaction while perceptibly apprising a newly promoted young man that stood a short distance from them. She turned and faced Laird and said, "Send back one league of your finest men to make certain that the delivery is unmolested on the trip back to us and tell them to finish the annihilation of any of these Nastazi that have not joined us in the consuming of the Kaav."

Laird answered, "Yes, my Queen I will begin the preparations."

She cut him short, "Do it now!"

He answered quickly, with the flicker of fear in his eyes that the queen enjoyed so, "At once my Queen," he stammered!

She then turned back to her evaluation of the fresh young man and added, "Send the young new lieutenant with the golden hair to my tent after you clean him up, he would service me tonight."

Her commander shook his head in immediate agreement and motioned to the young man to approach.

Then she added, "And tell him that when he comes to my tent just to do whatever I ask, but do not speak. Do you understand?"

"Yes queen Angelii," he muttered humbly. Feeling at a grievous loss as he was asked in the past to do just the same for his queen, he thought that he must have somehow displeased her. The thought soon passed though when he realized that if he had displeased her she would have most certainly have had him killed.

He told the young man to quickly clean himself up and go to the queens tent to do anything that she asks him to do, but do not speak a word. As the youth was returning from his washing he just muttered "Good Luck" to the lad; but as it happened, that was the last that ever saw that young man!

He then gathered the necessary lieutenants and gave the orders that would have many of his new recruits go to murder the people that they had until recently lived their previous lives with, powerless to deny the orders; the emptiness that he now felt was overwhelming. The Queen and her strange small bird were draining all that was good from their lives and their world and there was nothing that anyone could do to try and stop it.

As Angelii waited in her tent half clothed for this evenings pleasures her troops were beside themselves with the lust for battle and a desire to face the dragon that everyone was speaking of. They had sent several patrols out to reconnoiter the area and attempt to find the way to the dragon in the night, but none had been successful as of yet. This only tended to increase the bloodlust that was building in their hearts and this meant that the dragon was surely in store for a dreadful day of reckoning tomorrow. The strange thing was; that the pending danger towards another living being could easily wake the Piasa, but its own impending doom did little to resurrect the sleeping giant.

In a smaller pyramid at the edge of the village where in former days they had brought beans, wheat grasses and other items of their harvest to be processed, but lately had been used mainly for the making of the bags of hot wind and only most recently by the enemy for the production of the horrible enslaving herb that they were intent upon spreading, Nanuma and her students had finally finished preparing what they considered the best of the "wind riders" and it was now ready for flight. The problem was that it was now very late in the afternoon and they would soon have no daylight with which to see to be able to fly. Nanuma is the one that was first to state, "When the moon rises it may not be full, but it will be bright enough to see by and the stars should help you with the directions, even with the best of conditions you will need many hours of flight time to arrive at the place upon the plains that you have described, it is far to the North and West and you will need to fly most of the night in order to cover the distance."

Tecumseh agreed wholeheartedly saying, "Once again you are the bearer of wise advice Nanuma and I just want you to know how much we value your friendship."

Billi obviously agreed and the three all embraced as if it was their last time seeing each other and for as much as any of them knew, it just might be. (In fact it was.)

Tecumseh looked at Nanuma and Billi as she whispered to Nanuma, "Find all that are taking the Kaav and stop whomever you can and send as many as you can muster out to find where the evil drug is being produced and stop its production, wherever you find the plant destroy it. It is a scourge that we must free our people from. Do whatever you can to end its use and as quickly as you can and destroy all of the plants and seeds that you can find.

"Yes, I already have a plan in mind," Nanuma answered, her meticulous mental facilities already at work on the plan. Unfortunately the thoroughness of this plan might have actually been what doomed the vast majority of her people to certain extinction!

They repeated their parting gestures and Billi was hefted into the bag of hot wind by Tecumseh who then bounded into the basket to join her. They both looked around at the expert job that had been done in preparing the balloon with even more admiration for Nanuma and her girls. The balloon strained at its moorings as they did a quick inspection of the fire that burned in the embers basket just above their heads and they saw that at this time they would not need to add any more of the marvelous black rocks that they had found to burn in the bags of hot wind, as Nanuma had stoked it to perfection and the balloon seemed to be already at full capacity of the hot air that powered the craft, but when the need arose they had much more loaded. Tecumseh gave the sign and the moorings were loosed. They had to hold a very firm grip in the basket, as well as to each other as the craft seemed to leap into the cool evening air and additionally they had a small bit of good fortune at the beginning of the flight as the wind that was coming out of the south was pushing them precisely in the direction that they wanted to travel.

Billi stared deeply into her man's eyes and asked, "What now my love, how do we find our way?"

Tecumseh answered in as comforting a tone as he could muster, considering the amount of fear that he felt in his heart for the Piasa, as he said, "The moon will rise in a short time and we will be able to see the land much better by then, the stars will also guide us for as soon as we can see the North Star we will be able to use it as a beacon and it should lead us directly to where we need to go. Until then just lay here in my arms and let me hold you for we do not know if we will ever have this chance again."

She fully agreed with her man and just answered with the soft calling of his name. They lay there, fully enamored with each other and made love slowly, deeply and softly as if this was their last night together, for who knew what waited for them on this next morning.

With the finish of their loving union they lay in each other's embrace and continued to watch the sky and soon both drifted off to sleep. It must have been a beautiful sight, two young people very much in love drifting off in a balloon guided only by the winds of fate to try to save their friend and meet their own destinies.

After a short time they were both awakened by a refreshing of the night's breezes. They looked up and could now see a three-quarters moon had risen and the stars had begun to show themselves and there in the beautifully clear night sky they saw the North Star, their guide back to reuniting with their friend. Tecumseh got up immediately and began to make adjustments to their altitude in order to get the most speed that he could out of the craft.

Billi asked if there was anything that she could do to help and

Tecumseh told her, "Keep on the lookout for large river that will work its way to the west. We will follow it upstream for a time and after we have followed it for a number of leagues we should be able to see the huge mountain that appears to have been cut in half, this will take most of the night and into the morning, once we have passed the mount we will be nearly atop the glen of trees where the Piasa is trapped in his unwholesome sleep."

She looked into his eyes and said, "I do not know what tomorrow is to bring for us, but I am glad that I am facing it with you my love."

Tecumseh gently caressed her lovely face in both of his hands and whispered adoringly to her, "And I feel the same my love, I am ever thankful to be able to share my love with you and whatever fate has in store for us together!"

At the desired altitude the winds took them with unrealized and surprising speed. They settled into a warm embrace and gazed out over the beautiful scene that lay before them for it was truly a breathtaking night and theirs was truly a wonderful world.

Enormous and unstoppable changes had already been set in motion and the decisions and actions that had been made that day would shape theirs and many others entire futures!

Back in the present day, nestled in an enormous complex of caves in Southern Illinois, was a large brown Dragon that humans had at times called Quetzalcoatl, Yinglung, Drachenstein, or even now Granger, who was attempting to explain to a young boy with the name of Nathan Bellows some of the history of the young man's kind in an effort to enlighten him towards the mistakes that his predecessors had made in life and in so doing, not only save the young man's people, but hopefully to be able to save this lovely world that this dragon who was also called by some humans "Piasa" called home.

The Piasa had chosen young Nathan after observing him for a number of years and deciding that he had the qualities that would enable him, not only to listen to and learn from the entire story but also to convince others of the truth of what he had discovered. This, the dragon hoped, was the way in which to reach the humans and teach them how not to make the same mistakes that their ancestors had fallen victims of.

Nathan had been listening intently for hours with nary a word said until now when he finally said to the great brown dragon, "All of the people that you have been telling me of have seemed to be very advanced in some way or another. The Phoenicians and the Amazons seemed to know all that there was to know about the land and the seas, the people of Atlantis had created technologies that were far ahead of their time and the Nastazi through their network of trading and communicating with all of the people of the world seemed to know all about people and the interactions that exist between them, but it seems to me that you are trying to show me that they all had a great weakness that as of yet I do not understand. What is it? Can you tell me what it is that I might be able to help my people understand how to keep the present times from becoming the last days? I see on the news the weapons that we have and the terrorism that is taking place and I hear of the prophecies that are supposed to be coming true and it has begun to place a fear, deep in my soul that I cannot dispel."

"Yes, yes little one, it seems that I was correct about you; you are the one to teach the humans and I will tell you all, but you must hear the entire story to fully understand the importance of what I say, for although the different peoples considered themselves experts in many particular fields of knowledge, they did not know enough to understand that there is always more to know and one must never close the mind to the gathering of new knowledge. Furthermore, one must always strive to accept ones place in the world and perform your deeds of responsibility within the "Natural World." You will hear all that I will say and the end is near so try to be patient as I endeavor to complete my tale." Just then the great dragon flinched as he heard a sound somewhere near the front of the caverns that he thought that he recognized as that of the metal used in human weapons; he was ever so hopeful that he might be wrong on this occasion!

Back at the entrance to the caverns were the two men that fancied themselves as hunters. In truth, the type of hunting that they performed; baiting places with food for days only to wait for a hapless dear or hog to wander across this unexpected plenty just to be shot as they were about to enjoy their newfound windfall was truly only interspecies murder, and yet they labored under the false idea that it was some form of sport.

They had stopped at the mouth of the cave to each partake of a drink from the whiskey bottles that they each carried. They both stared at each other and made a great illustration of the lack of fear that each was attempting to show the other, as they also made a last inspection of the very large caliber rifles that they both carried. The one that called himself Burt said to the one known as Gill, "Even the biggest lizard on the planet won't stand a chance against this elephant killer," He patted his Browning A-Bolt WSSM .44 Magnum as he snickered.

"Especially when they are taking thirty rounds in a nine second burst," Gill retorted as he patted his automatic Kalashnikov AK-47 automatic rifle affectionately.

They both decided to relax for a moment and took another gulp from their bottles in an attempt to fortify their nerves before entering the cavern where they felt that their next trophy awaited. This time it seemed to take somewhat longer than it had in the past, but at last the time seemed right and they began to gather themselves for the "hunt," finally they turned, cocked their rifles and slowly walked further into the caverns entrance.

~~~~~~~~~~

The boys, Danny and Bill saw that the two hunters were readying to enter the cave and looked at one another as both recognized the similarities that their current style of living their lives had with these two horrible men, they then looked at each other nearly shivering in dismay; both realized at that moment that they must make a change in their lives, to save themselves!

Danny and Bill had somewhat calmed from the tremendous fear that they had felt only a short while ago, mainly due to the realization that if the monster wanted to harm them it would have done so and there would not have been anything that anyone could have done to stop it, however the horrible demise that they had initially imagined did not occur. This proved to the boys that the dragon was far more complex than either had imagined, he had begun the process of introspection within the two. This thought process was wholly new to these ill-raised boys; it would serve them very well for the rest of their lives and it seemed to have almost immediate results.

As they watched the two surly looking hunters disappeared into the mouth of the cave.

They knew not exactly why that they did what they would do next, but they found themselves headed right back to the same cave that they had just been told so forcefully to stay away from by the most frightening beast that either had ever seen. They made their way quietly back through the thick woods to the clearing that was just in front of the entrance; the one that they had only recently scrambled out of in great fear for their lives. They slowed and stopped when they saw the two ragged looking hunters standing at the entrance of the cave, but upon seeing them enter the dark mouth of the cavern they suddenly had no doubt that they must follow and do something to somehow warn the dragon. Why they needed to do this was not altogether clear to the confused pre-adolescent boys, but they truly knew that they must.

This was new territory for either of them, as they had for all of their lives been takers not givers and here they were for reasons still unknown about to help a being that they so sorely feared just moments ago. It felt very strange, but it also felt very right!

They followed the sounds of the obviously impaired hunters down the corridor deeper into the cave. It was utterly dark with absolutely no light to see anything at all, yet they continued and after a short while of following the sounds that the would-be hunters made and having absolutely no problem with locating their guides ahead of them in the hallway Bill turned to Danny and whispered, "How will they ever sneak up on the beast as loud as they are?"

Danny whispered back to Bill, "They do not really know what kind of magical being they are facing."

They both stopped for several moments and stared at one another, both realizing that some sort of change was taking place within them, though neither one of them fully understood, still they both seemed to fully welcome what was happening to them.

Deeper down the corridors of the massive cavern a great and ancient beast listened to the muffled sounds that he heard, for a time he seemed quite concerned, but at last he showed an understanding smile. He judged the distance of the noises and weighed the time that it would take for them to finally get down to where he and Nathan rested, then he turned back to the young boy and continued his story.

～～～～～～～～～

Back in the great Nastazi village that in ancient times was known as Nakokia, or in current times Cahokia, the escape of Nanuma and her young students had gone unnoticed by any of the occupying army of warriors that the malevolent queen Angelii had left in place. Some had heard the sounds of what they thought was some sort of great beast, but their fears had kept them from timely investigation of the sounds and so they missed the event that the sounds were actually connected with. This was another stroke of vast good fortune for the Nastazi who unknown to them were soon to run out of this positive luck they had so enjoyed.

Nanuma and her students obeyed what Tecumseh had told them and after helping to launch the wind rider that carried him and Billigana off to their fate of the attempted rescuing of the Piasa; they continued their efforts by quietly leaving the village and going towards the bottoms to make every effort to locate Trevlon Takan and the remainder of his force. They hoped that they would join them and give whatever assistance that they could offer and as part of this they had carried along with them the few weapons that they could find that they thought might help along with two of the remaining balloons, in hope that they may be used to help to win the battle that they felt was certainly in their immediate future.

The huge bags were very bulky and cumbersome and did not offer much to help promote silent travel. Upon the entry to what was considered "The Bottoms" they were immediately surrounded by a group from Trevlon Takan's small force. Fortunately, he was among the men closest to the small group of young women carrying the huge loads and lead by the old medicine woman Nanuma. He instantly recognized her and her students and let out a joyous howl of recognition, "Yeoww, some of the good of the Nastazi still survives." He said, "Can you men not see them struggling, help them with their burden and let us take them to our camp?" He pulled one of his young lieutenants to his side and added, "Take a handful of men with you and go back the way that they came to make certain that they were not followed," Trevlon Takan instructed, as he was always a very sound commander and at no time ever took needless chances.

As they made their way back to the new Nastazi encampment Nanuma told Trevlon Takan of the orchestration of their escape by Billigana and their joining with Tecumseh and relaying all that Tecumseh had told her to articulate to the king. She also added something that she had noticed, "The force that they have left to occupy the village was not overwhelming, it is in fact about the same size that remains of what I can see that you have remaining, though she had not really seen the entire of Angelii's remaining force her point was very true, for the odds at this time had gotten far better. Also they are concentrated surrounding the pyramid where they are producing the Kaav powder and spread very thin throughout the rest of the village," She offered. Nanuma had her sound military traits as well!

"Yes, this is what my scouts have told me and your confirmation is most welcome news," The King said. "We were waiting for more information about any more of our people that are still loyal and especially of news about Tecumseh, Billigana and the Piasa. Thank you for giving me the news that I have been anticipating, you have made me realize that the time to act is now." He rose from the respectful sitting position that he and Nanuma had been enjoying and said forcefully to his men. "Nastazi men gather to me now, we are about to begin the fight to reclaim our village, our people, and our future. We must act now before it is too late; come in close and listen to my plan," He knelt down on the soft and fertile bottoms soil and drew a carefully conceived gorilla action that would culminate with an all out attack on the huge pyramid that the outsiders had taken to produce their evil powder. After explaining it several times and showing the plan on the map that he had drawn on the ground with the explanation he finished by saying in his loudest of warrior-king challenge voices, "Remember, today we fight not only for our future and our homes, but truly our right to exist. The Nastazi will not ever become slaves to anyone!"

He was rewarded with a resounding cheer from his force of not quite two hundred men and a deep feeling of what would be considered today something akin to patriotism. He directed them to begin immediately and turned to Nanuma to tell her that she and her girls could remain here at this camp in hopeful safety, but was not surprised to see that Nanuma's entourage had all gathered themselves bows and as many arrows as they could carry. Nanuma smiled at her king and said, "It is our village and our future too, I believe you will see that we can be of much more help than you would ever imagine."

The King smiled deeply and said, "I believe that you will be and I thank you."

They embraced for a short moment and smiled knowingly at each other and after assigning two groups to hunt down the plant being grown and destroy it were off to fight what for all that they knew would be their final battle.

Meanwhile, deeper into the village Melanie had recovered somewhat from the huge dose of the Kaav powder that she had taken earlier and was now full of what she felt was a marvelous energy and with it a desire to do as the object of her new found adoration, Angelii had of asked her. She made her way on slightly unsteady legs, down to the pyramid where the processing of the enslaving substance was taking place in order to make certain that production levels would be sufficient to meet the additional needs as Angelii had instructed her to do.

She labored under the illusion that she had been bestowed a great rank and so wielded much power, but in reality the workers did as she asked with such promptness because it was well known that she was Angelii's concubine and to offend her would be to risk a horrifying death at the hands of the evil queen upon her return, and that little bird was always around to spy out whatever the queen needed to know. In fact unbeknownst to Melanie, the strange little bird Elgin was even now discreetly following behind her to make certain that she was doing as she had been instructed. This was a second timely stroke of good fortune for the Nastazi who, at this point in time could use any good fortune that they might happen upon, but sadly it would not be enough!

Melanie entered the vast main room of the pyramid and immediately saw a number of huge packages of the Kaav powder that were ready to be shipped to the much larger army that Angelii had taken to address the Piasa. She looked around for a moment and asked the warrior who appeared to be the one in charge, "Is this Kaav ready for travel?"

He turned slowly and answered her in a somewhat exaggerated tone, but just within the range of respectability saying, "Yes, Queen Consort Melanie, I was about to gather a detail to speed it to the army of our queen, but I thought that I would wait until I saw Elgin the bird as I have heard that he keeps a watchful eye on such events."

She, at first glared at the man for she was not certain that she liked the title that he had just given her, but after thinking it over for an instant decided that she did find favor with the new title and the perceived power that it bestowed. She said, "There is no need to wait on the bird, he will know when it has left and I am certain that he will keep a watchful eye on its progress."

This produced a quick grin on Elgin's face as although he did not know exactly how the young human girl knew, but what she had said had in fact always been entirely true.

Melanie looked at the warrior with an unusual newfound sense of power and gave him an order. "Ship it to Angelii and her army immediately; the bird will keep track of it as always." With that, the warrior submissively did exactly as he was told.

Melanie very much enjoyed this new feeling that she had discovered, she had never before felt such power even as the former queen of her own people and she enjoyed it immensely and so did the wicked little bird in the shadows behind her. All that she said was true; he thought and continued thinking that he may have some other use for her before he ended her life, as he had done so many other times to so many other naive human maidens. As he dwelled on these thoughts, the ancient consumer of human life looked on with uniquely soulless eyes and was deeply pleased with all that he had contrived in dealing with this latest group of people.

He alighted next to Melanie and spoke to her with only the power of his mind and said, "You ache for her, do you not?'

Melanie did not understand how the bird could speak into her mind, but answered, "Oh yes, I ache for her to my very core!"

"Let us retire to your quarters and I will take you to heights of pleasure that the Queen Angelii cannot even dream of," He said as he stared deeply at her with those strangely empty eyes.

She, herself was most surprised at just how quickly she agreed to the weird bird's request, but Elgin was not surprised in the slightest. He spent the next several hours enjoying himself with her; shifting shapes into forms of beings and strange animals that she had never before even known existed and with this he guided her erroneously driven mind into a deeper enslavement than one could ever hold hope of possible escape. It produced in her pleasure that she had never known; though she was unaware that he was drawing the very life force from her young body by just his mere touch. He merely relished in her newness and youth, also the strange enjoyment that he got from using one of the humans up and then discarding her as just a fragile, decrepit and old beyond her year's shell of the former self. He laughed at the strange attraction that they always seemed to develop with their unparalleled willingness to do any and all that he ordered of them.

Although he was not aware of it now, he was making the first real mistake that he had made when it came to his sex games in over four hundred seasons and it would be most costly, not only for his progression into his own evil fate, but beginning the final actions that would put an end to the huge numbers of people that had called this land their home for so long.

As this unholy alliance transpired inside the second largest of the Nastazi pyramids the attack to reclaim their village was started by the remnants of a once great Nastazi army. Group by group they encountered and defeated their foes, beginning on the outside of the village and quietly working their way towards the middle and the pyramid where their greatest challenge awaited them.

The pyramids grand entry hall seemed as the only obvious entrance and the warriors that Angelii had amassed, including the Sunomayans and Pawnee (their ancestors in any case) had this entrance guarded fiercely and would have obviously taken many lives of any army who would attempt to enter this way, but fortunately the Nastazi had always built into their pyramids a number of secret passages that were intended for use mainly for escape, but a passage could be used in both directions could it not? Try as they had the occupiers of the pyramid had not been able to locate any but the obvious back escape on the other side of the pyramid and had filled it with well hidden archers behind large stones.

King Trevlon Takan in his teachings prior to ascendancy to the throne had been through much of their cultures priestly training and included within these teachings was the secrets and locations of the doors in all of the pyramids. The king placed a very formidable looking force at the front entrance with instructions to begin to set up the large bows and other siege machines that would convey their coming attempt at this entrance and to posture as though this was in fact their plan, but as his men took part in this charade he gathered a good third of his men and placed them at two other secret passages that he showed the commanders how to open. Their entry into these two passages would enable them to approach the occupiers from the rear in the great hall where they would have little or no protection. Using polished mirrors of silver to communicate his signal to attack he made certain that all was at the ready and finally when all was as planned he gave the signal to begin the assault.

～～～～～～～～～～

As King Trevlon Takan prepared outside the pyramid the huge stockpile of the deadly Kaav powder was finally ready to leave. The Pawnee where aware of the apparently small force outside that looked as though they were intent on a suicidal frontal attack on their extremely well fortified position and prepared for some killing time, while they sent the group with the enormous shipment of the Kaav powder out the back passage that had been apparently left unguarded, with the certainty in their minds that this would help to build the strength and courage of their army in order to face the monster that they had been sent to conquer. They had the confidence of those whom had never known defeat and it was about to cause them to commit a most dreadful error. They created a cave in type booby trap at the roof of the back entrance that they could spring upon their departure and at that time most of their force departed with their treasure trove of the dreaded Kaav plants concentrated drug out the back exit that they felt was not guarded.

～～～～～～～～～～

The Pawnee caravan was preceded out the back of the grand pyramid by a fairly sizable contingent of heavily armed warriors, they exited carefully and showing extreme caution as great warriors (which unfortunately they

Words of the Piasa

were) will always do. The leaders that began the forward point of what was now becoming a very long column carefully scanned the thoroughfare that led away from the pyramid and towards the waiting cover of the nearby forest. They saw not one Nastazi warrior within the expanse of the broad thoroughfare and could only imagine that their ruse was working to perfection for they knew that the Nastazi had been duped into attacking the main entrance in the front of the pyramid and would charge headlong into the waiting ambush that awaited them there for they had left behind warriors that outnumbered the remaining Nastazi still three to one in a very well entrenched position with instructions to kill all that attacked and then to join them from behind.

The leader of the armed guard for this very important delivery, Temigin considered all that he knew and could see; and knowing also that his queen's strange little bird was always there to warn them of possible dangers gave the signal for all to follow as he made his command to continue to the waiting tree line and the supposed safety they would find there.

The Nastazi were not as absent though as Temigin suspected, as the raiding party with their powder of enslavement left out the back end of the beautiful Nastazi village and began to approach the thick glade of the magnificent river forest and the cover that they desired in those trees, they were being watched by hundreds of pairs of eyes. Eyes that belonged to Nastazi archers, some of the finest shots to have ever mastered the use of the bow, further their bows were some of the very first to experiment with steaming and re-curving of the bow itself this made them the most powerful one man weapon in existence at the time. It was now becoming apparent who was really the victim of the ambush; the Nastazi had proven to be shrewder than the Pawnee, the Sunomayans or even Angelii and her cohort Elgin had suspected for they had spied what was about to happen upon their entry into the grand pyramid and made the instant and correct decision not to concentrate on the secret escape doors, but instead to relocate their planned attack into an ambush just inside the tree line behind the pyramid, west of the village towards the river.

Just before this time while still around at the front of the majestic pyramid King Trevlon Takan had given the instructions and even went so far as to show himself at the front of his warriors so as to further convince of his subterfuge, although he was careful to have kept himself and his valuable brothers in arms just slightly out of the range of the usurpers that had occupied his temple and strove to control his village and his people. Though his archers had a slight advantage because of their superior weapons and the great numbers of arrows that their king had ordered them to make; they were just keeping the enemy hiding under cover and unable to even rise for a shot for the most part, as those that did were greeted by the whistling of a swift Nastazi arrow. Most found their mark, but those that did not conveyed the message of what would happen if they poked their heads out from behind the stones where they now hid. In this way the small fraction of the Nastazi force was able to keep the six hundred or so of Angelii's brood fully occupied and of absolutely no assistance to their retreating comrades.

The Nastazi king had created what appeared to be somewhat of a standoff as his troops seemed to not be able to navigate the broad expanse of open ground to gain access into the pyramid and yet at the same time their enemies now found themselves pinned down within their defenses, unable to move. They found themselves in somewhat of a stalemate and this suited King Trevlon Takan perfectly for he had given the orders, "Approach only if you can, do not make haste as we will wear them down carefully!" You see, things were going just as he had planned for he had also stated in further orders, "You first three groups in the front lines." He said as he pointed out the specific warriors that he was speaking to (about thirty men); "I am very proud of you; you are truly the greatest fighters in the land. I want you to stay here under the command of Noran and continue as you are performing so very well. We leave you with an abundant number of arrows. Do not stop until your arrows are gone or our enemy is finished! The rest of us must go now for it is time to spring our trap; take heart that you are making this ploy possible and know that we will return in a matter of just a short time; victorious!"

With that a mighty cheer arose from all of his men and that was followed by renewed flights of arrows at their antagonists and a stealthy parting of ways for the remainder of his men, the accompanying females which did not stay in the camp, who followed Nanuma and himself.

They made their way to the outskirts of the village with but one more look behind to ensure that all was as it should be and at this point he bade Nanuma to go through the village with her accompanying ladies and while remaining unobserved find every bit of the remaining

Kaav that they could and destroy it. He had given these orders with an honorable notion to keep them away from the coming bloodshed, but also in knowing that Nanuma and her girls would be most thorough in their endeavor; and this they were. Nanuma and her girls accepted the task wholeheartedly.

Outside the village just a short way was a wide creek that made its way around their village and actually ran parallel to the great river for a good distance; this occurred both naturally and with some assistance from the Nastazi's labors. It would, however enable them to out flank their antagonists and be the closing door of the trap that they had planned for their enemies that they had heard call themselves a number of different names Pawnee, Mayan, Sunamayan and who knew which, if any were true, though what the king did now know was that the trap was about to set appeared to be working and he would now possibly be able to save the remnants of his beloved people.

His group made their way to the creek and the canoes that they had left there and they piled in as quickly and quietly as possible. They were fortunate that this creek unnaturally flowed north for a short way because of their slight redirecting of the stream many years ago in order to facilitate water for their crops, because of this they were able to travel great distances with very little paddling or noise. The king looked ahead and thought quietly to himself, "I know that I must destroy this evil plant where ever I can find it and stop the making of this horrid powder that they derive from it, but yet I am very concerned about what Nanuma has warned me of. They do seem to really need this horrible thing and I am not certain that all will be as strong as Mandi has been. May the Great Spirit guide me in my actions," he thought to himself.

The Nastazi party arrived at the prescribed location and they all began to silently land their canoes and disembark. They gathered quietly as well as efficiently and immediately sent out scouts to locate their enemy and their own forces that most likely would join them soon from the parties earlier sent into the great pyramid as spies and to cover the secret exits.

The situation could not have occurred anymore fortuitously, for they had landed in a position where they were in the very thickest of woods between the footpath that led away from the village and the creek. None of their enemy would be able venture out this way for as they traveled to attempt to gain an advantage on his warriors the enemy was certain to run head on into the rest of his force that he had sent earlier and so they were now surrounded; the king was happy with the occurrence of events as this was almost too easy, he thought we are outnumbered, though we have our enemy at great disadvantage, but he considered this not without a certain amount of dread.

Next, one of his scouts came back with word that they had contacted his other forces, he immediately gave the sign and his men closed ranks for the battle that was now nearly upon them. His men closed the distance between themselves and their enemy as they crept closer and closer until they could now see clearly the footpath and the long line of enemy warriors that traveled upon it, sometimes two, three, or even four abreast; comfortable in their perceived safety in the forest. The two groups continued drawing ever closer together and then it was heard by all, the high shrill of a Northern Raven, the sign that King Trevlon Takan had chosen was now given and echoed throughout the forest.

It was as if the woods had come to life around them, the Nastazi's exploded from the mists and their enemies were engulfed with arrows from every direction. Those who did not drop to the ground dead immediately panicked, but had no direction to run for it seemed as though the woods had now become filled with arrows from every direction, all finding their marks in the enemies of the Nastazi's. As the enemy fell and the Nastazi parties drew together, the last of the enemies that remained, Temigin and several that had been in his forward group actually attempted to continue their fierce (although drug enhanced) aggression. They were dispatched with the short throwing spears that the Nastazi warriors kept on their backs for close fighting; Temigin was pierced by seven or more; it had been a slaughter.

King Trevlon Takan was quick to congratulate his men, but immediately ordered them to gather all of everything that looked like the Kaav. He told them to put it all in the pathway that his enemy had just been traversing and ordered them, "Burn it all, burn it now!"

His warriors did as they were told immediately and with great vigor and pride, but the king looked on with a morbid trepidation for even though he was now not fully aware of it for he did not yet understand the strength of the hold that the terrible drug had upon his people, he had just doomed vast numbers of his people to a before now unknown and horrible death, but before he was to know this, it was done.

In another part of their wondrous homeland that occupied the best parts of the Mississippi Bottoms Nanuma was scouring the village with the help of her girls trying to find every last bit of the insidious and evil plant; and while she had her misgivings about it she did what she had been told by her king to do; though she would surely obey; she worried about the repercussions of all that depended so upon the hideous substance so fully, still she burned all that she found as well.

They both had discussed it and knew that the evil weed must be destroyed; there was no doubt in either of their minds, but after they had done what they had agreed they would do they were overcome by a terrible foreboding, as if they had done something that was atrocious to their people; and in fact they had performed a function from which most of their people would never recover, they had just unwittingly doomed most the people that they both loved so much to disappear from Mother Earth now and forever in the unavoidable and most unpleasant death of made possible by addiction.

When this day was done the only Kaav that remained was with Angelii and her swollen brood of warriors. They were as a great calamity of action and violence and it was exactly this kind of environment that Angelii loved and had always lived within. Her men were all seriously under the influence of the Kaav from which they found remarkable strength for fighting and any other activity that she was pleased to order them to undertake. Her force had grown immensely in the past few lunar cycles as had always been the case, but this army had grown so much more quickly than she had ever before seen; so quickly that they were going through the Kaav at a rate like she had never experienced before, she did not worry though, as she had much more than they would need arriving from the newly vanquished territory tomorrow or the next day. "My strategies are all being fulfilled as planned, tomorrow Elgin will return with more Kaav and we can begin to enjoy our new subjects properly," she thought to herself with an undeniably sinister smile growing across her face that now exhibited an excess of malevolence which blended with her extreme beauty and changed the reaction by those who viewed her from want and desire to absolute and undeniable fear.

Angelii had unknowingly found herself in a state that I have seen many humans that had attained great power unintentionally find themselves having fallen into, she and her strange and ancient bird friend, well he was a bird most of the time in any case, but he could take many forms it has been found. The two had unknowingly made a terrible mistake; they had unwittingly let themselves slip into a state of complacency. He was back at the supposedly conquered village having his way with the poor misguided and very beautiful queen Melanie, allowing himself this pleasure of her use and following demise. You see, he felt certain that they had deceived the Nastazi and that their shipment of the much needed Kaav was on the way to queen Angelii and their newly inflated army. He had let his attentiveness slip as it had not for hundreds of seasons; for he felt certain that with this newfound legion of slaves now under their control that Angelii would not only be pleased, but that she would also be busy with her own pleasures. All is as it should be he thought; though they were both laboring under false illusions for they had never before dealt with a dragon and had yet to experience the strength of the human/dragon bond.

What was so unfortunate was that such a promising and advanced race of humans was to suffer the consequences of the evil that these two had created and brought to bear upon an unknowing people's. I once again began to recognize another type of mistake, a similar type of mistake that I had seen cost the Amazons, the Phoenicians, the Atlanteans and now I fear the Nastazi (or as they are known today Cahokians) so dearly.

Tecumseh and Billi awoke just as the majesty of the rising sun began to show on the fabric of the huge bag that carried them inside the huge basket that had been their home for possibly the last night that they would spend together for as much as either one of them knew. The sun had just begun to peek over the horizon and show the ground below them and as if guided by fate; the balloon had taken them to just where Tecumseh had visualized in his dream.

Off in the distance you could see the huge mountain that appeared as though it had been scoured on one side and only one half remained. Nearly below them and stretching out both ways into the distance they could see the muddy and turbulent waters of the river that he had envisioned and off far into the distance were visible several of the small hammocks of trees within one of which they knew for certain that they would find the Piasa.

To their surprise and delight as Billi gazed around them in all directions she found directly behind them several leagues in the distance the camp of Angelii's army; they had overtaken and passed the Piasa's pursuers.

As the sun continued to rise it shed more light on not only the beauty of the tall golden and vibrant green grasses in the plains below with the shimmering colors that seemed to wave back at them from the rocks in the approaching mountain, but it also showed that they had indeed been seen by the unnaturally wakeful warriors that occupied that camp which was now behind them but would doubtless follow them as quickly as they could. Would they be the ones to give away the Piasa's position? Would they be the tool used to facilitate their friend's death?

They were experiencing a tumultuous storm of conflicting emotions, but still knew one thing for certain. They must get to their friend and they must find a way to awaken him so that he might have a chance to defend himself or all would be lost.

As if in an answer to prayers that they had only just begun to reflect upon the wind increased and began to push them even quicker towards their friends' position. Billi and Tecumseh were jubilant and grasped each other in a warm and loving embrace thinking now that perhaps they might indeed have a chance after all. If Trevlon Takan had been able to successfully defend the village and they would be able to save Granger from the hideous fate that Angelii's minions had planned for him, then maybe, just maybe they would still be able to save their people and things could go back to being as good as they had been before the rescue of this malicious stranger.

Unfortunately, this was not what was to happen!

The increased wind was indeed a blessing, but shortly Tecumseh realized that while they were making far better time and headway, they were indeed approaching the glade where the Piasa lie at a much better pace, but unfortunately they did so from far too high above him and were now in danger of flying right over him and passing him by. This would have been a disaster they feared; their friend would die asleep and unwarned if they did not do something quickly. Tecumseh pulled the control rope that released some of the hot air that was still being provided by the marvelous burning black stones, but it was far too little and Tecumseh could see that it was obvious that they would soon overshoot their friend who he could now spot, mainly because of the intense bond that the two shared, by many leagues if he did not do something right now. Billi saw a very strange look in his eyes, as if something other worldly had taken him over. She was so confused, she meant to say something to help her man regain control and protect himself, her and the Piasa; she then realized that he had an idea and believed that she, in fact knew what it was and she tried to open her mouth to say that she agreed but all that came out was. "Do it!"

Tecumseh scrambled up the rope on the side of the balloon as quick as a cat and once he reached the top of the bag he immediately produced his knife and shoved it into side of the bag. He loosed his grip on the rope and slid down the entire length of the tremendous bag, slicing it widely open as he came down. He landed back in the basket next to Billigana having sliced open the bag from top to bottom. They both looked at each other with a mixture of terror and resolve as they embraced and the balloon began to quickly fall back to the earth. They both felt as if the flight that they were taking had now turned into a fall as they could both see the ground rushing up to meet them far too rapidly for comfort; still they held each other with all of the love and determination that they possessed.

Suddenly they felt the impact, they heard tree limbs snapping all around them, broken branches tearing at the cloth and piercing the basket though nothing seemed to be slowing their fall. Suddenly it seemed as though their own weights had increased tenfold, as they watched they could see the ropes stretch to their limit and then finally begin to retract as they reach their limits and did not break, but instead pulled the basket back upwards again. The entire apparatus bounced several times in the huge Poplar tree stand where they had landed and then thankfully came to a rest.

They both looked at one another accessing any damage that may have occurred and when they were satisfied with each other's health both sat back and let out a sigh of relief. "The great spirit has been with us on this day," Billi said.

"Or the spirit of the Piasa," Tecumseh was quick to interject.

Billi looked at him, not yet quite fully understanding, but agreed saying, "I just hope that we can find him in time to return the assistance."

Words of the Piasa

When they had gathered themselves sufficiently they began to climb over the side of the basket that was dangling precariously in the treetops. While beginning their climb downwards they started looking for their friend and to their surprise they did not need to search for long, for he was directly below them. He slept the deep, unchanging, nearly eternal sleep that is known only by slumbering dragons.

They clamored down the ropes and branches to join with the Piasa and as they approached him they could see that he had taken on a strange earthy looking color, one that they had never seen even with the myriad of colors that they had seen produced within his multi-faceted and all seeing eyes or even the many varied hues that they had witnessed take effect within his wondrous dragon's hide.

They made their way down the last few steps of the tremendous roots that somehow seemed out of place for this type of tree and as Billi fell against Granger's flank she leaned against him and touched his side. She was shocked and backpedaled away from the dragon not knowing just exactly what to do; she turned to Tecumseh in tears and said, "He has turned to stone, our friend is no more." She whispered again, "He is of stone."

"Wait, my love," Tecumseh grabbed and held her trying as he might to comfort her, although his heart was also breaking, "he is but sleeping, I have seen him as this before.

"My love, you are brave and wonderful and I appreciate your trying to comfort me, but something has happened to him, something terrible. For I know stone when I touch it," she broke down sobbing, feeling that they were now helpless and wholly alone to face the approaching mob.

"Billi, take heart's my true light." He told her, holding her tightly in his strong embrace and looking intently into her eyes with an engrossing and undeniable love. "We are far from lost; for this is how I saw the Piasa for the first eleven seasons of my life. We just need to find a way to wake him before all is lost."

She gazed at him through her tears in warm appreciation, but she was beginning to feel as though their end was approaching; yet she managed to say quietly, "How do we start."

"Of this I am not certain, "Tecumseh said. "There is not time to attempt the dreams and I really do not think that I can possibly sleep now."

They began to walk around the giant mound that was their; now helpless friend. They had to find a way to reach the dragon, a being that had been known to sleep for hundreds or even thousands of years at a time. They were far beyond the point of desperation!

Now Billi and Tecumseh were within a distance that would take no more than a small part of the rest of the morning for Angelii's brutal-looking hoard to cover and the space between the brave Nastazi couple and their foes had already begun to increase in their eccentric agitation. Their enemies were obviously frantic, whether merely from the influence of the malevolent drug that had now become the main focus of all of their lives, or the surreal warrior's excitement that some feel before an impending kill cannot be told, but they had gone from something of an organized fighting force to a stampeding mob during the last few days. Angelii did not care about their behavior right now, as long as they obeyed her every command, which they always did; besides she had been busy with a parade of new companions that she had been inviting to share her bed. Sampling the new blood she liked to call it, but unfortunately for many of them she was not easily pleased and as another aspect of her pleasure, some were quite often not ever seen again.

Her group was fast approaching where she had been told by her malevolent bird companion that she would find the Piasa. Elgin had described the area and it's landmarks that he had remembered in great detail nearly a moon ago when he had manipulated the dragon into the consumption of the enormous amount of the horrific plant and he had related the details to her very specifically when she had last seen her bird-sorcerer friend and she recognized that they were growing very close.

She bid her carriers to stop and sit her litter down so that she could comfortably climb out; you see at this time in this land they did not have the advantage of the marvelous animals that the humans later brought from afar and tamed in order to ride that are known as horses. They did not arrive until several hundred seasons past this time, when the humans rode them and dragons would have most likely eaten them. Quite possibly we dragons had something to do with their original disappearance from this part of the world in any case, as in the distant past there were a good many horses abiding in this land; however there were also many more dragons than now exist and as I mentioned before every action taken has a consequence in the balance of "Mother Earth" and her resources or nature as you humans now call it; in any case Angelii then stepped out of her litter and ordered a counsel.

She gazed around their camp and could see that those under her control had been very busy preparing the weapons that she and Elgin had told them that they would need; she could spy in the distance four of the huge crossbows that they had instructed them in building. Though they would be very cumbersome to aim, she felt certain that they possessed the killing power that would be needed. She had been told that this was a great "brown" dragon and though she had only ever encountered a "green" that it did indeed tower over all men and animals that she had ever known; she did not know that the "brown" was actually over twice the size. In any case she held the flawed notion that it would be easily stopped with the weapons and manpower that she now had at her command. She could also see towards the beginning of the columns the troops that were armed with the huge oversized spears that had been tipped with the new metal points, they appeared to be more than a match for any armor; man's or dragon's and the spears were the length of any three men so she was confident that they would be able to reach their target. She also had over forty thousand fanatical followers that would do anything that she commanded; this she knew to be her greatest asset and believed that she was now leading them wisely just as she had done in the past, but the one component of her plan in which she was most confident was the large amount of the black burning rocks that she had commanded her troops to bring, she knew that if she could surprise the Piasa and confront him while he still slept that she could make a fire so hot that even a being such as he would have no chance. They would dispatch the Nastazi's last hope and return to a new village that she would call her home for a time, one which would have been purged of any trouble by the time that she arrived in order that she could concentrate more fully on the pursuits that she preferred.

Her lieutenants began to arrive in the normal efficient short times from her command that she had grown accustomed to; all but Laird. She scanned the gathered faces and asked, "Where is Laird, why does he not obey my command?"

Several answered weakly that they had not seen him until it was obvious that he was truly missing. Angelii looked deeply into their faces and gauged that they were all being truthful and said as she pointed at the two closest to her, "You two go and find him and bring him before me at once!"

They answered immediately, "Yes my queen," hefted their weapons and quickly disappeared into the throng of warriors that was before them, seizing what they considered to be a fantastic opportunity for advancement within the ranks.

She turned to address her commanders and spoke to them clearly, "In a short time we shall encounter a beast like none that you have ever seen before, your people may know it as the Piasa, it is also called the thunderbird in some cultures, it has many different names throughout the world, but it is naught but a dragon and make no mistake, we are here to kill a dragon, an ancient beast that has outlived its useful time on this world and does nothing save for feed on your young and weak; be aware that we are dealing with a monster, a monster that is huge and strong and filled with deceit, we dare not do anything but take him by surprise, as I have seen his type in the past and they are crept up upon with ease. Elgin and I came across a green dragon sometime past and had no problem killing it, though this one is somewhat larger in size from what I have heard. We will approach it using all of the stealth that we can muster and kill it with fire. If we turn this into a battle we will still kill it, but many of ours may die also. So let me tell you again; for the best success in our quest to kill this beast we must approach it with as great a quiet as possible, those who do not carefully obey, you must kill of your own accord so that they do not give us away understood," she looked at them with the glaring question in her eyes?

They all looked somewhat lost for a moment, staring around at each other with vacant expressions upon their faces, until one of the lieutenants close to Angelii boldly drew out his gleaming long-knife and said in a terse and very low, but audible whisper meant to inspire his fellow warriors, "I for one will enforce strict silence ordered by my queen, for the good of all!"

He was answered with a grisly cheer from all!

Cheering, roughhousing and the types of revelry seen in ancient times before a great battle and quite familiar to what you see in today's world before a sporting event such as football seemed to overcome the queens followers for a few moments and she watched in morbid appreciation of the control that she knew that she held over one and all of them. She left them to their frolic for several moments, but when she again spoke there was immediate and complete silence.

"We are about to leave to meet the challenge of your lives," she spoke resolutely, "Not, but your finest efforts will be expected, or tolerated. I am authorizing a double portion of Kaav, now before the final march. Remember, the future of you all depends upon the end of this beast. If we are victorious there will be great reward for all, but if we would fail it means the end of everything that you all hold dear and the end of your precious Kaav.

This final threat was the most feared by all that were there, for all of the other things in life had grown pale in significance when compared to the Kaav plant that she had introduced them to and the incredible superhuman feelings that it bestowed upon all that partook of it. She looked at her group of seconds in command and gave an approving nod towards the stockpiled Kaav that was always kept under extremely close guard. They approached the stocks and began to dole out double shares to the over anxious warriors that acted strangely like children who have been promised sweets. There was then a time of organized pandemonium as her instructions were carefully followed, preparing her army for the final onslaught on the dragon, who slept deeply several leagues away, unawares.

Back in the Nastazi village where unknown to many, events were occurring that would reshape the world that all people knew for ages to come; as in many of the occurrences that future would for those that survived or for their descendants would later become known simply as destiny. To produce this fortune several things happened at that time, while they did not seem to be very closely related at the time they occurred had in the end a great influence upon one another and they also occurred nearly simultaneously.

King Trevlon Takan returning with his army of protectors of their village, his warriors still practicing the stealth that their king had taught them and had just afforded them such a one-sided victory, began to appear from all sides of the forest on the North end of their village. Only to find that the force that had occupied the pyramid had decided that their only way out of the trap was to go out the way that their comrades had gone, as they perceived (although inaccurately) that the force attacking the front of the great structure was too great to overcome with a frontal assault.

They had gone from turmoil within the pyramid and now ventured towards the rear of the pyramid only to be greeted by the caved in mess that their comrades had left behind. They felt, however that they had a stroke of good fortune as they saw a small opening and with so many men to bring to bear upon it soon had it large enough for several men to get through at once; and this they did only to reach the outside and meet their doom.

The warriors loyal to Angelii fought with that unreal drug induced ferocity and were so numerous, but the Nastazi though outnumbered once again, possessed the element of surprise and with the additional power of the greatest archers in existence exploded from the low lying morning fog that was common near the great river onto their enemy from all sides. Once again the air was filled with the sounds of the powerful bows and the whistling of arrows through the air, most of which found the mark that they were intended for and the Nastazi that came in close fought with a fierceness of those that were ready to give their life for their homes, which is exactly what they were doing, even if some of those that they were fighting were their own former neighbors that had been recently lost to the vicious wiles of the evil queen, her strange little bird and the horrible poisons that this evil pair had exposed their people to. The fight was fierce with hundreds, perhaps more losing their lives on this day, it was bloody and it was the final act of many of whom used to be known as the Nastazi; many died on this morning, all of those loyal to Angelii who remained in the village, but sadly also was the fact that many of them were those who called Trevlon Takan their king.

The king's force was once again victorious, but this time it had cost them much more dearly and left him and all of his surviving warriors with a most vacant feeling, a feeling more of resignation to the fate that all could now see was unfolding around and through them. He was now left with but forty men at arms, Nanuma's students and the rest of the women of the village, the Nastazi now numbered just short of one hundred if you did not include the thousands that were under the spell of the dark queen Angelii.

They gathered themselves and began to make their way back into their village, as the king thought to himself about what was there that he could do to protect what was left of his people and his village from the onslaught that he knew was inevitably to come. He was so proud of his men and knew for certain that they were the best army in the land, but they were far too few. They would have to settle into the great pyramid that had the spring for a water source and stockpile as much food as they could until the attack came. They would need more arrows and weapons; and oh how his mind raced, he would need to have Nanuma and her girls begin with the preparations as he was aware of their great skill and speed at producing items of Craft, in this case arrows. There was so much that he must strive to accomplish in the few short days that they would have until the horrible attack that he knew was forthcoming would arrive. He had always been a man who was very sure of himself and confident of his abilities, but now all that he could manage to think about was where could he find the help that he knew they needed, if only he knew what had happened to Tecumseh and Billigana for he could surely use the help of their dragon now, as his warriors were just too few!

The king was absolutely correct; he did need help, though the need was far more immediate than he could have ever dreamt for a large force of Angelii's brood that had been busied for quite a time with the planting and growing of the plant that was the cause of their problem and they had now combined with the legion that Angelii had sent back several days ago and were not an hour from the village; they had naught but slaughter on their minds.

This is when time seemed to speed up just a little too much for those involved.

Melanie, former queen of the Nastazi and former faithful, loving young wife to King Trevlon Takan, but now traitor to her people; seeming soulless concubine to not only the evil Queen Angelii, but also now to the strange being that had been seen as a malevolent small bird by most and regrettably as many different beings by a chosen few; she now had even becoming a protector of the cursed drug that had now managed to enslave nearly all of her own people. She was all of these things, yet now she appeared from the side of the pyramid where her husband and former love of her life the king Trevlon Takan planned his final defense of the village; where both of them had lived, loved, grown and so recently called home.

Her eyes met his and for an instant he thought that he could see a glimpse of the old Melanie, the wonderful young girl that was full of kindness and goodness and an undying love for him and his people.

She then seemed to become wrought with turmoil and averted her eyes to speak to him, "What Angelii offers is not as bad as you say," she stated, attempting to sound most convincing. "They never experience any type of sickness and can always be depended upon to do what they are told, there have been times, I am certain that your reign could have used such qualities within its subjects."

The king could only shake his head and answer mournfully, "A Great leader needs not command, but inspires his subjects to follow through his values and actions."

Melanie answered this with, "Angelii's subjects would die for her upon her mere request!"

King Trevlon Takan answered saying, "Yes, as mine would; the difference between us is that I would never ask."

As the king answered her he could see her haunted gaze return and he took several steps closer. He whispered, "I do not know where I failed you, but I hope that you can forgive me for what is to come."

"I do not know what you mean," she spoke it as a statement, but it was certainly more of a question.

The king continued, attempting to reach her and find the former woman that he had loved so much for so many years, "I fear that our people's days are about to come to an end."

"This is why I have come to convince you. Save the people that you have left, join with us and save everyone, save yourself," she blurted out feeling a flood of her old feelings begin to overwhelm her as she collapsed into a corner sobbing!

King Trevlon Takan looked upon her with a great pain remembering the wonderful life that they had formerly shared but now knowing that his feelings towards her that still remained were no longer mutual he made the decision to set her free. He took one more last look at the one woman that he had ever considered his soul mate and with a great deal of deeply felt pity he walked away from her answering his call of duty towards his people.

The group of butchers that Angelii commanded was now on the outskirts of the city with a massive bloodlust, outnumbering the remaining Nastazi more than twenty to one!

Words of the Piasa

Melanie looked up from her painful sobbing to see the man that until recently had meant everything to her walk away in obvious pain, she tried to search deep within her heart for the goodness that she knew he had always seen there. She realized that she owed the man that had always been so gentle with her in love and so kind to her in the life which he had provided for her some effort at the possibility of his survival. She lost herself in her considerations, but began to fade away as the massive host of Angelii's warriors began to enter the city from the North and East.

~~~~~~~~~~~~~~~~

Within the sight of the mighty half mount they had used as a landmark; hidden in a large glade of trees that was as an island in the beginning of a sea of tall grasses which started here and continued to the west for thousands of leagues; Billigana attempted to offer advice or guidance to her man, Tecumseh on something that she had really no experience to speak of, save for the love that she knew she felt for the Piasa and the love that she certainly knew that he felt for her. She had asked Tecumseh to perform different acts; to touch the stone monolith that their friend had become in many different conceivable ways, they screamed at the top of their lungs, pounded sticks onto flat rocks that they had found in the area that created a booming noise which they knew they must soon stop or be quickly detected by the approaching horde, but all was to no avail.

Tecumseh continued to pace around the giant stone that was what had become of their friend. He thought to himself that the only other time he had ever faced this situation, the initial time that he had met the Piasa, the actual thing that he remembered about the ordeal was the intense fear that he had felt at the closeness that he had come to death from the attack of the huge female Shush that had intended to kill and eat him and the way that he was saved from this certain death by the Piasa that lay frozen in stone before him then as now. He was not exactly sure how the Sunomayans would be able to harm his friend and savior, but he was certain that if there was such a way that the wicked Angelii would definitely know of it, for she had a formidable and undeniable knowledge of evil.

He continued to dwell on his attack by the bear when he was years younger, but could not seem to reproduce the same feelings and emotions that he knew he must have experienced on that day just five seasons ago that to him already seemed to be so far in the past; though to his friend the Piasa he was sure it would have only seemed the blink of an eye. Although he feared that a similar situation may soon be upon them he felt obligated to share his thoughts about the experience with Billigana.

Tecumseh told her quietly, "I feel that the situation that awoke this great being when we first met may again be upon us soon."

"What is it my love and how may I help," Billi answered him quietly?

He just held her more tightly and looked deeply into her eyes with an appreciation that is unmatched by even the greatest of loves that mankind has ever known. They both took a moment just to enjoy this time with each other and absorb the freshness of the morning air as they looked through the light mist that still hung within the outstretched branches of the white-barked trees towards the glowing outline of the rising sun and they both knew, even without the exchange of words the depth of their devotion. They both felt that if they were to die, the love that they had known together had been reason enough for the short lives with which they had been blessed and knew that nothing else was as important as that.

However, they both had fighting spirits and did not have the desire to just give up; especially with so many depending upon them for they felt certainly that they had to try whatever they could think of to save the Piasa and consequently the remainder of their people.

They had tried as many of the physical methods as they could think of so for a few moments they were void of any new ideas that they felt had any merit when suddenly Billi had an idea, "The only chance that we have is for you to reach a dream state once again." Billi stated, but she had more to this idea than her trusting man could realize.

Tecumseh began to protest, until the sense of her idea convinced him to cooperate. She lay down next to him stroking, caressing and soothing him with all of her wiles in order to get him relaxed enough to fall into the light sleep that would enable him to enter the dream state that they now needed to achieve so badly.

Unnoticed to Tecumseh she had positioned him in what was obviously the crook of the dragon's foreleg and she then covered him with varied branches, moss and leaves making him invisible to all eyes save hers. Tecumseh had mentioned something that she thought may be able to save her man and the dragon with the only sacrifice being her. Had she not known a wonderful life and been blessed with a love that few people had ever known? To sacrifice herself to save the Piasa, her people and her love was a small price indeed and one that she was very willing to make.

She grabbed Tecumseh's bow and quiver of arrows and quietly clamored up onto the stone that she knew was her friend the Piasa. She had made the decision to protect her man and give him as much time as possible to achieve their only possible salvation. In doing this she perched down behind the magnificent crown at the top of the dragon's skull that would give her excellent cover until her quiver of arrows was emptied and she would then await the fate that she could sense was nearly upon her, hoping that this action would provide the needed time for the dragon to awaken and provide the salvation that they so desperately desired.

Nanuma had been very busy, but was still very involved in gathering information upon the progress of the defense of their village with the use of her numerous young and athletic students. Most of them were gifted runners, as many are in their youthful years and nearly all of them were agile young girls. The two who were young men were somewhat different than most of the other young boys of their age in that they looked upon the females somewhat differently and instead of the normal hormonal lust that the other boys of their age were tend to feel, they rather wanted to fit in and take part in most of the activities that the young girls were apt to be participating in, such as the production of clothes to wear, spinning, cooking and gossiping. This was fully understood by Nanuma and the young ladies under her tutelage, for on occasion this happened in nature, even in the animal kingdom and so it was understood and bothered no one in particular; however this unfortunately seems to have changed in modern times.

What was different about these two young men, Trellon and Quinz, was that the type of passion that many of the other boys had for hunting, fishing or the pursuit of the young girls was awakened within these two by running like the wind. Both were faster at running than anyone else in the Nastazi population and the two competed with each other constantly for bragging rights to say who was faster, though as of yet there could be no clear winner as most races were very close and they seemingly split the wins. Because of this remarkable talent that both possessed Nanuma had asked them to be her eyes and ears. Though she used some of her young ladies in the same way, these she usually asked to make shorter trips in and around the village. The boys however she had entrusted with what she considered the very important matter of watching towards the north, towards where she knew that Angelii's main force had disappeared in pursuit of the Piasa and from whence she also knew that they would soon return unless some sort of miracle happened and the Piasa was reached. She was confident in their ability to remain hidden; for between her teaching of hunting skills and the kings constant training of the need of stealth and elusiveness needed for combat in their forest the two had become quiet experts at staying hidden and just because they happened to be somewhat different than the other young men, this diminished not their abilities in the warrior craft.

For these reasons Nanuma had chosen these two for this huge and dangerous obligation; that she had entrusted them with this and her knowledge of their tremendous abilities is why she was so very concerned when she saw them returning to her in such extreme haste, so unnerved she was certain that they could not be returning with anything considered good news.

As they came to the end of their run and Nanuma hurried out from underneath the wooded shade of a roof that surrounded the base of the pyramid to meet with the boys and find out the news that they obviously felt was so urgent; the young men quickly approached her and she motioned for some of her girls and asked them to bring some water.

Trellon screamed immediately, "No! There is no time, the enemy is upon us."

Nanuma motioned for them to come and said, "Come with me and we will take cover. Tell me what you can!"

Quinz was obviously very frightened and was just making a negative moaning sound, he finally said, "We must not stop, if we are to escape."

He stared deeply and questioningly at Trellon and at once Nanuma now fully understood what she had only suspected before, the two had always been together, their lives and fates were connected with the sort of physical relationship normally associated with man and wife and then Trellon spoke as quickly and as clearly as he could.

"We could not come when at first we discovered them far to the North for we were surrounded. They are many, many more than our people now number and we will not stand any chance against them in battle. We were fortunate enough to have been able to hide within their midst with the help of the forest, but we had no chance to escape until we were nearly upon the village," His eyes pleaded for her understanding. "They will be here soon, to stay is to die!" He embraced his mentor and teacher, the only mother that he had known since being orphaned as an infant. "Please come with us," he begged Nanuma.

She only looked at him with understanding forgiveness and whispered, "Go if you must." She then raised her voice saying, "Any of you that wish to escape the coming battle, go with these two. There is no shame in surviving so that you may have the chance to fight another day." She then turned back to Trellon and again whispered, "But my place is here, defending my village and my people."

She watched as Quinz anxiously pulled on Trellon and with final fleeting farewells the two once again began their graceful gallop to the safety of the South and to no surprise she witnessed none of her girls follow them; instead choosing to join in meeting the fate of their friend and teacher, no matter what that might be.

As they watched the two young men disappear into the forest at the base of the great bluff to the Southeast of their village, they had the very unpleasant shock of coming under an incredibly fierce attack by a massive and unexpectedly large number of insane looking warriors. Men that had very obvious experience in this type of war, berserkers who fought for the enjoyment of the spoils, as they swept through the small band of Nastazi women they killed Nanuma and the other older girls ruthlessly in the most hideous of ways, not wasting the arrows that it had taken them time and effort to make, but bludgeoning and hacking the women to pieces and capturing unharmed for the most part the younger ones for their later perverse enjoyment, while the very young ones they intended to keep until they became of use as slaves or possibly just kill for fun later. It was an appalling example of how low man could actually sink, while still imagining themselves as humans.

They had quickly wiped out Nanuma and her apprentices sparing only the four youngest and most nubile for a most certainly horrible fate that surely awaited them, as they were passed to the back of the columns towards the litters that followed the main group to be thoroughly bound and stacked with the other stolen spoils of their current rampage. The repulsive force then continued up the two main thoroughfares of the village for they were in no real hurry and made no real attempt at concealment for they already felt that their victory was at hand. The massive group of marauders with nothing but pillage, conquest and rape in their minds approached where the good king Trevlon Takan planned to make the final defense of his people's home.

He had gathered his men into the pyramid across from that which had just so recently been defended by the Sunomayans and Pawnees whom had been forcefully recruited into Angelii's horde and his warriors had so soundly defeated. He saw the benefits of the massive structure of the Great Pyramid knowing that the spring that ran beneath it as it did the sister pyramid of the Priests next to it would be absolutely essential to their survival if they would become besieged, though somehow he did not envision that as happening. He could now hear the noise of the approaching mass with his own ears and now knew the truth of what his scouts had been telling him for some time now. The force that was coming was huge and overwhelming; the remaining Nastazi did not stand a chance.

The King then decided to do the only thing that he considered right to do at this time, he turned to address his people, he stated as clearly and as compassionately as possible, "The enemy is nearly upon us and is far stronger than I could have ever known, I must stay here and defend our homes and my people, but any of you who wish to attempt to make the safety of the forest have my permission and blessing for it is not cowardly to survive against overwhelming odds to continue to live" saying this he gazed over the faces of his people. They were as grim and determined a bunch as any commander has ever seen and to the person not one moved to take flight, not man woman or even child that was present of the Nastazi that remained made any movement save to raise their hands in support of their king. Then from many places in

Words of the Piasa

the crowd came the calls, "To the King!" Or perhaps, "We will die with our King!" Many supportive statements were exclaimed such as this, but they had all the same message; they had chosen to stay with their king and defend their homes.

The King Trevlon Takan or "emissary of the Great Spirit" as his name was said to mean addressed his people from the heart saying, "Any king or man can have no greater love for his people than that which I have for you, I would do anything to save all of you and if we are to die together than I will give my life in defense of you and feel the great honor for the loyalty that you have all shown me." He held his bow and war club aloft and howled, "We will all die as proud Nastazi, let us be remembered as such," but then something wholly unexpected happened.

From around the corner of the temple came a small lone figure that all instantly recognized. She was met with a strange mix of emotions, some unappreciative jeers and some unforgiving gestures, but she approached and offered what she considered a solution.

She now thought that she should at least attempt to save the lives of her former husband and people. While calling it a change of heart may have been too generous, as the choice that she was to give them would forever enslave them under the power of the Kaav plant should they agree, in her drug addled state of mind it probably seemed to her that what she was doing was correct. She pleaded with the king, "Show them when they come that you are partaking of the Kaav, join us and save yourselves," she pleaded as she approached to within reach of her former lover and king.

He abruptly turned to face her and knocked it from her hands as he stated, "We would rather die as free beings than to live as slaves!" Trevlon Takan had spoken the heart of his remaining people.

As the Kaav spilled over the hard packed earth below the steps where they now stood Melanie grimaced and turned away from her former King and love to see what had caused the great agony that she now felt pierce through her back and deep into her heart; the first arrow and she turned back to the King as he looked past his once true love to see the first of wave after wave of arrows that Angelii's horde would now discharge at the remnants of the once great, but now doomed Nastazi people.

Everyone joined in his exultant war cry and they made a glorious charge to fight this devastating enemy ferociously and bravely, but alas none survived to pass down to new generations the glory of these once great people; for those that had remained in the village, sadly their end was abrupt, overpowering and horrendous. The army that had been gathered by the drugs of this evil queen killed the Nastazi in hideous ways, skewering people together and leaving them to die impaled hanging from trees, beheading them after offering them quarter and the horrible rapes that they insisted performing upon the many beautiful Nastazi women that always ended in death. It was a most horrific ending for a once noble people! Yet these Nastazi that had just been butchered had also unknowingly secured the beginning of the fate that was soon to come for their destroyers, for they had destroyed all of the Kaav drug that had just been harvested from all of the known plants in the region save the small amount that was still with Angelii's huge horde of what could now only be referred to as slaves. They had destroyed the Kaav for the evil that they knew that it possessed not thinking, or knowing that it would take several moon cycles for the plants to re-grow to the size that they could once again be harvested, nor did they know about a state later to be known as addiction or that the conditions experienced from the withdrawals from this horrible drug that the evil Queen Angelii and her malevolent magical bird had created resulted in death most all of the time. Even this evil pair did not know for they had only created it for its power to enslave and once they began the administration of the wicked crystals they never once stopped. The Nastazi did not have any idea how badly the vileness which they had destroyed was really needed; but greatly needed it was. Just a small number of Nastazi escaped this horrible massacre, but they were to witness an ending of their people and those too of some other tribes that the evil duo Elgin and Angelii had enslaved that was perhaps more hideous than the horrible atrocities that they had seen even within this bloodbath, the piteous dying of a human begging for a drug that they had no hope of obtaining, the erasure of all and any pride, decency or humanity that the person had ever known and the witness's inability to help in any way was as horrible a death as anything that has ever been ever imagined!

~~~~~~

Words of the Piasa

Angelii had been taking advantage of her position, as she was known to do, by being carried within her huge litter that needed the strength of eight adult men to bear. Inside the pompously decorated and most comfortable coach she had ordered another of the new young soldiers to lay with her during the travel and do her bidding. The sexual nature of this order that they received was always found to be quite exciting by the new recruits and they enjoyed it immeasurably in the beginning. It was only when they finally realized that if they did not please her that it would mean the end of their life and that was when the excitement began to change to a deep fear, however by that time it was already usually too late; this seemed to add an extreme and exquisite pleasure to the malevolent queen's satisfaction!

She rang a certain bell and began to search again for her clothes and while the young man asked why she stopped and she began to dress four very large, very ominous-looking brutes pulled the young man from her presence and usually dragged him off into the woods, never to be seen again.

She jumped lightly down out of the "Queens Carriage" as it was called and beaconed for her light travel litter to be fetched to her. She was beautifully dressed, although as casually as any there had ever seen her. She wore simple doeskin shorts that had been sewn with some sort of a golden thread and they were very short and very tight, with a light nearly translucent camisole-type top that was very flattering to her ample bosom. Her hair held the straggled carefree curls caused by the romps that she had just been enjoying and her skin glowed with what seemed to be an overabundance of female hormones that seemed to say "Look at me I am made for loving," but she also possessed a sinister stare that would strike real fear into the heart of most men; not unlike a Black Widow Spider would gaze at her mate for several terror filled moments just before devouring him.

Her litter, which was one quarter the size of the larger one that she spent most of her time within still required four strong men to carry and was every bit as luxurious as the other; was brought to her and she began to slowly ride about to investigate the progress that her forces had made. Overall, she looked somewhat pleased and beckoned her lieutenants to come and meet with her once again. She ordered a slow walk by her bearers with her coach towards their goal and all gathered around her when she halted. She said, "Soon we will see the beast and hopefully it will still suffer the deep trance that Elgin has told me of placing it into, if this is so then we must build a very hot fire around it as quickly as we can, use all that will burn hot, the black burning stones, the yellow stones and that black jelly that you have shown me burns so well anything to make this fire hotter for I would rather murder it in its sleep than have to fight this beast as I have heard that he can become most formidable. If it is accompanied by any person of any tribe, kill them immediately!

All of her lieutenants agreed heartily, not merely from their blind obedience towards their queen, but for the love of the kill that they had all so morbidly developed. They all seemed at this time to increase their pace towards their prey, trudging through and flattening the tall grasses that made up the landscape in this part of the land, they now headed directly west and had long left the cover of the forest behind them. Before them lay the flat prairie for as far as the eye could see, from horizon to horizon save for the small growths of forest that seemed to have been overgrown and surrounded by the grasses so that they stood as mere occasional lonely islands of the ancient forest that had once been there. They grew ever more sparse as you headed towards the western horizon until it appeared as though they just quit and were replaced by the great tall endless grasses.

The group called themselves an army, but to the trained eye it was quite obvious from their lack of discipline, uncouth noise, and the way that they just meandered towards the same point that they were nothing but a huge mob, but they were also a mob intent on the enslavement or destruction of any who opposed them. They were headed for what appeared to be one of the largest hammocks of trees within sight and though it was still nearly at the end of their view, it was just that, now within sight and they approached it ominously. The sheer numbers of the approaching horde mangled and flattened the graceful grasses of the plains and turned them into a smashed and matted wasteland, it was as sad a sight that you could imagine with the first individuals of the multitude parting the golden wavy grasses to pass between as a spirit through the foliage and after the passing of the masses all that remained was thoroughly destroyed badlands. It was enough to bring a tear to the eye of even a dragon from the mere memory of such abuse and lack of consideration for our beloved mother earth.

It was this hoard who now approached Billigana and her entranced mate as she made her valiant attempt at protecting her man and her friend the Piasa from this crushing force. She realized that this effort would most likely be in vain and cost her and most likely her two companions their lives, but they had done all that they knew to be possible in attempts to wake the Piasa without success and it appeared that the end was bleak and was drawing ever nearer.

From a great distance away, emerging from out of the forest that all had left behind emerged a small shape that appeared to be very determined to join the group. It was flying no more than the height of a man above the matted prairie and could soon be recognized as the small and strangely attentive bird that most of the warriors engaged by this evil duo feared terribly. It was known by all as Elgin and was far more than a small bird; but evil incarnate, he neared and was soon to rejoin the group.

Billi was at something of a disadvantage where she was, as she could not see outside of the hammock of the thick trees, while this was unfortunate she had not had a choice, she had not chosen the place for defensive qualities as she would have liked. She so wished that there was some way with which she could see the approaching masses before they were right on top of her and surrounding her and her friends as was obviously about to occur. She was just doing what she might to keep the evil throng away from her love for as long as was possible in order for him to have just the few extra moments needed to awaken their powerful friend, for if Granger could just be revived it would change everything! Though as she made herself as secure as possible atop her enchanted friend, she could feel only the cold stone that told of the continued unending sleep which she felt certain was to be her people's doom. At least she had lived long enough to have known the wonderful fulfillment of loving Tecumseh and now she would give all of the protection that the remainder of her life would allow; she readied her and Tecumseh's arrows, that might number close to fifty in all and waited, for now she could just begin to hear the clamor of an uncaring and raucous force approaching, with this she notched her first arrow and peered into the thick green forest that engulfed her, purposefully waiting for what was to come.

Elgin, the ancient malevolence which now exhibited the form of a native lark bird indigenous to this area, but known to be able to become whatever form it found to its liking at whatever time it chose had lingered to enjoy the thorough ecstasy that he had taken from the sexual gratification he had forcefully taken from the Nastazi queen; leaving her physically and mentally ruined. He had always found it amusing that something that was so enjoyable for one would leave the other so near death.

Elgin had flown lazily for most of the morning, but had only now increased speed slightly upon seeing the close proximity the slaves had to the Piasa and seeing for the first time in days, his main plaything, the one who presumed to call their bond a partnership and even sometimes love; Angelii. Circling down from above them, Elgin landed upon the roots of an upturned tree directly in front of the path that Angelii was progressing upon and immediately caught her gaze. He stared deeply into her eyes in a manner that she had not before seen, she then experienced something towards Elgin that she was most unfamiliar with; she now began to feel a deep and virulent fear!

As she approached the tiny bird, she imagined that she saw him shift into many different types of beings; an eagle, a huge sloth, a mountain lion with saber-like teeth, or was it a bear the images were all so fleeting and she could not tell if they were real or some sort of fleeting dream, but she felt a strange malice being emitted towards her that she had never felt from Elgin before. She grew ever closer to the tiny frame of a bird that she knew first hand was actually a being of tremendous power and when she was finally just within range to speak quietly to him she offered a strangely timid greeting that surprised all within earshot, save the little bird. "Elgin, we welcome your timely return," she said meekly.

"I come to warn you not to disturb the dragon, for we are not certain of its power and there have been many tales of its capabilities," the small bird said quietly, but firmly.

"Yes my love, but those are but tales; in the many seasons that you and I have comforted each other we have not seen any that began to live up to what has been said about this beast."

"Love," he screeched as he stared at her menacingly, "You are but a comfort and convenience and you will not speak thusly to me."

"Oh, well you certainly seem more than just comforted when you spend time in my chambers," she said trying to remind him of the pleasure which she provided for him.

"Do not judge yourself as of any importance woman," Elgin scowled at her as he spoke to her in such a way as she had never before experienced! Once again she felt the fear that she had just so recently been initially touched by, as she thought for a moment that she saw an incredibly huge and angry beast, though none save she seemed to have seen the apparition, or was it? She knew of his magical powers and certainly of the extremes in shape that he could attain, but did she know anything of his background or history before their meeting? Did she even know where he had come from? All that she actually had known about him for the vast amount of time that she had spent with him was that which he told her and this was precious little, save that he stated that he existed everywhere. She did not exactly understand what he meant by this but did know that at times, he appeared to take different forms, although she had not always been certain of this, believing that it might just be the effect that his incredible power to please had influenced her imagination. You see he had been forever a part of her imagination and development, for she had been with Elgin since she was but a very young girl, before she even knew the hair and bleeding of a woman. Somehow, also her being involved with this being had lengthened her life into hundreds of years; far longer than any normal woman and even though she had labored for so long with the assumption that she knew this strange being, at this very instant she realized that she did not really know anything about him at all.

Although she now began to experience indifference in him towards herself that she had never before seen and it made her feel small and insignificant, for she had for her entire life been cast in the role of the all-powerful queen that could have anything that she ever desired, someone who's every word was an order to be followed under pain of punishment or even death, but now she was beginning to understand for the first time where the real power truly was; it was with Elgin, the strange magical being that she had given and committed herself to early in her life and now she had the peculiar, but distinct and undeniable feeling that he was now finished with her forever.

Elgin gazed at her as a disappointed parent may have looked at a child and could see that she was uncomfortable, that she felt she may be cast aside. This amused him; the humans always formed such useless emotionally bonding attachments. Elgin had believed this one to be an exception, stronger and more powerful than the others, but alas she had now dissatisfied him also. There are others that would amuse him even more than this one had, even though she had been superior most times, he thought to himself conceitedly it will be interesting to search for others and the viewing of her current pain merely added immensely to his enjoyment of the situation.

His taste of this last young human maid had become the catalyst towards a decision; he had decided to move on, for he had tired of this human woman and the soulless slaves that they had produced. He cared not any more, for he had always been capable of the creation of slaves wherever and whenever he went. All that he desired now was to observe this creature that he had heard of for so long, the creature that the humans called the Piasa; he desired to meet a dragon and to reach new heights in the creation of a new, even more powerful slave!

He once again looked at Angelii and told her as plainly and painfully as he could, "You and I are now finished, but you will most likely need my help with this creature."

She stared back with tears in her large aqua eyes, knowing the finality of what she had just been told. She offered weakly, "We have developed many very powerful weapons, but would always welcome your magic Elgin." As she spoke she inched closer to the strange little bird body that housed the prodigious being that she knew to dwell within.

"Come no closer to me!" he spoke sternly, "I do not wish to harm you."

He stared at her as she resumed her distance. "You must not let this creature escape, nay or even take flight into the air. I have heard many tales of these beasts and they are mighty upon the wing and it is told that they can even breathe fire. It would be best if you secure it while it is not awakened as of yet for once you have awakened it there will be a very difficult struggle that you may not find yourselves capable of winning. Take my advice and surround the island of forest and advance in from all sides with the greatest of stealth in order to burn the creature to death."

Angelii replied, "As always, your advice is what we shall follow."

She turned to her men and said in a voice gruff with the projection of an attempt at the regaining of power and status and said, "Approach from all sides of the hammock," she realized as she was giving the order that this would take some time to accomplish and corrected. "Surround the hammock of trees before you close for the attack." Elgin spoke this advice knowing that it would never succeed, yet feeling that a first assault from these minions would assist him in weakening the dragon to more easily serve in his own desires.

She glanced at Elgin as if for approval and he told her quietly, "Tell the morons to keep quiet."

"And keep quiet," She yelled as she fought the terrible aching inside her that she just wanted to burst into tears. She did not know what to do or where to go and so she immersed herself into the coming fight, wanting to kill, if only for the extreme and delicious feeling of power that one such as herself felt when having taken a life. She ached for what she knew was close to happening, totally lost in her new-found though unwanted solitude. She did not yet know the scope of her coming isolation and so she could not see that it would have become more than she could ever bear!

―――――――――――

Tecumseh had fallen into a state that he had never before known; he was far more than sleeping or even having succumb to a trance, for the condition that he now found himself entered into was much closer to death than either of the former. He had found the nether-world that exists between life and death, a realm where there is nothing and yet there is all, there is none living and yet you are somehow in touch with all beings within, with all good and every evil, nearly able to touch them all, but somehow just not quite able to take the final step. He could feel exactly why he sensed in his large and powerful friend a morbid fear of this place that he had heard called "the Nether World."

Tecumseh felt that he was being called in many directions at once and had to fight to resist the many different influences that pulled at his very soul. It took all of his will power that he was able to gather, but he managed to finally concentrate on the task at hand and he was able to visualize Billi, the Piasa and himself at last. It was again as if he were floating above his comatose body and had begun to drift ever higher, increasing his view as he seemed to advance. He drifted up past the enormous body of the Piasa, that was still impressive even in the evil enchantment that he was now a prisoner within, he rolled upwards past the Piasa's body as if traversing a small hill, was still able to discern his gigantic wings and mighty limbs; and as he rose even higher he was able to see the mighty crown of his friend at the top of the mount that his huge body had created. This had furnished an excellent small fortification that his love Billigana was obviously trying to take advantage of. At this point he began to feel a fear like he had felt but one other time in his young life, the time that he had nearly lost his life to the Shush and also on that day met the Piasa. Though this was not the same it was somehow far worse, for he did not fear for his own life, in this he had some control and it was up to him to protect himself, but trapped within this dream there seemed to be nothing that he could do to save his beloved and he could see ever more as he continued to rise that his love was now surrounded by those that would be of the ultimate demise to her. He continued his slow ascension and though he could see that while she had found herself a well protected spot for defense, the woods were beginning to fill with the enemy from every conceivable direction.

She was surrounded with absolutely no chance of escape and their numbers were far too great to have any possible hope of slipping past, it was just a matter of time until they were discovered and all killed, yet he was entrapped in an inescapable near death trance from which he could not extract himself; he just seemed to drift higher and higher only enabling himself to further assess the hopelessness of their situation.

But that is when it finally dawned upon him; it was this feeling of fear, this is what had allowed him to touch the dragon the first time that they had met. Would it work when the fear was for his beloved and not himself? Would he be able to accomplish anything in time to save their lives, for he could see that he was just below his beloved though well hidden, he was for the most part unprotected? Would he even be able to communicate with his magical friend? All that he could feel was the extreme fear that he felt as the masses of murderous slaves tightened around him and the ones that he loved. He refocused putting every bit of effort from all corners of his soul into the calling upon his friend the Piasa.

~~~~~~~~~~

Billi also felt a deep and consuming fear, but at the same time she held deep within her a loyalty and protective instinct that can only be born of deep and enduring love that few actually are blessed enough to have known. She readied her weapons as best she could and went about making the preparations for her defense, as brief as it was likely to be. She had heard the oppressive noise of the huge throng of the marauding rabble for much of the morning as they drew ever closer, then suddenly something changed and there was only silence. No sounds from the animals of the surrounding woods, nor birds in the trees or sky and especially from the huge numbers of the disorderly legion that she knew to be fully enclosed upon her now. This new silence displayed a cohesiveness that the rabble had not shown before and this made her already deep fear only worsen, but she was already committed and knew of no other way that she was now able to proceed, she notched her first bolt and made ready.

Just at that moment, she felt as though a wave of belonging or even of recognized love may have just passed through her. She did not really understand exactly what it was, she just knew that she was doing exactly the right thing; she could have been doing nothing more noble or more in line with the proving of her love for her man or her people than what she was doing right now! She let her trained eyes scan the forest in search of her first target, but somehow she sensed something had changed incredibly. She saw her first painted Pawnee face break through the thick foliage of the forest hammock and it was far too close for her comfort, she knew that she should lose her first arrow to protect her love, the Piasa and herself for as long as was possible, but for some reason, unknown to her, something seemed to be staying her from the firing of her bolt. She once again felt something pass through her; a feeling of extreme well-being that seemed to pulse through her from below. All she could manage to think about it at the time was how very out of place it felt to her considering the current situation.

Suddenly the inevitable began to happen, just as she had seen the second of what was soon to become hundreds of possible enemy targets, that would have simply overwhelmed her even if she were able to fire every one of her less than fifty arrows, one of the aforementioned targets must have gotten a glimpse of her. This could not have been easy for she was afforded a remarkable amount of cover behind the stone crown of the enchanted dragon and the shot took her by surprise.

What happened next nearly shocked her from her perch above the rest of the humanity that now occupied the forest island. When the arrow from her enemy's weapon hit the dragon's crown in front of her, the bolt still shattered as she expected, but it did not make the sound of hitting stone. It made a sound altogether different and at the same time from below she heard a strange, barely audible half grunt-half snarl as if one of the village dogs were being bothered from a sleep that did not want to be disturbed. She looked down upon where she was standing and she saw a change coming over the stone precipice where she had taken refuge, for what had moments ago been a massive granite-like stone was now changing; it was changing into something recognizable to her, something that she was very familiar with, something that she had touched and even caressed; the dragon was coming back to life, it had again become the Piasa that is what she now supposed must have stayed her hand!

Somehow they had achieved what they had striven for; they had wakened the Piasa!

But what of Tecumseh, he had been even more exposed than she had been? Her question was answered as if the Piasa could hear what she had been thinking, which as a matter of fact was exactly what he had been doing. She quickly felt herself rise high into the air as the Piasa's body again adopted the nimbleness and fluid movement of a living magical dragon. What happened next, I am certain surprised all who witnessed it, for with a quickness and gentleness that dragon's have never been known for by humans, the Piasa grabbed the still unconscious Tecumseh and tenderly placed him within his dragon's crown next to his beloved Billigana, far safer from the imminent assaults.

For a moment the enemies attack was delayed, for none had ever witnessed so majestic a scene as the reawakening of a slumbering dragon; they were in possession of several moments that were simply lost in the awe of what they were now witness to. As the dragon rose out of its enthralled sleep it seemed to be growing ever larger, nearly doubling in size. The Piasa seemed to be surrounded by some sort of magical aura that danced with energy and life, his eyes flashed every color ever seen and even several that had not been viewed before by man as he looked around to take stock of the situation that he now found himself within.

Once that he had made his human friend safe he began a low, rumbling and altogether terrifying sound. It was more of a projected guttural gurgling than anything else, but soon grew into an unmistakable roar, stopping all of the would-be attackers exactly where they stood.

~~~~~~~~~~~~~

Billi began to see that Tecumseh was recovering from the deep effects of the trance that he had pushed himself into, albeit very slowly; she had no idea at this time of the incredible strength of the effects that were suffered upon one with the visit to that place called "the Nether World" by the few humans whom had known it, or of the rareness of ever finding your way back from this place once again. For now, she was thankful to have her man back in her arms and somewhat more secure than he was, only a few short moments ago; even though at this time they were still anything but safe.

She noticed that with the roar that the Piasa was sounding, the imminent attack had ceased for the moment and she began to once again notice a small amount of hope returning. She looked around them and all below where they had been just moments ago she now saw that the hammock had filled with treacherous looking heavily armed men that seemed to have come prepared for an intense battle, yet they had all momentarily stopped their advance upon seeing and hearing the magnificent creature before them. With this faint glimmer of hope she now allowed herself to even think that they might still be able to escape and somehow become the salvation of their people. "There just may be a way," she allowed herself this unique comforting thought, as she began to see her man actually come back into the real world, but the very next instant the hope was again diminished for she saw at this time emerge from the foliage not far from her and Tecumseh, the evil little bird known as a blight-lark that had seemed to be involved in everything that had gone wrong for her people since they had made the mistake of rescuing Angelii and inviting her into their village; what seemed like so very long ago. In reality it had been not even an entire year, but one that had transpired most rapidly and had seemed to have gone entirely out of the control of any of those whom she had cared for.

His surprising appearance here and now enabled her to realize that it had been this creature all along that had been the initiator of all of the evil which had been blamed wholly on Angelii and while she knew that Angelii was by no means blameless that the true source of and the definite originator of the evil was now looking at her.

However, Tecumseh and herself were mainly ignored by the hideous little creature, as its attention was fixed entirely upon the Piasa. It seemed to actually flash images of different shapes and bodies that it distorted to its own form as it gazed at the Piasa; truly it seemed fascinated by the awesome creature before it, as if he had never before been in the presence of a dragon.

This fact was most likely true as well; for though the evil beast Elgin had lived for many ages and the lifetimes of many humans it was by no means as ageless as the dragon and in fact had only begun to exist at the beginning of the age of humans; the beginning of the end of the age of the dragons and magic.

Although the Elgin beast had heard many tales of the Piasa and of its great powers and even its compassion for the insignificant humans that were so convenient to use as slaves, it had as of yet in its lengthy existence not had the opportunity to test its wiles on one, or even to battle this supposed magical creature, save a green that he and Angelii had murdered a short time ago through trickery. However, that green was nowhere near the example of a dragon that this tremendous brown happened to be as it could have been easily brought down by the men at arms which the Elgin creature and Angelii had under their control at the time; no the green and the brown dragons were as different as night and day; far different from one another in not only size and abilities, but also complex thought process and the powers which they possessed. The Blight-lark recognized this as a very different creature than any that he had previously encountered.

Words of the Piasa

The armed men surrounding the Piasa and his two passengers had been frozen in the observance of the magic existing before them; while Billi and Tecumseh struggled in their attempts to understand what was happening before them and to stay under cover as the dragon moved from position to position. You see, the dragon could not decide upon which form that the Blight-lark was going to actually assume; as he knew within the depths of his soul that the creature was capable of any one of those projected and so for now the Piasa's enemy could not actually be clearly seen!

All looked as the dragon felt that they should, save the tiny bird that was alighted behind the evil queen. This tiny being exuded an incredible aura of malice and although it was now very tiny, the dragon felt certain that this would soon change.

As told the Piasa did not really know fear, save possibly the unexplained anxiousness that he had felt in the presence and crushing grip of the black dragon, but something about this creature told him to beware. He knew that there was more to this small shape shifting bird than was obvious at first glance and just as the Piasa had made the decision to leap into the sky and attempt a timely escape he heard the evil little bird scream with startling power, "Kill them!"

Upon that, it was as a spell had been broken. A barrage of spears and arrows began to hiss towards the Piasa and his two young human companions; at precisely the same time that the Piasa leapt straight up into the midday sky, it appeared that the Blight-lark had begun a change too. Fortunately for the Nastazi youths and their dragon friend the Blight-lark had never seen a Black dragon or any of the more formidable creatures that Granger had encountered in his long past, for it began to take the shape of a giant ground sloth. This was a creature that while not as ancient as the dragons, was indeed an ancient being full of its own power and magic, in addition the Blight-lark still had the power of control over the many slaves that Angelii had provided and continued to order them to attack the Piasa and his passengers. Fortunately it did not have the power of flight, as a black would have had.

~~~

The Piasa strove mightily to rise above the flight of the many missiles that arched their way, but was unable to remain unscathed, although he did manage to avoid the huge timbers that had been launched by the devices that they had constructed, unfortunately wave after wave of arrows still rained upon them from every direction. They bounced off the hardness of his scales as though they were in a torrent of hail, yet they traced closer and closer to the friends who sat behind his magnificent crown; still the young humans remained untouched. As they grew closer to the top of the column of fired missiles and they finally began to thin, the inevitable finally happened, an arrow found its way between two of the dragons crown plates and sunk deep into Billigana's chest.

It was as though it had pierced all three of them at once. Tecumseh had never imagined the possibility of his young bride being taken from him, especially with an act of war. The placement by the dragon atop his crown had not compared to the shock of what he had just seen happen and he had not even been close to being able to protect his woman because of the horrible trance that he had somehow placed himself into. He felt as though he had failed his woman completely, as though he had let the Piasa come between him and his true love.

This untrue thought lasted, but an instant when he realized that the Dragon also felt her pain and he knew then that the dragon would do anything to save Billigana. Still, he felt as though he had failed her and it made him feel so very alone, as he finally became fully aware and free of the effects of that fearful place that he had been; he just held her body tightly, lovingly in his arms, weeping at her loss.

Shockingly, he heard her speak, "Tecumseh, you are squeezing my breath away." She whispered as she opened her eyes and gazed lovingly up at him. Even the Piasa became aware of their good fortune as he continued to struggle for altitude and to finally emerge from the range of the weapons that had been aimed at them. Through some extreme good fortune the bolt had pierced her through the upper right center of her tiny chest but hadn't struck any vital organs. Tecumseh and his great brown friend could not believe their good fortune.

"Granger, we must get her to safety as quickly as we can," Tecumseh urged frantically.

The dragon grunted in agreement and with several tremendous strokes of his wings headed east to the security of the forest that lay in that direction.

Below them the hoard of Pawnee, Mayan and now Nastazi slaves still strove to strike them with all manner of weapons, but they were now out of range.

Tecumseh was very relieved by his woman's good fortune, but was certain that she was in dire need of medical aid. In the conditions that they were now in he considered it too dangerous to even attempt the removal of the arrow. The mighty strokes of the dragon's wing beats made any kind of treatment, save holding her impossible. The young Nastazi warrior tried to remain strong, but after a few moments of the dragon striving for the east and the cover they both felt they would find there he broke down, "Granger, we have no time you must find someplace closer to land or she will die."

The Piasa quickly agreed and just comforted the young man with his thoughts saying, "She is heavy in my heart and I will find us a place to be safe." With that he made a diving motion towards another hammock of trees where they could have a short period of wellbeing.

As they swooped down low and alighted within the middle of a small clearing that the Piasa had picked, they did not realize that they had passed over hundreds of their foe that had hidden in the tall grass as they were warned to do so by the Blight-lark, Elgin. His gift for the manipulation towards evil was indeed unmatched.

Granger landed and gently placed both of his companions upon some wonderful thick, soft moss that looked as ancient a plant as the Piasa and Tecumseh went immediately to work on his love. You see, the Nastazi women were not the only ones that possessed exceptional healing powers, for this is an area that Tecumseh's mother had schooled him in from a very young age and Tecumseh, like many of his personal peers had well documented expertise in these matters.

First he removed the arrow by carefully cutting off the barbed arrowhead on the front of the shaft that had passed entirely through her and delicately sliding the arrow back out the way it had entered, fortunately Billi had seemed to have passed out again by this time. He was amazed at her luck, as it had not seemed to have struck any of her vital parts and even had caused what he considered a minimal amount of bleeding. Once again he was struck by her good fortune as he discovered that the moss that the dragon had placed them upon was the same that his mother had shown him would stay the bleeding of an open wound so many seasons ago.

He took off her blouse and could easily see that the arrow had entered above her ample right breast towards the middle of her chest and exited between her backbone and shoulder blade, he could not help but think that she must have indeed been protected because of the goodness of her soul. Finally he was able to gather not very far from where he and Billi were placed, several of the large dark purple leaves that his mother had always referred to as Condrit; which he had been taught would keep a wound dry and promote healing, these he crushed and strapped tightly against the wound.

As Tecumseh searched for appropriate vines to make his plan work, the Piasa edged his way towards the edge of the hammock in order to have a better view of their approaching attackers to make every attempt at the judgment their distance.

~~~~~~~~~~~~~~~

The blight-lark had not only managed to make plans that had a huge number of his minions at the exact place where the Piasa and his charges had been forced to take refuge, but had managed to have them once again surrounded in a very short time.

Though he had never before seen a dragon such as this, there had been tales of them like that which he now encountered and now the evil little bird desired to make the enslavement of the Piasa his crowning achievement. The blight-lark had succeeded in achieving dominion over all other creatures that it had ever encountered and now had an overwhelming and pervasive need to enslave this most majestic of beings, the Piasa. Had he known more about dragons, he may not have been so quick to assume that this was a possibility, but in any case this was to change his orders concerning the humans that accompanied the dragon for he now wanted them captured, as they may be of use to assist somehow with the enslavement of the Piasa. They approached the new location of their prey with a continued urgency, still bristling with weaponry and though most of their troops lagged behind, though still they possessed the overwhelming numbers that would make it quite easy to capture the two young Nastazi's.

Angelii was one of the first to break into the barrier of the trees with her small band of very loyal followers and had but one thing on her mind, the impression of the Blight-lark and finding a way of regaining its favor as she entered the thick grove with a fierce determination and mayhem on her mind. Behind her crouched a throng of menacing warriors with a terrible and ancient looking sloth that was easily as large as the Piasa. It was becoming quite obvious now that a horrific confrontation was near taking place.

～～～～～～～～～～～～～～～～～～～～～～～～

The Piasa gently poked his enormous head trough the thick canopy of the glade, only to be taken aback by what he saw, not one half a league away stood before him a creature at least as large as himself that looked more powerful than any that he had seen in all of his travels around this world save perhaps for the dragons of his own race. It was the same that he had seen the strange bird creature change into and had instantly caught his eye and stared back deeply into his own.

The thing seemed to have some sort of strange ambitions that he was unaccustomed to; for you see enslavement is totally alien to a dragon. In front of the huge repulsive creature were hundreds of the warriors controlled by the queen called Angelii and he saw her just now slipping into the cover of the forest, her lethal intent obvious. This would mean that danger to his friends was only moments away and so he ducked his large head back into the brush and quickly made his way back towards where Tecumseh was nursing his love as best he could.

The dragon whispered quietly, "The enemy is upon us, we must depart at once!"

But before they were able to gather themselves completely they heard the hissing of arrows in flight towards them. The crouching of the mighty dragon blocked all of the lethal bolts so that they could do no harm, but they now saw that they were under attack and most definitely within their enemies range once again.

The Piasa acted with lightning speed, surpassing anything that those preset were aware that he could perform and gathered the two young Nastazi's into his protective maw. He bolted across the hammock of trees that was entirely occupied by the advance of his enemy as they attempted to block his escape into the open sky. In but a few instants he was entirely across the glade to where he found an immense and ancient looking tree that he judged to be of sufficient protection to offer his friends the defense that they would need while he attended to the tasks that he could see were necessary for him to now perform. At this time a realization came over him that he was now involved in events that would have great effects on the futures of all involved.

He placed the mortally wounded Billi and her brave protector Tecumseh inside the hollow of the great old tree and pushed another younger, but very dry dead Oak tree in place in front of the opening. Leaving Tecumseh enough room to view, escape if the need arose and fire from if necessary, he grunted a somewhat loving sounding grunt, communicating his intent upon return and then turned to attend to the pressing matters that he knew to be of great and fateful importance which now lie before him.

This dragon could not understand the types of beings that desired to enslave and have dominion over others, but he had seen it before in the vile Black dragons of his kind that he remembered to have existed in the past. It was very unfortunate, but it seemed as though this sort of evil was not confined to only the hideous black dragons for there seemed to be some other origin of this despicable conduct, or perhaps it was just part of the natural world that he could not fathom. In any case, it was something that had to be stopped and a Brown Dragon was very proud and diligent in the care that he showed towards his precious "Mother Earth" and all of the good beings found there.

There had been awakened within him a feeling towards this human kind that was hard for a dragon to explain, but he wanted only the best for these humans and was of the mind set to protect them and see them well into their future. A sudden and fierce determination began to overwhelm him as he checked his friends safety one last time and then turned to face the overwhelming force; that which had been ordered to capture the Piasa and those that he held in such close regard; but the dragons course was now undeniable, for you see, the dragon was just now learning the meaning of the human concept of love and it was a very powerful motivator indeed.

The Piasa made his way to the edge of the woods. Over the many ages he had grown to most generally like and appreciate the humans for their complexities and the innate goodness that he had found most of them so capable of, but this group had been influenced in a terrible manner by the creature they called Elgin and this Piasa now understands that whether it is a horrendous creature such as this evil shape shifting being or that malevolence which can be sometimes grown in the hearts of man, evil does exist and at times surely needs to be battled. These once good and proud people had been robbed of their initial goodness and this had been replaced by an all-consuming selfishness that none so much as even realized possessed them; save the creature Elgin and perhaps the even more unfortunate Angelii, who was recognized by this dragon to have once been a very warm person capable of much goodness. The intricate situation that the Piasa now found himself involved in had some most saddening aspects, for as he thought of the past goodness that he was certain that she had once possessed he came face to face with Angelii and perhaps two dozen of her most loyal and fanatical followers.

She saw the Piasa at just the same instant that he spied her; even possessed by her strange rage she was strikingly beautiful and the dragon could see that with a slightly different emotional demeanor, she would have been a truly wonderful human, but she had the bad fortune of being influenced by possibly one of the more malevolent forces that existed in our world from a most young and impressionable age. This troubled this dragon unquestionably, but he definitely knew what must be done.

Suddenly all became very clear as he heard Angelii exhort her men, "Make the poison work, aim only for the eyes and inside its mouth," as she loosed her first bolt directly at the Piasa's open mouth.

Her accomplices immediately joined her in losing a barrage of arrows, all well aimed at the points that she had told them of, only his extremely quick dragon reflexes saved a hit that may have been proven to become quite serious.

The attack of a dragon in a war-like situation is not something that many have survived to tell about for it is quite overwhelming and surprisingly rapid. Although he had seemed to expand to the height of six adult men and the length of over twelve, the dragon moved in the wink of an eye and knew that his first target must be the leader. He leapt upon her the very first instant of the attack and though it troubled him to do so, crushed her with his huge forepaw before her entire core of warriors so that all could see.

This would have been enough to have stopped their onslaught in most cases, but due to the influence of the Kaav and the manipulations of the evil creature Elgin they only paused for a moment and at once continued the assault. This truly deepened the sadness that the Piasa felt, but only reconfirmed the correctness of what he had chosen to do in order to save those that were the beings he felt needed his assistance and dare he think it; he loved. He pivoted on the place where he had just dispatched the queen and lashed out with his mighty spiked tail in an ark that encompassed the remaining warriors and mowed down all that stood there like a scythe, men, trees, brush all that was within the sweep of the ark of his powerful tail fell shattered and lifeless to the forest floor. This seemed to arouse something of a battle rage within the dragon that was an entirely new feeling to him and now with not nearly as mixed feelings, the Piasa advanced towards the outer part of the hammock to where he knew the Elgin creature awaited him, along with hundreds or perhaps even thousands of the dreadfully influenced human followers.

Parting the thick canopy with his crown and seeing the first viewing of what awaited outside was no surprise to the dragon for he had felt the intense magical power of the being know as Elgin upon first sight; the Piasa knew that this being bore only ill will and was an evil that the world was far better without. Like the Blacks that he had faced in the past they cared only for themselves and desired dominion over all they encountered. Granger knew that this was a being that must be conquered and destroyed, but as in the case of the Black Dragons of the past he did not know whether he possessed the power to do so and unfortunately it seemed that the entire fate of those on his beloved "Mother Earth" would be decided with the outcome of this event. He must find the strength within himself to succeed, no matter what!

The Piasa was different than those dragons of the past, though he feared that he would not be able to win the battle that was about to ensue to protect the humans from this hideous abomination of nature; the pure evil that this being possessed just might be too much for even the mighty Piasa, but because of the change that had occurred within him he knew he must try to find a way. The dragon began to exit the grove of trees and saw that he was within bowshot of the huge sloth-like creature that was the currently held form of the thing that the humans had called Elgin. There were thousands of the enemy warriors advancing upon the grove and all stopped in their tracks with the sight of the dragon coming towards them, for the sighting of a Piasa has long evoked fear in humans, as there was a time long ago that humans often fell prey to marauding Black Dragons or even the larger Greens. Though these types of dragons were now gone and this remaining dragon had come to know and appreciate humans, though they had no way of knowing this and saw only a beast that appeared in a blood-rage advancing towards them. It was yet another misfortune of this day though; that they did not realize that the intense glare of the Piasa was not aimed at the numerous warriors that filled the plain before him, but the Elgin creature; realized it may have saved many human lives.

The two behemoths locked in hostile glares aimed at one another as they approached with anticipation of the extreme brutality that was about to occur. The Elgin creature bristled with thick wire-like hairs sticking up on the top of the back of his head and all of the way down its back; they appeared to be turning into quills even as the Piasa approached, additionally the monster seemed to be continuing its growth as the dragon approached and this was now becoming a matter of real concern for the Piasa, as there are few creatures that can be seen to be larger than a dragon, but this one in fact now was and seemed to be getting even larger still.

The humans that were near the two huge combatants all fled in an attempt to save themselves from the horrible violence that they saw was about to take place, but for some there just was not enough time. The dragon leapt forward with a fierce charge that brought formidable claws, teeth and strength to bear on his huge opponent, attempting a killing bite on the huge neck of the Elgin-beast. Unfortunately the thickness of the body and the massive strength of the creature were too much for the Piasa as he was tossed aside by the creature as though he were a much smaller animal, not one whose weight would be measured in modern days by tons. Many of the warriors that had felt they had escaped far enough away from the two massive creatures were not and the dragon was tossed mercilessly upon them crushing many scores of bodies that had absolutely no chance of escape.

As the Piasa began to right himself and try to decide his next move the Elgin creature continued to advance towards the hammock where Tecumseh and Billigana were hidden. Granger made another attempt, this time coming in from the side and once again attempting the neck bite on the huge monster. This attack had the same effect as the first on the creature; none. The Piasa was once again tossed off by the massive strength of the Elgin beast; once again killing large numbers of the nearby humans with the tumble and slide that occurred from the nonchalant toss that he had just been the recipient of.

This time he had been tossed partially into the hammock of trees that he was trying to protect and was beginning to become greatly concerned as to how he could hope to defeat this wicked monster.

With the start of the battle between the two mammoth creatures the Pawnee, Mayans, the Nastazi and all of the other peoples that had come under the spell of the Elgin creature, his beautiful, conniving human pet that had supposed herself a queen, Angelii and their deceitful enzyme from the Kaav plant that gave the feeling of immense power as it fully enslaved you body and soul began to scatter everywhere to find safety. Unfortunately many were not fleet enough of foot or possibly just did not possess the good luck to escape the violence that occurred this day and were smashed into the prairie soil. Many others that were fortunate enough to escape from the broad range of the carnage that transpired only found after their escape that they would be overwhelmed by the excessive need for the Kaav that had become so important a part of their lives.

Most all of the humans that remained far enough away to have not been one of the hundreds that were trampled underfoot as the two giants battled for supremacy faced a fate that was still far worse; for you see the small amount of Kaav that remained was in a litter similar to Queen Angelii's towards the back of the column of warriors guarded by Angelii's most trusted lieutenants, every one of which she had personally "tested" and so you see they burned with a fierce loyalty to her and a willingness to give their lives to fulfill her commands. Her last command upon her departure for the front lines was to protect the Kaav at all costs and not to dispense any of the small amounts that remained until she returned. Unfortunately for all she would never again return; additionally the huge army had consumed the Kaav to the point that there was certainly not enough for the remaining army for more than even a day. They had been depending upon the arrival of the Kaav that had been grown and processed at the Nastazi village of Nakokia that they considered the newest of their conquests, but now because of King Trevlon Takan's orders to eliminate it and their valiant, though failed defense of their land, that much needed drug would never arrive.

This would lead to wide spread massacre within the ranks of Angelii's army of slaves. It began at the litter that housed the Kaav and huge numbers of the impaired warriors demanding their portion that they had become accustomed to. They were not allowed as per orders from the queen and for a time this held the mob at bay, but as time passed the throng began to become much more agitated until after a lengthy standoff the craving became too much even for one of the trusted inner circle of guards and he was seen reaching into the litter for a small amount for himself. This was seen by the masses and set off an orgy of violence that spread throughout the crowd, men who had been brothers in arms just moments ago turned on one another in a spell of hatred and need began killing and maiming each other. In a whirlwind of blood, selfishness and urgent need for this strangely enticing substance to which they had been introduced by their queen and the strange little bird many died that day, while in their haste to acquire that which they felt they needed so badly the litter was upset and the remaining Kaav fell into the grass and the dirt of the prairie. While many attempted its retrieval, most were killed in the attempt and it was soon lost to all who desired it as the Kaav was stomped into the bloody mud that was created where this horrendous atrocity took place.

Though this was a terrible way to end the many of the lives that ended on this day, what awaited the remainder of Angelii's minions and newfound slaves was something far worse; for those that still lived and still remained under the power and dreadful deceit of the Kaav plant. Yes these men and women would still mostly find death, only it would not come mercifully at the blade of a knife or even the stroke of a war club. No, it would not even kill all that it held within its treacherous grasp, though it would take the lives of over ninety percent of its victims.

Of the rest only a few continued to live any kind of a normal life, though they would be shells of their former persons, their bodies and minds ruined, the rest would have been driven quite mad and did not last long into the next lunar cycle.

The Elgin beast was approaching the Piasa with the same malevolence glowing in his eyes that showed even as a small bird and a visible bloodlust within its heart. A dragon is not accustomed to being at a disadvantage to other creatures, especially when it comes to size. This dragon now realized that he needed to quickly devise a plan with which to overpower this new and menacingly powerful adversary.

The dragon once again approached the Elgin beast, very slowly at first but then with quicker and with more unexpected movements in an effort to outflank his adversary.

The remaining humans that were still within sight of this rarely seen battle of two of the most fearsome creatures ever seen in nature could only watch in awe as they tried to put as much distance as they could between this horrifying clash of beasts and themselves in an attempt to save their own lives.

Once again they joined with a thunderous collision that sent vibrations through the ground and even the very air itself, as it resounded with the shock waves that the two created although this time the Piasa seemed to have gained a slight advantage, he had somehow fooled the Elgin beast and been able to get a firm hold of the back of his neck with his mighty jaws. The beast let out a hideous shriek and began to shake the dragon violently. A beast with the strength to shake something so large as a Piasa is an incredible sight, the power that this took is just unimaginable. What is more is the fact that even though the dragon had an excellent hold on the neck of the beast and possessed some of the most powerful jaws and most formidable teeth that this world has ever seen, the Elgin beasts skin was not being broken. Though what concerned the Piasa even more was the fact that the beast seemed to be gaining strength and even appeared to somehow, be growing larger still! The Piasa now realized that he was engaged in the most demanding battle of its extensive and ancient life.

Words of the Piasa

In the nearby hammock of trees enjoying the temporary safety that had been provided them by the Piasa, Tecumseh and Billigana listened to the calamity that was occurring outside. When he placed the two in the protection of the hollow interior of the ancient oak tree, behind the downed tree trunk that the Piasa had placed in the front of the hollow that had formed an admirable protective space for them he had in the haste of the moment also created a room that could be very difficult to escape from for one wounded as Billi was.

For a time this did not matter to them for Tecumseh had been occupied with the comforting of his seriously wounded soul mate. Making certain that the bleeding did not resume and in a few moments he was even able to coax her back to a partial state of consciousness. He was also fortunate enough to have gotten her to drink some water into which he had been able to have squeezed a small amount of the extract of the plants that grew near their great river which he and all warriors took with them into battle to help relieve pain from the wounds that they may receive. He held her tightly in his arms as she again slipped back into unconsciousness.

He could hear the thunderous sounds that were being made by the two monstrous combatants that were locked in a struggle that he was certain would be the deciding factor of his and most other people's fate on this world and though he had the utmost confidence in his friend the mighty Piasa; he had not even seen the monster that the dragon battled, he had a very real fear that the Piasa, himself, Billi and the entire world that he had always known and loved were doomed.

Suddenly something happened that even deepened his despair. He saw approaching from a short distance away several of the warriors that he was certain that he had seen with Angelii and her huge brood of ruthless killers. He only saw a few of them and he was relatively certain that they had not yet detected him and his mates hiding place, but his fear of the situation in which they now found themselves increased even more.

He assessed his situation; although the space between the two immense trees was quite small, he was relatively certain that he could squirm and somehow squeeze his way through it and getting Billigana's far smaller frame through the opening would not be anywhere near as difficult although because there was a very serious drop once outside of the protection of the trees he would have to exit first and find a way to gently lower his love to the ground. This was going to be impossible with a group of ruthless killers that had been sworn to the annihilation of him and all of his people waiting a short distance outside for them he thought. It would not be easy and it would not be in the most noble of warrior ways, but he must wait for his opportunity and utilize the tiny area of room that was available to him in the hollow of this majestic old tree in which he had been hidden and take them out one by one; hopefully unnoticed by their partners. That was his plan at any case, but as it does most of the time in war; that is not what happened.

He was patient, he was extremely quiet, and he was as careful not to be discovered as was humanly possible. He had spotted only three of his enemies and felt that his chances were very good, considering the tumultuous and ground shaking noise of the battle that was taking place not so very far from where they were hidden.

He chose the one that he could see was the furthest behind the others and observed his movement through the undergrowth. When he could finally see that he indeed had the perfect shot, even though it was at a fairly extreme range he drew back his formidable recurved bow. This forced him to use every bit of the room that was available to him on the inside of this grand old tree, but he was comfortable with the draw and the coming shot. He waited as the man moved slightly ahead; still he waited for him to entirely clear from behind some branches that might possibly deflect his arrow, finally the shot was clear and he took it. The shot was straight and true and pierced his enemies neck just above the collar bone, but this is when fate stepped in and something that he did not expect happened as so often occurred in this type of tense moment. The bolt had gone straight through its target and lodged into a small tree that he had been standing in front of obscuring it from Tecumseh's sight and although the man had made but a nearly soundless gurgle when struck and was killed instantly, he still stood there leaned against this small tree with the arrow pointing straight back directly at the position from where it had come, pointing unswervingly to where Tecumseh and Billi were hidden.

His three adversaries, who appeared to have been Pawnee before falling into the ensnarement of the Elgin beast, Angelii and their all consuming drug, had approached Billi and Tecumseh in silence as all warriors practiced, although this was not so necessary considering the riotous noise of the battle between the two giants that seemed to be growing closer every minute. However the three now appeared as ragged mercenaries that followed the orders given by leaders that they feared greatly and who held a power over them that was truly inescapable. Still the three that had been now numbered two; as the two in front continued their communication with hand signals as most experienced warriors will do in such situations even in modern times, those that had been in front shortly viewed their deceased comrade impaled upon the tree with the arrow pointing directly towards where it had come from; they immediately took cover and converged together for a conference that was certain to bode poorly for Tecumseh and his stricken mate.

They too had found a very large fallen tree to use as cover, however theirs lay on the ground and they could travel up and down its length for a good distance, giving them a number of good angles from which to fire. Once the arrow that had claimed the life of their comrade had pointed the way, it had been quite easy for them to spot the formidable defensive location that their adversaries occupied, though at the time they did not know if it was any more than one warrior that they faced; they did know that it was a very strong defensive location, but they could also see that their opponent was trapped inside as well. They began to devise a strategy as they waited for any chance at a shot, such as someone sticking their head out of the hole to make an observation. They also listened to the sounds of the battle of the two monsters that seemed to be growing ever nearer as they attempted to carry out their newly formed plan. They did not know the entirety of the situation, but they knew that this was at least one or possibly both of the Nastazi to be captured as ordered and also that the two were said to be connected with the dragon. Capturing them could be of great benefit for their leaders and most likely possible reward of extra Kaav they thought.

~~~~~~~~~~~~~~~~~~

Tecumseh knew that he had just suffered a great misfortune, but he knew not of what would happen with his friend the Piasa and only knew that he must be the one to save his Billigana, for his dragon friend was very much occupied with a battle that he knew the Piasa must win if his people were to have any chance at any sort of future.

He carefully lifted his head above the downed tree for a better sight of the situation and was quickly rewarded with two swift arrow shots; one that stuck in the tree just in front of him and another that made it into the hollow of the tree and stuck the length of his arm above Billigana's head. He immediately moved just a few feet from where he had been into the total shadow cast by the angle of the light coming down onto his stronghold, making him invisible from the outside and returned an arrow that hit in the fallen tree only inches in front of where one of his adversaries attempted to poke his head up for another look as they too both immediately dropped down to take cover. The Pawnee warriors and Tecumseh seemed for the moment to have reached an impasse, but this type of situation could change very quickly, especially with two of the great giants of Mother Earth involved in a massive struggle that seemed to be rapidly heading ever closer in their direction.

The Elgin beast once again threw the Piasa clear of him after just shaking his vice like grip from his thick and hairy neck. The dragon rolled end over end for a good distance from the force of the throw of the hideous sloth-like beast. The tall grass on the plains, the trees and the unfortunate humans that were still within the area were uprooted, torn asunder and smashed by the two battling giants; they were as death, stripping the land of all living things and making it appear as a great wasteland which seemed to prove to all that witnessed that this battle was to have a great effect upon the whole of the life on the entirety of "Mother Earth."

Granger, the ancient Piasa that had seen so much of life and experienced most all of the joy, bliss and terror that this world had to offer as he had seen the land shaken and torn asunder when the earth itself was shuddering. He had seen storms of such force that even a creature as large as himself or even one of the hideous black dragons that had existed in the past would need to hide from their fierce winds and blasts of what would later be called lightning. He had even seen the mountains explode and spew out ash and fire for as far as the eye could see, but he had never felt such an evil as this Elgin thing possessed and what was more is that he could now feel that the creature was somehow continuing to grow ever stronger, ever larger as they battled. As he again mounted a new attack an idea began to materialize in his mind, an idea that he felt certain could enable him to defeat the horrible Elgin beast, but an idea that also filled him with the darkest and most forbidding of fears!

The two of the Elgin beasts and evil queen Angelii's warriors that had the young Nastazi couple cornered had come to a decision. They would capture the Nastazi that had killed their comrade, as they may be found of value to the Elgin beast that they held such fear towards, for they knew that the evil thing wanted them alive. They had begun to feel certain that they could capture the couple that were said to have been with the dragon rather than to kill them with the plan they had now devised; using fire to roust them from their hiding place for if they were surrounded by fire they would have no other choices than to surrender or die in the blaze.

They began to prepare flaming arrows and build a small fire for the assault that would decide which would occur. They felt certain that anyone inside would exit the small stronghold if it began to blaze and they felt that whichever of the two monsters was to win the battle that was taking place so close to them, either would most certainly appreciate the gift of these two; and so they began to discharge their flaming bolts into the dry dead tree in front of their victims that had until now been protecting them so very well.

Inside the magnificent old tree Billi had begun to come around and actually show some signs of gaining a small amount of strength. This just saddened Tecumseh and made him feel ever more desperate for he had recognized the sounds and smells of the arrows as they had struck the dry old tree that their friend the Piasa had placed in front of them for cover and he instantly realized the deadly peril that they now found themselves facing and though he was gladdened to see her improvement, it also broke his heart to have to say what he said next, "My love," he spoke slowly and sweetly, "I am so glad to see that you are gaining strength, but I must now warn you that we have a decision to make."

"Yes, my love, I am not yet that far gone," she said with a faint smile. "I can still smell smoke when it is upon me!"

"Yes," Tecumseh said. "And I do not believe that they have any real interest in taking us alive."

The hot flames from the well placed arrows began to spread in the dry, old, once noble tree that now trapped two people that held one of the deepest loves for one another ever known in all of the times of man.

Back at the Nastazi village of Nakokia where the horrible slaughter of most of the remainder of the Nastazi people had just taken place, the former Mayan commander of the army was beginning to have troubles with the obedience of his warriors. His orders were to seek out and kill any survivors that may be hiding in the woods, which included the remainder of Nanuma's young group that were fortunate enough to have been at Nanuma's assigned tasks and escaped the carnage suffered by their friends; instead his men were all making it known in no subtle terms that it was now time for more Kaav and they would continue their warring ways only after they had gotten another taste of the substance that had so fully influenced their lives for the past number of seasons declaring that at this moment this was all that really mattered to any of them..

They had a major problem though, one that had already cost several of the commanders in the other army their lives, for the Nastazi had destroyed all of the Kaav that was available here in this village and once the truth was known, the only interest that the slave-warriors had was to quickly find Angelii and her strange little bird so that they could once again have that which they all craved so terribly. They already had a general idea of where they had gone to and an army of that size was easy enough to track for at this time they no longer cared about what few survivors may remain, the only thought left in their minds was getting more of the Kaav that they one and all had to have. With this in mind they all began to depart for only that remained of import now; it soon became as a stampede not unlike the great beasts that were later hunted to near extinction on these plains.

But alas, their fate had already been sealed with the destruction of the small amount of Kaav that had remained with the main army and the subsequent riot of the members of that portion of Angelii's army of slaves. The great tragedy was not only that both sides believed that the other would be their salvation with more of the dreadful plant, but none realizing that they needed it so badly that the physical results would become which was to kill nearly all of them, but in just a few short days time that is what occurred; some succumbing sooner, some later but all became the drugs undeniable victims!

Though they all left in a great haste searching for their comrades who held what they thought to be the remainder of the Kaav, thinking it to be just a short march distant, not one of them made it to what they viewed as their salvation; no instead they spent the rest of what could be considered their lives in an unmatched nightmare of desperation, murder and mayhem. That was for those who were fortunate enough to meet their end quickly, however for the percentage that held and did not die in the first few days, they did so with the addition of self mutilation, hallucinations and a slow hellish death that for some even took the rest of the season, into the bitter cold of the Northern winter ending as food for the carrion often while still holding onto the last essence of an empty remnant of what was once their life in hopes of just once more experiencing the hideous drug that did this to all of them as they watched the animals feed on the puny remnants of their flesh that still remained.

~~~~~~~~~~

As the Piasa watched and assessed the Elgin thing, for what it had become now defied explanation, it was not like any being that the dragon had ever encountered; for it now had in fact grown larger and looked more like a combination of the sloth and also one of the huge saber toothed cats that had existed in this area some time ago, but with the thick leathery hide like what humans called dinosaurs or even one of the hippopotamus that modern men made homes for in what they called zoos. Although the lack of freedom that the beings that occupy these human constructed homes enjoy could only referred to by another human term that I have come to know and that is prison. The only saving grace is that the ways that the humans have multiplied and occupied all of the livable areas of "Mother Earth" in modern times they are probably saving the creature from the disappearance suffered by so many other creatures, particularly nearly all of my kind; save myself and a few that I know of in the North and East.

The presently huge Elgin-beast now began to quickly approach the dragon; a creature that has been feared by all on "Mother Earth" for all of time; with the obvious intent of slaughter on its mind and once again Granger felt that alien feeling of fear, but although rare he had felt it before and only one other situation other than the presence of a black dragon had ever produced it. That was the act of going to that netherworld that he and but few others had ever been able to accomplish; and although he knew how to get there with the use of his mystical wiles and felt that it might be his only chance against this ever strengthening spawn of evil, the very consideration of it filled him with a deep dread that he was not certain that even he could overcome. He had felt certain for a great while now, that if he returned there he would never again find his way back out again; within this place one was lost entirely with no way of finding your way, where you were at, how to go back to whence you came there was no up or no down, no passage of time, there was nothing and yet you were everywhere at once. You could not clearly see anything nor could you really hear anything coherently, you only felt, you felt the cold, the helplessness and the moans of the lost and trapped souls. The thought filled him with an unequalled foreboding!

The beast was approaching even faster now and because of the direction that he had so effortlessly tossed the dragon the thing was now bringing its wanton destruction ever closer to his close human friends Tecumseh and his wonderful little mate Billigana. The Piasa was beside himself with anxiety; he needed to make a decision at once.

He leapt upon the Elgin-thing again trying to gain a superior hold upon the creature's neck that by this time had increased in size to have become a formidable stretch for even the huge Piasa. The dragon dug his claws into the back of the monster and rolled in an attempt to redirect their battle away from his human friends.

The Elgin-beast sensed this desire in the dragon and roared as an evil laughter understanding at once what the Piasa was trying to accomplish and just to thwart his obvious desire the Elgin-beast lifted the Piasa completely off of the ground, a being that by today's standards of weight would be well over one hundred tons, and threw him towards the very direction that the Piasa had been attempting to guide the struggle away from.

The dragon crashed back onto the ground with an earth shaking rumble, smashing and snapping trees, rendering the ground and displacing a huge amount of earth until finally coming to rest not far from two of Angelii's brood that looked to be preparing for some sort of assault. This immediately changed with the close proximity of the two fearsome monsters and their cataclysmic battle. The two warriors had an instant change in priorities and scattered; by this time they too felt a great need for the Kaav plant and ran in two different directions both seeking the same false relief and soon to feel the effects that the lack of their deadly habit caused; a need that had been so maliciously begun in them by the once very beautiful Angelii and this cruel evil that its followers knew only as Elgin, but of course they had also only ever seen it as a small, strange finch-like bird, not as the very essence of evil within the world that the Piasa now recognized it to be.

The dragon Granger, later known in the tales told by the very few survivors of this terrible time of demise and destruction, as the Piasa quickly scanned the area and seeing all of the destruction that this battle had caused to the beauty of "Mother Earth" while knowing of the great suffering and loss of human life that his adversary had caused and also knowing that if it was not stopped now there may be no force that could put an end to the suffering that it caused, made the most important decision in his lengthy existence. He decided that he could defeat this vicious evil in only one manner, he would have to take him to the nether-world, between life and death, where both existed yet nothing really had form; the horrible place that struck fear even into the heart of a dragon; that place that while difficult to enter was far more complicated to leave; that place where all that filled the nothingness was the wailing of the multitudes of so many lost souls.

It was his only chance! The Piasa leapt forward, surprising the Elgin beast and bowling it over as he grasped a death grip upon the evil thing with his teeth, claws and all of the power that was at his very formidable command. He then held onto the creature with all of his might as the gathering of the sparkling lights mixed with black darkness surrounded the two gargantuan creatures. The last sight that the Piasa was able to glimpse of was the protective stronghold where he had placed his human friends Tecumseh and Billigana still intact, but with the great dead tree that he had placed in front for protection now burning vigorously.

Suddenly they were in the eerie silence with only the whispers of tortured screams the surrounding nothingness of the netherworld somewhere between life and death. The Piasa hurled the Elgin-beast away from himself with all of the strength that he could muster and for several moments he saw the monster tumbling away into the void, howling with bitter hatred that momentarily covered the other muted cries, but soon the hideous creature disappeared and its cry just blended with the sounds of all of the other trapped souls inside this horrid place.

The dragon, perhaps the very last of his kind now found himself floating helplessly in a ghastly place that no living being could still possess the remainder of his own free will, this place that for so long had even struck fear into this very dragon, one of the most fearless creatures that had ever existed in our world. Yet he was just as lost with no inkling of how he would find his way back; still that fear is not what filled his mind, for all that he could think of now was how his human friends were about to perish in an unintended trap in which he had placed them, a trap in which they would be burned alive!

Tecumseh could see the flames beginning to grow and was very aware of their plight; he thought that he could wedge Billi through the opening and toss her to the ground, unsure of how much more physical damage that she may incur between the flames, the long fall to the ground and their awaiting attackers or if she even had any chance of survival at all. If he tried to climb through the opening first he knew that there were two enemies outside that were intent on his death as certain reprisal for the fate of their comrade, but his love for Billigana was very strong and as much as it dictated that he should make some attempt to save her, even more it compelled him that he should not let her die alone. He was unsure of what just exactly what to do, but he knew that he had to make a decision at once!

He had heard the distant rumblings of the huge struggle that he was certain that the Piasa was embroiled in and he could feel that it was a struggle against the evil Elgin beast though he could not fathom just how that small bird could possibly challenge the dragon, there must have been more to that bird than he had known; but that was all that he could sense at this tumultuous time as his Billigana and himself were also in a struggle for their lives. Suddenly the sounds and the trembling of the ground were directly upon them even to the point that he thought that they might become swept up into it, he stood to peer out through the growing flames and could see that all of the trees nearly to the point of where they were entrapped had been stricken down by some enormous force and then he heard a hideous howl and so gathered himself around Billi to be able to protect her from what was coming. He looked towards the noise and what he saw sickened him and filled him with dread; he saw the Piasa locked in mortal combat with as appalling looking a creature as he had ever seen, but as he watched the two of them disappeared in a mixture of strange twinkling lights and a mixture of deep unparalleled darkness. He knew that they had gone to the netherworld and along with the disappearance of the Piasa went any hope of rescue.

He knew then what he must do if they were to survive and he quickly gathered Billi into his arms as he twisted her long beautiful brown hair into a huge knot and loosely tied it as close to her head as he could as he said, "I must drop you to the ground to save you, please try to roll and cushion your landing!"

She looked up at him weakly and replied, "There is no time left my love, I am nearly gone save yourself."

He kissed her and pushed her through the opening as quickly as he could and then followed immediately behind her. The flames licked fiercely at him, but he was through the opening quickly enough that the inferno only caused a very few minor burns. His leap at the top of the opening had propelled himself somewhat further than where Billi had landed, but he could see that they had both been very fortunate because the battle between the Piasa and whatever horrid evil that he had fought had pushed up a massive mound of soft earth that had ended just below the tree where they had just been trapped, good fortune had smiled on the two pure hearted Nastazi yet again.

Tecumseh swiftly checked the condition of his soul mate and as he did so she slowly opened her eyes and smiled, but said nothing. He gathered this to be as good a sign as he was likely to receive and scooped her into his arms to carry her further from the flames. As he walked away from the burning tree he saw something else that struck fear into his brave young heart anew; the embers from the burning tree had traveled to the tall grasses of the Great Plains and had begun a wild fire that could conceivably burn for days and many, many leagues. They were somewhat safe within the barren destruction created by the battle of the two giant creatures as there was not much fuel to burn, but with the wind coming from out of the west as it normally did in this part of the land it would burn all the way to the river and possibly even cross the river they followed to get here and possibly even burn its way all of the way back to the Green Lands that they knew they would cross to get back to their home; in any case it was most likely soon to be burning their wind rider which was, once repaired their transport back home. He just drew Billi back further from the flames and tried to make her as comfortable as he could, sat with her in his arms and rested, trying to decide his next course of action.

The Piasa had never felt the emptiness such as that which he was now experiencing. Though he was plagued by barely audible wails of misery, he could not see anything but the grey nothingness of the between worlds where there existed nothing, only the barren lifeless void to which there seemed no escape. The one vision that he did have was that of his human friends trapped in the burning shelter that he had placed them into. The brown dragon was utterly lost, just as he had feared would happen if ever he had attempted this dreadful place again, he was now trapped without escape! He had made the promise to himself that he would not ever come into this place again for he had feared exactly this happening for many seasons; as it had happened to so many of his kind that he had seen trapped before, now at last it had happened to him. Though the vision of his human friends burned within his mind and seemed the only connection to the real world that remained. He knew that somehow he must concentrate upon that image and find the way back to the world that he knew and loved; he was certain of that being his salvation. He also felt an urgent need to save the two humans that he had become so close to and try to make right all of the wrongs that he felt he had allowed to happen, for it was he whom had placed them into the trap that would soon become their doom and he whose role it would have been to shield them from the monstrous malevolence that had been called Elgin. Though they now seemed safe from the evil of that beast it seemed that they would soon perish from the direct action of the brown dragon that had professed to love them.

Though the Piasa burned the thought into his own mind, he was having no success; he could not get the picture of the flaming tree from his mind and concentrate upon his friends, hence he could not make the jump from his desolate trap.

As he was nearing his end and he could feel his resolve beginning to weaken for possibly the final time is when the horrid image slipped from his mind and he instead pictured the two young Nastazi lovers and the purity with which they gazed at one another. He saw there the unselfish and unconditional love that was, in fact the purest that he had ever witnessed. He gazed at them and reveled in their unmatched adoration and felt something that nothing had ever been able to cause within him before, he realized at that instant that he loved the humans; this was a feeling without equal, one that he had never before realized (although he felt that this may not have been the first time that he had felt this way, in the past he had just not known what it was called!) The Piasa knew now that he loved humankind and the Great Spirit had planned for him to become their benefactor. His heart ached with the love that he felt for all of humankind, but especially for the two young Nastazi that he had placed into the tree that was now becoming their doom. He shut his eyes tightly to the pain, for there was naught to be seen in any case.

Tecumseh had felt that he could just sit rest and wait to decide on his next move until something happened that forced him to take immediate action! A subtle change in the wind changed the way that the plains were burning around them and it became obvious that they would soon be completely surrounded by the hot flames of the rapidly burning high plains grasses. He had to act at once! He saw the lift of the compressed earth that they were currently hiding behind and quickly judged that it would hold together sufficiently if he were to dig a small cave into the side of the rise. Then he did just that, ever so quickly to avoid the approaching inferno and he then pushed Billi into it, sliding in behind her and throwing earth up behind him as best he could to protect them both from the heat. His real concern though was if they would be able to breathe the intensely hot air and so he pushed the soft earth that he found up into the entrance to entirely close them inside of his newly created grotto.

Fortunately, the fire came quickly and was over within but a few short minutes as the prairie grasses burned hot, but fast and though the noise was deafening and the breathing was extremely difficult for a while, it was over in just a short time. When the din from the conflagration subsided he began to slowly reopen his hurriedly constructed sanctuary and when he judged that it was finally safe Tecumseh slid out of the makeshift shelter and gathered his love into the protection of his arms and began to inspect her; for a moment he worried that the experience may have been too much for her in her seriously weakened condition, but after several moments of fawning over her and trying to clean her face with the loving application of his own saliva he was rewarded with the loving smile that he recognized so well. It was very faint, but she had made certain that her man saw that she was still with him, although at this time she made only the slightest of sounds.

He knew that he must gather her immediately and begin the long trek that would lead them to safety, but he had a real concern as to the amount of water that they had in his half empty skin and the length of their upcoming journey. He convinced Billi to take as long a drink as she could handle at the moment and then took a small sip himself. He then cinched the skin to his deerskin britches and gathered Billi into his arms and began the long march of carrying his soul mate to the river and their only hope returning home; all the while hoping that this barren wasteland of nothing but still warm ash would not last for long; but sadly, at this time, it stretched as far as his eyes could see.

The Piasa had drifted painfully in the void; for how long he did not know, when he felt a new sensation, for that matter it had been the only sensation that he had felt since his entrance into the netherworld. His eyes sprung open in anticipation and to his utter delight he could now see. What he did see however was piteous, for he was right back at where he and the horrendous evil that had been known as Elgin had been battling and their struggles had been all that had kept this area from the fiery conflagration that had obviously occurred. All of the tall golden grasses that had previously been surrounding him during and before the battle had been burned to the ground and he saw no living being of any sort for as far as he could see in all directions; except for the tree, for there not far away was the remaining scarred trunk of the tree where he had placed his friends for their own safety he had thought at the time. He approached the black husk and peered inside, expecting the worst, but to his surprise it was empty. He knew that had they been able to escape for he would have seen something of their remains even after such a hot burning and so he was somewhat relieved. However they would still be stuck in the middle of leagues of desolation with Billigana mortally wounded; he had to find them soon!

He began to search for any signs of his two human companions but saw nothing at first. As his search began to widen though he finally saw something that he thought was a definite positive sign. It appeared as though they had dug into the side of the embankment that the struggle between himself and the Elgin beast had created. This seems to have been where they had avoided the flames during the firestorm that had obviously taken place not so very long ago and if they had been able to have avoided the flames they must have lived. Their bodies were nowhere to be found so it seemed only obvious that they must have survived as they were most resourceful, these two.

His search continued once again and soon he located another sign, he saw one set of footprints; Tecumseh's and it appeared as though he was carrying something, so he felt that Billi must still live and that Tecumseh was carrying her to find sanctuary. This gave the dragon at least some comfort; for the dragon had seen these tracks before, it was definitely Tecumseh of this he was certain; he was attempting to carry his love to safety. This in turn truly produced a tremendous amount of grief that the dragon once again felt, as it appeared that the fire that had burned here in the Piasa's absence had been very large and unfortunately, it was many leagues to the river that was his way to the village that he called home or for that matter the water that they would both need to survive.

The dragon had to locate them and offer assistance as soon as was possible, lest they perish in this desolation! He arose into the air while at the same time flying as low to the ground as possible in order to attempt to follow the tracks, for they were very vague, even for his exceptional vision, an eyesight that had been hued from ages of hunting from the air for nearly all of his prey. The prints were very faint though, as though they were far from fresh. This the Piasa found very disturbing, for he was uncertain of exactly how much time he had spent within the "Nether World" and this concerned him immensely; but on he pressed searching for his human friends.

───〜〜〜───

Tecumseh had walked for all of the day in the hot Midwestern sun; only pausing for short rests and to give his love another drink of water when he felt that she had the need, still nursing what little water that remained by only taking the smallest of sips for himself. He had been closely watching her and was very concerned that he had nothing to feed her and the heat from the sun was so weakening; even though she was being carried he could see that it was draining the little strength that remained in her small, beautiful body. Though what was really disheartening was that although he had walked all day at as great a pace as he could muster, knowing that he had to have covered quite a distance; still for as far as he could see there was nothing but the lifeless grey desolation of the fresh ash. He had so hoped to see the beginning of the rolling hills that marked the vast land before the great river and the first promise of water that he was aware of; a region that his people called Hozho'Anasazi, or "the beautiful land of the Ancient Ones." Today it is known as The Ozarks and though it does not reach as far to the North as it once did, it is still a substantial and beautiful part of our great land; it begins today in Eastern Oklahoma and includes parts of Northern Arkansas, most of Missouri all the way to the Mississippi River, or Great River as the Nastazi referred to it. Continuing on the other side of the river to blend into the "Smoky Mountains," it was a beautiful land with the promise of not only water, but shelter and food.

Tecumseh was most certain that he must make that land, yet he feared that his strength was nearing its end and though she was being carried he knew that Billi's strength was also nearly spent. So he decided that he must find a pace to rest, if only for a short time as he knew the travel would be much cooler during the night and any of the predatory animals that would normally be a danger to him and his love would most likely have been driven away by the fire, he would probably not need to worry about the bear or the cougar until he reached his goal of the Ancients Beautiful Land. For now what he needed was just a short rest to regain some of his strength and then he would press on into the night. Although he was not aware of it at this time, an unaided walk to where he desired to go would have most likely taken him more days than they would last; time that he did not possess.

The sun had already dropped down to near the horizon when he finally had his first bit of good fortune for quite some time it seemed. He found a large flat boulder that looked as though it did not really belong where he had found it, as it appeared to have been shaped by water as in a river. Additionally after the sun had dropped the temperature had gone down quite a lot and so he was now concerned with Billigana's protection from the cold, but to his good fortune, not only was the boulder nice and comfortably smooth, it was also still very warm from the experience of the fire and the strong Midwestern sun. He lay his love down and comforted her with the last of the water from the skin.

Tecumseh was very strong and approaching what would be the prime years of his manhood, but carrying his beloved for all of the day had sapped his strength immensely, as the ordeal had also drained his woman. He once again checked Billigana for any sign that she may be able to give him as to her condition, but did not see anything that was different. His stoppage of her bleeding and mending of the wound seemed to be holding up, but he knew that she needed more healing herbs, a poultice upon the outer surface of the wound, food and water.

He again picked up his water skin even knowing that he had given her what had remained and inverted it in an attempt to drain whatever might be left in it to drop into Billi's beautiful, even though chapped lips in order to try to convey some little bit of hope to her in this most difficult of times. Trying to give her enough hope to hold on; for this he was rewarded with a weak smile and he knew that he had done everything that he could do for the moment. He then lay down next to her and caressed her for the added warmth that he could add and fell into a deep sleep almost immediately.

Behind the brave young Nastazi lad, the Piasa had no idea of just how much that he had closed the distance between himself and his human friends. Had he realized that they were now within twenty leagues of his current position he would have continued his flight, for he knew that he must be overtaking them and also by the occasional tracks that he discovered recognized that he was indeed following Tecumseh (thankfully still apparently carrying Billigana). Unfortunately the sun was dropping below the horizon and the dragon must soon stop for lack of the ability to see the ground on this, as of yet moonless night.

He glided on ever more slowly as the great expanse of black burnt prairie continued to meet and blend with the darkness of the sky, but shortly the only manner of distinguishing between the two was the beginning of the appearance of the first stars of the evening. The Piasa prolonged this portion of his flight for as long as he dare, but finally he dropped down to the barren ash-filled earth for fear that he may pass his human friends in the darkness.

As the dragon alit amid the great, but now invisible cloud of ash that his mighty wing strokes had created he indeed felt weary from the trials that he had recently endured and had the passing thought that he must be careful not to sleep again for he had slept for too long a time already and it had cost his human friends and acquaintances a momentous price, he judged from all that he had seen, though it did not matter for he had made the decision that he would find his friends and would again be under way just as soon as the light of the moon or the sun would allow. Had he known just how close that he had come to his reunion he may have continued on afoot, but alas, the wind was blowing lightly from out of the west as usual and so he did not receive their scent and as a result; he did not realize that he had stopped no more than ten minutes flight away from them!

Something akin to warrior spirit increased within Tecumseh this night, for although he had faced many challenges in his young life and by most would have been thought to have risen to them very well; on this night he was faced with saving his love. The one whom he knew was his one and only soul mate, the one with whom his life could never be complete without and it was a challenge that he would not fail! As soon as the nearly full moon broke into view over the horizon he was awakened. He knew not how long that he had slept, but felt greatly renewed and much more fresh albeit deeply sore in every muscle of his body. He decided that he must take advantage of the cool of the night if he was to succeed on this most vital of endeavors, he also decided that the finding of the green rolling hills would be more quickly achieved by heading more to the South as he had heard from some of his elders that had explored this way that the green lands filled more towards the west in this direction, it may save them days of travel he felt. He stroked and caressed Billi again, conveying renewed hope and that he was once again going to be on the way to safety. This time there was no reaction except his detection of her light and very shallow breathing; he knew that time was of the essence. He picked up his empty water skin in the hope of possibly refilling it on the way, for he felt that if he could not succeed on this night that he would no longer have any reason to go on living.

He then gently lifted Billi back up into his strong young arms and continued on, refreshed further by the light breeze from out of the west that seemed to carry the faint aroma of subtle familiarity. Though he could not place it exactly, he found it somewhat comforting. Sighting the stars and determining the exact direction that he must travel he strode off into the darkness, determined to save Billigana. As he began his journey anew he found himself wondering; what could have happened to the Piasa? Had the evil Elgin beast; for Tecumseh although he did not know how, knew this to be the thing that the Piasa was battling was indeed that evil small bird; had it killed the mighty dragon?

Had the Piasa's worst fears been realized? Yes Tecumseh had felt it, he knew that the thought of going into the netherworld; that place where the Piasa had even inadvertently shown a young Nastazi warrior how to come to. The thought of entering this place again had terrified the huge and otherwise fearless dragon. Perhaps there was something in that place that Tecumseh had not seen, or perhaps there were deeper parts into which no one or nothing could find the way back out again. Perhaps it was something even more terrifying, for the young man did remember one thing about that place; that was the undisputable feeling that he was being appealed to in some powerful way to remain. The hopeless appeal of innumerable lost souls begging for him to show the way out, pleading for someone or something to put an end to their suffering, pleading for even the release of death, for even this they could not achieve; they were trapped in a place unlike any other, neither life, or death only the extreme infinite void with no depth, no direction, only the lament of all of the lost souls and the pain of isolation that existed in this place. Perhaps the dragon's worst fear had come true! He strode on into the night as an emergent fear of that place had come to occupy his mind as well.

~~~~~~~~~~~~~~~~

Deeper and deeper into the cave the two drunken "hunters" had stumbled. They had their flashlights, but had decided that it would be too risky to turn them on save for very short flashes only to once more find their way if they had come to an obstacle; though this only managed to make them ever more noticeable as they wound deeper and deeper into the cavern and loudly traversed over the ever increasing numbers of large rocks and boulders that had been washed down into the cave over the years by the rain waters that had formed it. They had supposed that they would quietly sneak up on the mighty beast that they had heard may occupy this cavern and become famous, and probably very rich for being the first ones to have finally proven that something like this actually existed.

For all of their lives they had been exposed to stories about the Piasa that the Native Americans had said was a part of these woods; stories of Sasquatch, or Bigfoot that had as of yet not been proven, even UFO's and the aliens that were said to have occupied them, but now they had the chance to be the ones that would finally have the proof that they felt the world needed; a body!

Their minds were filled with thoughts of talk shows and magazines, of the money that would inevitably come their way and the notoriety that would be theirs for just another day in the woods of drinking.

Burt whispered hoarsely to Gill, "Be quiet now, I think that we are getting close to that thing," and then fell down to one knee while again drunkenly stumbling on loose rocks.

"Quiet yourself," Gill chuckled, as he slipped upon the same loose rocks, just catching himself upon a huge protruding boulder on the wall that he was leaning upon.

Burt, who had been drinking the more heavily of the two now

decided to light his flashlight, so as to see if there may be any crevices or other dangers ahead of them, for now it seemed that they could begin to hear the low rumblings of a sound made by the dragon; he knew that they were almost upon their quarry and it would soon be time to act.

He showed the light ahead on the trail which they would follow and gave a thumbs-up sign to Gill. He shut off the light and they were both once again consumed by the blackness, yet on they pressed, as the reward that they imagined pushed them to an unequaled act of evil and yet they could not even distinguish that the needless murder of another creature was anything but the taking of a trophy, and so on they pressed!

Close behind them now were Bill and Danny; the Piasa's protection of the little newcomer and it's sparing of them when it had been so obvious that all the dragon would have had to have done was to put forward the slightest of effort and they would have both been toasted cinder's; removed from this world and most probably for what was a just cause, had changed them in an undeniable manner. This creature that they had before considered a monster had seen something in them and had chosen to forgive them.

They felt as if they must now return the kindness that had been bestowed upon them; they had to protect the dragon from the needless killing with the drunken hunter's high powered rifles and this is exactly what they meant to do. How they were going to succeed in this was still something of a mystery, but they planned on stopping them in some way. They had one thing working in their favor and that was this total darkness. Fortunately, they could hear the drunks ahead of them quite clearly and knew that they were now approaching closely to the decadent pair.

That is when they spotted a flashlight turned on only a short distance ahead of them. The two hunters had stopped for some reason and were attempting to whisper amongst each other, but unfortunately for them it was coming out far louder than they had anticipated.

Bill and Danny froze and measured the distance between themselves and the two impaired villains. They had not discussed what their plan might be, for they did not have much of a chance facing the high caliber rifles that the pair ahead of them had in their possession, but they both felt a newfound since of righteousness and knew only that it was up to them to stop the planned cruelty from occurring. The light was doused and the two boys continued their quiet stalking of the gun carrying ruffians ahead of them. They were considerably quieter than the two further on and this made it easier for them to close the gap totally unnoticed.

The four continued to edge their way down the black corridor for what seemed to be an eternity; Burt and Gill stumbling drunkenly towards what they felt for certain would be their crowning achievement; the most remarkable trophy ever taken by any type of hunter, a beast that had been only legend would now be proven to exist by these two hypothetical hometown heroes. They would prove that dragons existed with a body and in their opinion, this was the only way.

Behind them were two young boys that had recently undergone an incredible change of heart. They had changed from two vandalistic bullies to young men with a functioning conscience with just one act of mercy shown by an incredibly powerful being that did not need to show such kindness. At this time they did not even realize the magnitude of the act of fate that they were about to perform.

The four continued traversing the dark corridor, two in back as silent and cunning as a snake on the hunt and the two ahead bumbling and stumbling; drunk not only with the bourbon that they consumed, but the expected promise of the false future that they perceived was about to be awarded them with so little effort. This would become the most crucial of days that any of the four had yet to experience, as it was to change forever the courses of all of their lives, yet not at all as they would have ever suspected!

Suddenly Danny grabbed and pulled on his older friend's shirt. "Stop," he exclaimed as quietly as his excitement allowed, "Look ahead of our redneck friends, I see something."

Bill raised his gaze from the useless study of the dark ground before him and whispered, "Yes, I can see a light ahead."

For a few moments more Burt and Gill did not notice the light coming from the small fire that the dragon had made from the coal that was prevalent in most of the grottos in this part of the land. The Piasa had easily made the fire with but a short burst of his dragon's breath in order to sooth the young Nathan as he spoke to him. The dragon had also chosen this part of the cave with that comfort in mind for it had a marvelous circulation of fresh air out the roof of the cavern at this point; for a long while the dragon felt comfortable with his arrangements, for the dragon had no concerns about his own breathing, he did know however that this young human needed good fresh air to survive.

All of these choices the Piasa had made were very obvious now to young Nathan and that only added more substance to what the dragon was trying to convey to him. Nathan could sense an actual feeling of compassion from the otherwise terrifying looking being.

Back in the grotto that lead to the cavern where the Piasa spoke to young Nathan, two men that professed to be hunters slowly made their way around the corner and at last they could get a peek of the huge beast that they had proposed to take.

It was an incredible sight; there ahead of them sat the fiercest looking creature that they had ever seen; it was easily thirty feet tall though his head disappeared into the shadows, save his magical multi-faceted eyes that seemed even from this distance, in the near total darkness that they were now completely immersed in, to be staring right through them in silent menace. His wings were folded at each side, but could be seen to be able to more than fill the cavern if unfurled. They were tipped with wickedly sharp looking claws as were the forelegs that seemed to be folded across his mighty chest. He sat on massive legs that were as big around as any oak tree that either had ever seen, these too were tipped with the most huge claws that these men had ever dreamt could have existed and upon them balanced a long and muscular body that faded into the darkness behind him, though the occasional movement belied the existence of a huge tail that was much longer than the height of the dragon. The entire body seemed to be covered with thick scales that had an unusual opalescent sheen, not unlike that of oil floating on water. The dragon had the look of the ultimate predator and seemed to be looking directly at them, inviting their challenge.

Sitting in front of the colossal beast was ten year old Nathan Bellows, obviously enthralled and captivated with what he was hearing and astonishingly showing absolutely no fear towards the creature that filled so much of the cavern before him!

Burt and Gill sat staring; neither of them seeing the others' mouth agape in utter amazement, for this was a sight that few men had ever seen. Moments or even minutes passed, they did not know; but finally the two began to communicate, if only by signs as both approached the fallen rocks ahead of them to rest their powerful rifles for as precise aim as was possible. Still, the Piasa's eyes bored into them; though he continued speaking softly to the young boy who sat dwarfed by the dragon on the boulder before him.

Bill and Danny had gotten quite close to the two armed men and now began to frantically weigh their options. The two men in front of them were both large adults that easily outweighed the two young boys by over one hundred pounds each and they had nothing that could be considered any sort of trusted weapon. They were now in a moment of time whereas both seemed at a total loss as to what course of action to take. With the faint light they could now see the repulsive men lay their massive weapons upon the rocks in front of them and begin to sight them in using the only available light in the cavern, a light provided by the dragon for the comfort of the other young boy that shared space in the cave between the dragon and the self proclaimed hunters.

The dragon had now taken on a different sort of manner, or so they now perceived for the deep multi colored eyes of the beast continued to look directly at the two marauders, without so much as a movement of his head in their direction, while at the same time he seemed to be able to see past them to where Danny and Bill hid as well, even though it was utterly black down the passageway in which they all now traversed, but he did not take any action even though the two boys were certain that his vision pierced the dark and saw every move that was made by all before him. Incredibly, the boys could "feel" the compassion that the dragon held towards the young Nathan that they themselves had been harassing earlier in the day and in some deep way this made them both feel a great shame; additionally a developing since of the desire to atone for the malicious acts that they had performed during their most all of their young, troubled lives.

It finally came to them; Bill and Danny both realized just what the small act they could possibly save the day with and their weapon of choice lay at their feet. They each squeezed the other on the shoulder and bent swiftly down to grab one of the many small pebbles that littered the floor of the cavern where they stood, though they were but tiny rocks and would be considered much less than perfect for an assault on a much larger adversary, they should suit their needs just fine and they did not hesitate, they picked up their missiles and launched!

Ahead of them at that very instant were two misguided would be famous hunters that did not actually realize just what kind of being that they now had in their sights, but felt that the only method of proving that the legend actually did exist was to kill it in order to have a body to show everyone.

They had drawn the bolts of their weapons and cocked them on the way inside the cavern, something that no legitimate hunter would ever do because of the inherent safety rules concerning hunting with guns and the danger of walking around with such a weapon ready to fire. The last communication that they exchanged was Burt whispering to Gill, "You take the right and I the left, we will shut those glowing eyes forever!"

The instant that the pebbles were released from the hands of young Bill and Danny the Piasa moved like lightning; he dropped his enormous wings entirely around Nathan to protect him from what was about to occur. At the same time he nimbly turned his massive body as quickly as one of the tiny ground squirrels or chipmunks that one would see in these woods or hills, the difference only being; he was as tall as eight grown men!

Tecumseh had traveled at a good pace throughout the night, not realizing that he was now again increasing the distance between himself, and the Piasa. For all that he knew he would not see the Piasa again ever, for he now believed that his dragon friend had become lost in the netherworld that stuck such fear into the mighty creature, or perhaps even worse, killed by the evil thing that he had been battling. In any case, he thought that the salvation of the situation and the saving of his precious Billigana were now entirely up to him, so he continued his trek, attempting to maintain as quick a pace as humanly possible.

Soon he was greeted by a magnificent sunrise, made so not only from the beauty and magnificent colors that could be seen, but by the fact that he could now see on the horizon the rolling hills that he knew would lead him to the land that had been his goal to reach and as the sun rose into the cloudless sky he not only felt that he could see the lush greenery of life and plenty that the land possessed, but he even felt the promise of what lay in store for them upon their arrival.

He had chosen to change his direction to proceed further south when he had resumed his walk during the night and because of this he was now far closer to the land that would offer water, food, shelter and perhaps their salvation. The remaining problem though was formidable; he still had many leagues to walk and once again he felt the weakness beginning to overcome him. He had partaken of no food or water for too long a time and he was asking so much of even his strong, young body, yet he dug down deeper to renew his efforts with a warrior's commitment. On into the sunrise he trudged, but he staggered, no longer able to maintain a direct route through the vastness of grey and dusty ash.

He continued to will himself forward as the sun rose ever higher into the bright morning sky, increasing the temperature and though it could not lessen his resolve it was now beginning to fully sap his remaining strength. The thought began to seep into his mind that he may have been fighting a losing battle! He pulled the buckskin shade from Billi's face as he continued to walk, but saw no sign of recognition, or even life. Yet he was comforted by the fact that he could still feel the beating of his lover's heart, this was one thing that Billigana did possess and he indeed found enormous comfort in this realization. He could feel his face curl into a smile of approval for at this point he felt that they would be alright. Unfortunately, he then turned and swooned; he collapsed into unconsciousness, with Billi falling atop him in a bundle of humanity lying in the increasingly hot Midwest morning sun and although he thought that he could now see the rolling hills that marked his desired destination, he was still many days walk from it for a young, greatly drained Nastazi warrior!

The Piasa had merely rested during the cool of the night, for dragons sleeping needs are far different from any other being in this world. At first light however, he was once again lifting his remarkable mass up into the chilled morning air with as much ease as that of any butterfly that one might see alighting in the exploration of a field of wildflowers. Except that what he viewed was as different from that image as could have ever been imagined; as far as his powerful eyes could see there was only the grey/black desolation that remained after a recent wildfire conflagration and with the comfort of the night's gentle breeze he was now faced with another major problem! The trail had disappeared for the tracks that he had been following which he was certain belonged to his friend Tecumseh, who must certainly be in great need of the assistance of the Piasa by now, had been erased, they had been covered by the same gentle breeze that had been such a comfort last night and the dragon now had no way to track the humans that he had grown so fond of and desired to assist so greatly.

The young man could have chosen several different directions to travel, yet the Piasa did not believe that Tecumseh was as knowledgeable of the land to choose correctly, for he was but a young lad and could not be that familiar with these lands at this tender age; could he? The dragon did not discover until later of the many stories passed down verbally by the boy's father, mother and all of the elders of their tribe that did indeed convey much of the geography of their great land through knowledge gained from generations of trading and living throughout this grand and glorious realm.

The Piasa believed that Tecumseh would have only been familiar with the direction that he had come following the course of the river with the hot air balloon for with less than twenty seasons he would not have known of the lush green hills that actually reached out much farther to the west that lie to the south and would have been much closer to him and far easier to reach. The dragon surmised that the young Nastazi would have known the direction of the river that he had followed to reach this land and probably needing water by now would have gone in the direction that he was certain of; unbeknownst to him though would have been the fact that the balloon had skewed his perception of the distance that he had traveled and he would not know that this direction would have added a great distance to his compulsory journey. For this reason the Piasa chose to follow east as his choice in directions, for he knew that Tecumseh and Billigana would be in desperate need of help in the following of this course, or any course which they had chosen.

He made his choice and began to fly towards the river that is known today as the Missouri, knowing that the best direction would have been for Tecumseh to have headed Southeast of where the dragon had seen his last tracks, as this direction would have led them to a land of rolling hills and plentiful waters and game far more quickly; but alas he did not believe the young human was aware of the existence of this place.

He drew himself ever higher into the clear sky and traveled into the northeast towards the river where he felt Tecumseh had come from, knowing that he would discover his friends before he would reach it and his flight would allow him to make contact in a short time and assist as was needed. Once at the proper altitude for best view of the largest section of the land below him, the dragon began to make wide sweeping arcs so as to view the widest possible portion of earth as possible and carefully flew in a large searching pattern.

The Piasa continued this wide sweeping pattern for several hours in the direction that he had supposed that his friends would have taken, but to no avail. He had already covered an area larger that his human friends could have traveled in several days when it began to dawn upon him that perhaps he had underestimated his young Nastazi friend; perhaps in some way he had known about this beautiful green land that the dragon knew to exist in the south. It was most certainly much closer to where the tracks that had last been seen were located.

The dragon continued his long swooping passes, rising and falling to view different portions of the ash covered ground as he searched for what may have been telling signs of his friends, until he finally decided that something was wrong. He had progressed to the point where he could now see the mighty river that Tecumseh would have sought on the horizon and yet still there were no tracks; no sign at all of his friends passing or of the passing of any living being on this wide horribly scorched grasslands. "I must have chosen the wrong direction," the great Piasa thought, as he instantly turned back in the direction that he had come. "I can only hope that I have not squandered the only opportunity to help my friends!" He made every attempt to increase his airspeed, covering ground in a remarkable manner; still he had wasted hours of time that must have been very precious to his friends.

He knew exactly where he had spent the blackness of the night upon the charred ground and decided to veer to the south and east from that point and once again began his wide sweeping arcs of flight in an attempt to spot his friends.

He was most puzzled as to why he could not feel the bond that he had shared with the young human; perhaps Tecumseh even believed him to be dead? On he flew!

―――――

Feeling the warmth of the morning sun on her lovely face Billigana mirrored her names meaning of true morning light as she awoke feeling surprisingly good for all that she had been through in the last several days. She saw Tecumseh in a deep sleep beside her and began to gaze around at her surroundings. She now remembered about the huge wildfire and could now see the enormous scope of its destruction, as she was surrounded now by the blackness of ash for surrounding her as far as she could see. She began to fill with desperation and continued to turn and look behind her, to her surprise she then saw something that actually gave her some amount of hope. It had been behind her, but she now could see the lush rolling hills of a land that promised rescue and though the hills just barely showed on the horizon to the southeast she knew from what she had heard from her elders from a very young age that the water and food that they both needed so dearly was now very close at hand, but on further contemplation she decided that it was still quite a way from where they now rested; much further than she could hope to navigate in her weakened condition. She decided to begin to formulate a plan, for though she did not feel confident in her ability to make the trek in her current state, she knew that it must somehow be made.

She lay there for some time and thought of the many different possibilities, none of which seemed at all promising. Could she take the skin and walk to the bountiful green lands ahead of her? If she did make the long walk there in her weakened condition, how long would it be until she found water? Would she be strong enough to make the long march back? The skin was very light now, but filled with water its weight would increase significantly, should she find the water and merely bring back a small amount? Nothing seemed very promising to her at this point.

She lay down once more, wondering for how long she must let her soul mate sleep and if he would have the strength to continue once she awoke him? She thought to herself once again, "Oh my Piasa, what has become of you? We need you now like never before!"

~~~~~~~~~~~~~~

Spiraling downward to gain speed while still covering as large an area as possible the Piasa could now finally see the large mat of green rolling hills that had not been visible just several moments ago; feeling as though he would only have a real chance at seeing the young Nastazi couple if he was able to pick up their tracks in the black ash of the wildfire burn, the dragon began to edge ever westward in hopes of finding some sort of sign before the young humans made it to the green forested land. Once that they had reached the vast green region there would be a significant increase in the difficulty of spotting them and while the beautiful lush forest would offer them water and fill other needs that they had, it would also expose them to dangers that would become ever more challenging in their weakened condition. "Or" thought the dragon; "Perhaps the reason that I can no longer feel their presence is that they have succumb to this awesome challenge already, for they really are quite fragile these humans."

Saddened, but still dedicated to finding his friends or at least what had happened to them the Piasa continued his search. Though his direction was somewhat indistinct, he still tried to view the area where the beautifully forested land met the black ash of the recent conflagration though even with the gift of flight the land was still so very large, so large that it even dwarfed the efforts of a mighty dragon. His melancholy began to deepen and grow ever more intense!

Though it had seemed as though the morning had passed, one look up into the sun proved that it was not yet midday when the dragon realized that he was most likely due east of the last place where he had seen the tracks and this began to increase his sorrow considerably, for it was not sensible for Tecumseh to have changed directions and he felt certain that the young warrior would not have made that type of foolish choice without cause.

Soaring back and forth from above the lush green hills with their promise of life's necessities, food, water, a shaded shelter from the ever strengthening sun and then turning back out over the desolation of the black burn of the tremendous wildfire, so recent that some places still smoldered with the remaining embers from the flames that had engulfed the plains such a short time before; he glided methodically in an attempt to view as much of the terrain below as possible, but was beginning to experience a good deal of remorse as he was now realizing that he was headed much further south than where he had last spotted any signs of his human friends when something marvelous happened!

As he continued his, as of yet fruitless search he felt something familiar; suddenly the Piasa could feel the voice of Billigana pleading with him to come to her. She was alive and the "bond" that he already shared with Tecumseh now was felt for the first time between himself and Billigana. He could see in his mysterious dragon mind's eye where Billi had come to be deposited by her love and in this vision he could also see young Tecumseh laying next to her, tattered and full of ash. He also appeared to be completely exhausted and seemed to have fallen into the sleep that only those who have used all of the strength that they had possessed can have known; but they were both alive!

The Piasa wrenched to his right, gaining the correct direction and began to descend directly towards his human friends that had been through so much. Though he was still a great distance from them, he was now headed directly for them. He sped to their aid, for it pleased the Piasa to the utmost to assist these two, as they represented all that was good in humankind. Their doubtless and undying love, not only for one another, but for all that they came across; the respect and harmony with which they treated their "mother earth" and the kindness and fairness that they tried to show all creatures, animals or plants, young or old. These were the qualities; the dragon knew, that were what would save the humans from their worst and most potent enemy; himself!

For that has been what has become the downfall of all of the races of humans that have shared this beautiful world with the dragons; whether speaking of the mighty Amazonian warriors that had existed so long ago and did not fully understand the complexities and traps of their "***natural world***" and believed that they could make use of such a powerful force that they found to exist in their world as the "between" place, without fully understanding all of the dangers that dwell there and the impact on their culture if misused.

Or perhaps I can refer to the magnificent culture of Atlantis that was so far advanced, so long ago, even sending their creations into the vastness of the skies to challenge the dragons and all of the birds for a place in the heavens, only to finally be denied. They also had great abilities concerning the creation of what you today refer to as "***technology***," yet they once again, like the Amazonians leapt at the opportunity to utilize these abilities without having developed the wisdom concerning their use that was necessary for the required control; and as a result of this pursued the goals of creating weapons of immense power while at the same time even striving to control the occult power of the crystal skulls that had not been created, but merely found by them; without the full knowledge of their dangers; the choice of this pathway cost them the lives of most all of their culture as well as many of the beings that shared this world with them at that time.

Now I; the dragon that the humans have called Piasa had to attempt to bring the message to what remained of the Nastazi people, or what many of the humans of present day call the "Cahokians." They would need to learn that their worst threat would come from the "*evil*" that can come from many places that no one really understands, but can manifest itself within the hearts of man and must; nay, can only be quelled with resources that we have available to ourselves every day; that of consideration, respect and love. These can be powerful tools of change and the pathway to a happy, harmonious life!

The dragon alighted gently upon the black earth next to the young Nastazi woman Billigana, who by now was crying with relieved joy and her loving soul mate Tecumseh who was still locked within the deep and all encompassing sleep of the totally exhausted.

It is an incredible sight to see a creature with as fierce an appearance as the Piasa gently nuzzle a fragile young woman in order to comfort her at the end of an ordeal that would have been too much for most and to tenderly place a young exhausted human into such a large, powerful mouth that bristled with the tremendous number of long, sharp teeth that the dragon possessed and place him delicately into the space between his folded wings atop his back, and that is what next occurred. Next the dragon bent down and just as carefully picked up Billi and delicately placed her next to her man, within the softness of his out stretched wings; wings that belonged to a being whom was so concerned about the comfort of his passengers that he even bent the tips of the vast wings curling above the two in order to shield them from the hot midday sun. This having been done the dragon then walked them to the green safety on the horizon, covering the distance in a fraction of the time that the young Nastazi's ever could have, even in the peak of health!

Back in the depths of the cavern fate took some rather unusual turns, and as it often does it happened very quickly; the two young boys with a newfound attitude towards life threw their not so formidable missiles at the malicious hunters Burt Aarons and Gilbert Hayes, who planned to kill one of the wonders that the world had ever experienced; merely for the proof that the dragon had ever existed. They did this with no thought of what wonders the being may have been able to perform or what the implications of the beast's death may hold, also with no concern at all about the safety of the young boy Nathan Bellows that was now being protected by the mighty creature's wings and body, yet they would fire their weapons in any case.

However, at the instant before they took their shots they were struck on the back and head respectively with the speeding rocks that had been thrown by young men that though they were small in stature, had become newly large on conviction! The instant after the rocks struck; the weapons fired with deafening, simultaneous cracks, and because of the rocks thrown by the boys, the aim of both men had been ever so slightly affected; instead of the eye shots that had been planned one now struck the dragon on the back of his well protected scaly neck and one round missed the target completely, however the result was the same for both bullets trajectories. Their high velocity made them begin to ricochet wildly around the cavern!

The Piasa had Nathan under his enormous wings and while they had a leathery appearance, the magical essence of a dragon's being in fact made the membrane that seemed more thin and pliable for flight, actually became of such denseness that they were impervious to the ricocheting projectiles, thus Nathan was very safe, but to their misfortune the same could not be said for the two who had just fired the shots. The bullets found their way back to near where they had originated and while they did not strike either of the initiators of this fateful action, the causal effect was even worse. The bullets struck the roof of the cavern together in close proximity to their point of origin, causing a cave-in that trapped Burt and Gill right in the spot where they had fired with a riotous amount of near deafening noise and suffocating dust.

Though the two had both been most fortunate that they had not been crushed to death by the falling rocks Burt was now trapped in a standing position against the boulder that had been his gun rest only moments before and Gill once again the less fortunate of the two had both of his legs crushed and broken underneath himself as he had fallen forward into a forced prone position, now directly laying across the path that they had walked upon to gain their ambush point. Neither of the reprehensible men was going any place without the some major form of assistance from what would take an obviously large number of their human friends.

Or perhaps a brown dragon! The Piasa searched into the darkness once the sounds had told him that the projectiles had ceased their murderous travels and the cave in was now ended; his keen eyes told him immediately what had happened when he saw that the two disreputable men had been the ones who had suffered the most from the results of their own actions.

The Piasa slowly unwrapped his protective embrace from around young Nathan and viewed his guests to appraise their conditions. "Are you harmed," the dragon questioned young Nathan?

"No," Nathan replied, and then added, "Thank you for your protection."

"We of this world will all need one another's protection in time and the sooner that you can make your kind understand this, the better chance for survival will exist for us all!" The Piasa said; his eyes beseeching for the understanding that he knew must come for this world to become safe, but after several moments of gazing into the young man's eyes he realized that it was something that would occur most likely one person at a time and while he was happy at his reaching of young Nathan he realized that there was still much to do; he turned towards the piteous moaning of the self proclaimed hunters.

The dragon approached with the fewest of steps and was immediately upon the two. His head hovered above the two malicious gunmen taking in and appraising all that had befallen the unfortunate souls.

Behind the dragon glowed the fire that he had made for the sake of Nathan, but in front of him and beyond in the cave was a darkness so total that even the dancing light of the dragons eyes improved the view only slightly.

The Piasa hovered over the two for several moments as Burt and Gill began to cower thinking that they were about to become food for a monster that they had only heard about in frightening tales of the terrifying magical beasts of long ago, tales that had in their minds had not ever been proven to have the least bit of substance, until today!

The Piasa began to lean down and investigate the two as if deciding where to take the first bite or possibly even eat them whole, as he could have easily done. Suddenly the Piasa looked up, directly into the pitch black corridor where Danny and Bill were hidden and stated in a low rumbling voice. "I see that you have returned to my chamber though bidden to be gone," he stared directly into the eyes of both young men! They were shocked, for they had been frozen in immobile silence surrounded by utter darkness, certain that they had not been seen when the dragon spoke looking directly at them both.

Danny stammered, "I, I, we came to warn you of the men and their guns."

"Yes, I can sense in you both a change of heart," the dragon answered steadily. "That is something that you must spread throughout your kind if we are all to survive." He then motioned with his massive spikes atop his powerful head to behind where he stood and said, "Thank you for your attempts at changing the aims of these hoodlums, it is appreciated. Now put your selves behind me to where it will be safe and let me try to help these two misguided souls." They instantly scampered around him as quickly as their sight would allow and drew into the main corridor where they stood humbly at a distance on the other side of the fire from Nathan. The three exchanged glances; the knowing glances of people that were privileged to be witness to something akin to a miracle.

Burt was attended to first, as he had just been pinned between the slab of boulder and the cavern wall; he also did not seem to be nearly as badly injured as his partner appeared to be.

The Piasa merely approached him and began to touch his entrapping boulder as Burt could only cower in feared anticipation. To Burt's surprise, he was not at all harmed as the dragon merely leaned against the boulder and he was subsequently freed, surprisingly uninjured for the most part!

Gill was next!

As they watched, the Piasa once again leaned down to Gill as if thinking of crushing him into his massive mouth and sharp teeth, but that was not his intent, he seemed to appraise exactly what he was about to do for a short time and then exploded into the boulder, sending it rolling down the corridor without further harm to either of the men.

The wailing was loud and immediate; Gill having been freed of the crushing weight of the boulder from off of his legs could now feel every one of the multiple compound breaks and fractures in his awkwardly contorted legs. As the man wailed in pain the dragon once again leaned further down; this time touching the man on his back with his muzzle, saying softly to him, "I am going to help you, however I cannot heal you if you do not accept my assistance. Do you understand?"

Gill continued his wailing, now as much from the incredible fear that he felt at the particularly close proximity of the huge beast that he had just moments ago attempted to kill, as from the incredible amount of deep pain that he was now experiencing.

The Piasa could see that he must take the initiative if this human was to be saved and curled around to place his head between the cave wall and the grimacing man. He placed his nose directly in the face of the now terrified Gill and spoke with such assurance as to make the man unable to deny his instructions. "Open your eyes and speak with me human," he said steadily.

For a moment Gill seemed to close his eyes even tighter and there was a tentative silence except for the slow, steady, melodious, almost comforting breathing of the dragon, until finally the pained man began slowly to open his eyes.

They were watered and filled with a horrible suffering, but they seemed to instantly be captured by the magical gaze of the Piasa. The dragon held this stare for a long time as everyone in the cavern waited with intense anticipation. Burt fearing the worst was about to happen to the unprincipled man, while Nathan, with Danny and Bill now included knew that the dragon was Gill Haye's only possible salvation.

Gill was lost in the enchanting gaze of the Piasa and seemed to also in some way lost in time, yet he could now sense that his only hope of ridding himself of the horrendous pain that he felt throughout his entire body lie in the great beast before him. Dragon and man shared a time in deep reflection with on another although at the time only one realized just what was actually happening; The Piasa delved deeper into the very fiber of the man before him with the miraculous multi colored all affecting, though little understood eyes, while Gill seemed at first to struggle against all that the Piasa would try to accomplish. However soon the struggle eased and finally stopped and with that acceptance began to be seen in the face of the stricken man. Then as the life again returned into his gaze once again being shared with the dragon he succumbed to his feelings and pleaded, "I am sorry for what I have tried to do to you; will you please help me?"

The dragon felt relief, for he desired deeply to free this man of the pain that he was now suffering, even though it was self inflicted and filled with a malicious intent. He looked ever more deeply into the man's eyes with his luminous kaleidoscopic, magical vision and urged forth a very comforting, "Yes!" Then, they both shared their deep gaze for what seemed to be a very long time until the Piasa finally whispered comfortingly, "Release to me human."

Gill relaxed as though he had just fallen off of a high precipice and exhaled with a loud whooshing sound as the space between himself and the dragon began to fill with a radiance of growing connected light that danced with every color known and every hue attainable of the blend of these colors. It was as if the totality of all lights had been harnessed by the Piasa in order to help this pitiable human that, as far as the other humans in the room could ascertain really did not deserve this magical beings help, nor the help of anyone for that matter. In any case; a magical event now occurred, for the dragon's assistance was now offered; and accepted.

It was nothing short of miraculous; the light grew as brilliantly as the stars in a clear night sky and then slowly subsided while at the same time came the brilliant multi-faceted lighting of that "between" place that the Piasa had not only the power to travel to and dwell in, but also a strangely all consuming fear of. When it had disappeared and only the slight glow of the small fire behind the Piasa remained Gills legs had once again become reshaped into their normal appearance and he had stopped his lamenting. The dragon's head still hung where it had been a moment ago, but he now appeared to be quite tired as if he had been the conveyor of some sort of energy that was nearly too much to bear. He looked down at Gill and said nothing merely appraising the results of his attempt to assist the human in the use of the "nether region" that held such promise for many, but also held the hidden misery of countless numbers of lost souls. He had also felt that he had somehow enabled an unwanted presence to once again make a contact with him; this was a presence that he had not been in contact with since their great battle many a human lifetime ago that had cost the Nastazi people so dearly in the past; a contact that he did not ever desire to regain! Once again he felt that terrible feeling that he knew the humans call fear; not so much for what might happen to an old dragon, but moreover for just what he may have now inadvertently released upon and guided towards the modern world!

Gill, having been laying on the ground grimacing in agony only moments ago and with the subsidence of the brilliant lights he now found himself able once again to cope with his situation and what is more, he was no longer terrified of the huge, fierce looking beast that occupied the massive space before him. Surprisingly he now felt a surreal kinship to the dragon that was impossible to explain; yet it was undeniable for he felt it as deeply as he had ever felt anything. He looked up into the Piasa's magical stare and for the first time recognized the deep compassion that was there and finally understood the depth of his misguided ways and said, "I can now see that you are our only hope for I now know that you have witnessed many of my kind fail and you now fear that we may cause the downfall of the entire world with our next failure. We would all benefit greatly from the lessons that only you can show us." He had also come to know now that in some inexplicable way he and the dragon had now "bonded" and he now understood the Piasa's good will and benevolence towards mankind; he also now understood that he desired to save mankind in order to save his own home "Mother Earth." It was ever so clear now; he turned to Burt and said in a new moment of supreme clarity; "How could we have been so wrong? This magical being is our only hope; we must listen to him if we are to save our homes, our lives and those whom we love.

Burt had nearly seen too much to take in. First the boys and their small stones that prevented what could have only been known as the ultimate tragedy of the death of this incredible creature followed by Gill's miraculous healing and the communication of this incredible beast with them in the attempt to change the ways and values of mankind in order to try and save the world from the one thing that had the greatest potential of destroying it; mankind himself!

Bill and Danny had supposed that they would be remaining back out of view for this entire encounter, in the shadows beyond young Nathan and the small fire, forgotten when suddenly the Piasa spoke softly, but firmly saying "Daniel, William, come here and join us for there is much for all of you to accomplish if you are to be able to effect a difference.

They thought that they had been forgotten, but now they began to realize that the Piasa had intended to include them as much as anyone here, they were very grateful and felt most honored as they joined the newly formed group.

"There is much for all of you to do, if you are to be able to sway your kind and have any hope of preventing a catastrophe that will end life for all of us who call "Mother Earth our home, come outside and confer with me for a time."

They all gratefully obeyed the dragon and formed an interesting little group as the dragon led them swiftly to another exit and outside of the huge cool cave to where the they all then found their way out into the warm midday Midwestern sun; following the Piasa for a short distance to another small shaded grotto with a delightfully fresh running stream tinkling through the side where huge boulders and rocks that hid the cave had collected. They all found great comfort under the canopy of trees that provided them with their shade and the coolness of the fresh water and for the next several hours all listened to the Piasa as he told them of ideas that he had and had offered to many of their own kind over time as to how the stories and warnings that the dragon had made known to young Nathan would be of most impact and benefit to their fellow humans. His words and teachings were the same as he had, in past times told a young Nastazi prince and his beloved Billigana, though at this time he added the story of the Nastazi; told of the resident evil that can be found in many ways and places and of the unfortunate inherent spiritual weaknesses that resides in most humans hearts. With this he also told them of how these things could be countered with the simple acts of understanding, kindness, respect and love and he attempted to make it as easy to understand as possible.

The Piasa sat with Nathan, Bill, Danny, Burt and the recently saved Gill and related them the tale much as he had told it so many years ago to Tecumseh and Billigana after a similar type rescue and bonding experience.

~~~~~~~~~~~~~~~~~~~~~~~~~~~~

The Nastazi couple of whom the Piasa had referred had both long ago been rescued by the Piasa, unfortunately the act coming too late to save the remnants of their people, as the Piasa had somehow been manipulated into the consumption of a large amount of what was later discovered to be the very plant that had become the downfall of these wondrous Nastazi people, though it was meant to kill him, while this was not achieved it did manage to place the dragon into a coma-like sleep for a length of time that was enough that his friends were then taken advantage of by an evil duo.

They had been given the Nastazi names meaning "One that travels path that is crossed by the Panther" Tecumseh for the male and "True Morning Light" Billigana for the female and this dragon has always felt that their names definitely pointed towards their involvement in the formation of fate. They had just walked for a large number of leagues through the burned out remnants of the prairies where the great battle that had helped to result in the downfall of their people had taken place; until they were able to enter into the forest and rolling hills of a land that would one day be known as the Ozarks toward an oasis type glen nestled between several small hills that had a small pond made by several large boulders that had fallen across the fresh spring fed stream that happened to be flowing through this cool, green alcove in the beginning of hundreds of miles of rolling hills that was not at all unlike this very spot where the Piasa now had his small group gathered.

The two had made it to where the place of their salvation could now be sighted upon the horizon; however with this wondrous place within their sights Tecumseh's strength had now come to an end.

This is when the Piasa finally heard Billi's call, viewed them and dove down to assist. Soon after the dragon had settled the two easily down to the soft grassy earth within just a couple of steps from the headwater of the stream and only a short walk to the pond where Billi immediately took advantage of the situation that she felt certain had saved her man's life and filled the water bottle with the cool, life giving fresh water and promptly began to wash Tecumseh's face and give him; at first only small sips of water, but after a few moments as he seemed to regain some strength she allowed him deeper draughts as she comforted him in her warm, loving embrace.

His eyes finally opened and he saw the dragon and was able to speak with him for the first time in many moon phases; since just before all of the past tumultuous events had so recently taken place. He asked the Piasa, "What happened to you, we thought that you had died?"

"My friend," the dragon sighed, "I cannot say. I may have been duped, or perhaps it was just fated, but I was somehow persuaded to eat a plant that while not even that tasty, I somehow felt that I needed to devour this unusual herb in large amounts and upon doing so I was somehow placed into the most inescapable of sleeps; one that I was not able to wake from until your calling and perceived danger of you both. At that time I was confronted by most of the worst examples of your kind that I have yet to see and then the most evil of beings that I may have ever encountered.

The thing was called Elgin by those who served it and I am not certain just what it could be called other than the very essence of wickedness, but I do know that it's power was derived from pure evil, whether found naturally in this world or just manifested within the hearts of men and I know also that it had the ability to change to anything that it desired. Battle as I could there was no way that I could have hoped to have matched it's ever growing power, I only succeeded in saving myself and possibly the futures of us all by taking it to that place which I fear the most of anything within this world and stranding it there. Had it not been for the memory of you two, I should not have been able to have found my way back out again and for this I wish to thank you both.

"So we have saved one another," Billi said. "For you have just once again certainly saved the both of us," Tecumseh chimed in.

Billi's wound was beginning to heal and had become sealed from the herbs and treatment that Tecumseh had administered in those first crucial minutes and incredibly her strength seemed to be returning somewhat when she thoughtfully questioned, "Well what now?" Billigana asked the two beings that she felt the most closeness and love for of all whom she now knew in this life, "Our people have been massacred and most likely our village is also destroyed, with any possible survivors more than likely scattered, so what can we now do?"

The dragon looked at both of them with a deep conviction and told them, "You still have one another and are living examples of the love that will one day be the salvation of your world, you have more than most and must find a way to continue on."

Billi and Tecumseh exchanged loving embraces and looked deeply into one another's eyes and knew at once that the Piasa was correct and shared in unison with the dragon, "Of course, we still have each other and the unwavering friendship of the Piasa!"

"Before we continue there are some words of advice that I must offer you," The dragon offered gently, "I would offer to tell you of what I have learned of your kind to this point, if you care to here the story!"

Billi looked at Tecumseh and could see that he was beginning to feel better. She nodded her delicate head and queried of the gracious brown dragon, "My friend, we have long to listen to all that you have to say and will, but now we are both famished as we do not have your superior constitution."

The Piasa then realized just how right she was and admitted in something of a chagrined state, "Of course, you cannot have eaten for several days and I had forgotten the regularity with which you humans must feed."

Tecumseh looked up at him with a question in his eyes saying, "I will build a fire."

The Piasa immediately took the hint and offered, "I will find you a whiskerfish or something as delicious, that you may burn him before you consume his flesh!" The dragon had taken Tecumseh's hint and gone to hunt for his friends, even if he was never to understand this human practice of putting fire to a perfectly good meal.

The dragon carefully rose and walked several steps away before gently rising into the air, following downstream of the brook that he had chosen to light next to for his human friends.

In just a short time he was back with a whiskerfish that would have fed Billi and Tecumseh for the rest of the moon's cycle, he then carefully deposited it onto a fallen log at the outer perimeter of their camp.

Tecumseh rose tiredly and the dragon could see the sorrow in both of his human companions at the loss of so many of their friends, for they had in fact lost everyone that they had known and every member of their families save him; a dragon. A being that was not even of their kind, he felt that they were greatly troubled and he meant to try and help.

Tecumseh walked towards the huge fish and managed a small smile saying, "You are very generous my friend, but my woman and I could not eat this in the rest of the season. Please share the rest with us after I cut some for cooking."

The three all shared a smile of those who belonged together. It was a very memorable moment, a beginning to a new age as the three shared deeply in the appreciation of each other there, on that afternoon in the beautiful green alcove, directly after the passing of the entirety of several of humankinds races and the demise of a truly heinous evil, they all took great comfort in the presence of one another, their ongoing survival beginning a new age between man and Piasa and yes; love.

Tecumseh began to cook as Billi rested against the now prone dragon that eyed the rest of the whiskerfish that Tecumseh had let remain, but did not touch it at this time. As they settled in the dragon once again spoke.

I have lived for many of what your kind considers ages and thousands untold of your lifetimes and so have seen many of your people's triumphs and as well with that, most all of their failures; so began the tale that the dragon had begun to recite to his human friends.

"I have known glorious sailors from a land across the great seas that called themselves the Phoenicians. My closest friend among them called himself Ebirius and he sailed the great sea to the East with his companions Durages and Flaxon.

They were accomplished sailors, as the warrior race of women that they chanced to become acquainted with had once been, but something that I did not witness had taken place within this group of humans that did not appear to be quite natural within the world of "Mother Earth." They had somehow changed and begun the practice of the enslavement of all of their men. All of the chiefs were women; all of the fighting was done by the women; all of the considerable power that was exercised was done so by women. There was no give and take, no cooperation no discussion of wants, needs or desires save by the decree of the queen or one of those who would serve her or even aspire to be queen."

"While the Amazons, as this is what they had called themselves," the Piasa continued, "Were evidently masters of the forest in which they lived and could create the most stout and comfortable of dwellings using living trees and plants and were supreme lords of the jungle, over all living creatures, they did not fully understand or appreciate the powers that were part of their "Natural World." Especially unknown to them were some of the trickeries and entrapments that accompanied one of the more potent of these natural wonders."

"They had discovered that place of which I have so tried to warn you of," The Piasa went on, "They had discovered tools and methods of achieving the netherworld with far too much ease and because of this had not developed the proper respect that this supernatural domain warrants. As a result of this, they caused the disastrous passing of nearly their entire culture into its permanent inescapable torment. I was far removed for the most part of this happening and so was only witness to the very end of the calamity unfortunately. What I do know though, is that they unwittingly brought this destruction upon themselves and this was very unfortunate, as I felt that they had much to offer to all that dwell here on "Mother Earth."

"From the Amazon's example I would hope that you can learn the respect of your "Natural World." For if you do not respect its power you can become its adversary, or worse, its prisoner!" The dragon said as his eyes pleaded that they listen and understand. "The poor Amazons were a magnificent race of superbly intelligent and even beautiful warrior women that in some way began to travel down an unnaturally unbalanced path by totally subjugating and entirely enslaving their men before I had the opportunity to become acquainted with them by way of my Phoenician friends Ebirius and his comrades Flaxon and Durages. They were the first humans that I had ever really become acquainted with and you may have called them early sailors and explorers. They had discovered a female of your human kind that was a princess of the Amazon's who had been taken to this land that was not her land by those who would do her ill and as fate would have it she would not have been rescued unless the young Phoenician sailors would have discovered her; as they did, far from their own land as well. However they were on a self driven quest at that time and they happened to run across one of the most attractive and good willed of you humans that I have had the pleasure of knowing, judging by the reactions of all of the humans that I saw come into contact with her. She was called Desiree and she had gotten into a bad situation with some of the less than honorable humans that will sometimes attempt to force their ways on the other more noble of your kind. But I digress; Ebirius and his friends rescued her from the clutches of these evil men and at her request bore her back to her home across the sea with not even a small amount of my assistance. This is where they and I met the Amazons originally.

With all of their great mastery of the magnificent forest where they made their home and their vast knowledge of the ways of the world and even some of the secrets of our own "Mother Earth" they had not the wisdom to use this vast knowledge properly and the result was their obliteration as a culture. Their aberrant behavior towards their own men was a sign that I wish I had discovered in time to have assisted for it was to be the beginning of their path into a horrible fate. Nearly all of them were tricked into the disappearance in the netherworld that has claimed so many of my kind."

"They lacked the wisdom to use the vast knowledge that they had accumulated about our precious "Mother Earth" correctly and this was their doom. They did not respect **Nature**!

Granger, the ancient Brown Dragon known by some as the Piasa, by others in distant lands as Quetzalcoatl, Phoenix, and Yinglung or by a host of other names continued his tale....

"After some ages I again was awakened from a long slumber and desired as normally to quench my hunger that accompanied my lengthy sleep." The dragon settled down curling around his two friends conveniently blocking the chilly evening breeze that had begun to blow from out of the north. "I began to frequent a marvelous little cove that I had revisited for several days in a row as the fish that dwelled there were fat and tasty. Every day I spotted this marvelously unafraid girl that was of no tribe of man that I had ever known and as time passed I became intrigued with this beautiful, playful young human girl."

"Soon, I communicated with her and shortly after, you could say that we became friends. Her name was Shawna Ree and she called her people the Atlanteans. I soon found that these people had found ways to make what they called tools that were very advanced to the point that your modern kind now possess and I believe refers to them as "***technology***." They had found ways to make their lives much easier while at the same time becoming far more productive, as they seemed to enjoy saying. Their creations encompassed every facet of their lives; they had even found methods to match the flight that I and some of the other creatures of our world enjoy."

"Unfortunately, they had included in their artful studies and wondrous creations; pursuits that appear to be unique to your kind as far as I can tell, the development of weapons; increasingly destructive and unfortunately for them, ever more difficult to control."

"They also made use of a group of skulls of your mankind seemed to have not made, but found I know not where; skulls that were made of natural crystal and seemed to possess some gift for the conduction of certain very powerful forces," the dragon exhaled a forlorn sigh, but continued on.

"Though they were not the creators of the skulls and did not really grasp all that need be known about them, they seemed to have learned how to use the skulls to conduct an enormous energy that they had discovered could be made to pass through them; yet as they did not fully understand exactly how to fully control this energy this would soon become their ultimate downfall. As Shawna's misguided father attempted to threaten, or even destroy me with this hideous weapon Shawna had warned me to get as far away as possible. This I did, as I had made this promise to her previously, though I had every intention upon returning to her after I had flown out of range of her misguided family and associates and then circle back to meet her at our preset secret cove soon later."

"I did not, until then realize just how successful the Atlanteans had been at the creation of this horrid weapon: the entire island home of the Atlanteans and all of her people disappeared in one gigantic flash of light that was accompanied by a tremendous shock wave that knocked me from out of the sky and unconscious into the sea many leagues away just moments later. The people of Atlantis, including my friend Shawna and all of the beauty, architecture, technology, art, orchids and treasures that they had been fated to have created, even what I believe was the last living Monoceii, were no more!"

"The people of Atlantis had created "***technology***" yet in their haste to use that which they had created denied them the development of the necessary wisdom to control its use properly; this was their doom! Once again, a wonderful people with so much to offer and yet again doomed to a horrible extinction, but unfortunately a fate that was also self-inflicted." The mighty dragon lowered his gigantic, horned head and released a long, low and utterly forlorn sigh; the expression of futile and heartrending sadness.

After a very long silence; a length of time so long that the young Nastazi couple began to feel that their giant friend may have once again slipped into dragon sleep until Billi quietly asked the Piasa, "Have we saved ourselves as a people with the defeat of the wicked Angelii and her wicked beast, or are we doomed to a similar fate as the people's that you have described to us?"

The dragon again opened his eyes, glowing with a combination of admiration, hope and love and told her, "I have seen just what you and yours consist of and it is not you that needs to change, but the unfortunate remainder of your people's that have not discovered the loving ways of living life that enables one to live in harmony with Mother Earth. It is they that will finally tempt the fate of our mother and believe me when I tell you that she will always have the last word, for she shall always remain after all that dwell here are gone. Only she and time are constant, all others; even some as ancient as myself who are long enduring but are finally doomed to share the humans future and are also at risk to become impermanent!"

The Dragon continued striving to make a point that he was just beginning to fully understand himself.

"What I have seen though with some of you humans is the identity of some of your people grows so much in tune with the mother earth that she allows not only your survival, but even prosperity for ages of time, though unfortunately all of the people have found some way of losing sight of what was the gift that they once possessed and somehow became a people who were lost."

Billi and Tecumseh just gazed at one another, certain of their love and happy that they still would share a future together and hopefully someday even a family, but at a loss as to what to do about this problem that the Piasa was attempting to explain to them. This was an uncertain issue that seemed to be a problem with a solution that would span many lifetimes and require the learning and application throughout entire future cultures.

The dragon curled into a more comfortable position and lay on his side; offering part of his softer underbelly for them to become more comfortable on for he knew that they must be exceptionally tired as he was aware that the humans had not the kind of stamina that his kind were blessed with and so he made them a convenient place in which to rest for the night. As they settled in and grew silent he covered them with one of his massive wings to keep off the night mists that were so common in this land that would someday become a vacation paradise. He merely rested while his young friends slept deeply through the night and fully enjoyed this wonderful time spent with those who had shown him what they called love.

The Piasa spent this night and many, many others in the company of his Nastazi friends and saw them, as humans were apt to do finally age and become "old," as humans were observed by this dragon to do far too quickly. Though they had enjoyed, after their horrendous episode with the evil Elgin beast and his consort Angelii, a most wonderful and very fulfilling lifetime together, even spending much time with the Piasa exploring many of the wonders available to them in their "Mother Earth," that the Piasa had previously promised to take them to, they were never blessed with child and the dragon could not help but wonder if that did not have something to do with the horrendous experiences shared so young in life and how this may have effected them. True, it showed the dragon just what types of beings that these humans were capable of becoming, but it must have certainly demanded some sort of a price from these marvelous souls that did indeed possess certain frailties and it appeared that at least Billigana or perhaps even both of them had been deeply scarred, both physically and emotionally by the crisis that cost them most all of their people and the disappearance of their entire culture; though through her amazing strength of character she rarely let it show. She was indeed a very special human!

Finally the day came on the eighty-first year of our acquaintance, when although she was still very active and nimble for one of her years she watched the sun sink below the grassy rolling hills on the western horizon and told the love of her life, Tecumseh, "There seems to be a great tiredness in me this night my love, shall we sleep?"

Tecumseh, several years her senior, but still very fit seemed to feel it too and agreed most willingly to join her under their soft worn skins. They wrapped into one another's bodies and drifted off to sleep; never to again awaken. When this dragon found them the next morning he was very happy for them and the life that they were so fortunate to have shared together, yet knew that these were humans that exhibited all that was well and good in their kind and as a for that matter qualities that one should strive to exhibit at all times in all beings.

Though missing them intensely as he would for the rest of his time in this life, the Piasa prepared the bodies as the Nastazi had been known to do, placing them atop a large pyre of grass and wood and setting them afire; with the added touch of the use of his own fiery breath. After he had silently said his farewells and the blaze had burned down to a smolder, he blew their ashes into the magnificent lake next to which they had made their home; a lake known today as the "Lake of the Ozarks!"

Back in present time the Piasa was finishing his story of the Nastazi people to his small gathering of souls whom he hoped would be able to communicate the lessons that would need to be passed and learned from in order to save their world and he finished by saying, "The poor Nastazi had to learn the most difficult example of them all; they had to recognize their own inherent ***weaknesses as humans*** and how to deal with them while also discovering that there exists evil in the world that must always be combated, no matter what it's source and from what I have been able to discern, you must strive to live your life in the manner of a man whom I had never the opportunity to meet as I was amidst a great slumber during his short thirty three seasons, but he is said by many of your people today to be a prophet, or some say even the Messiah; he was called Jesus Christ and although his and my destinies did converge, I have been told that he lived a life that was the perfect example of a loving existence and that he not only died for the people of our "Mother Earth," but also has devotees that are known to practice his teachings. You may hopefully reach your kind by teaching them the proper ways of living through him; or even teaching the reverence towards "Mother Earth" practiced by the Cherokee or Sioux or one of the other indigenous tribes as they are now called that once inhabited this great land."

The Piasa sat in the comfort of the lovely green grove that most humans noticed he had a special gift in finding, having just finished the retelling of his association with the young Nastazi couple Tecumseh and Billigana and the lesson that it taught about the reasons that their people had not survived when he began to have a most uncomfortable, but not wholly unrecognized feeling. One that was very faint at first, but continued to grow, ever more malicious and unstoppable!

Though the Piasa had felt the presence since quite a while ago inside the cave with his assistance of the injured human Gill Hayes, he was somewhat taken by surprise at young Nathan's anxious voice warning the brown dragon, "Granger, there is evil stalking us that I cannot see, but feel it growing ever closer!"

"Yes, my young friend," the Piasa responded. "My assistance of Gill Hayes allowed a connection that may have guided an evil back to me that I was hoping to never be confronted with again; we must now make all haste!"

"All of you get back into the cave as quickly as you can for there is soon to be great malice here that I will make every attempt to shield you from," the dragon said as he gazed with his multi-faceted eyes deeply at young Nathan and then briefly at all of the others.

Nathan offered, "My friend is there anything that we can do?"

The Piasa looked thoughtfully at the group and after but a moment's hesitation said, "I shall need some luck, but do not believe that there is much that you can do in this case, but remember to pass on all that I have told you and strive to live your lives by these lessons which you have learned; if I can somehow save a future for us all it will be in your hands to protect; now go!"

The dragon watched his comrades disappear towards the cavern, down the stream when he noticed a horrid increase in the sickly feeling of evil that he had noticed since he had helped the injured human in the cave. Suddenly he turned and looked behind himself to see a small, but malicious looking bird making its way up the stream intently, his eyes already locked on the Piasa in a dreadful and hungry stare.

The Piasa locked eyes with the strange, evil looking little bird wondering once again how something so small could house so much cruelty and wickedness.

The Blight Lark stopped and seemed to alight upon a gnarled root that's very appearance seemed to invite malevolence. A dark veil seemed to envelop the bird and much of the surrounding area; not the multi-faceted bright lights as seen when the Piasa ventured to the "between" world, but a dark malevolent veil that has sometimes been associated in modern times with the demon Naberius, (14.) or many of the other similar modern demons mentioned in current and historical literature.

As the Piasa appraised the situation; his former and regrettably now recurrent opponents image seemed to take part in many varying pulsations and bizarre changes; what at first appeared as a small dark brown lark slowly changed into a much larger jet black and insidious looking crow. The veil darkened and changed until what the Piasa now saw seemed to have taken the shape of a multi-headed canine, a horrendous wolf or dog that began to stare at the dragon with malicious, hungry eyes as if sizing him up for a most vicious attack.

Once again the Elgin beast seemed to disappear into the dark haze before the straining eyes of the Piasa, but this time it was different; this time the entire darkness seemed to possess an irradiated evil, a sort of deep buzzing that existed, but could not readily be seen, yet was so obviously present; it could readily be detected by the way that it shriveled the vibrant lush green of the leaves on the beautiful trees in this oasis so quickly into the dry crusty brown of death, by the way that it made the fresh spring water begin to bubble and steam of sulfurous fumes and in the dead colorless pallor that it forced upon even the rocks within its reach. But then it began to move, it alighted down from the root where it had been into the stream with a tremendous hissing splash that began to tumultuously boil the surrounding water and fill the clearing with a foul steam that smelled of thousands of putrid corpses of many sorts of beings, the stench of death. It then began making its way pitilessly towards the Piasa.

The Piasa had seen much in his long life on "mother earth" and was not easily taken aback by anything that he saw, but was astonished by what he saw next even though he had seen the shape changing powers of this strange beast in the past and this ability was no surprise.

As the thing made its way slowly down the boiling stream towards where the imminent battle would ensue, the steam seemed to somehow clear away a portion of the darkness and for the first time he could see what it was that he truly was about to face; he saw two multi-faceted, bulbous eyes staring at him out of the darkness of the evil cloud that it had created and just as before it seemed to be growing as it approached him. This growth was also no surprise to the dragon as he had seen this demon do this before and the thing was once again quickly approaching the size of the Piasa, by the time that they met would surely surpass the dragon in size, but what the dragon saw next produced a response that the dragon was altogether unfamiliar with; it produced an undeniable fear!

Before the Piasa and quickly closing on him he could now see a huge mantis-like creature unlike any he had ever seen in his long, full life. It approached carefully, yet quickly and seemed to be viewing not only the dragon in front of him, but the entire area with those bulging eyes that seemed to be able to see all about and even behind him. The beast had two very powerful looking mandible pincher/claws that appeared to be horribly powerful, the narrow thorax part of its body seemed to be compact but very hard as it's skeleton was on the outside of its body protecting its insides from harm. Continuing behind that, it's powerful abdomen sprouted six very powerful and heavily armored legs that seemed to be too powerful to damage or even produce any kind of pain or injury upon. The thing exuded the embodiment of a purely evil power.

Words of the Piasa

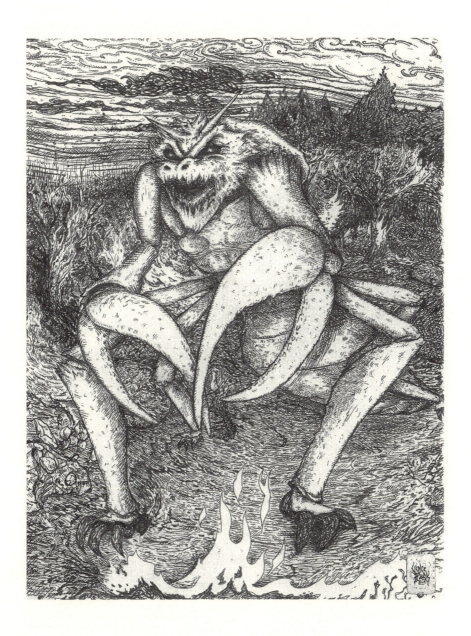

The dragon had to think fast! In their last encounter this monster had grown very quickly to a nearly unmanageable size and the Piasa had no doubt that the same thing was going to happen once again. This mantis creature was obviously the newly chosen shape from what the Piasa had first seen as an evil looking little bird that had changed experimentally into many different entities and the dragon feared that this may just be the ultimate, possibly undefeatable incarnation!

When, in the past the few times that the dragon had been confronted by such an overwhelming and forceful being such as the huge and horrible black dragons the trick that the Piasa had been able to utilize had been the taking of his nemesis into the "between world" – that place that even the Piasa feared, the realm where so many souls and in fact most even of his own kind now found themselves trapped inside of for eternity, this place that his human friends would someday call purgatory, or limbo.

What was very unfortunate for the Piasa is that he had already used this reliable ruse on this adversary and the evil thing had managed to find its way out once again, no doubt using the dragon's earlier entry into the realm as some sort of beacon to follow and had found its way to where they now both stood.

The Piasa had few options remaining and even less time to ponder his course of action for as he watched, the mantis creature leapt towards him covering what in today's time would be considered about three hundred meters in only a few seconds; he was suddenly on the Piasa!

The evil Elgin beast had an obviously simple, but very difficult to defend against plan. It grasped the dragon's head in those horrid and overwhelmingly powerful pincher/arms as it bit at the Piasa's exposed throat going for a death bite that was all too dangerously available. Fortunately, this was not the first time the dragon had been in a situation in which he had to protect his neck, although this was the closest that he had ever been to not successfully being able to do so.

As the two struggled the beautiful brook and vale that had just moments ago been covered by bright sunshine coming from a beautiful Southern Illinois spring morning that showed the new life and promise of the new season had begun to change; slowly at first, but now ever more increasingly rapid. The birds and small animals had long disappeared and the plants had now begun to lose their new luster under a more and more ominous sky as clouds had appeared and had grown deeply dark in mere moments; they seamed to grow ever more menacing as the one sided struggle continued.

Under the changing skies with the winds quickly growing to gale force, Granger, as he was known by some human's, curled his head down into his chest and used the weight of his enormous tail to twist and pivot around in order to escape the grasp of those powerful pinchers and hopefully mount some sort of attack of his own and it worked beautifully save only one aspect of his plan.

He could not twist free of the insurmountably powerful grasp of the mantis creature that his nemesis Elgin had become. Elgin, the evil that could become whatever he desired to become it seemed; and who was still increasing in size as the two continued their struggle was the Piasa's ultimate nemesis of this long lifetime.

The Piasa, though he could not see very well because of the coverage that was occurring by the huge body of the beast with which he was now locked into mortal conflict; knew that on the other side of the brook in which they battled there was a granite outcropping that was actually the beginning of the mount that housed the cavern where so much had taken place earlier upon this day. With his powerful legs and tail still free, the dragon pushed powerfully and threw both of the combatants into the solid rock wall with a tremendous, ground shaking thud.

Rocks and boulders were torn from their resting places of centuries, landslides occurred and inside the cavern where he had asked his human friends to go to for safety the loud noise was accompanied by tremendous cave-ins that while they did not injure the dragons friends did alert them to the desperation that the Piasa must now be suffering outside.

Had the Piasa finally met a being that as more powerful than him; if the thing could defeat the Piasa then what of the humans, what could they do? The humans that the dragon had just counseled recently were now confronted with a huge decision, Nathan, Danny, Bill, Burt and Gill had to decide whether to continue to hide in the cave and await their fate, or show the dragon that his words had reached them and changed them to the core.

Each of them had been awed, grown spiritually and had been changed by the Piasa; of that there was no doubt, however they all still faced one inescapable truth and that was the fact that against such a monster as the Piasa now faced they had very little chance of overcoming, or even slowing the creatures assault on their dragon friend. They all stared at one another wondering what they could possibly do when young Nathan broke the forlorn mood and said, "We can be of no help in this cave; we must go and see what assistance permits itself that we can offer!"

All of his comrades quickly agreed and the group made its way back to the mouth of the cave, but what they observed when they reached the outside was absolutely terrifying. The Mantis creature had the Piasa clamped in its tremendous and powerful claws; it had become even larger than the Piasa and seemed to be slowly continuing its growth; additionally as the monsters power seemed to be growing and the Piasa's seemed to be on the wane there seemed to be a definite negatively harmful effect upon the surrounding weather. What had been a beautiful spring morning in the hills of Southern Illinois just moments ago was quickly turning into a dark, stormy and very malevolent looking day; the natural world was obviously being directly affected by the struggle taking place by the two before them.

The humans exited the cave and had never been faced with anything like this that they were now confronted with, the horrendous changes in the weather since their entry into the cave, the two before quite recently, unknown creatures battling before them, they did not at this time realize exactly what effect this battle would have on their future but did realize that there was one thing they needed to accomplish as quickly as they could or all that they knew, valued and treasured would be lost forever. They must free the Piasa from that terrible grip or they would all perish on this day; this they all understood without question.

Gill was the first to spot it, perhaps because of the intense gratitude that he must have felt toward the dragon and possibly some amount of guilt knowing that it was the act of saving him that had shown the creature the way to find the Piasa once again. He pointed at a huge tree trunk that had evidently been overturned by the struggle between the two behemoths that was dangling near the edge of the cliff wall some fifty feet over the two struggling creatures, but was being held fast by only some of its remaining roots that had not broken. He pointed to it as he told his companion Bill, "Your rifle; shoot those roots or we are all doomed!"

Words of the Piasa

All of the group then saw what Gill was talking about and possibly felt some small inkling of hope at last as Bill took aim and fired.

The report of the rifle was deafening and had an immediate although unwanted result. The Mantis-creature / Blight lark that was actually the embodiment of the purest of evil turned to look at the group and most especially Bill who had just fired the rifle and said maliciously, "Your weapons can do me no harm, especially if you are incapable of hitting me with them, you shall enjoy my attention shortly and for much longer than you would ever desire," the evil beast rumbled repulsively. With that he turned back to the dragon and clamped towards his neck with the powerful looking mandibles for the final killing bite.

The rifle rang out once again, this time the largest of the roots was cut and the smaller ones that were not yet parted could not take the strain, the tremendously heavy tree trunk slid down the face of the cliff gathering a great deal of speed as it came. The mantis released its grip on the Piasa and tried to step out of the way of the careening log; just then the dragon kicked.

The mantis known as Elgin by some and simply as evil by most others was kicked directly into the path of the huge tree trunk as it came to the bottom of its plunge down the cliff. The motion of kicking the blight of evil into the path of the tree had also taken the Piasa out of the path of destruction if only just barely and for a moment it seemed as though all would now be safe, as the Mantis creature seemed to have been crushed by would have been a tremendous weight of the huge old tree. The dragon closely watched his adversary as he approached it carefully, for any signs of life.

In only a moment the dragon's worst fears were confirmed, the Piasa turned and gave a desperate look of warning to his friends and immediately turned his attention back to the mantis creature as the thing again opened its eyes and looked up hungrily at the dragon; at that same instant the wind again increased and the storm clouds worsened over their heads. Lightning bolts began coursing throughout the entire area as the rage could be seen building in the face of the being that some had in the past called the Blight Lark, but this evil has been referred to by many names in many different cultures; suffice to state that was just evil incarnate.

The Piasa attacked at once, again pouncing on his enemy, but although stunned by the huge tree and seemingly temporarily incapacitated the mantis/creature had still continued to grow. It was now approaching one quarter larger that the immense size of the Piasa and showed no signs of slowing its enlargement. The dragon thought to himself, "I cannot defeat this thing with my power as he surpasses me in this measure, however I can use the "between" place just once more and possibly defeat it in a slightly different way; I believe that I can make use of the nether world and trick this creature just once more; for believe that I can trick it with "time."

Though not entirely certain that it could be done, as he had never attempted it, the dragon decided that he would take the Blight/lark to not only a "where," but also a "when" that was just what the Piasa strongly believed would be all that could defeat this thing. Quickly, while the mantis was still not yet fully recuperated from the smashing of the tree trunk the tell-tale multi-colored flickering of the lights of the nether world surrounded the Piasa and his foe.

Instantly they were transported to the image, place and time that the Piasa had conceived in his mind. They materialized on an isle somewhere to the north of what is now called South America in an ocean now known as the Atlantic in the middle of the raised hallway on the tallest inhabited point of that island; they were in an open hall that was surrounded by carved totems topped with "Crystal Skulls" and in the middle near a huge weapon was a thirteenth and much larger skull that seemed to be drawing power from all of the others. They had been brought to a time long ago, into the hall of the Atlanteans during the buildup of the power for their great, but unwisely produced weapon, just moments before these wondrous peoples demise. The dragon slammed the mantis to the ground below him and he immediately began to flicker with the lights of the act of traveling "between."

The Piasa, also having a great concern for his human friends and not wanting to risk being followed back to his friends thereby placing them in danger if his plan was unsuccessful, thought to himself as he progressed, "They have through their contact taught me what I so treasured about them; experiencing and being exposed to the wonderful humans that I have known over the time that I have known them has finally resulted in me, a dragon learning what sets the humans apart from all of the other beings; he then willed himself to materialize once again into a huge dragon shaped boulder in a place somewhere in the Midwest that was commonly referred to as "The Bottoms," someplace where he had found comfort once before; as his first understood, newfound act of supreme love.

Behind him the blight lark/mantis creature was obliterated in an immense explosion caused by Atlantean technology that had grown entirely out of their control at some time in the distant past!

Remaining behind in the clearing so recently selected by the Piasa remained the group to whom the dragon had just spoken his last known words; Nathan, Bill, Danny, Burt and Gill all sat resting from what had been an especially draining yet copiously enlightening experience. As they recuperated they saw the dark storm clouds begin to dissipate; the life and color begin to return to the trees, grass, bushes and even the water as they could all now feel the explicit and totally uplifting renewal of their individual spirits.

They all somehow felt that they would never again see the Piasa; but at the same time they all knew that he had given them the keys to the well being of all human kind. They needed to live their lives wisely following the truths that the Piasa had enlightened them with; but also spread the word of these teachings in order to enable all of mankind to understand and to also practice these simple truths that would protect their "Natural World." They now could all feel deeply, the importance of how well they both respected and treated their natural world; they now realized that we needed to stop the pollution and unbridled use of her bountiful supplies which were rarely replaced; the over use of which would in turn damage her greatly; also they needed to show restraint and good judgment in the use of the formidable technology that they were now able to create, especially that which was meant to do great damage as a weapon; and perhaps most importantly of all was to recognize the weaknesses that many of their kind had become burdened with and strive to help one another stay strong and avoid the failures that these frailties can lead to and if ever confronted by a fellow man who has become stricken by these downfalls, then to help one another recover and again become whole. The dragon had told them of an example had he not? The man that the Piasa had mentioned had been called Jesus! The group joined hands and did something that none had ever done before; they prayed; and after long soul searching and prayer, they embraced one another, shook hands, wished each other well and went their separate ways.

They all left with two new missions emergent within their minds; to live their lives as an example of what the Piasa had taught them and to touch as many people as they could with this newly found inspiration. And so, if you are blessed to hear the words of the Piasa, will you be able to be touched by the love that took so many ages for the Piasa to realize; will you be able to consider the prudence of his message, for it is a message that is meant to save us all!

Websites: Name / Website

1.) Piasa – First recognized by the Illiniwek Indians of the American Midwest- Their people began to call the bird the "Piasa", which meant "the bird which devours men".   Pg. v
http://www.altonhauntings.com/piasa.html
http://www.polenth.com/myth/namerica/piasa.html

2.) Modern Dragon Discoveries /Animal Planet   Pg. 10
http://animal.discovery.com/guides/atoz/imaginary.html
http://www.chinavista.com/experience/dragon/dragon.html

3.) Quetzalcoatl   Pg. 10
http://www.crystalinks.com/quetzalcoatl.html

4.) Gas'hais'dowane – Horned Serpent   Pg. 10
http://www.polenth.com/myth/namerica/horned.html

5.) Chinese winged dragon   Pg. 10
http://www.polenth.com/myth/asia/yinglung.html

6.) Phoenicians   Pg. 14
http://library.thinkquest.org/J002807/Time%20and%20Time%20Again/Time%20and%20Time%20Again/phoenicians.html

7.) The Bermuda Triangle   Pg. 57
http://www.byerly.org/bt.htm

8.) Atlantis Pg. 104
http://www.crystalinks.com/atlantis.html

9.) Atlantean War birds Pg. 112
http://paranormal.about.com/od/ancientanomalies/ig/Most-Puzzling-Ancient-Artifact/Ancient-Model-Aircraft.htm

10.) Crystal Skulls Pg. 141
http://www.world-mysteries.com/sar_6_1.htm

11.) Nazca Plains - Peru Pg. 181
http://www.crystalinks.com/nazca.http

12.) Meramec Caverns Pg. 181
http://en.wikipedia.org/wiki/Meramec_Caverns

13.) Bighorn Medicine Wheel Pg. 195
http://solar-center.stanford.edu/AO/bighorn.html

14.) Naberius – Demon Pg. 439
http://en.wikipedia.org/wiki/Naberius

Appendix:

1.) Nicholas Fletcher – The first young adult that Nathan felt confident in the recitation of his remarkable story. Chosen for his honesty, listening ability and the fact that Nathan knew that Nicholas would believe the truth even if he was told something as fantastic as the story that he knew he had to recite.   Pg. v

2.) Nathan Bellows - An ordinary (or so he thought) blond haired, freckle faced ten year old boy who when he succumbed to what he thought was only the normal yearnings of the young to play in the woods and explore where he had not been before was actually fulfilling destiny; not merely his, but the Piasa's and perhaps all of us!   Pg. v

3.) Piasa – The Piasa is a North American dragon, first seen by settlers painted on rocks overlooking the Mississippi river near Alton, Illinois. It has four feet that end in sharp talons, wings, and is entirely covered with thick scales. This is not unusual in Native American art as also worshipped and reproduced in this hemisphere are the dragons heads of the Gas'hais'dowane often found on the totem poles of the American Northwest and Quetzalcoatl that has been pictured and worshipped by the Mayans, Toltecs, and Aztecs of old world Mexico and central America and there have been suggestions that the original accounts of this creature by some were not altogether accurate, despite the numerous different sources found in both our Western hemisphere and Chinese (Yinglung) and European (Drachenstein) descriptions of nearly identical creatures. Whether the older tales are correct or not, the Piasa (dragons of all sorts) is a definite part of the both ancient and modern folklore of many areas. The original rock art in Illinois was destroyed, but a recreated version can still be found in the area today; unfortunately upon a billboard.   Pg. v

4.) Bill McGraine - Teenager that was a product of a broken home and going down the wrong path in life, but upon their encounter with the Piasa experienced an unexplainable and remarkable change in character.   Pg. 9

5.) Danny Newton - Same as Bill above, Danny was on a very negative path in life that would be positively changed by his meeting of the Piasa.   Pg. 9

6.) Mayans- Well known culture that controlled much of this hemisphere who were long time trading partners with the Nastazi.   Pg. 14

7.) The Osprey - Ebirius's very well built and fast ship; built by his grandfather who was patriarch of their family of shipbuilders. Pg. 16

8.) Ebirius Saluur - Young Phoenician sailor/adventurer who the Piasa once met and was bonded with; he and the dragon and shared part of their lives together.   Pg. 16

9.) Elburt Saluur - The grandfather of Ebirius Saluur; he was a master shipbuilder.   Pg. 16

10.) Durages Hammil- Shipmate and one of Ebirius's two best friends; from a family renowned for their abilities in navigation and celestial research.   Pg. 21

11.) Flaxon Ceals - Shipmate and the second of Ebirius's two best friends; from a family known for their abilities with training animals and knowledge of plants and herbs.   Pg. 21

12.) Desiree Perseii - Princess of the Amazons – rescued by and fallen in love with Ebirius.   Pg. 27

13.) Andrea Perseii - Physically formidable and very beautiful Queen of the Amazons.   Pg. 28

Words of the Piasa

14.) Gruumens - Race of malicious, barbaric men who coveted much of the Amazon's and were known thieves. Pg. 28

15.) Raginites - Race of insolent men who commonly stole from, kidnapped and committed even worse mayhem against their neighbors; thought to be the descendants of the men who escaped when the all female rule began with the Amazons. Pg. 30

16.) Therasil Zerca - One of high priestess's of the Amazons; very ruthless and powerful. Of ancient ruling bloodline and desires very much to be queen. Pg. 31

17.) Druii - The name the Amazons have given their religion that practices the worship of Mother Earth and Nature. Pg. 45

18.) Saapwin - The incredibly powerful, crystal pointed lance that Ebirius used to kill the black dragon and protect the Piasa when they met: translates to "the life drainer" in the Amazon's language. Pg. 54

19.) The Bermuda Triangle - See furnished website. Pg. 57

20.) Charondele Helms - One of the Queen Andrea's largest and most trusted officers. Pg. 60

21.) Victoria Pearce - Another of Queen Andrea's most trusted circle of officers. Pg. 60

22.) Zin-Darlya - Spy/warrior allied to Therasil. Pg. 69

23.) Jenal al Arrief - Old former high priestess allied to Queen Andrea. Very accomplished and most outspoken about restraint on the use of the Realm until it was better understood. Pg. 70

24.) Nuuns - Ancient Amazonian sect of priestesses that attempted opposition to the sisterhood. They attempted telepathy in conjunction with the Realm and were ousted for this dangerous practice centuries ago. Pg. 71

25.) Tamara Sate` - Queen Andrea's young, naïve, yet very ambitious consort. Pg. 77

26.) Quellenar - Device designed by the Amazon's to prevent prisoners who had the ability from attaining the Realm. Pg. 79

27.) Neandra-Luz - Former high priestess who was very much in favor of the use of telepathy and the Realm together as a weapon. Fully loyal to Therasil. Pg. 81

28.) Kristine – Trusted long known warrior and possible former lover of Therasil. Pg. 81

29.) Talya - Top rated; most exceptionally talented in war craft of Therasil's warriors. Pg. 87

30.) Aliceria - Trusted warrior in Therasil's camp. Pg. 88

31.) Lorna - Trusted warrior in Therasil's camp, who is also an incredibly huge, rather sadistic woman. Pg. 88

32.) Anna-Suz - Therasil's most highly trusted messenger Pg. 90

33.) Katlena Beez – Proud Amazonian; dispatcher of Neandra-Luz who unfortunately was rewarded with the fate of being one of the last remaining of her people, in an empty homeland. Pg. 98

34.) Burt Slade - Present day redneck/hunter/drinker that began by stalking the Piasa before a great realization. Pg. 103

35.) Gill Jess - Present day redneck/hunter/drinker that began by stalking the Piasa before a great realization the same as his partner. Pg. 103

36.) Shawna Ree - Atlantean girl who was the daughter of one of the most formidable scientists that existed in the Atlantean culture; though the technology frightened her and she made every attempt to separate herself from it, she unfortunately had her life thoroughly entrench within it, ultimately becoming an unknowing pawn within the fate that was to occur. She became one of the dragon's closest friends to that date and was sorely missed. Pg. 105

37.) War birds - Jet airplanes that the Atlanteans had already apparently developed 10,000 years before their appearance in the Twentieth century. They were very fast and heavily armed. Pg. 112

Words of the Piasa

38.) Atlantean Death Beam – An apparent laser or particle beam weapon developed ages before even being considered in the twentieth century. Pg. 112

39.) Optiscopes - Extremely efficient, long range viewers created by Shawna's father in a more peaceful time. Pg. 114

40.) Mount Sienna - The mount in the middle of the Atlantean home island. Pg. 115

41.) Blowing Rocks - Dangerous to enter secret cave where Shawna chose to hide the Piasa. Pg. 116

42.) Aunt Rea and Uncle Selvin Ree – Shawna's aunt and uncle who had saved her life as a young girl. Pg. 117

43.) Alsaruns - Ancient enemies of the Atlantean people. Pg. 118

44.) Orchid's Nest - Forest on the island of Atlantis; filled with beautiful orchids and thought by some to be enchanted. Pg. 121

45.) Ursalas - Unicorn: called Monoceii in dragon tongue; this one was believed to be the last one of her kind in the world. Pg. 124

46.) Daryell Ree - Shawna's father; a great creator of Atlantean Marvels. He would today be considered a very accomplished scientist, but somewhat obsessed with the defense of his island home. Pg. 126

47.) Cavetti Reales - Atlantean prince who Shawna's father desired for her to wed and though he is totally smitten with Shawna she does not love him. Pg. 130

48.) Crystal Skulls - Carved representations of human skulls thought to be nearly impossible to recreate even with our current technology that have been found worldwide even in recent times. They are said to channel some sort of strange energy and are the objects of study and hearsay even today. Pg. 141

49.) Norander- Nastazi word for dragon like being that had been spotted in their lands in ancient times. The name means "Thunder Lizard." Pg. 151

50.) Shush - Nastazi word for "Grizzly Bear." Pg. 153

51.) Naomi - Tecumseh's mother. Pg. 154

52.) Tecumseh Osuwage - Young Nastazi boy who bonds with the Piasa and grows into manhood in this tale. His name means "One who has crossed the path of the Panther." Pg. 154

53.) Noran - Friend of Tecumseh. Pg. 154

54.) Cherniko - Friend of Tecumseh. Pg. 154

55.) Zendla- Honored Nastazi elder woman. Pg. 154

56.) Himreal Gerez- Noran's father; a high ranking Nastazi warrior and close friend of Tecumseh's father. Pg. 162

57.) Chonaka - High ranking Nastazi warrior and Himreal's fishing partner. Pg. 162

58.) Kurlhii Osuwage - Tecumseh's father; very high ranking Nastazi elder and one of few to be considered for king. Pg. 163

59.) Billigana- Young Nastazi girl who become Tecumseh's lifelong love. Her name meaning, "True morning light." Pg. 166

60.) Digis- Nastazi word for "Panther." Pg. 169

61.) Incas- Ancient Indian culture that predated the Mayans and considered them a very warlike, threatening culture, as they were! Pg. 180

62.) Oaxintaal - Ruthless Mayan commander; supposed friend of the Nastazi, but possessing a hidden agenda. Pg. 186

63.) Hure'Tan- Mayan second in command. Pg. 186

64.) Zauhn- Ambitious, purely evil Pawnee chieftain. Pg. 188

65.) Pawnee- Malicious, warring people who had bad intentions towards the Nastazi people's homeland. Pg. 188

66.) Kharzin Atol- Doomed Nastazi king. Pg. 190

Words of the Piasa

67.) Nanuma- Honored Nastazi elder woman, teacher.   Pg. 191

68.) Tonnel- Nanuma's former sweetheart, who happened to have developed a relationship with a different dragon than the Piasa now known as Granger.   Pg. 191

69.) Ka-Nick Anick-   Strong drug related to Bella Donna that the Pawnee leaders had their warriors partake of to increase strength and stamina. It also had bad side effects.   Pg. 194

70.) Nakokia- Nastazi word for their village; it means "People's Home."   Pg. 194

71.) Medicine Wheels- Stone wheels constructed in the ground by Nastazi's, Mayans and other Native Americans that assisted in guidance, seasonal needs and celestial viewing.   Pg. 195

72.) Atlatl- Mayan weapon that was a bronze tipped spear with a lever to assist in its throwing; achieving greater velocity and accuracy.   Pg. 196

73.) Cobaltons- Nastazi word for the highly valued sapphires traded to them by the Mayans.   Pg. 202

74.) Wakan Tanka- Nastazi name for the "Great Spirit/or God." Pg. 202

75.) Sha'siang - Billigana's mother.   Pg. 206

76.) Lake Genesee- Oxbow Lake to the north of their village where Tonnel met the green dragon with which he disappeared strangely in an episode earlier in Nanuma's life.   Pg. 212

77.) Chartil - Green dragon, or later called Piasa that had begun a relationship with Nanuma's former love interest Tonnel long ago.   Pg. 214

78.) Angelii Zarteen-   Especially beautiful, yet somehow very strange young woman who was at first rescued by Tecumseh and Billigana, but then attempted to enslave all of their people with the assistance of a misrepresented drug and a being of pure evil.   Pg. 243

79.) Elgin- The Blight Lark. A shape-shifting being that housed a soul of pure and unparalleled evil. Representative of the evil that can be found represented within man in so many circumstances. Pg. 245

80.) Chickwa-   Nastazi word for Meadow lark; referring to the small bird first recognized as and called Elgin. Its small size could not long hide the evil residing there.   Pg. 245

81.) Mandi, Tanya and Coi-   Young apprentices of Nanuma's; Coi Le Serre- being the strongest willed of the three; who was able to fight off the effects of the drug although she was forced to partake of it by Angelii's minions, very close friend of Mandi and Tanya who did not have the strength to fight the Kaav at first, though Mandi did also in time.   Pg. 246

82.) Kaav- Strangely healing, yet insidiously addictive drug that was the tool which Angelii was to use in her enslavement of most of the Nastazi and many of the other people's with which she came into contact with; so powerful that it even had an effect upon the Piasa.   Pg. 250

83.) Melanie Takan- Nubile and trusting young wife of the new king Trevlon Takan who was quickly and wholly corrupted by the wiles of Angelii.   Pg. 253

84.) Trevlon Takan - New king of the Nastazi people after the deaths of the old king and many of the more ranking elders; was including Tecumseh's father during the surprise attack by their old enemies, the Pawnee.   Pg. 254

85.) Leona - One of Nanuma's most trusted apprentices.   Pg. 260

86.) Berry Falls - Beautiful location on the horseshoe lake to the north of the Nastazi village that was a romantic spot for many, but where other more unfortunate things also happened to have occurred.   Pg. 272

87.) Noodling – ancient method of catching catfish practiced at first by Nastazi's and other ancient indigenous people and still practiced even today; though mostly for sport.   Pg. 272

88.) Cahtar- Friend and fishing companion of both Tecumseh and Noran. Pg. 273

89.) Makai- Stated name of the people whom Angelii said she had come from. Pg. 287

90.) Mount Rushmore- Though not named in this saga this is in fact the mount to which they referred to. Pg. 299

91.) Tatanka - Nastazi word for what is known today as the American Bison. Pg. 307

92.) Gondel - Large strange metal arch for which the Nastazi had traded for that rang like a tremendous bell when struck. Pg. 313

93.) Sunomayans- A large portion of Angelii's enslaved army that were said to have once been Mayans. Pg. 341

94.) Temigin - The highly trusted/ often tested former Pawnee warrior that had been awarded the task of guarding and taking the newly produced Kaav to Angelii's army that would soon face the Piasa. Pg. 341

95.) Trellon and Quinz- Two Nastazi boys that could be noticed were different from the rest of the young men of their age; their people recognized them as being what we label today as homosexual, but in their culture they were not chastised or ridiculed for this; they were just accepted as being "different." They were also very fast runners and so they were naturally used as messengers. Pg. 359

96.) Condrit - Large leaved, purple herb used for antiseptic properties. Pg. 380

97.) Hozho'Anasazi - Nastazi phrase meaning "People's Charmed Land" naming an area of the Midwestern U.S. that occupies parts of Missouri, Arkansas, Oklahoma and Kansas; today called the Ozarks. Pg. 404

98.) Naberius - Trickster demon that makes false promises, often appearing as a Three Headed Dog or Raven, often with an accompanying dark mist. Pg. 439

Manufactured By: RR Donnelley
                   Momence, IL USA
                   January, 2011